Natalie Chandler was educated at St Chad's College, Durham and currently works in behavioural education, specialising in social, emotional and mental health issues. She is a Curtis Brown Creative alumna and was previously selected to be part of the WoMentoring scheme. She lives with her partner, dividing her time between London and rural Lancashire, and enjoys greeting every dog she meets.

NATALIE CHANDLER

BELIEVE ME NOT

ACCENT

First published in 2022 by Headline Accent
An imprint of HEADLINE PUBLISHING GROUP

1

Cataloguing in Publication Data is available from the British Library

ISBN 978 1 4722 9172 1

Typeset in 11.25/15.25pt Bembo Std by Jouve (UK), Milton Keynes

Printed and bound in Great Britain by Clays Ltd, Elcograf S.p.A.

HEADLINE PUBLISHING GROUP
An Hachette UK Company
Carmelite House
50 Victoria Embankment
London EC4Y 0DZ

www.headline.co.uk
www.hachette.co.uk

To Mum and Dad, with all my love –
because of you, everything is possible.

Chapter One

Even before it became clear she was being held prisoner in a cell masquerading as a hospital room, she knew something was missing. Something physical. Something vital.

What, exactly, she had no idea.

The fluorescent lighting burned into her eyes, their weighted lids begging to close again, but she fought the tempting return to darkness. Her surroundings were blurred, a fluid film mottling her vision, but rapid blinking only cost precious energy and she failed to raise her heavy head from a pillow that smelled of sweat and fear.

The bedsheets were too tight, trapping her legs in an efficient bind. She forced herself to be still, drawing deep breaths into tense lungs as her grip tightened on the blue blanket drawn nearly to her nose. The breaths flooded her with that unmistakable hospital smell, a medicinal tang mixed with antiseptic cleanliness, faint undertones of disinfectant not quite masked by a subtle floral air freshener.

She groped around the narrow bed, feeling the cold steel of rails confining her, searching for a drip's needle in her arms, the coarse rasp of a plaster cast or the sticky pads of a heart monitor. Nothing. Just a gentle pinch of her index finger, a small plastic clip displaying several numbers that meant nothing.

'Mrs Newman? Megan?'

The voice startled her, too strident in the hushed quiet, and she bolted upright. A wave of vertigo swept over her and the room swam, a carousel of distorted images.

'Have some water.' A woman came into focus, standing beside the bed. A plastic beaker of water was placed carefully into Megan's weak grip, the head of the bed slowly raised.

It took concentration to raise it to her lips, an effort to swallow, but it seemed to help. The spinning sensation slowed, allowing her sight to clear. She blinked again, trying to clear the last of the blurriness, but it clung defiantly, sepia tinges at the edge of her vision.

The woman took the empty beaker from her. She wore medical scrubs and a reassuring smile, dark hair slicked back into a neat bun.

'My name's Gemma. I've been your nurse since you were admitted.'

'Where am I?'

'This is the Grosvenor Unit.'

'Was I in an accident?'

'Not an accident, exactly. You had a knock to the head, but there's no long-term damage.'

'Then why am I here?' Megan heard her voice rasp, as if her vocal cords had been strained, her throat raw and sore. She stroked it, searching for swelling or the sting of bruises. The water beaker was offered again, refilled, and she welcomed its soothing coolness. 'I feel strange.'

'That'll be the medication.'

'Why am I on medication? How long have I been here? What day is it?'

'Your doctor will explain everything. Let me check where he is.'

'Don't leave me!' Panic swelled from nowhere.

'I'm only down the corridor, love.' Gemma squeezed her hand. She was shorter than Megan, more athletic, and she radiated the sort of capability Megan had always prided herself on. 'You're safe here. Just press this button if you need me.'

As soon as the door closed gently behind the nurse, Megan pushed herself off the mattress and sat fully upright. The dizziness returned with a vengeance, frightening in its intensity, and she nearly lunged for the call button, but it took only a few moments to subside to a fuzzy dullness.

She found herself focusing on another button attached to the wall, larger, red, like a panic alarm should look, but she was distracted by a jolt of clarity, reminding her something was missing. She could sense a loss, something of great importance, but it remained stubbornly beyond her grasp. Trying to reach for it only made her head spin again.

Gingerly, she explored her skull, searching for the head injury Gemma had so casually mentioned. Her chestnut hair was greasy and lank. Through the tangles, she identified a painful spot and what felt like a wound closed with surgical glue, which stung sharply as she pressed too hard.

As she recoiled, she became aware of a strange, uncomfortable tension in her lower abdomen whenever she moved. Raising the synthetic material of the hospital gown, she was confronted with a large wound, the path of a surgeon's scalpel stretching across her bikini line.

She ran a tentative finger along the healing scar, conscious of a dawning familiarity at the sensation. She knew what this was. The skin was still tight and tender to touch but there were no stitches or raw-redness. No evidence a surgeon's hands had plunged into her open abdomen.

It had been the strangest sensation, staring at the fabric screen obscuring her view, the urgent tugging and fumbling inside her, careless violation of vital organs that should never have known the sure touch of human fingers. Stef clutching her hand, sweat beading on his forehead. At last, the cry, severing the hush of concentration as the slippery bundle was pressed briefly to her chest. Startled eyes, a slick of black hair, tightly clenched fists.

Luka.

Luka, the child she had never craved until, one day, it was suddenly the most important thing in the world.

Megan was certain she had devoutly planned her pregnancy. She would have consumed a myriad of antenatal books, taken up yoga, swum daily, listened to foreign audio books to encourage an ear for languages, even broken her coffee addiction. She would have done everything right because that was how she ran her life. Scheduled, organised, dedicated to whatever task was being undertaken.

So why was she here, in this hospital bed, without her baby?

She fumbled for the call button, pressing it repeatedly, increasing the pressure until she was almost punching it, free hand gripping a hank of her hair. Finally, the door opened, but it wasn't Gemma she saw first.

Stef's usual beguiling grin beamed at her, but his striking grey eyes quickly slid away, as if he was uncomfortable with what he saw. As usual, he hadn't bothered to lace his Converse or iron his

4

T-shirt and his messy flop of dark hair remained untamed. He was uninterested in designer labels or status symbols, entirely at ease with himself.

'Stef, you're here!' She flung her arms out to her husband, a dry sob clawing at her throat. 'I don't know what's going on. Stef, what's happening to me?'

He crossed the room to her in swift strides, bending to allow her to wrap her arms tight around him, clinging to his salvation. His familiar smell – citrus and bergamot – comforted her, defeating the reek of sweat and chemicals that clung to her skin. He felt firm and strong against her protruding bones and paper-thin skin.

'Don't be scared.' He pulled back, taking her hand in his reassuring grip. His platinum band matched her own, now too large for her finger. Against her alabaster colouring, his olive skin appeared permanently kissed by the sun of all the foreign shores they had explored together.

She raised her eyes to his and saw clouds in their smoky depths. 'Where's Luka? Haven't you brought him?'

He squeezed her hand, a momentary shift in his careful expression.

'Is he OK?' she persisted. 'Is he not allowed to be in here with me? They shouldn't separate mothers from their babies!'

Stef gently pulled free from her grip, and she saw the red marks her fingers had left. 'How long ago did you wake up?'

'I don't know! It doesn't matter. Who's looking after Luka?'

'I've visited every day. Did you hear me talking to you?'

'No. What does that matter? Where is Luka?'

'Have you seen the doctor yet?'

5

'Stef, what is wrong with you? Answer me! I want to know where our baby is. Tell me who he's with!'

'Let me fetch you a coffee.'

She waved her hand abruptly, dismissive of her favourite addiction. 'I don't want coffee! Where's the doctor? Maybe he'll tell me what the hell is going on. I need to see him.'

Stef was already heading decisively for the door. 'I'll ask Gemma while I get your drink.'

'Hurry up, for God's sake! Luka might be in danger.'

The door banged carelessly behind him, sending a sharp spike of pain through Megan's aching head. Time passed that could have been seconds or minutes, perhaps even hours. Too long. Megan's gaze remained rooted to the door, her fingers constantly fidgeting with a lock of hair, tugging at it whenever her attention began to drift, her unconscious method of calming herself since infanthood.

When the door finally opened again, it wasn't Gemma or Stef but another man who strode to her bedside. A tanned stranger with honey-coloured hair greying at the temples and a dusky-pink linen shirt tucked precisely into chinos.

'Hi, Megan, how are you?'

Megan only just prevented herself from seizing his pressed sleeve. 'Are you my doctor?'

'I am. My name is Dr Barnard Macaulay. Most patients call me Barney or Dr Mac.' His American accent was rich and smooth even though he spoke quietly. 'I'm from California, but I work solely in the UK now.'

He had a ready smile, the very straight, very white teeth of American dentistry, but she didn't care about his name or his home state or his bedside manner.

'My baby isn't with me. I need to know where he is. No one will tell me and I don't understand why.'

He took a seat by her bed, unhurried, no flicker of concern at a missing infant. 'Megan, we need to talk about your condition and why you're in hospital.'

'But what if my son's in danger?'

'No one's in danger.'

'How do you know?' Megan demanded.

Stef chose that moment to return, juggling two enormous Costa coffees, causing them both to turn their heads.

'Megan, do you know who this is?' Macaulay asked, gentle voiced, as if speaking to a young child.

'Of course I know! This is Stefan ... Stef ... my husband.'

'I've already met Dr Mac, sweetheart.' Stef handed over her usual order, large cappuccino with an extra shot, blithely unaware of the reason for her agitation.

'We don't usually allow hot drinks, Mr Newman. They can be a safety risk.'

Stef's jaw set. He'd never liked being told what to do. 'I didn't think—'

'What do you mean, a safety risk?' Megan demanded, the flare of rage taking her by surprise. 'I won't burn myself, I'm not stupid!'

Macaulay gave her another smile. 'It's just procedure, to keep everyone safe. It's fine this once.'

'I'm not allowed coffee again until I get out of here? You've no right to do that!'

'Of course you can have coffee. It just won't be as piping hot as you're used to.'

Megan took a gulp, as if the cup would be snatched from her

7

any moment, clutching it tightly, drawing comfort from its heat. The familiar smell enveloped her, nutty and earthy, coaxing tentative buds of memories to the surface – the rush of pleasure each morning at the first velvety sip, cappuccinos shared with friends in steamy cafés, winter's chill chased from her fingers by the warming comfort. Normal life, beyond these claustrophobic walls.

Then she remembered where she was and what the most important question was.

'Where is my baby and why the hell am I here? How long have I been away from him? I don't know what's going on!'

An unreadable glance passed between Macaulay and Stef.

'Megan, there's no easy way to explain situations such as these.' Macaulay leaned forward, resting his elbows on his knees. He indicated to Stef to take the chair on the other side of the bed. 'Three weeks ago, you attempted to commit suicide. You sustained a serious head injury and internal bleeding, which meant you required an emergency hysterectomy.'

'That's not what my scar is from.' Megan interrupted. 'I gave birth via C-section.'

'At the time of your suicide attempt,' Macaulay continued as if she hadn't spoken, 'you were experiencing an acute psychotic episode. You believed your husband was trying to kill you, and when you have seen Stefan since you've been hospitalised, you've attempted to harm him.'

'What? No. You're wrong. Why would I do that?'

'Your psychosis required immediate treatment. As you weren't able to consent, Stefan signed the paperwork to section you and bring you here to the Grosvenor Unit. The Grosvenor is my London psychiatric practice.'

'I don't understand—'

'You've been kept heavily sedated, for your own safety as well as others', which is why you're so confused. We've now started reducing the sedation. The next step will be getting you stable enough to be discharged home.'

'What are you talking about?' Megan's voice rose in disbelief as she was finally allowed to speak. 'This is madness! I'm not violent. I'd never hurt Stef!'

'Psychosis can come and go. Sometimes you're not in control of your thoughts or actions. At the moment, the medication is preventing many of your symptoms, but we can't keep you on such high doses for an extended period of time.'

'You still haven't answered my question! Where is Luka? I want my baby!'

That glance again between the two men before Stef took her hand gently, as if she were an object of extreme delicacy.

'Megs, we don't have a baby.'

A moment of painful silence. Megan struggled to spit out the rush of words crowding her throat. Gasping for the necessary air to speak, she snatched her hand free, searching her husband's familiar face for the giveaway, for the joke, unable to comprehend why he was being so damn facetious. Didn't he understand how he was enraging her?

'What are you saying?' she managed to wheeze. 'Of course we have a baby.'

'We don't have any children, sweetheart.'

Another ragged breath. 'Stef, listen to yourself! You can't just deny Luka like that! If you think this is funny . . .'

'Megs, I'm not denying anything. We don't have a baby.'

'Are you out of your mind? His name is Luka. He was seven

pounds two ounces. He was born by emergency C-section. You were there! You held my hand the whole time!'

Stef was becoming a stranger before her eyes. Everything that she knew so well was changing. Why was he telling her these lies?

'Who are you, Stef?' she demanded.

'What do you mean, who am I?'

'You're not my husband. You're acting like someone I don't know!'

'Don't upset yourself, Megan.' She barely noticed the doctor take her coffee cup, handing it to Nurse Gemma, who hurried discreetly away with it.

'I hadn't finished that!' Megan seized a lock of hair, tugging at it. 'I need to see my son. I need to know he's all right.'

'Calm down, Megs.' Stef caught hold of her hand again, grip tighter this time. She watched him place his own coffee out of reach. 'This isn't helping.'

'Why is no one listening to me?'

'Megs . . .'

'Stop saying my name! I know who I am! Why don't you know who our baby is?' Megan knew her voice was rising, but she was in control, assertive. Pushing Stef aside, she threw back the sheets, swung her legs out of the bed. Better to be standing up, show them she wasn't an invalid who required pacifying.

Stef moved as if to corral her but was beaten to it by Macaulay, who gave the red button a sharp smack as he stood to meet her, arms spread wide, palms open. His lips were moving, no doubt reassuring words, but Megan couldn't hear him above the echoing noise suddenly filling her head.

Gemma was back again, this time proffering a small plastic

tray. Someone was screaming, a high-pitched howl that made the hairs on Megan's arms stand on end and her throat ache. A tortured sound of suffering.

As Macaulay slid the needle into her skin, the noise abruptly stopped.

Chapter Two

S tef averted his gaze as the nurse manoeuvred Megan's limp body on to its side, removed her pillows and drew the sheets over her, raised the side rails. Her eyes slid closed, as if her eyelids were too heavy to hold up. The nurse checked her vital signs, made notes on the chart, before quietly taking the used syringe away.

'Sorry you had to see that.' Macaulay's voice sounded too loud in the new silence, his tone brisk, business-like.

Stef focused on Megan's hand, which was hanging loosely over the edge of the mattress, the hand that could have killed him. Her lips were slightly parted, her breathing slow and even, her face almost childlike. She couldn't have looked less of a threat at the moment, but he had seen the madness within her, the violent rage even he wasn't strong enough to fight.

He shook his head to dislodge the memory. 'How long will she be like this for?' he asked.

'The sedation lasts a few hours.'

'I'll stay with her.'

'There's no point. She won't be aware you're here.'

Stef stepped carefully away from the bed, expecting sudden movements to startle Megan awake. 'I thought she was going to attack me again.'

'If it helps, she's not in control of how she's reacting.' Macaulay moved to tap his pass against the door's security fob. 'I have a few minutes, come get coffee with me. We haven't had an opportunity to talk yet.'

Stef's instinct told him he should remain by his wife's side, where he belonged, but he couldn't bear the prospect of sitting silently by her motionless form for hours with only his conflicting thoughts for company. He nodded acceptance of the invitation and strode after Macaulay, casting a final glance back at his wife so he could watch the door close securely.

'I was hoping that would go better.' Stef didn't bother to regulate the accusation in his tone.

'It happens. There's a lot of information for the patient to take in, many questions they want to ask. It can be an overload.'

'She didn't understand what was happening.'

'That's the effects of the medication. It will lessen as we reduce the dosage.'

Stef hadn't visited the dining room before. The Grosvenor would not call it a canteen: the napkins were cloth rather than paper, there were glasses instead of plastic beakers, walnut tables and matching chairs. No touch of Californian cool in the very British decor.

It had felt wrong to casually sip coffee as he sat by his sedated wife's bedside, so he'd just held Megan's hand, babbled nonsense she hadn't heard. He'd avoided coming here for her first cappuccino. It had taken longer to nip over to Costa and he had needed that time to gain his composure.

He took a seat while Macaulay brought the drinks. China cups and saucers, of course. The American raised one eyebrow.

'I miss real-sized coffee cups.'

'Quite a change from Los Angeles to London,' Stef observed, unsure why he was wasting time with small talk even as he spoke. This was the first time Macaulay had afforded him an audience since Megan's admission a week ago; each previous encounter had been an efficient, professional lecture about treatments or symptoms, delivered at speed before the psychiatrist strode off to attend to his next concern.

'London has some better opportunities.' Macaulay's reply was blithely unconcerned.

'You haven't been here long.'

'You've done your research, Mr Newman.'

'I don't like risky investments, so I made sure I got plenty of information on you.' A lie, but he needed to sound in control, like he usually was, in the more familiar character of the successful businessman. He was uneasy with this new role he found himself in and he did not want Dr Macaulay to see it. 'Please, call me Stef.'

Macaulay acknowledged the invitation with a courteous nod. 'I haven't been called an investment before.' He laughed. His teeth really were excellent, even if the smile was false. Stef calculated him to have at least ten years on his own thirty-eight but in appearance they could easily have been contemporaries.

'I'm investing my wife's health in you, to be blunt.' Stef took a gulp of his flat white. It was too hot, but he welcomed the burning sensation on his tongue. 'I chose you because everything I read said you succeed where others fail.'

'What else did it say, Stefan?'

14

'That you sail close to the wind.' Stef added a note of challenge to his tone, but Macaulay didn't rise to it.

'Your wife is safe with me; you don't have to worry about that. I have the luxury of taking on very few patients at any one time, so I can give each one my full attention. It does mean my fees are somewhat higher than those of other psychiatrists—'

'The money doesn't matter,' Stef interrupted. 'I've gone private for a reason. I can pay whatever's necessary. I just want Megan back to normal.'

'We try not to use the term "normal".'

'Why? Because she won't be? She's never going to be the old Megan ever again?'

'I'm not necessarily saying that, but this is a complicated process and results can vary between patients.'

'Sounds like you don't expect her to make a full recovery.'

Macaulay downed his coffee like a tequila shot. 'The definition of "full recovery" also varies. After the onset of psychosis, the brain reacts differently than it did before. In some cases, this is temporary and reversed once recovery is complete. In others, some long-term changes remain.'

'You mean she could always be affected by this?'

'I'll do everything I can to reduce that probability.' Another perfect smile. 'Trust in your investment. Megan needs to see we're both working from the same page. I need your support as much as you need mine, Stefan.'

Stef gritted his teeth at the condescension as much as the pronounced use of his full name. He had shed that name years ago, determined to banish the ghosts that haunted the old identity. 'Understood.' He drained his own cup quickly. 'What happens now?'

'You go home; I'll introduce Megan to her treatment plan once the sedation wears off.' Macaulay stood without further explanation, his sales pitch complete. 'Have yourself a good afternoon.'

Stef was left feeling distinctly wrong-footed, and it bothered him more than it should. He had never liked being talked down to, but he reassured himself this was probably typical of dealings with highly educated, clever doctors, so different from his usual daily business. They didn't have time for long explanations. Their brains worked much quicker than that of the average person and they just expected you to keep up.

That made him think of his brother. Isaac's IQ had been in the genius range. Maybe he would have been a doctor too, if things had been different.

Stef shook his head, abruptly shoving his chair away from the table, searching each pocket for the car keys, even though he put them in the same one every time.

His brother was the last person he wanted to think about.

Once again, Megan wasn't aware of waking up so much as gradually coming back to her senses. Her mind replayed the scene – Macaulay coming at her, syringe raised, ready to plunge it into her skin – and she cringed away from his ghost looming over her. She looked for the site of the needle mark on her arm, prodding the little pinprick to check it was real. Her ears rang, as if she could still hear her own screams, and her wrists burned with angry red weals, evidence of unforgiving material cutting into her skin as she fought against it. She didn't remember being restrained but, somehow, she recognised what the marks were.

As before, Gemma was almost immediately in the doorway.

'You OK?' Gemma asked gently.

'Think so. Thirsty.'

Gemma poured from a jug on the bedside table, hovering while Megan coordinated her fingers to grasp the beaker securely.

'Am I awake?' It was hard to be sure, even as she felt the water trickle into the cracks of her arid mouth and smelled the clean linen of Gemma's spotless uniform.

The question didn't seem to trouble the nurse. 'Yes, love, you're awake now.'

'What happened? Why was I injected?'

'You got a bit distressed; the doctor gave you something to calm you down.' She had a pleasant West Country accent that spoke of Cornish beaches, cream teas and lazy summer holidays, at odds with the fragile atmosphere that clung to the room.

'Did they say where my son is?'

'No idea, love.'

'Have you seen him? Has Stef brought him to visit?'

'Not that I know of. Your husband's gone home now, but he'll be back again tomorrow. Been here every day since you were admitted.'

Megan stared at the nurse, struggling to process her sentences, unable to summon her initial panic at realising Luka's absence. It had been replaced with a dull sensation, as if emotion had become impossible, clouded by a heavy fog not unlike a vicious hangover.

'I need to see the doctor from before. The American? He must know where my baby is.'

'I'll page him for you. Do you need anything else?'

'I need my child!'

'How about a cup of tea?'

17

'I don't want tea. I want the doctor.'

'I'll see what I can do. Try to stay calm, love.'

The door closed behind the nurse and Megan saw it was secured; entry and exit permitted only by a pass-card. She looked to the window, noted the lack of handles. An air-conditioning unit sat above it, rendering the window the sole decoration amid the clinical white.

Being faced with the undeniable evidence that she was a prisoner didn't shock her. In fact, she couldn't bring herself to care at all. What did it matter when she was denied the most important thing in her world?

She had no urge to move but forced herself upright with a vague idea she might find an escape route somewhere in the soulless room. Sliding clumsily out of bed, she had to cling to the rails until she was steady on her feet. The floor was uncomfortably cold and a draught made her shiver, making her aware of how the hospital gown gaped at the back, leaving her exposed.

She took the blue blanket from the bed, wrapped it around her shoulders to preserve her modesty. Made a slow circuit of the small room, distrusting of each tentative step. The bed was secured to the floor, as was the small circular table by the window and its two chairs. She gave the window latch a tug, just in case, but it failed to move. There was no wardrobe, no locker in the bedside table. Nothing in the room was movable; even the controls for the bed and wall-mounted TV were attached. In one corner of the ceiling, a fish-eye lens watched over her, benevolent and threatening all at once, a priest surveying his sinful congregation.

It all seemed ridiculously overcautious, but hadn't she been exactly the same, in those first days after Luka's birth? Scared of leaving him with a blanket in case he suffocated, terrified he'd stop breathing if she put him down to sleep. So many ordinary objects a threat to his safety.

Where was he? He would be missing her by now. Would he even remember her when they were reunited?

'Hello, Megan.' The cheerful accent made her jump. She hadn't heard the doctor beep himself into the room. She wobbled unsteadily, grabbing the table for support.

'I can't remember your name.'

'Call me Dr Mac.' It sounded like an instruction rather than an invitation. 'Shall we sit and talk for a while? Table or bed?'

'Table, I'm not an invalid.' Megan wrapped the blanket more securely around her. The room wasn't cold, but she couldn't find any warmth in it. She took the chair nearest the window, watching Macaulay unhurriedly open a leather-bound notebook, uncap a fountain pen and settle himself in the other seat.

'Do you feel able to carry on our earlier conversation?'

'You mean am I going to freak out again?'

'I don't like to use that phrase, but we'll work through it if it does happen.'

'Work through it with a needle, you mean,' Megan snapped, surprising herself. She usually avoided confrontation, a desire fuelled by the years of past conflicts she had been unable to walk away from.

'Only if we absolutely have to. We don't inject patients for no reason.'

Megan took a steadying breath, nodding as if she trusted the assurances. 'You said I'd had a psychotic episode?'

'Do you remember what we talked about?'

19

'Some of it. I remember my husband denying we have a baby. I've no idea why he'd do that.'

'Megan, he was correct. You do not have a child. This is part of your condition; it causes delusions and hallucinations. Put simply, patients can't tell the difference between reality and their brain tricking them. That's what you're experiencing.'

'You're wrong! I have the C-section scar!'

'That's from your hysterectomy.'

'Why don't you believe me?'

'Because it would be wrong to feed your delusions. Let's talk about another topic; I don't want you losing control again.'

Megan realised she was shaking, on the verge of doing just that. She didn't want another needle, not when she was searching for answers.

'Why can't I remember things?' she asked with forced calmness. 'It's like my memory's been wiped.'

'That's also part of your condition. It should improve with time.'

'You said I tried to commit suicide. What did I do?'

'Let's not go into that now. We're going to have intensive therapy sessions – I'd rather wait to discuss traumatic events until you're better equipped to deal with them.'

Frustration flared again despite her best intentions and she had to grip the edge of the table to remain in her seat. 'You can't ignore my questions because you're worried I won't cope with the answers!'

'Give me time to work with you first. I'll keep a note of all your questions.' He gestured with his fountain pen. 'I promise we'll address them when I feel you're well enough. Shall we talk about your admission to the Grosvenor?'

'I don't care.'

20

Another smile, a parent indulging a child's tantrum.

'At the moment, you're on an involuntary section, a Section Two. That means we can keep you here twenty-eight days, with or without your consent.'

'I have to stay here for a month?' Megan heard her voice rise with shock.

'Hopefully not. However, there's another involuntarily section, a Section Three, if we decide you require more intensive in-patient treatment.'

'How long would a Section Three last?' She hardly dared ask.

'Six months initially, but it can be renewed indefinitely.' Macaulay held up his hand at Megan's horrified expression. 'I don't imagine a Section Three will be needed in your case, if you commit to treatment.'

'You mean I need to cooperate with you.'

'Only you can make that decision.'

'I don't need treatment! I don't feel mad.'

'You're not mad, Megan, you're unwell.'

'Then why don't I feel unwell? Psychosis is when you're out of control, isn't it? You lose your grip on reality. That's not me.'

'Shall I read your notes to you? So you can understand what's happened since you've been here?'

There didn't seem much point in saying no, so Megan threw up her hands and sat back in her chair. Macaulay unlocked his briefcase and withdrew a slim file.

'I can read it myself.'

She saw a moment's indecision before he slid the file across the table, relaxing back as if they were skimming the papers over Sunday brunch.

It took too long for her eyes to adjust to the text and, even then, she could only focus on certain lines that seemed to jump from the page.

Megan was transferred in an acute psychotic state, requiring restraints during transportation. She was previously admitted as a trauma emergency to St Mary's A&E following a suicide attempt.

She is unable to respond to direct questions and is experiencing severe hallucinations, including a belief that people are trying to kill her.

Megan has frequently attempted to harm herself, including tearing at her skin with her nails and clawing her eyes.

Megan is displaying severe delusions involving her husband and her family.

Megan has been witnessed attempting to rip out her own hair.

That was the final straw, especially when she found she had habitually grasped a lock of hair as she read. It stung, and she remembered her head wound, hurriedly releasing her grip.

'I'm not trying to rip my hair out! I just tug on it if I'm stressed, I don't pull hard.' She looked up abruptly at Macaulay. 'This is absolute crap!'

She threw the file across the table to him, tried to push back her chair before remembering it was attached to the floor. Macaulay showed no alarm as he returned the file to his briefcase and stood.

'I'll give you some time to think over everything we've talked about before Gemma brings your medication. Our first therapy session will be tomorrow.'

'You can't go now! You haven't answered my questions! Where is my baby?'

The door was closing softly behind him before she could move to prevent it. She flung herself at the handle several moments too late, jerking it impotently. Her prison held firm.

Chapter Three

Megan had hoped her first therapy would take place in a different room, away from the cold, claustrophobic walls that kept her trapped within their sterile grasp. Somewhere peaceful, where she could breathe. But Macaulay buzzed himself in, carrying his leather notebook, and settled at the small table.

'Good morning, Megan.' He indicated the chair opposite him. She hated how his eyes appraised her coolly, as if searching for flaws.

She slumped into the seat. Clothing had been unnecessary in the days she had been sedated, so now she had to wait for Stef to bring a bag when he visited. Until then, she was stuck with the gown, though Gemma had found her a towelling robe. She drew it tighter around her, dropping her chin to sit on her chest as she folded her arms.

'How was your night?'

'I thought I'd dream about Luka, but I didn't.'

'Patients often report that the medication prevents them from dreaming.' No reaction to Luka's name. 'I'd like us to get to know each other today. Why don't you tell me a little about yourself?'

There was nothing she wanted to share with this man, but she struggled to direct her foggy thoughts to provide even the blandest of information. 'There's not a lot to know. I'm thirty-six, born and raised in London. Stef and I have been married seven years and we live in Newington Green. Luka is our first child. I read architecture at King's, but I work with Stef now, managing his property company. I have one sister; she's married to Eve, who's also American, actually, and they had my niece two years ago.'

'Very concise.'

'What else do you want to know?'

'Your sister is Sophia, yes? And she has a daughter?'

'Yes. Amelia. Or are you going to deny her existence as well as Luka's?'

Macaulay gave the condescending smile that was already becoming familiar. 'Sophia has visited regularly. I've met her several times. She tells me you two are close.'

'We had to be, growing up as we did.'

'Would you like to tell me more about that?'

'Not particularly.'

'I notice you haven't asked for your parents, Megan. Are they still alive?'

'My father is.'

'How long ago did you lose your mother?'

'Years ago.'

'Were you close?'

'No,' Megan said shortly, determined to elaborate no further. 'Why are you asking about my family but ignoring all my questions about my son?'

'It's information that will help along the journey.'

'The journey to being allowed to go home?'

'If that's your primary aim, yes.'

'Of course it's my primary aim. I need to get home to my baby.'

Her declaration went unacknowledged. 'How many years are there between you and Sophia?'

Megan couldn't prevent an involuntary hiss of frustration. 'I'm two years older.'

'Not a large gap. Do you get along well?'

'Generally, yes.'

'These questions aren't part of a test. You can speak freely.'

'What if I don't want to answer them?'

'You don't have to, but that would make your primary aim rather difficult to achieve.'

'If I don't talk to you, you won't let me go home?'

'I need to be able to trust that you and your family will be safe.'

'I could just be telling you what you want to hear.' As soon as the words were out, she realised it was a stupid thing to have said, but it was too late and she was too angry to apologise.

'That's true, but people have tried before and not succeeded in fooling me.'

'You make it sound like a challenge.'

'I'm challenging you to work with me, not against me. Some of my questions will seem strange and invasive, too personal. They're not for me to pry into your private life; they're designed so I understand the root of your condition, to guide your recovery.'

'So, I will recover?'

25

'Hopefully, if you trust the process.'

'I'd have more trust if you didn't keep drugging me.'

'The medication is necessary at the moment.' Macaulay capped his pen, no smile this time. 'We'll stop there for today. Thank you for talking with me.'

Megan watched the door lock engage, tempted by the whispered idea of a sprint for freedom the next time it opened, but swiftly dismissed the thought. Quick movement was impossible. Her limbs resisted any demand for response, heavy weights pinning her down. She didn't even have her phone to order an Uber.

Where *was* her phone? She hadn't thought to ask for it. She was sure it would contain photos of Luka. She stabbed the nurse bell rapidly.

'Everything OK, love?' As ever, Gemma appeared within moments.

'Can I have my phone, please?'

'Your husband's got it safe for you at home. We don't allow phones in here.'

The slap of frustration hurt. 'Why not?'

'Doctor says they compromise treatment. Won't do any harm to have a rest from social media.' Gemma checked her watch. 'Ages till dinner yet. Fancy a cup of tea and a biscuit?'

'I'd rather have my phone.'

'Not my decision, I'm afraid.'

'But I need it!' The old Megan would have discussed the issue calmly, shying away from conflict, but this new Megan seemed to have a hair-trigger temper.

'I'm sorry, love.' Gemma didn't react to the sudden flare of anger. 'Let me get you that tea. Won't be a minute.'

Megan didn't respond, her mind still fixed on her phone, forgetting she despised tea. Gemma's comment had reminded her about social media. She would have posted Luka's birth on Facebook; it was her strongest link to old university friends and former Londoners now scattered across the world. If she could access it, she would be able to prove the platitudes wrong once and for all.

It seemed the phone would not be returned to her while she was in the unit. The only way to leave the Grosvenor was to show she was well enough to go home. She could do that, play by the rules, passively submit to get what she wanted. Once she was home, there would be no more games. It wasn't as if you could hide a baby.

If that was what she had to do, she would act her part. She had always liked having a goal to work towards.

Stef wasn't alone. Megan could see him speaking to someone out of view and hope bloomed in her chest. She scrambled to her feet, forgetting to tug her dressing-gown belt.

'I see you've embraced the current fashions in psychiatric chic.' Her sister grinned as she entered the room, pushing in front of Stef. Winded with disappointment, Megan turned away to salvage what little dignity she had.

'Don't worry. Your PJs were the first things I packed.' Stef waved her familiar overnight bag, looking pleased with himself for remembering.

'How's it going?' Sophia kissed her cheek as if they were meeting for coffee.

'Are you not looking after Luka?' Megan demanded. 'I thought you'd have him.'

27

Sophia cleared her throat, taking care in unwinding and folding her pashmina. Usually, it would have been discarded on the nearest chair. 'Stef's got your Kindle, but do you need something else bringing in?'

'Don't you ignore me as well!'

'I'd fetch your sketch pad, but they have a rule about pencils, apparently,' Sophia chattered on. 'Presumably you can't make a weapon with wax crayons ...'

'Thanks, Sophia,' Stef interrupted tightly.

'Where is my son?' Megan almost shouted.

'Keep your voice down!' Sophia hissed. 'For God's sake, Megan, do you want to be tranquillised?'

'I want someone to answer me!'

'We don't have answers! Just sit down before you bring the nurses running. I don't fancy visiting a vegetable again, it's disconcerting.'

Megan didn't have the strength to prevent her sister steering her to the bed, practically forcing her down on to the mattress. 'I wish I understood what's happening to me,' she whispered, almost to herself. Her visitors seemed content to pretend she wasn't talking to them.

Sophia sprawled next to her, as if the confrontation had never happened, all lean curves and supple limbs, bronzed skin and artfully scrunched bleached hair. Her snub nose, scattered with just the right amount of freckles, and dazzling amber eyes gave her the look of a self-assured starlet who knew they could have whatever they wanted. A complete contrast to Megan's English rose appearance: porcelain complexion; fine, delicate features that demanded gentle handling; the long-necked, graceful figure of a ballet dancer and the elegance that went with it.

'Bed's comfier than expected. No wonder this place is costing Stef a fortune.'

'As if the money matters!' Stef said sharply.

'I'm joking! Chill your beans, or whatever it is the kids say now.'

Megan flinched at the sudden increase in volume, despite the familiarity of their bickering. She and Stef rarely found cause to argue, but he enjoyed squabbling with Sophia. Her younger sister had taken all of their mother's temper, whereas Megan's character had developed from years of refereeing their blazing rows.

Sophia helped herself to the uneaten orange from Megan's very healthy lunch. Organic and paleo-friendly was the order of the day when it came to Grosvenor food, a distinctly Californian influence.

'Shall I tell you about Amelia's latest dramas? They're much better than soap operas.'

'Where is Amelia? Is she with Luka?'

Sophia airbrushed the second question effortlessly, barely pausing. 'Eve's taken her to the zoo. She's been impossible today, absolutely crazy. Oops, sorry.'

'For fuck's sake, Soph.' Stef rubbed his palms across his face.

Megan rolled her eyes. 'Words aren't *verboten*, you know. I'm well aware Amelia is absolutely bonkers.'

Sophia flicked a defiant strand of pith in Stef's direction. 'She's adopted a potato. I have to keep swapping the damn thing before it sprouts those horrible white tentacles. You try finding identical baking potatoes. She refuses to wear shoes. Wellies are OK, sandals just about acceptable, but actual shoes, forget that. And don't get me started on the bloody hat.'

'What hat?'

'She found it at Camden Market, crocheted monstrosity of a beanie, bright yellow with pink flowers. She won't leave the house without it on her head. I compromised by putting it in her little backpack; ten minutes later, she was still screeching. The neighbours will be calling social services – they're already unsure about lesbians having children.'

'We don't need to hear all your drama, Soph,' Stef interrupted.

'Oh, shut up. You should have seen them at the windows when Amelia had her hat meltdown. Good thing Eve—'

'Sophia, enough,' Stef said firmly.

'—was carrying the pushchair or she'd have given them the finger.' Sophia continued as if he hadn't spoken. 'What the hell's the matter, Stef? Am I not allowed to have a normal conversation? Would you rather we sit in silence and meditate?'

The two glared at each other, neither prepared to back down. Sophia carelessly popped another segment of orange in her mouth. 'How are you getting along with the lovely Dr Mac, Megan?'

'He mentioned you two had met.'

'He's been quite chatty when I've visited. More than you, anyway.'

'Sorry I couldn't join in a gossip session.' Megan looked to Stef. 'Do you know when I'll be allowed home?'

Stef chose that moment to tie his shoelaces. 'It's up to Dr Mac.'

'Will you ask him? It's driving me mad, not knowing anything. I don't even know how I tried to kill myself.'

Sophia froze midway through dissecting another segment. 'You don't remember?'

'Not a thing.'

'Why the hell not?'

'The doctor insists it's part of my condition, but I think it must be the medication or maybe whatever my head injury was. Soph, you must know what happened?'

'Dr Mac needs to have these conversations during your therapy,' Stef intervened. 'We can't talk about it.'

'He tells you what you can and can't say to me?' Her voice rose in disbelief.

Stef sat up straight, crossing his arms and earning a scornful glare from Sophia. 'He knows what he's doing, Megs. He's the best in the country for psychosis.'

There seemed no other option than to accept that. What else could she say? Clearly, Macaulay issued the commands, and Stef seemed to be following orders, for once.

The remainder of the visit was filled with anecdotes of Amelia, wallpaper dilemmas for a new property and TV updates on reality shows Megan wouldn't dream of watching. She remembered to nod and smile in the right places, made the effort to add the odd comment when it seemed she'd been silent for too long.

Thirty minutes passed without incident; she hadn't screamed or tried to hurt anyone. Stef and Sophia busied themselves gathering coats, squabbling about traffic and Stef's erratic driving.

'Bring Amelia next time.' Megan managed to get a word in as they said their goodbyes.

Sophia's smile faltered. 'Best not while you're here. You know how loud she is, she'll disturb the other patients. When you're home, OK?'

More like she doesn't trust you around your child.

31

The voice was immediately recognisable. It was one she had heard before. As clear as if Megan had spoken out loud, strident enough to make her jump. She spun away, ostensibly to retie her robe. The sound seemed to echo around the bare room. Surely everyone had heard it, so insistent was it, but when she slyly looked, Stef and Sophia were entirely unaware.

They won't hear anything they choose not to.

Chapter Four

Before

One of the few things the brothers agreed on was how fortunate they were to be non-identical. Rarely spotted for twins, they didn't share that fabled bond. No sixth sense, no mirroring, no finishing of each other's sentences or agreement of thought. Even as toddlers, they had done their own thing.

Stefan was the gregarious, sporty one, popular with his peers and mildly exasperating to his teachers. Isaac preferred his own company; he was quiet and studious and his intellect was recognised at a young age. A scholarship to Dulwich College followed. The family could comfortably afford the day fees of the local private school, a twenty-minute walk from home, but Dulwich was beyond their means and Isaac was duly dispatched to that elite world.

In prep school, Stefan's popularity had kept Isaac's bullies at bay, an inconvenience Stefan tolerated to prevent his peers learning too much about his brother's fragility. The snide comments and mocking laughter made him burn with the same humiliation he had felt when he was denied the advantage of public school, an opportunity he would have fully embraced, unlike Isaac.

At Dulwich, Isaac was on his own, no stronger twin to hide behind. Public-school boys were encouraged to fight their own battles; a bit of name-calling and the odd scuffle were to be expected. It was character-building, a sentiment Isaac's father liked to echo.

Drowning amid the prides of alpha males who ruled their competitive, ruthless world, Isaac took refuge among library tomes and in the classrooms of sympathetic teachers who raved about his abilities. He told no one of his trials, and no one bothered to ask. Quietly, gradually, he withdrew from the wider world and its threats.

Still smarting and unable to find sympathy for his twin's problems, Stefan detached himself, keeping to the rugby pitch and the squash court; cricket and athletics in the summer. Isaac was put forward for his Cambridge interview a year early and went up to Trinity to read bioengineering, a seventeen-year-old academically advanced beyond his years but, internally, a damaged, brittle child. Indifferent, Stefan did just enough to get by in the classroom, an easy smile appeasement for acceptable essays and last-minute revision and an effective shield against the dark clouds that followed Isaac.

'You can't go through life coasting along,' his father regularly declared.

Stefan shrugged, careless of the warning. 'It's worked so far.'

'You're perfectly capable of achieving more. Look at your brother and his IQ.'

'I'd rather not, thanks. I'm doing fine, Dad. I'll get my grades for uni, don't worry.'

'You'll get a shock at Durham. I wish you'd tried for Oxbridge.'

'Not interested. Durham's more fun.'

'Life can't always be fun.'

''Course it can.' Stefan laughed, a determined study of nonchalance.

His final year of sixth form was proving to be a blast. He'd been going out with Megan Crawley from the other end of Marlborough Avenue since last Christmas and, although they'd known each other since early childhood, this was new ground. He'd been the one to take her virginity, an unexpectedly sensual experience, very different from his previous trysts, and one that had left him, for the first time in his life, helplessly in love.

It helped that she was far more beautiful than she realised: high, regal cheekbones, hair the colour of polished conkers that lay in waves down her back, a dancer's precise movements, legs that seemed endless. She spoke of Royal Ballet School dreams gone unfulfilled, replaced with a new passion for sketching, her feelings of responsibility towards her mother and her desire to travel the world, fascinating him with her quiet capability.

'We'll go together,' Stefan promised. 'When you finish your A levels, we'll take a few months backpacking.'

'Who says we'll even be together then! Everything will change when you go to Durham.'

'It won't,' he said fervently, believing his every word. 'Nothing will change.'

Of course, it did. A disturbance one night, shaking Stefan from his sleep. The sound of frantic movements from his parents' room, hissed words being exchanged. Stepping into the hallway, shivering in just his boxer shorts, he saw they were dressed, but not in their normal neat fashion. His father was sockless and wearing his golf trousers; his mother's hair was a tangled mess.

'What's happened?' he asked.

They seemed shocked to find him there, as if they had forgotten all about him.

'Isaac's ill, Stefan,' his father finally said. 'Hopefully nothing to worry about, but we need to go to him.'

'Is he in hospital?'

'Yes, but we don't know the details yet.'

'Shall I come with you?'

'You stay here, you need to look after Orion.' Their golden retriever hadn't even bothered to see what the commotion was about.

'What's wrong with Isa?'

'We're not sure. We need to go, Stefan, we'll call when we can. You'll be OK, won't you?'

Stefan nodded, because what else could he do? His parents were gone in moments, barely pausing to find shoes and coats, distractedly telling Orion to stay when he finally roused himself to investigate.

Stefan joined the dog on the snug's sofa, wrapping his arms around the warm, familiar body. Orion cuddled close, tongue lolling happily, and was asleep again in minutes. No such comfort for Stefan; sleep had abandoned him. He sat, staring into the dying embers of the log burner, and somehow he knew this wasn't just a case of glandular fever or appendicitis.

Something had changed in his family that night.

When Isaac eventually came home, his left arm was swathed in bandages and Stefan couldn't prevent himself staring at them, imagining the damage his twin had inflicted upon himself. Always thin, taller than Stefan, he was now skeletal. Grey skinned, bruises under both eyes, hair unwashed and lank with grease. He was silent, shying away from Stefan's uncertain greeting as if fearing violence, unable to make eye contact. Some unexplored part of Stefan bade him to ask the question their parents refused to answer – why had he made such a determined effort to kill himself? – but he tamped it down, wanting to discover more first.

Isaac didn't leave his room. Their mother made his favourite dishes but he ate only cereal. It wasn't talked about. At the dinner table, their parents chatted with forced casualness as they ignored Isaac's empty place. Stefan's enquiries were met with vague details of depression, anxiety, replies that were too easy, and he gave up asking questions no one seemed prepared to answer honestly.

After another week of tiptoeing around, he decided there was no point putting his own life on hold. Any queries about his twin were handled with a shrug and a vague reply, leaving the enquirer to draw their own conclusions about a sudden illness, a struggle to diagnose. Cancer, maybe. How awful for the family. They would give Stefan a sympathetic smile or a pat on the shoulder and hurriedly change the subject, exactly as he wanted.

Arriving home one Friday from school, eager to collect Megan from her piano lesson, he shot straight down to the cellar without announcing his return, to pinch a bottle from the wine racks.

He didn't hear his parents enter the kitchen and begin their usual routine of preparing dinner together until he was at the top of the cellar steps, the stolen bottle stashed in his boot bag. He froze, unable to think of any explanation for being down there if he was caught. His father was precious about his expensive wine and a lecture would steal valuable time with Megan.

'We should have insisted on him being tested again,' he heard his mother say.

'The paediatrician said years ago he isn't on the spectrum. That won't have changed. This isn't something we can stick a label on.'

'We have to do something.'

'What do you think I'm trying to do?'

'I don't think you realise how serious this is.'

'Of course I bloody realise — not like I can ignore what happened!'

'We don't know what happened; only Isaac does.'

'I've got a fair idea, and so do you, if you stop burying your head in the sand. We need to get him proper help, not more damn tests, before it's too late.'

'Is that why you can barely bring yourself to speak to him?'

'I don't know what to say to him.'

'He needs to know we support him. You've seen how vulnerable he is.'

'He needs to stop this nonsense!'

Stefan was growing uncomfortable in his crouched position, but he didn't dare move and expose himself. He heard a sharp bang that sounded like a pan being slammed down, then his father calling after his mother and their voices fading.

He wasted no time in escaping through the kitchen door.

Chapter Five

The voice stayed with Megan through the following days. It was comforting, in a way, company through the never-ending hours waiting for nothing. Stef visited dutifully each afternoon, inconsequential small talk carefully screened for controversy, his body relaxing only when his thirty minutes were up.

They're hiding Luka from you.

The voice sounded like her own. It didn't sound evil or angry, a little forceful maybe, but the real Megan lacked natural authority and a little vigour inspired by the voice was no bad thing.

'Want to come for a walk?' Gemma asked.

Megan looked up in surprise from her Kindle, noticing she hadn't turned the page for quite some time. 'I can do that?'

''Long as I come with you, sure.'

You could run away! Gemma won't be able to stop you on her own.

Megan seized on the idea. 'Where can we go?'

'Just down to the gardens, but it's outside, at least.'

She wanted to hurry before the offer was withdrawn, but her limbs wouldn't cooperate. Her movements were agonisingly slow and clumsy as she struggled to zip a hooded top and coordinate her feet into untied trainers. She realised with sinking hopes that she would never manage to outsprint Gemma if she made a break for freedom.

She expected the nurse to hold her arm as they left her room, take her elbow like a police officer escorting a prisoner, but although Gemma stood noticeably close, she let her walk alone. It almost felt like trust.

There were just two other rooms on the corridor. Megan attempted to peer through each window but saw only the still, silent forms of people in bed. Like her room, their doors were barred by entry fobs.

'How many other patients are here?' she asked.

'Not many. Ours is a very small unit. We share the building with a couple of other therapeutic practices.'

Gemma guided her down the stairs, linking arms in a way that felt friendly rather than restraining. The ground-floor corridor seemed to be offices, closed mahogany doors and the sound of distant discussions behind them, but no physical evidence of other staff.

Gemma beeped another door, and they were outside. Megan stopped abruptly as the air touched her face. She could hear traffic and birds and rustling trees. There was a scent of fresh coffee in the air, just discernible above the city smells of exhaust fumes and fast food. Sounds and smells no Londoner was ever usually aware of, but Megan now felt acutely sensitive to them. She inhaled the memories of her life before the Grosvenor.

'How's it feel?' Gemma smiled.

Megan closed her eyes, let the breeze lift her hair, felt the spring sun touch her skin. Any lingering plans to run slid away. 'Free,' she whispered.

40

She looked around the small garden. Well-maintained borders, daffodils and crocuses peeking through. Neat lawn and crazy paving, dotted with benches. The building was handsome, red brick, not the seventies ugliness she had been expecting.

'Thank you for bringing me out,' she remembered to say.

'Just ask. Any time I can, I will.'

'Hopefully I won't be here much longer.'

'Fingers crossed for you, love.' Deliberately neutral.

'How long have you worked here?'

'Couple of years, since Dr Mac set up the practice.'

'That's not as long as I thought.'

'He practised in the States before he moved here. Years of experience – you're in safe hands.'

Megan watched a butterfly settle on a scarlet tulip, wings vibrant with colour and shimmering delicately in the soft breeze, envying its freedom. The voice had quietened amid the sounds of normal life. She tilted her face up to the weak sun and felt herself smile.

Stef was sorely tempted to let the call go to voicemail when he saw Macaulay's name on his phone screen. What the hell had happened now?

'What's wrong?' He reluctantly picked up, realising the conversation would be no easier if he delayed it.

'Good afternoon, Stefan,' came the unhurried voice. 'Nothing's wrong. Please don't worry.'

Stef expelled the breath he hadn't realised he'd been holding. 'Apologies, I didn't mean to be sharp.'

'I'm calling about the next steps of Megan's treatment. How would you feel if she was discharged?'

'Is she ready for that?' Stef probed. 'I expected she'd be an in-patient for weeks.'

'I don't like to keep patients here too long. It further distorts their grip on reality, the longer they're away from the real world and their regular lives.'

'But she's not herself.'

'And she won't be for some time, but she's managing.'

'It seems a bit soon,' Stef insisted, determined to be heard. 'What if she doesn't cope?'

'We have the option of readmission, but it's rarely necessary after the initial assessment period. I know this is a bit daunting for families, but she's still your wife, Stefan. You're not bringing a stranger into your home.'

'She feels like a stranger.'

'And that's a little struggle of your own to overcome. Megan needs to feel she's still loved and accepted by you.'

'I didn't mean it like that—'

'There are some things I need you to prepare for Megan's return home.'

Irked at being spoken over, Stef searched for a pen, finding only a highlighter. It was hard to read on the Post-it note but, as usual these days, he was unprepared.

'You need to gather any sharp objects, medicines, painkillers, kitchen and bathroom cleaners – anything Megan could use to hurt herself or others. I've emailed you a list. Lock them away somewhere secure. Remove any tablets, laptops or computers if you can; she needs to be kept away from social media. Then message the people she's most likely to contact; let them know about Megan's treatment and why it's important they don't answer any questions she might ask. Do you have a landline?'

42

'Yes, but I can delete the contact list ...' Stef felt a sudden chill as he realised what Macaulay was saying. 'You don't want her talking to her friends?'

'We don't want any setbacks caused by someone saying the wrong thing.'

'God, this sounds like I'm policing her.'

The statement was ignored. 'You also need to think about anything that could be used as a ligature, and make sure you take all door and window keys.'

'So she can't escape or jump,' Stef said dully.

'This is short term, Stefan, remember that.'

Once again, the use of his full name made Stef's shoulders tighten instinctively, ready to fight off the memories that hovered. 'Anything else?'

'Not for the moment. If you can complete those tasks today, I'd appreciate it.'

Stef affirmed his commitment – because what else could he do? – and said goodbye, staring at the blank phone screen for too long after he ended the call. The email list pinged into his inbox, but he didn't open it immediately. He had never imagined he would need to clear his home of anything his wife could use to hurt him or herself, but it brought back more unwelcome thoughts of his brother. He couldn't bear to go through that again.

He shook himself firmly, banishing Isaac along with his full name, and retrieved a storage box from the garage before setting about his task, trying to be methodical, continually referring to the list. Upstairs first: bathrooms and master suite, his office, up to the second floor to Megan's study in the rafters, which he escaped from as quickly as he could. So many little items he'd

43

never considered remotely harmful. The kitchen was his biggest challenge. There was far more than the Japanese knives and the cutlery set. Over an hour, and the pile on the island continued to grow.

Stef was not, by nature, an organised man. Megan was the one with the weekly planner, the appointment diary and the strict schedule. His property business was successful thanks mostly to her. He made the big decisions, the impulsive purchases, took the risks and earned the gains, but it was Megan who analysed profit margins, organised the trade bookings and ensured that relationships remained cordial.

Now, she wasn't even allowed tweezers for her eyebrows. A sharp pencil was a banned item. There could be no unsupervised cooking or gardening. Everything was to be locked away after each use. God, it was a minefield.

He'd always preferred disorder to rules and spontaneity to schedules, but now he wanted to cling to the comfort of routine, a craving for familiarity. No more uncertainty, no more tiptoeing around, steeling himself for the next episode.

His phone ringing made him jump, so very loud in the silent house. His heart was still pounding as he snatched it up.

'You OK? Sounds like you've been stabbed.'

Stef slumped onto a breakfast-bar stool, taking a calming breath. 'Hardly funny, given the circumstances, Soph. What's up? I'm busy trying to decide if a whisk is sharp enough to be a weapon.'

'I wondered if you wanted me to come with you tomorrow, to collect Megan. Dr Mac just rang to say you'll need support. Insurance in case you go mad too, I assume.'

'I didn't know he'd call you.' In the back of his mind, it

registered that doctors didn't usually discuss patients with multiple relatives, but he was too distracted to give the thought any attention.

'Not like there's anyone else, is there? Were you intending to tell me, or did you expect I'd find out via my crystal ball?'

'I've only just found out myself. I'm still getting my head round it.'

'Don't you want her to come home?'

'No . . . I mean, yes! I don't know. I'm thinking how hard this will be to manage once she's home.'

'You're hardly relaxed even while she's safely locked away!'

'I thought you—'

'I know what you thought. I may not make millions, like you do, but I'm not actually stupid.'

'If she finds out . . .'

'She has to find out at some point! It's not exactly a secret that can be kept for ever.'

'I know!' Stef raked his fingers through his hair, realising it was damp with nervous sweat. 'But not while she's like this. I can't lose her.'

Sophia was silent for a moment. 'So, shall I come with you to the Grosvenor?'

It was tempting to grasp her offer of security, but he was still wary of Sophia's lax tongue. 'No, we'll be fine.'

'What if she grabs the wheel while you're driving?'

'I'm taking a cab.' He didn't want to admit he'd already thought of that scenario.

'If you're sure.' He thought he detected a note of relief. 'I'll visit once she's settled.'

'Will you bring Amelia?'

An uneasy pause. 'Bit soon, I think.' Another pause, even more awkward. 'Do you think she'll cope at home?'

Stef shook his head to dislodge his very similar worry. 'She'll still be on medication and daily therapy with Dr Mac.' It didn't answer the question, but it was the most reassuring reply he could summon.

'I wouldn't mind a bit of therapy with Dr Mac,' Sophia sighed.

'Not sure your wife would be too keen on that.'

'Lesbians can appreciate men's attractiveness as well,' she scolded. 'Eve fancies Hugh Jackman.'

'I think *I* fancy Hugh Jackman.'

They both laughed, grasping the moment's relief.

'Good luck,' Sophia said when they'd sobered.

'I reckon I'll need it.'

Megan waited, because that was what she did now, weighed down by a thick, suffocating cloak she had ceased attempting to evade. Before, she could never tolerate being idle, needing to be absorbed in a book, or music or drawing, but now she could sit motionless without any realisation that hours had passed. Time had become meaningless.

'Do you need anything?' Gemma asked, her pass beeping against the entry pad as she poked her head in. 'Something to drink? Biscuit?'

You need your son. Ask her for that.

Megan did her best to ignore the voice. 'No, thank you.'

'Doctor's on his way now.'

'We've already had therapy today. He just talked about what psychosis is and the sort of delusions people have. He says my delusion is the baby, but he's wrong.'

46

Gemma offered an uncertain smile. 'Not my area of expertise, I'm afraid. I just do as I'm told. He won't be a minute, anyway.'

He'll lie to you again. He wants you to think you're mad, then you'll stop asking awkward questions about Luka.

Megan gritted her teeth against the baiting and willed the voice to let her think for herself.

The beep of another pass announced Macaulay's arrival. 'Good afternoon, Megan. Did you enjoy the gardens? How do you feel?'

The lack of pauses for answers told of his lack of interest in the answers, but Megan responded regardless. 'A little less foggy, I think.'

'Excellent. We're continuing to slowly reduce your medication.'

'So I'll feel normal again soon?'

'It's a gradual process, but these feelings of being weighed down and time slowing will lessen.'

Megan sighed, annoyed at his vague platitudes. 'Are we having another therapy session, Dr Mac? I thought we only met once a day.'

'I've come to ask a question. How do you feel about going home?'

A jolt of electricity ran through Megan's body and for a moment she couldn't find any words, couldn't remember what to say. She gaped for rather too long, trying to corral her racing thoughts, almost falling over the words when she could finally speak. 'That's all I want. Please let me go home. I'm ready.'

'You think you'll be OK?'

'Of course. I know I will. I can really go home?'

'There'll have to be a meeting to discuss changing your section, and you'll need to commit to your medication and a therapy session every weekday.'

'I don't need a daily session.'

'I'm afraid that's non-negotiable. Altering your section carries a risk.'

Megan would have agreed to any condition at that point. 'When can I go?'

'Tomorrow. If everyone's in agreement, we'll organise the paperwork, then Stefan can take you home.'

You've done it! You'll be free of this fucking prison. Tomorrow, you'll find Luka.

Triumph swelled through Megan's veins, a momentary high she felt sure would last for ever.

'Thank you, Dr Mac,' she said politely, as if nothing had changed.

Chapter Six

Time was standing still again. The meeting, it seemed, didn't include Megan.

It's wrong of them to talk about you when you're not present. They could be saying anything.

Megan agreed she should have been invited, if only to defend herself against the imagined slights.

'Don't look so worried.' Gemma had brought another tepid cup of tea she wouldn't drink.

Don't let her patronise you!

'I'm not worried,' Megan snapped. 'Is it always like this? Waiting for your fate to be decided by other people?'

'Patients don't usually go into section meetings; it's next of kin who represents them. Because you didn't give consent to the original section, see.'

'So my opinion doesn't matter.'

'I thought you'd be happy to be going home.'

'I'm angry I'm not allowed to be responsible for myself.'

'You don't have to argue with me, love, I'm just doing as I'm told.'

'There's no one else to argue with until this meeting's over,' Megan said helplessly. 'Sorry. I shouldn't be taking it out on you.'

'Want to play cards while you wait? All's quiet at the moment.'

Megan couldn't think of a reason to say no so she watched passively as Gemma shuffled and dealt, stared blankly at her hand.

'I miss my baby,' she whispered.

'Oh, love, I'm sorry.'

'Do you believe he's real?'

'It's not for me to say.'

'I'm not making him up, Gemma, I swear. I'm not a liar.'

'No one thinks you're a liar.'

'They do. They look at me like I'm talking absolute crap. No one listens to me!'

'Megan, I listen to you.' Gemma took her hand, her tone becoming urgent. 'But you need to listen to me now. If you start shouting and screaming, they won't let you go. You could end up here for weeks, and that's no good for you. Look at me. Breathe. In for five, out for five. Come on, do it with me.'

Don't give them a reason to keep you here.

Megan submitted, trying to copy the nurse's breathing, closing her eyes as she focused on counting. The roaring in her ears seemed to increase with each shaky inhalation.

'That's it. Well done.' Gemma kept hold of her hand. 'Keep breathing.'

Megan did as instructed, helpless to do anything else. Pins and needles robbed her fingers of feeling as her head pulsed with pain. A band tightened around her chest, forcing her to gasp for air. Time passed that could have been seconds or minutes, Gemma's calm voice barely registering.

She was being led over to the bed, a sleepwalker guided back to safety. She didn't resist; the bed felt secure, grounded. Gradually, the sensations faded, leaving her limbs leaden and her eyelids too heavy to hold open.

Gemma pulled the covers over her. 'You'll feel better when you've had a nap, before you face everyone.'

Megan knew she wouldn't sleep, but it helped to close her eyes again and concentrate on her breathing.

The next thing she was aware of was a hand squeezing her arm. A baby's tiny nails lightly scratching her skin, the surprising strength as the little fingers tried to grip her flesh, urgent for her attention.

She opened her eyes to Stef.

'You OK, sweetheart?'

Megan struggled to process the question, no adequate response forthcoming. Her skin still tingled, the memory of Luka's touch lingering, even though she could see Stef's hand resting where the baby had grasped. Pain coursed through her head as reality fought against fantasy.

She struggled into a sitting position, wincing at the tug of her abdominal scar, her tether to Luka. 'Have you had the meeting?'

Macaulay nodded confirmation. 'We've agreed you'll be transferred to a Section Seventeen. This means you can leave the hospital, but you must remain at home, apart from attending any required treatment here, otherwise your discharge will be revoked.'

'So if I don't follow the rules, you can change the section?'

'If that were to happen, we would move to Section Three, the six-month in-patient treatment we talked about.'

Megan flinched at the unspoken threat of the sinister Section 3. 'I'll do whatever you want.'

★

Her clothes felt foreign against her skin. Gemma had encouraged her to dress each day, but she had stubbornly remained in pyjamas, unable to see the point.

'You're allowed to be happy, love,' Gemma said softly, as she helped pack her scant belongings into the overnight bag. That bag had made so many trips: weekend breaks to Dublin or Paris, hand luggage-only adventures for five nights in Tangiers and Belgrade, driving tours of the Highlands in autumn and Dartmoor in spring. How demeaning for it to have been demoted to a hospital carry-all.

'I *am* happy. I just can't remember how to show it.'

You're scared, aren't you?

'And I'm scared,' Megan admitted.

Gemma's arm slipped over her shoulders, and Megan was surprised by how reassuring the gentle squeeze was. 'Nothing's ever real while you're in here. You'll see what I mean when you get home. Tell me what you're scared of.'

'So much. I'm scared Stef doesn't love me any more. I'm scared of never being myself again. I'm scared I've lost my son.'

'Everyone has fears when they've been through something like you have, only natural.'

'I thought getting out of here would change everything. Like the cloud would lift and the world would be sunny again.'

'Don't forget you're still on a fair bit of medication. That will affect your mood.'

'Shouldn't it make me happy?'

'No, love, it makes you stable. Only you can make you happy.'

'I don't think I know how to do that.'

'It'll come in time. Just remember, you're stronger than you think. Now go on to your husband. He looks worried you don't want to leave.'

Megan glanced through the window at Stef waiting in the corridor, bouncing on the balls of his feet, looking everywhere, but at nothing.

What's he so anxious about?

She paused in her tasks, observing the fretful lines furrowing Stef's forehead. His discomfort was even more obvious because Stef didn't get worried. He was the one who found it simple to say everything would work out, a follower of 'what'll be will be' and 'everything happens for a reason', while she habitually preferred to worship at the altar of detailed plans and finite schedules.

Does he want you to stay safely locked away?

'Good luck to you, Megan.' Gemma hugged her, a real hug that felt like a friend's. Megan held on for a moment, using the nurse's strength against the voice's doubts.

There was no sign of Macaulay as Gemma beeped them out of the corridor, down the stairs and to the front door this time, not the garden exit. Megan was grateful not to see him, itching to escape his undisguised analysis. The front door, a majestic original announcing the building's former status, was buzzed open, and she was free. A fresh wave of vertigo washed over her, forcing her to clutch at the rail until Stef took her hand and coaxed her down, step by step, as if they were both afraid of what awaited them.

The pavement felt too hard after cushioned lino, abrasive beneath the thin soles of her ballet pumps. Immediately across the road, she saw the Costa Stef must have bought her first cappuccino from. How strange that normal life had been going on out here, just on the other side of the red bricks. From her room at the back of the building and the sheltered garden, she had been able to imagine they were in a quiet, leafy West London side street, away from the hustle and bustle of the main city thoroughfares. Not just a few hundred yards from High Holborn.

Stef held open the door to a waiting black cab.

'Where's the car?'

'Cab was easier than finding somewhere to park.' He cupped her elbow, helping her in. She remembered just in time to stoop and avoid banging her head on the roof, but needed a nudge to put her seatbelt on.

It wasn't a long journey to Newington Green, a route she knew well, but she couldn't look away from the normal lives going on as if nothing had changed. Two teenage boys astride BMXs, loitering on a corner, identities concealed by dark hoods. Students carrying Starbucks cups and thick textbooks, continuing vital conversations as they weaved through the crowds. A woman in an abaya haggling over prices at a fruit stall as her toddler strained to touch the colourful display. Men with shoulders broadened by their suits striding confidently down the pavement, assured everyone would move out of their way. Buses coming and going, spilling more people. Horns and revving engines and near-misses as bicycles forced their way through. Everyday London, her home – so why did she feel like an ethereal observer, watching from another reality far removed?

Abruptly, it was too much. She closed her eyes against the sudden onset of motion sickness; after the stillness of the unit, everything seemed to be moving too quickly. She didn't look up again until she heard the familiar crunch of tyres against the crushed basalt as the cab turned into the driveway of their double-fronted Victorian villa, a house her younger self would never have dreamed of one day owning.

Climbing unsteadily out of the car, for a moment she thought she was back at the front door of the Grosvenor. So similar: stained-glass panels, polished brass. It took too long to realise their door was a deep racing green, nothing like the unit's blue, and she let out a quiet noise of relief before she could catch herself.

'Coming in?' Stef had climbed the steps ahead of her and unlocked the door. He held it open as if showing off the familiar mosaic tiles of the double-width entrance hall, the wide, sweeping staircase curving up out of view.

Stepping inside her home, shutting the door on the outside world, Megan finally felt the jolt of happiness Gemma had promised would come. She closed her eyes and breathed in the familiar smells.

'Do you want to unpack your bag?'

Usually, she couldn't rest until everything was back in its proper place. 'Not yet.'

'I'll get the coffee machine going.' Stef set off decisively to the kitchen at the back of the house.

Go and find Luka. What if Stef's left him here alone?

Megan looked to the open doors around the ground floor, spring sunlight flooding through them, but she didn't want to start there. She made straight for the first floor. Climbing the stairs left her breathless and she had to grip the polished oak banister. She wanted to run up them, but her limbs wouldn't obey. It was like jogging in the swimming pool, a short-lived fitness fad she had quickly got frustrated with, only it was medication weighing her down rather than warm water.

55

The nursery door was closed, but she rushed in, eager to confirm Luka's existence, not quite daring to hope he might even be in his cot.

The walls were the first thing she noticed. The warm sunshine yellow she remembered had been replaced with sage green. A pleasant, calming colour, but not suitable for a nursery. The bright images of zoo animals she had carefully painted were gone; the shelves were full of books rather than toys.

Stef's desk stood by the window, where the cot had been, surface covered in papers and half-drunk mugs of coffee. A filing cabinet was in the changing station's place. The nursing chair had become a leather armchair. The sheep mobile ceiling lamp had vanished.

Panic surged, a tidal wave rising from agitated waters.

Why have they dismantled the nursery? Maybe they've moved it all to another room.

Megan rushed to each guest room, throwing open the doors, expecting to find the cot behind each one. When every room presented itself exactly as she had left it, she began tearing open wardrobe doors, even pulling out drawers in case a baby was secreted in spare bedding and holiday clothes. Her movements becoming frantic, she hurried into the master suite, riffling through the dressing room, checking cabinets in the en suite. Luka's name rose in her throat, desperate to be called, but she was too afraid of Stef hearing her.

She made one last dash back to the nursery, just in case it had been a hallucination. That was part of the psychosis, wasn't it? Maybe she'd just imagined the office furniture.

But, no. No baby, no answers. Megan sagged against the doorframe, defeat overwhelming.

What if they're right? What if he isn't real?

'Of course he's real,' Megan hissed back furiously before she could stop herself. She held her breath, forcing her protests safely back inside her head before she was overheard.

'Megs?' Stef's hand was gentle on her shoulder, but she still started. She hadn't heard him come up the stairs, so consumed was she in silently arguing against the voice's musings. 'What are you looking for?'

'I don't understand. Where's the nursery?'

'We don't have a nursery, sweetheart.'

'But I remember it! The walls were yellow. The paint was called Lemon Pie; you said it made you hungry and you insisted we stop for coffee and cake on the way home from B&Q. Why are you looking at me like that? Don't you remember?'

'Megs, this has been my office since we moved in. You said it should be sage green because it was stress reducing. We had a massive row in IKEA when we went to buy the desk and I wouldn't get the one that looked like a decorator's table.'

Megan blinked at the sudden memory of storming through the throngs to the IKEA café and buying a ridiculously large plate of meatballs, moodily stabbing them with her fork until Stef joined her and ate them for her, since she didn't actually like meatballs.

A smile jumped, unbidden, to her lips. 'I remember that.'

Stef smiled back. 'We haven't gone to IKEA together since. Mind you, we can afford better these days, thank God.'

'I love IKEA,' she said stubbornly. 'Did we not buy the baby stuff from there? Or did I go with Sophia?'

She felt rather than heard a sigh escape Stef. 'Megs, you're just upsetting yourself again. We didn't buy baby stuff; we didn't need to.'

She didn't feel upset. In fact, she didn't feel anything much, now the brief flood of emotion was gone, beyond a dull weight that seemed to be dragging her down from the core. Why were they doing this to her?

Maybe they've taken Luka because you're not well enough to look after him.

Of course! That made sense. He could be with Stef's parents in the Lakes. Safe and loved until she was better, until he could come home to her. Maybe that was the reason they were all denying Luka, so she didn't worry herself, didn't have another 'episode', as Macaulay called them.

You have to play their game. Go along with them. Make them think you're cooperating. Then they'll bring him back to you.

'Why don't you get into bed for a while? It's been an exhausting day.' Stef's hands were on her shoulders and she allowed him to gently steer her into the master suite, finally prepared to submit. At least this was exactly as she remembered: the feature wall of duck-egg-blue feathers she adored, handmade super-king bed, antique chaise longue that looked sophisticated but was so uncomfortable it was only used for Stef's discarded clothes.

Megan climbed under the plump, weightless duvet, the soft rustle of goose down luxurious after meagre hospital sheets. The Egyptian cotton smelled comfortingly of home as she lay down, snuggling deep away from the rest of the world.

'I'll let you sleep,' Stef whispered. 'Shout me when you wake up. I'll sort dinner.'

'I'm not hun—' Megan started to reply, but he had already closed the door softly behind him, eager to escape.

Chapter Seven

Before

Stefan usually remembered to bring the picnic hamper, so they had a rug to sit on and tumblers for the wine, but his haste meant they had to make do with sharing sips from the bottle. Fortunately, Megan was always well prepared and had remembered the corkscrew.

They were in their usual spot, at the back of the allotments that ran behind the Marlborough Avenue gardens. Beyond the carefully tended vegetable patches and brimming greenhouses was a patch of grassland left to provide a wildlife haven before it gave way to the thicket of trees protecting the gardens from train-line noise. The cover given to butterflies and hedgehogs provided equally good shielding for teenage romances, and they weren't the only regular visitors.

Megan hadn't befriended Isaac growing up. He had refused to play with the avenue's other children, declining invitations to birthdays or barbecues, but she listened thoughtfully as Stefan repeated his parents' conversation.

'It's awful for Isaac when he worked so hard to get into uni early.'

'He didn't need to try and kill himself,' Stefan muttered.

'It must have been too much for him. Maybe he felt out of his depth.'

'How should I know? He hasn't told me anything. Not a bloody word. I barely see him; he's locked in his room day and night.' He swigged deeply from the bottle, barely noticing the smooth, rich flavour of the expensive wine. A Châteauneuf-du-Pape, his father's favourite. Hopefully he was too distracted to count his stock.

Megan played with a lock of hair, deftly twisting it between slender fingers, her thoughts entirely readable. 'Have you asked him?'

'No.' He couldn't explain why not, couldn't admit he was afraid of the answer. Not knowing was easier. He didn't want to confront the demons that threatened his twin's life.

They shared the wine in companionable silence for a while until they were relaxed enough to lie back in the grass. Stefan leaned over to kiss her, feeling the tension slip away as her hands tentatively explored.

'Will Isaac go back to Cambridge?' she asked.

Annoyed at his brother interfering even in his seductions, Stefan sighed sharply. 'I don't bloody know! Probably – the 'rents won't let him throw an opportunity like that away.'

'I'd better not come to yours while he's there. It wouldn't feel right if he's on the other side of the wall.'

They usually had sex in his room; he had a double bed and his parents were content to feign ignorance. Stefan wasn't about to be forced into abstinence for the foreseeable future. 'Can we go to your house, then?'

'S'pose so. Sophia will be in, though.'

'She doesn't give a damn.' Stefan liked Megan's rebellious young sister. Sophia could start an argument in an empty room and still enjoy it. 'What about your mum?'

'She's out of it this week.' Megan looked away sharply, avoiding his gaze. 'She won't even realise we're there.'

'Thought she was going through a good period?'

'It can change at any time. Bipolar doesn't have a schedule.'

'Sorry, I didn't mean—'

'It's OK.' Megan got abruptly to her feet. Her mother was the taboo subject, the one topic that would make her shut down. The only thing she refused to share with him. 'Come on, before Dad gets back from work.'

She collected the empty wine bottle – littering was top of her pet peeves – and they picked their way across the allotments to her back garden gate. The garden wasn't completely abandoned, but it was untended and looked forlorn compared to the miracles the Newman gardener performed on their much larger patch.

Megan unlocked the kitchen door, two pink spots forming on her cheeks as they were confronted by unwashed dishes and a half-eaten saucepan of pasta abandoned on the stove top. The floor crunched with dropped cereal and toast crumbs.

'It isn't usually like this.'

'Doesn't bother me,' he reassured her, hugging her to distract from the ripe smell of the unemptied bin. She leaned into him, tilting her chin up for a kiss.

Once again, she pulled away before he could slip his tongue between her lips, but for good reason this time. Stefan jumped violently at the sudden crash that came from deeper within the house, followed immediately by raised voices, screamed accusations.

61

'Fuck's sake,' Megan hissed, the profanity made stronger by its rare usage.

'Is that—'

'Just go home.'

'No chance, I'm not leaving you with that kicking off.'

'Then go up to my room. Mum will flip out even more if she sees you. I won't be long.'

She practically shoved him up the stairs, but he paused long enough to see into the living room, at the scene of fifteen-year-old Sophia and her mother shrieking insults at each other.

'You're not a fucking mother!' Sophia bellowed. 'All you fucking do is sleep and cry and throw tablets down your throat. When did you last make us a meal or change the bedding or even wash yourself?'

Their mother was wavering on her feet as if drunk, dressed in a nightgown that looked like it belonged to an elderly relative. Her hair was a wild nest of tangles, her arms impossibly skinny, yet she wielded an ornament with manic strength as she stabbed it forward in emphasis of her own screams.

'You're not my daughter! You're the devil! The devil is in my house!'

Another crash as the ornament flew from her hand. Stefan started back down the stairs as Megan rushed into the room, worried it had hit Sophia, but from the smash of china and Sophia's enraged roar of 'You almost got me in the face, you mad bitch!', it seemed disaster had been avoided for that moment.

'Go upstairs!' Megan yelled, and it took Stefan a second to realise she meant him. He ran up the rest of the steps, closing her bedroom door behind him. As he sat on the neatly made single bed, he could hear the thumps and screams reverberating downstairs and Megan's pleas to stop.

Eventually, they did stop. He heard a door slam and went to the window to watch Sophia's slight figure sprint down the garden and disappear through the gate. Stefan crept to the bedroom door, wondering whether to sneak out while all seemed quiet.

He'd just cracked it open to check the coast was clear when the stairs creaked and Megan came into view, half carrying her mother. Tears ran down her blazing cheeks and she kept trying to brush sweat from her eyes without losing grip of the dead weight against her.

'Help me,' she whispered, raising her gaze to his. He had never seen such defeat in her.

He rushed to take her mother's weight. She seemed barely conscious, her eyes half closed, limbs limp. Megan steered them into the master bedroom, a room whose outward neatness couldn't disguise the lingering stench of unwashed bodies and stale bedding.

Stefan laid the woman on to the sagging mattress as gently as he could, stepping back so Megan could pull the faded covers over her. Together, they watched for a moment until convinced it was safe to move away.

Back out in the hallway, Megan pulled away when he tried to hold her, revealing a red mark on her cheek beginning to swell. 'Don't. Please don't pity me.'

'I want to comfort you, not pity you!'

'You can't, not about this.'

'Is she often that bad?'

Megan's lips jerked in a humourless smile. 'Depends how much Sophia winds her up.'

'Does she hurt you?'

'Not intentionally.'

'Megs—'

'Don't, Stef,' she repeated firmly. 'There's nothing you can say that'll make it better. It's just something I have to live with.'

'There must be something I can do.'

'Cure her, or get me a new mother? Which would be easier?'

'Don't be obtuse.'

To his amazement, Megan laughed, a real laugh, as if the whole event was already banished to the back of her mind. 'If only my school taught me to slip words like that into conversation.' She reached out and took his hand. 'She'll sleep the rest of the day now – she'll be fine till Dad gets home. Let's go and get McDonald's.'

Stefan allowed himself to be removed from the house, more shaken than he cared to acknowledge.

Chapter Eight

As the steaming water poured into the deep claw-foot tub, Megan watched the bubbles lather the surface, filling the en suite with the scent of pomegranate. She wasn't usually a fan of time-consuming baths and had insisted on the enormous walk-in rainfall shower, far superior to the functional main bathroom, but now she was desperate to soak and scrub away the hospital.

The water was hot enough to sting as she lowered herself into it, and she gasped as she lay back. Her skin tingled, more alive than it had felt in a long time. Taking a long breath, she sank beneath the surface, escaping into a comforting cocoon. This must be what being in the womb felt like. Safe. Protected from the rest of the world.

Her lungs burned with the effort of holding her breath, but she was reluctant to rise up into the world again. She tried to fight the reflex reaction, but it was no good and she gulped air involuntarily as she broke the surface. Her pulse pounded in her ears, her heart about to burst from her chest. Panic hovered, threatening, but she managed to regulate her breathing, sinking down to her shoulders again and letting her limbs float loosely until she was calm again.

'Megs?' Stef's voice came from the other side of the door, knocking. 'You OK in there?'

'I'm not drowning myself, if that's what you're wondering.'

An awkward silence. 'Shall I come in and sit with you?'

How are you supposed to think with him watching you?

'No, Stef, just leave me. I haven't had a moment unwatched in God knows how long.'

'I'm going to work on the bed.'

Megan sighed; clearly, he wasn't going to leave her completely unattended. She heard the rustling as he settled on top of the duvet, then the steady tapping of his fingers on his laptop. She let her head slip under the water again, this time leaving her mouth and nose clear.

She stayed there until the water grew cold; her fingertips were shrivelled and her hair was beginning to knot when she finally rose from the tub. After the hospital towels, the warmed bath-sheet felt wonderfully soft as she wrapped herself up, a comforting hug.

She didn't want to look at her body, afraid of what she would see, but she forced herself to stand in front of the full-length mirror, a penance she felt sure she deserved. She had always been slim, but now her ribs were prominent and her collarbones protruded from her skin in a way they'd never done before. Shadows lurked like bruises beneath her eyes, almost meeting cheekbones sharp enough to pierce. Her fingers slipped down to just below the slight curve of her belly; the scar was healing well and she didn't flinch with sensitivity when she stroked it, her strongest link to Luka.

Remembering her head wound, she separated her chestnut hair, usually thick, glossy waves that touched her shoulder blades but now rendered dull and brittle, until she found the injury site. She realised a small section of hair had been shaved, the soft regrowth hidden by the longer sections. It was difficult to see, but she managed to catch a glimpse and discovered the wound wasn't glued after all; rather, it had healed into a slightly raised ridge. It was smaller than she had originally thought. To her untrained eye, it didn't seem a traumatic wound – it was straight and precise.

The door opened quietly and Megan observed the reflection of Stef slip into the bathroom. They watched each other in the mirror for a long moment before Stef came towards her, reaching for the discarded towel and enveloping her in it. Hugging her from behind, he drew her against him, her spine pressed against his warm, strong chest.

She couldn't remember the last time they'd embraced. Tension so constant she had become unaware of it slipped away and she felt her body unclench as she turned, lowering her head on to Stef's shoulder. She breathed in the familiar scent of citrus and bergamot, comforted by the gentle planes of muscle and the impossibly soft bamboo of the eco-friendly shirt she had been unable to resist online.

You ordered a few babygros for Luka while you were buying Stef's present. You remember that!

Megan's head shot up as the thought reverberated loudly within her skull.

'What's wrong?' Stef sounded hurt by how abruptly she'd pulled away.

'Nothing. Sorry.' She picked up her hairbrush and started

mechanically pulling it through the damp strands, forgetting to be mindful of the head wound. Her hair greedily soaked up the oil she rubbed through the split ends, arid from lack of conditioning.

'Ready for some food?' Stef asked, bored as ever by her regimented grooming routine.

Megan had no appetite, but she nodded anyway. 'How long was I asleep?'

'Ages. You sparked out soon as you got into bed yesterday. Must have needed to catch up.'

'All I did was sleep at the Grosvenor.'

Stef shrugged. 'Maybe home sleep is different.'

There was truth in that, actually. For the first time, she'd slept naturally, genuinely tired instead of drug exhausted. It had taken too long to realise it was morning when she had eventually woken, slightly sweaty and desperate for a bath.

'Omelette, then?' Stef asked. 'Goat's cheese and Parma ham?'

Tell him you're not hungry.

Megan resisted the voice's magnetism. 'Sounds good. I'll be down in five minutes.'

Normal conversation. Roles reversed – she always cooked – but a typical exchange between a secure, loving couple.

Just like you used to be.

Stef took himself off downstairs and Megan shook off the furtive insinuation, returning to the bedroom to sit at her dressing table and reacquaint herself with eye creams, moisturisers, serums and toners. She had to concentrate on what was usually an ingrained habit, making sure she got each jar in the correct order, patting and smoothing the silky, cool products into her skin. Parched from the institutional air conditioning, it drank in everything Megan offered.

68

The range of choice the dressing room offered her was overwhelming – too many considerations. She fled with a pair of skinny jeans worn into comfort and a striped jersey bought in Montpellier a million years ago.

Before she took the stairs, she checked again, in case Stef's office had reverted to the nursery overnight. No, still the same. The disappointment was like a stab direct to the centre of her scar.

'Coffee's ready,' Stef said as she entered the kitchen-diner, the newest part of the house. He clearly wasn't enjoying the responsibility of not burning the omelette and was staring intently at the pan as if it would erupt in flames if he glanced away.

She poured them both large mugs of the Cuban blend, the full-bodied scent filling the room, and slid on to one of the island's breakfast-bar stools as Stef presented her plate with a flourish, even popping a sprig of parsley from the windowsill pots atop the slightly burnt eggs. By his own standards, he'd done well, and Megan's lack of appetite blunted her taste buds sufficiently for the bitterness of cremated Parma ham not to matter. Stef sat beside her, attacking his own plate with enthusiasm.

'Are you working today?' she asked, taking another small mouthful as he finished his serving.

'Only from home. Trisha has the office sorted.' Megan had hired the office manager and knew her unflappable efficiency kept Stef's spontaneity under control. 'I might do a few site visits next week. How's your omelette?'

'Fine, but I can't finish it. My stomach must've shrunk.'

'All of you has shrunk.' He grimaced as soon as he spoke. 'Sorry, that came out wrong.'

No, it didn't. He meant it.

69

Gritting her teeth against the sly voice, Megan forced herself to eat another couple of mouthfuls but couldn't tolerate more. Stef cleared the plates, even remembering to put them into the dishwasher rather than leaving them on the side as usual, and busied himself with his back to her, pouring fresh orange juice.

He brought the juice and a saucer to her, placing it down carefully as if it was fragile. She looked down at the saucer and realised he had used it to carry her pills.

Does he want you to think he's got nothing to hide, arranging them neatly like this?

Megan stared at the deceitful display for too long, until she noticed Stef hovering, watching her closely. One by one, she slowly pushed the pills between her lips and chased them with orange juice. They left a chalky taste in her throat she hadn't noticed in the unit.

'Where's my phone?' she asked once she'd drained the glass.

He avoided her gaze. 'Dr Mac wants you to have a digital detox.'

'I'm not a teenager!'

'Your phone's safe. I haven't read your messages or anything.'

'That wasn't what I was thinking. I want it back.'

'I'm just following orders.'

'You've no right keep my phone from me. I want to call your parents.'

'Why would you want to do that?'

'To check if they have Luka! Can I borrow yours?'

'I've left it upstairs.' Stef fidgeted with the salt and pepper grinders.

'I'll use the landline, then.' Megan strode to grab the handset from the side, struggling to remember which buttons to press. 'What's wrong with this thing? I can't find the contacts.'

'They got deleted when it did its last updates, fuck knows why. I've not had a chance to do them again.'

Megan slammed it down, hoping it would crack, but it held strong. 'Then give me my phone!'

'You'll have to ask Dr Mac about it. It's not my decision.'

'Is he coming here today?' she demanded.

'Yes, I've put your appointments on the fridge so you won't forget.'

She didn't bother to look at the printed schedule affixed by a magnet from Budapest. Stef poured a fresh coffee as if it would appease her. 'Will you be OK if I crack on with work?'

'I don't need babysitting.'

'Shout if you need anything.'

You need your phone to find your child, but he won't let you have either. What else could you possibly need from him?

'I won't need anything.'

71

Chapter Nine

Megan barely heard the doorbell when it rang, her senses numbed to the shrill peal even as it echoed through the house.

This was what she had been reduced to. Little more than an approximation of a human being, one who breathed and blinked and obediently swallowed tablets but, beneath the shell of plausibility, was completely empty. As far as she was aware, she hadn't moved a muscle since settling herself in the living room. The original fireplace sat laid but unlit, framed on either side by floor-to-ceiling bookshelves, the eclectic collection lovingly collated from countless hours hidden away in dusty bookshops. Rugs chosen in Turkey accented the oak floorboards and added softness to the room that the enormous corner sofa couldn't achieve alone, but sat askew and wrinkled, something Megan would normally never tolerate.

She expected Stef to shoot down the stairs and answer the door, take control, as he was doing of everything else. After a few moments, she realised it was a task she could do herself, and slowly got to her feet, grasping for equilibrium.

Macaulay smiled as she opened the door and she pretended it reached his eyes. 'Good morning, Megan, how are you today?'

'Good morning, Dr Mac,' she replied, robotic as a primary-school class greeting their teacher in unison.

'Wow, this house is really something. Incredible features! The colours of those floor tiles – original?'

'Yes, we had them restored.' Megan stood aside, reluctantly allowing him entry. She instinctively led him through the first doorway, into the more formal sitting room with its original oak panelling, painstakingly repaired, the wingback armchairs and the baby grand piano, rather than use the more homely living room. 'Is this OK?'

'Wherever you choose. This place is unbelievable.'

'It was a complete wreck when we bought it. It had been a home for delinquent teenage girls and they'd trashed it.'

'Must've taken some hard work.'

'By the tradesmen more than us.'

'You should be pretty used to that.'

'Our company was still in the early days when we found this place. It didn't have half the turnover it does now.' It felt important he know they had worked hard for their gilded life, that they weren't one of those entitled couples who sought Harley Street gods because the NHS was beneath them.

They sat facing each other, more distance between them than her hospital room had allowed. She much preferred the lack of proximity. Macaulay's eyes rested for too long on her as he unhurriedly furnished himself with notebook and Montblanc.

Remember you need to ask him about the head injury.

Megan sat up straighter, encouraged by the quiet reminder.

73

'I saw my head wound this morning for the first time. Will you tell me what happened?'

'You suffered a severe head trauma, serious enough that you were placed in an induced coma. Have you heard of a subdural haematoma?'

'I don't think so.'

'It's a bleed on the brain caused by a fall or an accident. You needed a drain inserted through your skull to remove the blood – that's what your wound is from.'

Megan felt the alarming tingle of pins and needles as she digested the information. 'How long was I in the coma?'

'It took almost two weeks until you were stable enough for the sedation to be reduced.'

'And then I ended up at the Grosvenor Unit?'

'Once you were fully conscious, it became clear you had escaped brain injury but were still experiencing psychosis. It took another week before you were well enough to leave the neurology ward, then you were transferred to us.'

'How can you be sure all this isn't from the head injury? Maybe it's the reason I can't remember any of the past few weeks.'

'You were experiencing psychosis before the injury and your tests showed normal brain function afterwards. The memory loss and confusion may be partially attributable to it but they're also common side effects of your condition and the medication.'

Megan took a moment to digest the sudden onslaught of information. 'What did I do to cause the head injury?'

'It was a fall.'

'I jumped?'

'We'll talk about that another time. Let's stick to the schedule for now. I'd like to talk more about your parents today. Shall we start with your father?'

Don't tell him about your family.

'I need water first.' Megan stood too quickly, forced to ride a wave of vertigo before she could make for the door. 'Would you like anything?'

'Sparkling water, if you have it.'

In the safety of the kitchen, she took her time searching the fridge for Perrier, rattling the ice tray loudly so he would know she wasn't hiding. She poured it slowly, enjoying the cubes crackling as the carbonated liquid hit them. Taking a lemon from the fruit bowl, she opened the knife drawer.

They weren't there. Not a single knife.

She stared at the drawer for rather too long, then quickly pulled open all the rest, moving rapidly round the kitchen. Nothing, not a thing she could use to slice the lemon.

Eventually she could take no longer without looking suspicious and she was forced to return, clutching two tall glasses, trying to keep her expression neutral as she processed her discovery.

'Why do you want to talk about my father? He hasn't been part of my life for years. He left when I was at uni.'

'Did you know why?'

'Another woman, I guessed. He never said, just went to work one day and never came back.'

'There's never been any contact? How do you know he's still alive?'

'I assume he is. I've no proof he's dead.'

'Was your relationship difficult?'

'More distant than difficult. It wasn't a happy home life for any of us.'

'And he didn't suffer from mental illness like your mother?'

Someone told him.

Megan froze, her gaze locking involuntarily with Macaulay's.

Macaulay raised an eyebrow, although his face remained impassive. 'Stefan and Sophia mentioned she was unwell. They wondered if there was a link between your condition and hers.'

They shouldn't have told him anything about the past.

'My mother had issues,' Megan felt forced to admit, unable to rally against the psychiatrist's deliberate stare or the voice's agitation.

'You haven't mentioned them.'

'Why would I? She just wasn't well. I don't remember noticing until we got to secondary school – I accepted it as normal, I guess – but by then she was quite unstable. Bipolar, the doctors finally decided.'

'When was she diagnosed?'

'I was about fourteen. She'd been declining for a few years, but my dad just said she was highly strung and had "problems with her nerves".'

'A familiar description of most mental health conditions back then.'

'I remember the mania more than the depression. It was like a whirlwind. She was impossible to keep up with but, just as soon as we adjusted to it, she'd crash and would refuse to get out of bed and wish she was dead.'

'Must have been hard, growing up in that environment.'

You're not on Macaulay's territory now – you don't have to play nicely any more.

Megan took courage from the reminder she was in her own

76

home now. 'We coped,' she snapped. 'It was easier once she was diagnosed and medicated.'

'And you continued to care for her after your father left?'

'What choice did I have?'

'You must have seen some distressing things.'

'Enough to know why Stef has hidden every knife in our kitchen.'

'I advised him to do that, just for now.' Macaulay sipped his water, blithely unconcerned at her kitchen discovery. 'Can you see any similarities between your mother's condition and yours?'

'No. I am not bipolar, Dr Mac. Do you not think it would have been spotted by now?'

'You admitted your mother went undiagnosed for years.'

'That was a different time. Mental illness wasn't talked about.'

'You didn't realise her illness at first.'

'Well, no, but—'

'But you couldn't be expected to notice it when you were so young? Or maybe the signs and symptoms didn't show themselves so obviously.'

'I'm nothing like my mother. I don't want to discuss my family any further.'

'What would you like to talk about?'

'My child.'

'Megan, we've been through this. I've explained that your belief you have a child is a result of your psychosis.'

'Then prove it.'

'How can I prove it?'

Megan opened her mouth to shoot back a response, then realised she had no idea what evidence could be given.

77

'I don't know,' she whispered, 'but until you do, I won't believe you.'

Macaulay had barely left before Sophia arrived, reverently bearing a bakery box. Megan didn't hear her key in the door, absorbed in her latest problem.

How can you prove to them Luka is real, since they can't prove to you he isn't?

'Megan?' Sophia's voice was uncertain, as if she had already spoken several times. 'Are you OK?'

Megan shook her head sharply to dislodge the voice before realising the action had alarmed her sister. 'Sorry. Miles away.'

'I brought treats.' Sophia held up the box. 'Let's have coffee.'

Megan's legs seemed to take for ever to respond. She felt Sophia watching her as she slowly moved to the doorway, focusing too hard on taking balanced steps.

'What are you doing in here?' Sophia asked. 'You never sit in this room.'

'Dr Mac came for my session. I didn't want to take him next door.'

Sophia nodded her understanding. 'Less personal in here.'

Megan felt a surge of relief that her sister knew her reasoning. She let Sophia lead the way into the kitchen, as though it was her house.

'You didn't bring Amelia?' She didn't hide her disappointment.

'Not today. The sight of the world's most hideous hat would have set your recovery back immeasurably.'

'I was looking forward to seeing her.'

Sophia looked irritated her wit hadn't proved distracting. 'I'll bring her soon, promise. And the bloody potato, of course.'

'When?'

'Soon, Megan.' An edge of frustration. 'Shall I make the coffee?'

'Go ahead.' She didn't have the concentration required to work the Krups barista machine. Sophia had no such compunction, setting the beans to grind before rummaging for her favourite cups. They had been an unrequested wedding present and Megan disliked the mismatched colours – every saucer was different to the cup – but Sophia loved the contrasts of fuchsia with aquamarine and indigo with lime.

'Sophia, will you tell me where Luka is?' Megan asked abruptly, watching her sister's back tense. 'I won't let on you've said anything, it'll be our secret. I just need to know who's looking after him, if he's OK.'

Sophia continued grinding the beans; they would be little more than dust by the time she finished. 'There is no Luka, sis, we've told you that.'

Megan ignored the insistence. 'I think he's with Stef's parents in the Lakes, so at least he's safe, but I don't understand why the nursery has gone.'

Sophia angled her body in a half-turn, not quite facing her. 'The nursery?'

'It's Stef's office now. He must have redecorated while I was in hospital.'

'There was never a nursery here.'

Even Sophia is lying to you now.

'Of course there was!' Megan's voice rose sharply, the wick of anger lit. 'I'm not fucking stupid.'

A cup slammed. 'Shouting at me isn't going to help!'

Megan swallowed the retort that rose too easily in her throat, holding her breath until she was certain the flame had been smothered. 'Sorry. I'm just frustrated, having no answers.'

Sophia was silent for several minutes, frothing milk and directing the stream of aromatic espresso into cups; busy movements.

'Do you remember much about the Grosvenor?' she finally asked as she worked, her tone stiff.

'Only the last few days. Anything else is a blur. I remember sounds. Screaming. There was a lot of screaming.'

Sophia gave the milk wand a thorough wipe-down despite usually leaving it crusted with white flecks. 'How do you feel now?'

'Like treacle,' was the honest answer. 'My head's full of it and my body's wading through it whenever I move.'

Sophia completed her miracles with the coffee machine and carried both cups to the table. Megan followed obediently, taking her usual seat. Sophia chose the head of the table, the chair Megan and Stef usually left empty when they ate alone, preferring to sit opposite each other.

Previously, this had been the room Megan spent the most time in. She'd never dreamed she would have a kitchen-diner designed specifically for her, and even when she wasn't trying out a new recipe she would usually be found on the Chesterfield at the far end of the extension, looking out into the garden with the bi-fold doors wide open, whenever the weather allowed. She had chosen everything in this room, from the dove-grey cupboards to the marble worktops and the Indian wood dining table. She'd decided on the exact positioning of the enormous Velux windows so light flooded in and the concealed induction hob that rose from the worktop at a touch. It was her sanctuary, and yet she'd barely set foot in it since returning home, since she'd discovered Stef's alterations.

'Dr Mac has made Stef keep my phone,' Megan said abruptly. 'I can't even text you.'

'That's annoying. Getting withdrawal from Facebook?'

Don't let them know the phone will be your proof. They'll only hide it away for longer.

'I haven't even thought about social media, actually,' Megan lied, heeding the voice's warning. 'I just feel naked without my phone.'

'I know what you mean. I couldn't find mine the other day and I really needed to call Eve. Then I realised I was talking on the bloody thing while I was searching for it!'

'Is Eve not home?'

'She was at work. Anyway, mad, isn't it, how you panic without it?'

'It feels like I'm not trusted. I'm not even allowed a phone, like I'm a child. That's a point – I wonder where my laptop and iPad are.'

'They'll be locked in the office with your phone.'

'Why?'

'Because if you're not allowed social media on your phone, you won't be allowed it on your other devices, will you?'

Megan hadn't thought of that, and it momentarily bewildered her. 'Have you got Stef's parents' number in your phone?'

''Course not. Why would I have that?'

'I want to speak to them, ask if Luka is with them. I'm sure he is.'

'Why do you need to ring, then?'

'To be certain! Do you think they'll be in the phone book? Is there even such a thing as a phone book any more?'

Sophia shrugged. 'I'll find out for you. Leave it with me.'

She quickly proffered the bakery box, revealing a row of brightly coloured macarons, delicate and perfectly round, beautiful matte shades of buttercup yellow, rose pink, lavender purple.

Megan stared at them as if they were foreign objects.

Sophia chose for her, placing a green pistachio treat in front of her. At the same moment, Stef clattered into the kitchen, no doubt to raid the fridge. He stopped in mid-step when he noticed his sister-in-law.

'Didn't know you were coming!'

'Did the carrier pigeon get lost?' Sophia rolled her eyes. 'I wasn't aware I needed your permission.'

Unabashed, Stef grabbed a couple of the confections. 'How was Dr Mac, sweetheart?'

'He asked about Mum and Dad.'

Sophia stopped with a raspberry macaron halfway to her mouth. 'What the fuck for?'

'He thinks I'm the same as Mum.'

'Like hell you are.'

'He said you'd both wondered if Mum's condition and mine were linked.'

Stef shook his head quickly. 'No, he asked us if there was any history of mental illness in the family, so we told him about your mum.'

He's the one who betrayed you.

'Do you think I'm like her?' Megan demanded, spurred by the damning conclusion.

'No, 'course I don't.'

'This is ridiculous,' Sophia interrupted. 'Dr Mac has no right bringing Mum and Dad into your problems. Dad's long gone and Mum barely knew we were her daughters, so what possible use are they to your recovery?'

'Macaulay knows what he's doing,' Stef argued.

Sophia smirked. 'Because he's the most expensive doctor you could find, that makes him the best?'

'His results are what makes him the best!'

'You think if you throw money at a problem, it'll all go away!'

'Since when do I think that?'

'Since you made your fortune.'

'That's bullshit, Sophia, and you know it!'

Megan considered letting them fight it out but decided it would appear strange if she didn't defend her husband.

'Soph, that's not fair.'

Sophia shoved the whole macaron into her mouth, glaring fiercely as she chewed. Then she gave a sigh and threw up her hands. 'You're right. Sorry. You're not actually a complete dick-head, Stef.'

'So relieved you approve of me.' There was no stiffness in Stef's tone; he was used to Sophia's sudden flare-ups. 'Let me have another of those.'

'Leave some for Megan!'

'There's plenty left!'

'I don't want any,' Megan tried to say, but neither of them seemed to hear her.

Chapter Ten

'The bloody Whitechapel house has standing water in the cellar!' Stef strode into the bedroom as Megan was hovering in the dressing room, unable to decide on the day's outfit.

He moved around her to grab a suit from his rails. That told her he was going to the site; he always dressed well whenever he went to visit a project. Said there was less chance of him being overcharged by his contractors if he exuded authority.

'I need to see for myself. I've called Sophia to stay with you. Will you be OK?'

You're the child now, aren't you?

'I'm not safe to be alone in my own home?'

Stef paused partway through knotting his tie. 'I can't leave you on your own just yet, Megs.' He gave an exasperated sigh as he ruined his attempt, tugging the tie loose and starting again.

'Where did you sleep last night?' she asked abruptly.

He moved to the mirror, taking great care in turning down his collar. 'The burgundy room. I went to bed late, didn't want to disturb you.'

The painting of the wine-red feature wall in the largest guest bedroom had caused a plethora of issues, not least splashes all over the floor that had looked like bloodstains, but it had been worth the chaos. They'd spent a laughter-filled weekend tackling the task themselves instead of asking the professionals, a challenge they hadn't needed to embark upon. An impromptu picnic of Brie and Shiraz had been devoured on the paint-speckled floorboards, hands stained as if a murder had occurred but glowing with satisfaction at their own labours.

And now Stef is using it to hide from you.

'You haven't slept in our bed since I came home,' Megan mumbled, fighting the urge to clasp her hands over her ears, block out the voice's taunts.

'I thought you might need space.'

'Why do you want to avoid me?'

'I don't! I was thinking of you.' Stef shrugged into his suit jacket. 'Megs, I have to get going. We can talk about it later.'

He kissed her as his phone rang again.

'I'm on my way, Trish, just waiting for my sister-in-law to arrive . . . I don't care if they've got another site to get to!' He raked his hand through his hair. 'Hang on, let me check where Sophia is.'

'I'll be fine till she gets here,' Megan said as he cancelled the call and dialled again.

He shook his head distractedly. 'Hi, any chance you can hurry up? I need to get to Whitechapel. How far away are you? Oh, OK, great. No, I wasn't ordering you around . . . See you in a few minutes.' He slid the phone into his pocket. 'She's two minutes away. I'll get going.'

Megan moved to her dressing table, giving her full attention to perfecting a high ponytail. She heard Stef trotting downstairs, the jangle of keys and, at last, the front door closing. Immediately, she was on her feet, and rushing. Sophia's estimates were notoriously inaccurate, a fact Stef had clearly forgotten in his haste, but she wouldn't have long.

In the office, she began her search. It didn't take long to realise that her devices, plus most of the kitchen, were in the filing cabinet, as it was the only thing that was locked. Before she started hunting for the keys, it occurred to her she could access Facebook on Stef's computer. His password was a complicated jumble, but she had used it often to access spreadsheets and was sure she remembered it. Attempt one failed. She paused and concentrated hard, visualising the combination before trying again. No good. The red circle tormented her, refusing her access.

Leave it! It will lock if you mess up a third time.

She backed away obediently. Hurrying now, she yanked open the desk drawers, rifling through the contents. They were full of paperwork Stef never bothered to file, old receipts and official headed letters, along with various detritus – stopped watches, spare shirt buttons, a creased photo of Amelia as a baby, curling Post-it notes.

Where else would he hide the keys? He wouldn't carry them with him; he was forever losing small objects. She tried the pen pot, felt around the edges and creases of the desk chair. Critically tracked her eyes over the carpet to see if it had been lifted anywhere.

'Megan, are you upstairs?' Sophia's voice yelled.

Megan shot out of the office and into the master bedroom before she called back. 'Yes, just getting dressed. Sorry you had to rush over.'

'Not to worry, I was only dropping Amelia at nursery.'

'Aren't you due at work?' Megan asked as she took the stairs to where her sister waited at the bottom.

'I took some leave when you . . . when you were ill.' Sophia worked for a drama company, running acting courses for children and adults, providing casting for TV and radio adverts, a job she loved and hated in equal measure.

'Then why's Amelia at nursery?'

'Because she needs routine and I need a break.'

Because she doesn't want you near Amelia.

'More like you don't think my own niece is safe with me.'

'Megan, it's not my decision! I'm just following instructions.'

'Whose instructions?'

'Who do you think?' Sophia was already heading for the kitchen. 'Coffee? Have you eaten?'

'I'm not hungry.'

'You've got to have something, Stef told me to give you your pills.'

'They're locked away in his office with everything else.'

Sophia found a bag of croissants in the bread bin, tossed two in the oven to warm. 'Which jam do you want? Raspberry or apricot?'

'I don't care.'

Sophia put both jars on the breakfast bar, fetched side plates. 'Keep an eye on the croissants. I'll be back in a minute.'

She's going to get the key.

Megan waited until she heard Sophia's footsteps on the stairs, then quietly left the kitchen and followed noiselessly, knowing exactly where to stand to avoid any creaks. With the office door wide open, she was able to crouch on the top step and crane her neck to see Sophia kneel and feel around on the underside of the bottom desk drawer. Her hand emerged with a key covered by a strip of duct tape.

As Sophia stood up, Megan hastened back downstairs, just in time to snatch the croissants from the oven. She was sliding them on to plates when Sophia returned with two butter knives and a cupped hand carrying the tablets.

Megan didn't want the pills; her mind was clearer, she felt lighter and less clumsy and she dreaded the heavy fog that would descend again as soon as the medication hit her bloodstream. She took her time tearing her croissant, anointing it with apricot jam, putting each small piece slowly to her mouth.

'Stef sounded stressed when he called,' Sophia said conversationally.

'One of the properties has flooded or something. You know what Stef's like, he wants to fix everything immediately.'

'Especially emergencies that will cost him money.'

'Maybe I'm one of those,' Megan said. 'I'm an emergency costing him money.'

'Why do you say that?'

Megan shrugged. 'Can we pick Amelia up at lunchtime?'

Sophia frowned at yet another sudden change in topic. 'I'll bring her soon, I promise.'

'I want to see her, Soph. I miss holding Luka in my arms but at least I could cuddle Amelia till he comes home.'

It seemed to take Sophia a long time to swallow her mouthful. 'Megan, you've never wanted kids. You've always enjoyed being free to travel and go out whenever you want.'

'Then why don't I have the implant or the Pill? I've checked; I don't have any form of contraception. Stef wouldn't have hidden that, would he?'

'You use that natural contraception app; you were struggling with the side effects of the implant. Look, you've got the scar from where it was removed.' Sophia took hold of Megan's left arm and showed her the tiny white mark on the inside of her biceps.

Megan touched the little scar. She couldn't check her phone for the app, but it didn't seem to matter.

'Don't you believe me?' Sophia asked, her tone becoming affronted, a relief from the excessive carefulness.

'I don't know what I believe any more.'

Sophia stood up, began gathering the breakfast things, picking up her sister's flake-strewn plate. 'You need to take your tablets.'

She'd been so close to the pills being overlooked. She'd even managed to hide them under the edge of her plate without Sophia noticing.

Let them win for today. They can have the little battle – the war will be yours.

Defeated, Megan fed them into her mouth one by one and waited for her mind to shut down for the day.

Stef returned after a couple of hours and immediately shut himself away in the office. Megan could hear him on the phone, striding up and down the room. Sophia left to collect Amelia, and Megan forgot to ask to accompany her. Not that she felt like jumping on and off buses back to Hackney; her limbs were leaden again and she had forgotten whatever had been so important to her earlier.

Staring at the living-room TV as it babbled nonsense at her, she registered an advert for nappies, a giggling dark-haired baby that looked so much like Luka.

89

Why don't you have any photos of him?

Memories of selfies in her hospital bed played across her mind. Luka cradled to her chest, picture after picture of him sleeping, yawning, lying in his bassinet beside her, eyes alert and interested. Determined to record every precious moment with him.

Filled with a sudden resolve to search for pictures, she stood abruptly and dropped the remote. The batteries flew from it as it skittered under the sofa. Megan was about to ignore it, but the voice spoke sternly.

You'll never remember where it is and you'll lose your temper again. Don't give them any ammunition.

The polished floorboards were uncomfortable against her protruding kneecaps as she lowered herself down to retrieve it. She thrust her hand under the sofa, shifting her weight awkwardly as she felt the pull of her scar, and nearly let out a scream as her fingers touched something soft and furry.

Snatching her hand away, she almost shouted upstairs for Stef to risk his digits to the unknown threat. Only the thought that it may just be a lost sock prevented her. Stef didn't need any more reasons to question her sanity. So she steeled herself and pressed her cheek to the floor to look into the shadows.

Her hand snatched the object before she could fully register what it was. It was dusty, fur stragglier than she'd seen it before, but she recognised it immediately. The first stuffed toy she had bought on learning she was pregnant, a soft white duck with blue beaded eyes and a bright orange beak, determined to be Luka's babyhood companion.

Quackles!

Megan caressed the downy fur, touched the velvety webbed

feet. Holding the toy to her face, she breathed in the scent she knew was her son's.

'Stef!' she screamed.

Running footsteps pounded down the stairs almost immediately and Stef sprinted into the room. 'What's wrong? What's happened?'

Scrambling unsteadily to her feet, she thrust Quackles towards him.

'I found him under the sofa!'

'Oh, God, I thought it was something terrible.' Stef grinned at the duck. 'So that's where he went! Good find. He's been missing for weeks.'

'You remember him too!'

''Course. Amelia freaked when she lost him.'

'Amelia?' Megan felt her forehead crease in confusion.

'She couldn't find Quack last time she came round. Went absolutely mental ...' Stef broke off abruptly. '...I mean, she was really upset.'

'Quackles is Amelia's toy?' Megan whispered.

'Most important thing in her world.' Stef's chuckle died on his lips as he saw her expression. 'You don't remember?'

'I remember Quack belonging to Luka. I bought him the day I found out I was pregnant, from that tiny shop in Covent Garden.'

'You bought him, you're right, but you bought him for *Amelia.* You took Quack to the hospital on our first visit.'

Stef crossed the room, taking her in his arms. His hand smoothed her hair as he drew her close against his chest, murmuring reassurances.

'It's OK, Megs, you'll remember in time. Your brain's just trying to recover.'

'But he smells like Luka. I know his smell.'

Stef gently took the toy from her. 'We can give it back to Amelia if Soph brings her over.'

The duck doesn't belong to Amelia – he's lying to you again. Don't let him take it.

Megan was almost overwhelmed by the order to grab it back. She clenched her fists so tightly she felt her nails cutting into her palm, managed not to seize hold of the duck.

'Get some rest, sweetheart. Do you want some music on?'

She shook her head wordlessly. There was no room for music now; every piece of her love was directed to her absent son.

From nowhere, sudden tears came. She was sure they were supposed to be hot, but maybe that was for angry weeping. Perhaps heartbroken tears were meant to be cold.

Megan curled herself into the tightest ball, buried her face into the sofa cushions and tried to weep, but already her eyes had dried, as if her emotion had never existed.

Chapter Eleven

Before

S tefan's first term at Durham flew by in a sea of parties, formal dinners, sports matches and the occasional lecture. Meanwhile, Isaac never returned to Cambridge. He remained at home, hidden away, the Open University his only connection to a world of academia far from the elite education he had previously known.

For Stefan, it was a relief to escape the cloud that now hung over his once-happy home. No one talked about Isaac's breakdown. The reason still hadn't been confirmed to Stefan. Isaac had cut so deeply he had permanently damaged nerves, but he had refused to admit exactly why. Stefan had long since stopped asking for more information.

Christmas arrived too soon, with a surprise at the gates of Hatfield College – his father's Range Rover containing not just his parents, but Isaac too.

'How's it going?' Stefan asked Isaac after greeting his parents and joining his twin in the back seat. Orion joyously leapt over from the boot, covering him in licks and hairs.

'Not great.' As usual, Isaac's voice was barely audible as he roughly shoved Orion back, sharply ordering the dog to sit down.

'Leave him alone!' Stefan snapped. 'I didn't expect to see you.'

'Mum thought I'd enjoy a change of scenery. Not sure why.'

'Megan's dying to see you,' his mother interrupted. 'She popped in before we left, she was so excited.'

Stef couldn't hide a smile at the prospect of being reunited with his girlfriend. He hadn't felt able to invite her up to visit, not before she turned eighteen, but he had defied her prediction that they would split up before the end of his first term.

'She comes round quite often,' Isaac said. 'She walks Orion.'

'You'd better not be rude to her.' Stef reached back to rub the dog's ears, encouraging him away from Isaac.

'Why would I be rude?'

'Boys, enough.' His mother's tone was a warning, to him rather than Isaac.

'She's very pretty,' Isaac said.

'Why the fuck are you eyeing up my girlfriend? Find yourself a woman, if you're that keen.'

'I don't want a relationship.'

'Do you ever leave the house?'

'I walk every day to use the library. People from Megan's school go there, but they never talk to me.'

'I bet you're not exactly inviting them to. Been to any parties on the avenue?'

'I don't like parties. I can't breathe when there are lots of people making noise.'

Stefan rolled his eyes. 'God, Isa, you're like a monk.'

'Stefan!' A glare from his mother.

'I know you don't understand me,' Isaac said calmly.

94

Stefan scowled and turned to look out of the window. If he was honest, he'd never understood his twin, not even when they were young children.

Finally home, he barely paused to fling his bag into his room before jogging up the street to Megan's smaller house, which was growing shabbier with each passing year. Her younger sister answered his knock.

'Oh, you're back.'

'Nice to see you too.' He grinned.

'Thought you'd have run off with a posh girl by now.'

'Your sister's enough for me.'

Sophia rolled her eyes. 'How cute. Suppose you want to come in?'

'No, I quite like standing on the doorstep.'

'Wait here, then.' Whether he was joking or not, the door closed on him and he had no choice but to stand there.

'Hi!' Moments later, Megan was in his arms, hugging him tightly. 'How was the drive down?'

'Shit. Isaac came with the parents.'

'Wow, that's a surprise.'

'Not a welcome one. He's such a weirdo.'

'He's your twin, Stef, don't be so hard on him.' Megan raised her school bag from her shoulder. 'Come on, I've got supplies.'

It was too cold and damp to go to the allotments, so they went back to Stefan's house. His mother greeted her like an old friend, making them both tea and asking after Mrs Crawley.

'She's on a low at the moment,' Megan said, matter-of-fact, 'but the doctors have got her medication stable now, so that makes it easier. And she sleeps a lot when she's down, so she doesn't need watching all the time.

She shrugged cheerfully, so accepting of a situation Stefan would have found impossible. He wasted no time extracting them from the kitchen; as soon as they were upstairs, door firmly closed against interruptions, they abandoned their tea in favour of chilled cans of Heineken.

'Have you thought any more about uni applications?' Stef asked.

'I can't come to Durham, Stef. How can I leave Mum? Sophia wouldn't look after her.'

'She'd cope.'

'I have to stay in London. I'll apply to King's and UCL and Imperial, maybe Royal Holloway, then I can still live at home. It's either that or give up on uni altogether.'

'You're too clever for that!'

'You don't understand how my life is, what it's like looking after Mum. Even leaving her for lectures is going to be difficult.'

'You're giving up the best years of your life for her.'

'That's how it is. How would I feel if I went to Durham and she managed to kill herself because I wasn't here to keep an eye on her?'

'D'you think she would?'

Megan shrugged. 'She tries regularly enough. Besides, it's almost a year away. I don't even know how my A levels will go. It's hard trying to work when all you can hear is crying and shouting.'

She took several long draughts from her can before putting it on the bedside table, sliding up the bed until she lay in his arms. Her lips tasted of hops and sweet chilli crisps, not that

Stefan gave a damn as she sealed her mouth hungrily against his. He let his hands run up and down the long curve of her spine until his fingers found her bra clasp, before pulling her on top of him.

Abruptly, he sat upright, pressing his finger to his lips. 'Shh, hold still. He's listening to us.' He could hear Isaac pacing in the next room, the creaking floorboards, his twin muttering to himself, then the turning of his door handle.

Stefan shoved Megan aside and snatched open the door as she hurriedly righted her clothes. 'What the hell are you doing?'

'Hello, Megan.' Isaac ignored him, looking straight past him.

'Hi, Isaac,' Megan said calmly. 'Were we making too much noise?'

'No, I just wondered what you were doing.'

'Catching up, that's all. Do you want to join us? Here, have a beer.'

Ignoring Stefan's ferocious glare, Isaac moved into the room. He accepted the can and popped the tab, but didn't drink. Gritting his teeth, Stefan returned to the bed, wrapping a possessive arm around Megan and drawing her back against him.

'I know you were listening,' he snapped.

'Don't make it so obvious what you're doing, then.'

'I've seen you at the library quite a lot this term, Isaac,' Megan interjected before Stefan could lose his temper. 'You can say hello. I don't bite.'

'You're always busy.'

'My house is too noisy to work in, so I get as much done there as I can.'

'Your sister is very loud.'

'She isn't keen on libraries. She only comes to meet me so we can walk home together.'

'I mean at your house.'

'How do you know?' Stefan interrupted.

'I hear her shouting when I walk past.'

'Probably my mum as well,' Megan said wryly.

'You have problems with your family.' It wasn't a question. Isaac nodded, as if confirming to himself, and took a tiny sip from his beer. 'So do I.'

Stefan scowled at him. 'More like we have problems with you. Get out, Isaac.'

'Don't be rude!' Megan said.

'It's fine. I don't like small talk anyway.' Isaac stood up and gave her a weak smile, unable to hold eye contact. 'Thank you for the beer, Megan.'

He left the can behind as he closed the door.

'Bloody waste.' Stefan grabbed it and downed half in one.

'You don't have to be so harsh on him.'

'He drives me mad, wasting away here, making my parents worry about him.'

'That's depression for you.'

'It's not fucking depression! It's way deeper than that. I don't know what, but there's something seriously wrong with him.'

'So he needs support, not condemnation.'

'He needs locking up.'

Megan's brow creased. 'What's that supposed to mean?'

'Nothing. Forget it, it doesn't matter.'

'It must matter, or you wouldn't have said anything.'

'Can we talk about something else?' Stefan attempted to raise one eyebrow, James Bond style, and failed. 'Or not talk at all?'

That was enough to make her laugh and distract her. Stefan pulled her down beside him, rolling over so she was beneath him, closing his eyes as her fingers worked to unzip his jeans.

He made sure he turned the music up loud enough that no sounds would carry to the next room.

Chapter Twelve

'I hate not being able to remember anything,' Megan complained, tugging hard on a lock of hair.

Macaulay's pen paused against his notebook, even though his face remained impassive. She was developing an increasing aversion to his refusal to react to her. Apart from an encouraging nod when she elucidated without prompt or the occasional frown as he jotted down his copious notes, he showed no emotion whatsoever. Entirely neutral; pleasant but bland; vanilla ice cream.

'Define "anything".'

'Attempting suicide, Stef's password, things about my niece. Yet I remember Luka's birth in clear detail. I know I've asked before, but are you sure there was no sign of brain injury?'

The writing resumed for a moment, the pen moving swiftly across the pad. She found his refusal to make notes on a laptop or iPad rather odd; she hadn't seen a doctor write in years.

'You had all the necessary tests.'

Did you, though? He could be lying.

'Then why do I have no memories from Luka's birth to

waking up in the Grosvenor Unit? You said it's part of my condition, but surely there must be more to it.'

Again, he ignored the mention of Luka. 'When a person suffers a trauma, their brain can react in strange ways. It can block out harmful or painful memories to the point where they are unable to remember anything about the traumatic period. It's a process called dissociation.'

'What was I traumatised by? Was it Luka's birth, because it went wrong? Is that what my brain doesn't want me to remember?'

The rush of questions went unacknowledged. 'Would you like some reading about dissociation?'

Megan wanted straight answers, but she clearly wasn't going to get them. 'If it will shed more light than you're prepared to, yes.'

Macaulay smiled, entirely overlooking her slight. 'I'm always pleased when patients show curiosity about their condition.' He sat back slightly, his gaze moving around the room. 'Your piano is a beautiful instrument. Who plays?'

'Me. I got my Grade eight during A levels,' Megan replied reluctantly, unwilling to allow him the subject change he so transparently orchestrated.

'That's quite an achievement. You didn't want to study music?'

'Music was an escape, not a career.'

'And now?'

'I haven't played since I came home. I can't find the right feelings, and piano always sounds terrible if your heart's not in it. Maybe I'd feel like playing if I was happier.'

'What would make you happy?'

'Apart from Luka? My niece. When can I see Amelia?'

A slight raise of Macaulay's eyebrows. 'Whenever you want.'

'You're not stopping Sophia bringing her to see me?'

'Not if Sophia is happy to do so.'

'That's not answering the question. Am I a danger to Amelia? Have I done anything to harm her?'

'No, you've done nothing to Amelia.' Macaulay sipped his usual glass of Perrier, still containing no lemon. 'This is a good time to discuss that part of your family.'

He wants to wheedle out all your secrets.

Megan sat up straighter, drawing her shoulders back. 'Sophia and Amelia have no effect on my mental health,' she said firmly.

'Oh, but they do. They form part of the basis of your emotional attachments. Tell me about Amelia.'

'She's a sassy little parcel of attitude.' Megan couldn't help but smile as memories of her niece made her resolve slip. 'Knows exactly what she wants, and she will get it, come hell or high water. She's so similar to Sophia. It's crazy that they aren't blood related.'

'Sophia isn't Amelia's biological mother?'

'No, Eve carried her.' A quick glance to check Macaulay was following the dynamics. He nodded understanding. 'Eve's egg and a sperm donor. Swedish, I think they settled on.'

'How do you get along with Eve?'

'I like her. She's good for Soph.'

'Do I sense a hesitation?'

'Only because you're looking for one,' Megan said sharply.

That got a reaction, if only a slight rise of one eyebrow. Megan fought the kneejerk urge to apologise.

'I get on well with Eve. She's very intelligent and I enjoy talking to her.'

'You feel inferior to her?'

'I didn't say that.'

102

You do, though. You've always been intimidated by how clever she is. She was always going to be a better mother than you.

Megan couldn't stop a flinch at the voice's sudden venom.

A slight flicker played across Macaulay's lips, as if he could hear the voice's malice as well. 'How is she as a mother?'

'What does that matter?'

'Just trying to understand the dynamics.'

'Eve's a good mother, but she didn't feel the same compulsion to have a baby as Sophia.'

'So the pregnancy was driven by Sophia.'

'Yes, Sophia can't have kids, not any more, not since—' Megan caught herself abruptly, hoping her slip hadn't been obvious. 'She didn't want to waste time. Eve is quite a lot older than her, and the chances of IVF success are low after forty.'

'You love your niece?'

'I adore Amelia. Stef and I both do. After she came along, it must have stirred my decision for us to have a child.'

Macaulay paused in his writing, clearly waiting for her to ask again about Luka. Megan forced herself to remain silent, holding her breath to ensure no words escaped.

'Megan, do you think your brain is getting confused between Sophia's family and yours?'

'Why would that happen?'

'It could be that you envy Sophia.'

'I'm perfectly happy with my life.'

'Stefan told me you never wanted children.'

Stef should learn to keep his mouth shut.

Megan blinked at the voice's defensive snarl as much as at the rapid change of subject. 'I never saw myself as maternal,' she admitted. 'I enjoy going out to eat and I love travelling. I suppose

I always valued my freedom to do what I wanted, when I wanted. Opportunities I never had growing up.'

'And do you remember that changing?'

She thought for a moment. 'No, actually. It must have been very sudden. That happens, doesn't it? Something just changes one day. Hormones or something.'

'That can happen.'

'I didn't dislike children. I just didn't want to be a mother, until suddenly I did.'

'How did Stefan feel about that, if he didn't want children?'

She couldn't find an answer to that, no matter how hard she searched her clouded memory. 'I don't remember. He must have agreed.'

Macaulay made more notes, carefully recapped his fountain pen. 'We have to deviate slightly from our normal routine today, Megan. I need you to provide a urine sample, to tell if you've been taking your medication. We'll test you once a week.'

He doesn't trust you.

Megan instinctively recoiled. 'You really don't trust me.'

'It's not about trust, it's about—'

'Safety, I know,' she snapped, realising there was no way of avoiding the test. She didn't fear the result, it was the invasiveness she wanted to protest against. 'I presume you don't need to supervise me?'

'If you could use the bathroom down here rather than upstairs, I'd appreciate it.'

Barely managing to refrain from snatching the small plastic container he held out to her, Megan stalked to the downstairs cloakroom, making sure she left the sitting-room door open so he could hear the sounds if he wanted to. She had to sit for what felt like for ever, unable to summon the urge to go, staring at the slate tiles she had so carefully chosen but now felt were too dark, too cold and foreboding for the small room.

Task finally awkwardly completed, she was nearly over-whelmed by the urge to hurl the sample against the taunting tiles.

Do it. Throw it.

She resisted the command, forced herself to keep her temper under tenuous control, before she was safe to escape the gloom and return it to Macaulay. This was part of the game, she told herself, firmly. She couldn't give them any reason to be con-cerned about her. The voice quietened, momentarily chastised.

As she watched him don latex gloves and unwrap a small paper dipstick, she found she was holding her breath, her shoul-ders rigid, fists clenched. Why the dread, the feeling of mounting guilt, when she knew she had dutifully swallowed every pill? Had the psychosis left her so paranoid she couldn't trust what she knew beyond doubt to be true?

The dipstick must have revealed the approving colour, for Macaulay smiled as if she had done something worthy of praise and made another note before re-sealing the container and handing it back.

'Thank you, Megan. It confirms the presence of the meds. I'll let you dispose of that.'

'It was only ever going to confirm,' she retorted, taking the sample too roughly. 'I've been taking the tablets, even though I despise them.'

'How does the medication make you feel?' Macaulay asked, unruffled by her attitude.

Megan searched for an appropriate word. 'Removed. Like

I'm distanced from everything. I feel as if I'm watching myself living all this. Nothing seems real. I keep expecting to wake up and everything will be normal again.'

'And what is normal?'

'None of this, of course!' Megan swung her hand in emphasis, noted with satisfaction Macaulay's flinch at the sharp movement. 'No meds, no therapy, Stef back to his usual self, my baby here with me. Life as it was.'

'Does Stefan seem so different to you?'

'A stranger in my husband's body.'

'Are you sharing a bed?'

A spike of anger coloured her vision. 'None of your business!'

'I will need to ask questions about your relationship, even if you find them intrusive.'

'I'm in no position to refuse, am I?' Megan retorted, surprising herself with such assertiveness. 'Stef is sleeping in another room at the moment. I don't imagine it will be for long. He's giving me space to recover from the hospital.'

'That's thoughtful of him. Is it what you want?'

She began to shake her head, say she wanted Stef back in their bed, but she found she couldn't. 'I don't know. All I really want is my baby.' Her fingers found the scar, touching it through her T-shirt. 'I know he's real, Dr Mac. There must be a reason why no one will confirm it. I suppose it's because you all think I'm not safe to be around him. I only want to know where he is and who's looking after him. Is that so much to ask?'

Macaulay held eye contact, his gaze entirely calm. 'Megan, you don't have a son. I know how much distress this causes you, but I am telling you the truth, as are Stefan and Sophia. You are not a mother.'

Megan felt herself recoil involuntarily, her palm pressed to her stomach, protecting the foetus that was no longer inside.

Why is he so determined to make you believe him? What's in it for him?

'You're wrong,' she whispered, closing her eyes against the questions she couldn't answer. 'I know you're wrong.'

As she got ready for bed that evening Megan forced herself to stand naked in front of the full-length mirror. She had to admit, apart from the slight swell of her belly above the scar line, she showed no signs of having been pregnant. No real stretch marks, just a few pigmented lines around her hips she was sure she'd had since puberty. Was it even possible to be pregnant without stretch marks? There were all sorts of creams and oils; maybe she'd used them.

'What you up to?' Stef came out of the en suite, a towel wrapped round his waist.

'Just looking.'

'For what?'

'Changes.'

'You need to eat if you want to see changes, sweetheart.'

Look how he talks to you, like you're an idiot.

Megan didn't bother correcting him or the voice. She flinched as he came up behind her, sliding his arms round her, but forced herself to remain still. His lips touched her bare shoulder.

'Is it OK?' he asked.

As she instinctively began to say no, she realised it was. Her body relaxed into him as he kissed his way up her neck, nibbling gently on her earlobe, his hands stroking her breasts. She

107

felt herself responding to his touch just as she had always done, and suddenly she wanted him desperately.

Turning, she wrapped her arms around his neck, mouth hungry for his, craving his tongue caressing hers. She dropped his towel to the floor and stroked him firmly, rewarded by a gasp.

'You're sure?' he whispered.

She replied by stroking him harder, eliciting a groan as he pressed her to him, lips on her nipple. Locked together, they stumbled to the bed.

It wasn't slow, gentle loving; it was frantic and satisfying and Megan could feel her orgasm swelling inside her. She cried out his name as she climaxed, and that was all it took for Stef to lose control, clutching her tight as the spasms shook his body. Gasping for breath, they sprawled in each other's arms as Stef pulled the sheet protectively over them.

'Love you, Megs,' Stef whispered.

'Love you too,' she whispered back.

'I'm sorry I let you sleep alone. I thought I was doing the right thing, giving you space.'

Megan propped herself up on one elbow, reaching to stroke his damp hair, the first time she recalled touching him voluntarily since her discharge. 'This bed's too big for one. It feels lonely.'

He kissed her softly. 'I've missed you so much.'

They lay together for some time in comfortable silence, neither really thinking, and for once the voice was quiet. Megan let her fingers trail over his chest, up and down his firm abdomen. She paused as she found an unfamiliar ridge, rough against his smooth skin, foreign to her.

'What's that?' She tried to raise the sheet to see, but Stef had already rolled on to his stomach to kiss her again.

'Just a graze. Caught the corner of the cellar wall at the Whitechapel house.' He smoothed escaped wisps of hair back from her forehead. 'You're twitching for a shower, aren't you? Go on, I won't be offended.' It was true Megan didn't like to go to sleep after sex without a shower, but it hadn't occurred to her until Stef spoke. Immediately she felt sweaty, unclean, and she rolled off the bed.

'Won't be long.'

'Liar,' Stef grinned. 'You've never managed a shower in less than half an hour.'

'You try having this much hair!'

She turned the shower up hot and closed her eyes against the fine spray as the powerful jets pummelled her skin. She took her time lathering her hair, mindful of the scar, enjoying the rasp of her fingers against her scalp. Her skin felt alive, flushed by the strenuous activity and tingling pleasantly from Stef's touch.

As the suds circled lazily around the drain, her eyes were drawn by a flash of colour. Small red splashes, just a couple, blending through the white foam.

Megan's hand flew to her abdomen scar, and she froze, watching the red dissipate in the flowing water. It took some courage to reach down and check, and she heard herself let out a cry as her fingers came away stained with a smear of blood.

'Stef!' she screamed.

Sounds of panicked movement came from the bedroom and Stef almost fell through the door. 'What? What's wrong?'

Megan pointed to the shower floor. 'I'm bleeding! My period must be starting. How can I be bleeding if I've had a hysterectomy?'

A look of panic crossed Stef's face. 'I don't know. Does it

mean something's gone wrong? Fuck, we shouldn't have had sex! I thought it had been long enough. Wait, I'll google it.' He dashed back to the bedroom and returned, clutching his phone. Megan felt acutely vulnerable, standing naked and wet at the shower entrance, even though Stef's attention was focused on his screen.

After a few moments his fingers ceased flying across the keypad and his eyes moved rapidly as he read.

'The NHS website says spotting or bleeding often occurs after a hysterectomy during the healing process.'

'It's not my period?'

Stef frowned, on uncertain ground now. 'I don't think you can have a period any more.' More rapid googling. 'No, it says not.'

'How am I supposed to tell the difference?'

He shrugged, distinctly out of his depth. 'You know more about that than me.'

Megan realised how cold she had become, her skin covered in goose pimples. She stepped back into the shower stream, letting the powerful jet flow over her head.

'Are you OK now?'

'Yes. Sorry, I panicked.'

Stef withdrew with no little relief, closing the door again. Megan watched another little splash of blood appear on the shower tray.

What if he's lying?

Chapter Thirteen

There was no sleep for Megan that night, only hourly visits to the bathroom to check how much blood she had lost before returning to bed to stare at the ceiling until she could stand it no more and got up to check again.

By the time Stef's alarm went off, she couldn't wait for him to leave. His mere presence was putting her on edge, a threat to this new consideration reverberating within her head, whispering to her throughout the night.

If you didn't have a hysterectomy, that proves you had a C-section. It proves Luka is real.

'I need to go into the office for a few hours,' Stef was saying as he dressed. Megan hadn't heard him speak, had to force herself to tune into his words rather than the voice's urgent murmurs. 'Sophia's on her way. I'll get breakfast sorted.'

Megan nodded distractedly and dashed to the bathroom for another check. Still only spots of blood, but it hadn't stopped, which encouraged her enough to dress and head downstairs to force down a few mouthfuls of toast and the standard handful of pills. Stef hovered, bringing coffee and offering Manuka honey as he tapped out emails on his iPad.

'I'll only be a couple of hours.' He dropped a kiss on top of her head, as if she were a child. 'Have a good time with Sophia.'

Megan heard a key in the front door as Stef left the kitchen, a brief conversation before the door closed again.

'Don't want!' a strident voice bellowed. 'Give me, Mummy!'

'You just said you didn't want it!' Sophia's tone was already exasperated. 'Now you want me to give it you? Which is it?'

'Want!'

'You can only have one.'

'No, Mummy!'

'Fine, one for each hand then. But that's it. And take your wellies off. You can't wear them in the house.'

Megan's legs wouldn't respond at first and, by the time she got to the doorway, a toddler whirlwind in pink wellingtons and a canary-yellow knitted beanie was barrelling towards her, clutching a rice cake in each hand.

'Amelia!'

'Meggie!' Amelia screamed, dropping both her hard-won snacks and launching herself at her aunt.

Megan dropped to her knees and flung out her arms. Amelia's little hands locked around Megan's neck, squeezing tight. She lifted the child into her embrace, feeling the impossibly soft skin pressed against her cheek, breathing in the smell of apples from the silken-gold hair tickling her neck. Her scar protested, but she didn't care.

'I missed you so much, Ami.'

'Meggie gone.'

'Yes, Meggie was away for a while, but I'm back now.'

'Biscuit!' Amelia was done with hugging, wriggling free to jump up and down as if splashing in puddles.

'You've just had rice crackers!' Sophia said.

'All gone!'

'Yes, because you dropped them on the floor! Take that hat off, and why are you still wearing your wellies?'

Amelia had already sensed the moment of weakness and made a run for the kitchen. As soon as Megan handed her an oatmeal cookie, she launched herself on to the Chesterfield to munch in peace.

'Soph, I think I've got my period,' Megan said quietly as they sat at the island.

'Yeah, so ... oh, right.' Realisation dawned. 'Can you even have a period now?'

'I don't know. Stef googled it and said it's normal to bleed after the op, but I'm not sure. Can you check it?'

Sophia carelessly slid her phone across. 'Help yourself.'

Megan wasted no time in accessing the Google app. 'He's right; it says bleeding is common post-op.'

'Are you googling something else?' Sophia watched as Megan's fingers continued to tap at the keyboard.

'I want to read about psychosis.'

'Are you allowed to do that?'

'Going to inform on me?'

Sophia shrugged. 'I've never seen the allure of being a grass. I'll make coffee.'

Megan's finger hovered over the Facebook icon. She would be able to access her profile through Sophia's. She touched the screen and the familiar timeline popped up – posts of work woes and spousal disharmony, pictures of toddlers baking and

113

cute cockapoos wearing bandanas, rants about the Tube and requests for holiday-spot recommendations.

'What's it say?' Sophia made her jump as she banged down the coffee cups to snatch Amelia's beaker before she flung Ribena everywhere.

The diversion gave Megan enough time to close Facebook and bring up another Google search. 'Psychosis is "a condition which affects how your brain processes information and leads to you losing touch with reality, causing you to see, hear and believe things that aren't real",' she read. '"The main symptoms are hallucinations and delusions."'

'Exactly what Dr Mac told you, right?'

'That's a thought. Can I google Dr Mac while I've got chance?'

Sophia hitched one shoulder. 'I won't spoil your fun.'

Megan tapped in his full name, speed-reading the links that promptly appeared. Controversial. Boundaries pushed. Boundaries crossed. Trust. Brilliance. Denial.

She hovered, uncertain which one to tap, no longer sure she wanted to know. Her stomach clenched as hot and cold flushes rolled over her, terror and exhilaration at the evidence other people had doubted the almighty psychiatrist as well.

Maybe you're not as mad as you think. Hurry up and read before Sophia takes the phone back.

As if mocking the voice, the phone immediately rang, an unknown number flashing on the screen. Sophia reached over and plucked it from Megan's hand, screwing her face up in a dramatic grimace.

'Fucking PPI.' She stabbed at the screen and slid it into her pocket before Megan could ask for it back. Megan thought bitterly of her own confiscated phone, locked away in Stef's office, along with her social life and social media.

Didn't you work out a way of getting access to it? It's the perfect time while Stef isn't here.

Amelia bounded over, hugging Megan's legs, as if sensing her spiralling frustration. 'Want Stef!'

'He's at work, darling.'

'Stef!' Amelia bellowed.

What about the duck?

Megan leapt to her feet at the sudden reminder of Quackles the duck, the perfect reason to be in the office, not even noticing the rush of dizziness that now accompanied any quick movement. 'Hang on, Ami, I've got something for you. One sec, it's upstairs.'

Hoping the toy was in the office, she hauled herself up the stairs to find it. Sure enough, it was propped up on the desk, bright blue eyes watching her contentedly. She caressed the downy fur, held it to her cheek.

From nowhere, a memory shouted its presence, something important, but it retreated again before she could grasp it. She stared into the toy's eyes as she tried to pluck it from her foggy brain.

You know where the key is.

Kneeling quickly, she scrabbled under the bottom drawer until her fingers touched metal, ripping it free. She slid the prize into her jeans pocket, irrationally proud of her achievement. Tonight, she would get her phone back and at last be able to see her Facebook photos of Luka.

Stef will know you've been in here – he'll see Quack is gone. What if he checks for the key?

The sensible solution was to leave a note explaining her reason for being in the room, so there would be no suspicion of an ulterior motive. She scrabbled in the top drawer for a Post-it note but found only old ones Stef had already written on. She grabbed one to see if she could use the back of it, but both sides were covered by a list scrawled in pink highlighter.

The first bullet point read: 'Hide all stabbing objects'. Underneath were 'Change computer password' and 'Find pills' and finally, at the end of the list: 'Stop my wife from killing me or herself!!!'

Megan stared in disbelief at the glib words, each bullet point hitting her like a winding punch to the stomach. She almost slammed the drawer and ran from her discovery.

You need to write the note or the plan will be ruined.

Actions becoming clumsier, she forced herself to search the drawer again until she found a few fresh Post-it notes underneath a photo of baby Amelia. Quickly jotting an explanation and sticking it in plain view on his desk, she started replacing all the riffled items. She gazed woodenly at the photo, a happy time, irretrievable now.

Look closely.

A realisation slapped her in the face. Nausea erupted, unannounced, and she only just made it to the main bathroom in time. There was nothing to bring up apart from a few bites of toast and her stomach spasmed painfully as she retched. It was over in moments but left her feeling too shaky to stand. Only the knowledge that Sophia was waiting got her back to her feet, and she clutched the sink as she rinsed her mouth of the bitter, chalky taste. Shoving the photo into her back pocket, she grabbed Quack and escaped downstairs.

'You look flustered.'

'I was sick,' Megan admitted. 'The meds make me nauseous. But look what I found.'

She held up the toy duck. 'Look, Ami, Quackles is safe! He was under my sofa!'

Amelia ran over and seized the duck, inspecting him carefully before delving into her backpack and producing a fluffy toy sheep. 'Mine!'

'Did you get a new snuggly?'

Amelia obligingly held the sheep up for inspection.

'Don't you want Quack?'

'Baby gone!' Amelia said.

'Your baby's gone? You mean Quack? He's not lost any more, look.'

'My baby gone,' Amelia declared, giving Megan pecks with the sheep's nose, as if it were a carrion bird.

'Yes, but he's here now.' Megan glanced at Sophia. 'I thought she was desperate to get her duck back.'

Sophia rolled her eyes. 'That's toddlers for you. At least this is better than the potato.'

Amelia charged off, making 'baa' noises, abandoning Quack.

'She gave me hell for days about the damn duck, now she couldn't care less. Maybe she has attachment issues.' Sophia picked up the dropped toy. 'Megan, what's wrong? You've looked like you're going to burst into tears since you came back down.'

Megan touched the photo in her back pocket, trying to decide whether she wanted to confront the reality or remain in the comforting darkness of the unknown.

Show her.

117

'Have you seen this photo before?' She made a rare snap decision and produced the picture.

Sophia glanced at it. 'Don't think so. Where's it come from?'

'It was in Stef's desk drawer. Is it Amelia?'

Sophia looked more closely. 'Yeah, guess so.'

'You don't know?'

'All babies look the same when they're born, Megan, unless they're particularly hideous. Some resemble celeriac, don't they? It must be Amelia. What other baby would Stef have a picture of?'

'I don't think it's her.'

'Do you have any other pictures from when she was first born?'

'They'd be on my old phone. I didn't have iCloud storage then. All the ones we had printed and framed are older, after she started smiling.'

Sophia handed the photo back with a shrug. 'I'm pretty sure it's her.'

Megan stared down at the photo, looking at the reddened, scrunched-up face, the shock of dark hair, clenched fists waving to the camera, and felt a rush of familiarity.

'How are my favourite ladies doing?'

'Stef!' Amelia shrieked, leaping on her uncle.

Stef swept her up into his arms and kissed the top of Megan's head. She shook him off in irritation, his touch suddenly abhorrent.

'I didn't hear you come in. You weren't long.'

'Trisha has everything under control. I just had to sign off on a few invoices.' Stef turned his attention to the squirming toddler, tickling her under the arms. 'How are you, Trouble? Happy to see Auntie Meggie?'

Amelia screamed with delight, wriggling frantically, managing to kick Stef in the groin and the ribs at once. He swiftly returned her to the floor, rubbing the bruise with a grin.

'Guess that's our cue to leave.' Sophia laughed.

She started rounding up her daughter's strewn belongings but didn't succeed in stowing the hated hat before Amelia snatched it. Amelia pounded off on an escape route through the house, Sophia in hot pursuit.

Megan took the opportunity to ask the question she couldn't stop echoing loudly in her head. The Post-it list she would keep within, until the time was right, but not this.

'Who is this baby?' She thrust the photo in her husband's face.

Stef frowned as he took it to examine. 'Where'd you get this?'

'Your desk drawer.'

'Why were you in my desk drawer?'

'I went up to fetch Quack for Amelia – I left you a note to say why I'd been in there. Who is the baby, and why do you have their picture?'

'It's Amelia. Who else would it be?' Stef attempted to straighten the crumpled paper.

It's not. You know it's not.

'That's not Amelia. Amelia is blonde!'

'She wasn't when she was born.'

'You think I don't recognise my own niece?'

'Clearly not, 'cos that's Amelia. What other baby's picture would I have?'

'It's Luka, isn't it?'

'No, Megan, it is not Luka. There is no Luka.'

'Stop saying that!'

'I have to say it! Sophia, tell her.' He turned to his sister-in-law as Sophia carried the thrashing toddler back into the room.

'Megan, I'm sure it's Amelia,' Sophia interjected, sitting her daughter firmly on a stool. She began pushing boots on to jerking legs, regardless of protest. 'Shall I take the photo with me if it worries you so much?'

Don't let her take it! You'll never see it again.

'No!' Megan realised she was echoing her niece as she grabbed the photo back from Stef, setting it safely on the island and smoothing it out.

'Quieten down before you set this one off.' Sophia gave a warning nod in Amelia's direction. 'We'd better go.'

'I'm sorry. I didn't mean to scare her.'

'You haven't. You know rampaging rhinos wouldn't bother her. Just time for lunch, that's all.'

'Have lunch here. Or I'll come for lunch with you.'

'Dr Mac will be here soon,' Stef said.

'We'll do it another day,' Sophia promised. 'See you soon, OK?'

She herded her daughter to the door, Stef following behind to see them out, as he always did. Megan turned to pick up the photo, put it safely in her pocket, and saw it was gone.

She scrabbled among the other items on the island, checked underneath all the stools, even pulled a couple of drawers open in case it had slipped through a crack. It was nowhere to be found.

They'll pretend it never existed now.

Overwhelmed by an exhaustion which chose that moment to rear its head, Megan could do nothing but sink on to a stool, grasp a handful of her hair and wish she could cry.

Chapter Fourteen

Before

'Don't be such a wuss, Isaac! The whole bloody avenue's going!' Stefan glared at his twin across the breakfast table.

Isaac kept his gaze fixed on the oak surface, spooning cereal slowly into his mouth. 'The avenue doesn't care about me. I'm invisible. No one will notice I'm not there.'

'Mum and Dad are fed up of making excuses for you every time you ignore an invitation.' Admittedly, it was a bit unfortunate they lived on such a sociable street; all the neighbours had been friends for years and regular invites to dinner parties and barbecues were issued to the whole family.

'Why are you so concerned about this particular party? You and Megan split up ages ago.'

Stefan gritted his teeth and tore a bite from his bacon sandwich. It didn't matter that his relationship had come to an amicable end soon after Megan started at King's College: he still loved her. Not even the St Mary's girls had been enough to tempt him since Megan had quietly told him she thought it was better for them to concentrate on their individual lives.

She had so easily sensed his increasing reluctance to come home for the holidays, though he had refused to be so understanding when she had said regular visits to Durham were impossible now her time was so limited. After a few weeks of bickering and unfounded accusations neither of them meant, Megan had made her decision and Stefan had had no choice but to accept it was over.

The Easter break was the first time he'd been home since, and he'd arrived to a birthday-party invitation. Nothing unusual in that, except for the host – Megan's mother.

'I'm bothered because Mum and Dad deserve the chance to go out together for once. One of them always has to stay behind to babysit you, and it's not fair.'

'You don't care about them, just about yourself,' Isaac whispered, as if afraid to express the words too loudly.

'Enough, Isaac,' their father interrupted. 'Stefan's right. You're coming to the party. I want your mother and me to both be able to enjoy ourselves.'

'No, Dad.'

'Did I give you a choice? You don't have to stay long, just show your face and say hello to people for once. I'm fed up of all the questions about you.'

'Just tell them I'm tapped in the head, like you usually do.'

'I do not say that!'

'Can we at least finish breakfast before we have an argument?' their mother demanded. 'Isaac, we have ties to Megan's family. It will look very rude if you don't attend.'

'What ties? Just because Stef went out with their daughter and you sometimes babysit their bat-shit-crazy mother does not mean we're tied to them!' Isaac went scarlet at his outburst, biting his thumbnail hard enough to raise beads of bright red blood.

'I said, *enough!*' A thunderous thump of their father's fist. 'Your mother spends a lot of time helping the Crawleys. Don't be so bloody dismissive of her.'

'Dad, I can't go to the party. I can't be with that many people.'

'Then I'm taking your computer.'

'I'm not a child! You can't confiscate my belongings!'

'While you live under my roof without making any contribution, I'll do exactly as I please. That's the deal, Isaac. We go to the party as a family, or your computer disappears till Stefan goes back to Durham.'

'I might be gone by Monday at this rate,' Stefan mumbled.

'Don't you start!'

Isaac's face was a mask of fear as he dropped his spoon into his half-full bowl and scrambled to his feet, kicking out at the dozing Orion as he nearly fell over the dog. Seconds later, the sound of him vomiting came from the downstairs toilet.

'That went well,' Stefan declared. He shoved the last of his sandwich into his mouth. 'Orion and I are off to help with the party prep.'

'Tell Megan we'll all be there later.' His mother offered a distracted smile, torn between comforting her fragile son and allowing him privacy.

Stefan grabbed the dog lead and hurried Orion along the allotments to Megan's back garden. It had been mown and weeded for the first time he could remember. Her father, leaning against a pair of hedge shears, already looked exhausted by his efforts.

'Oh, Stefan, didn't know you were home.'

'Megan texted me about the party so I decided to come

back for Easter break.' Stefan released Orion and watched him bound for the house in the hope of treats. 'Need a hand?'

'You any good with bunting?'

'I'll have a go. Megan about?'

'She's just come back with the shopping. Sophia!' He raised his voice to his younger daughter, who was setting out a table of plastic cups with an unusual enthusiasm that suggested she was keen to sample the punch they would contain. 'Tell your sister Stefan's here.'

Sophia rolled her eyes and poked her head through the open kitchen window to bellow, 'Megan, your ex is here!'

Both men went red: one with frustration, the other with embarrassment. Megan's dad made himself scarce and Stef busied himself untangling the bunting, making sure he looked hard at work when Megan appeared.

'Hi!' She came to the kitchen door, waving to him. 'You came!'

''Course I did,' he said awkwardly as she walked barefoot over to him. 'I've missed talking to you.'

'We still text often enough.' She changed the subject tactfully. 'I suppose Isaac's not coming?'

'Actually, Dad's told him he's got no option.'

'He won't like that. I still see him on his way to the library; he always looks scared of his own shadow. He chats now, sometimes.'

'Miraculous,' he said drily.

'He's better than he was. He's not like you, Stef; everything you find so easy is difficult for him.'

'Just how long have your little chats been?'

'Don't say it like you're jealous.'

'I am jealous. Sounds like you talk to him more than you do to me.'

124

'I see him more often than you.'

'That was your choice.'

'You knew my reasons. You said you understood.'

'I do understand, Megan, but you can't expect me to be pleased you're palling up with Isaac.'

'I'm not "palling up" with him. I feel sorry for him; he clearly hasn't got any friends. What's so wrong about me giving him the opportunity to talk to someone his own age?'

'Because I don't, you mean?'

'You label him, Stef. You don't even try to understand him.'

'Think I haven't tried? I did everything I could to support him when Cambridge said he couldn't go back.'

'Couldn't go back?' Megan's brow creased. 'What do you mean, "couldn't"?'

'I meant shouldn't. They said he shouldn't go back. Because he was so unstable.' Stefan paused in his battle with the bunting, unwilling to reveal too much of what he now knew about Cambridge. The confirmation of his suspicions, finally gleaned from eavesdropping on a whispered argument between his parents, still winded him. 'I know you identify with him because of your mum, but he's not like her. You can't help him.'

'I'm not trying to. I'm just, I don't know, being a friendly ear for him.'

'You're wasting your time.'

'That's my decision, not yours.' She glanced at her watch. 'I'd better get back to making sandwiches. There's a load to do. Thanks for coming to help. I do appreciate it.'

He offered her a reconciliatory smile. 'No worries. Watch Orion doesn't steal all the meat.'

Stefan watched her gracefully pick her way back across the

garden, hair still long enough to touch her belt, and he wanted her so badly he nearly allowed tears to flood his eyes. He scrubbed his hand roughly across his face.

'Your brother *is* weird.' Sophia appeared from nowhere, standing over him as he crouched down.

'Yeah, I know, thanks.'

'I've seen the way he looks at Megan. He likes her.'

'He can fuck off. Megan's not interested in him.'

'She isn't, she just feels sorry for him. But he doesn't know that. It's sad, really. Is he autistic?'

'You're too young to understand.'

Rage flashed in Sophia expressive face. 'I'm seventeen, dickhead, not a child.'

'Sorry,' Stefan mumbled, not wanting to argue with another member of the household. 'I've known you since you were little. I forget you've grown up.'

Sophia snorted impatiently. 'Whatever. Is he coming tonight?'

'Isaac? Yeah, unfortunately.'

'I bet he'll freak out. Doesn't he hate crowds? I remember him crying at a barbecue years ago because he had to choose which meat he wanted.'

Stefan shrugged, not giving a damn. 'I won't let him spoil the party.'

'All my friends are coming. Are you going to dance with us?' Sophia grinned at him, so at ease with herself, cheeky and alluring all at once. When had she stopped being the fearless little tomboy playing rough football with the avenue's boys to prove herself? He'd been so caught up in Megan that he had never noticed her sister's metamorphosis into womanhood.

' 'Course I will,' he said, and grinned back.

126

Chapter Fifteen

Macaulay's schedule gave Megan enough time to compose herself after Sophia and Amelia had left. She managed to hold it together until they were safely gone, before she fled upstairs, a kaleidoscope of images invading her mind, distorting her memory of the photograph even as she tried to bat them away. Stef followed, hovering outside their bedroom, as if expecting her to slit her wrists with her bookmark.

The doorbell shrilled only minutes later and Megan automatically hauled herself off the bed to attend to its demand for attention, as if it were a newborn baby screaming for milk.

'I'll get it.' Stef was already on his way down the stairs. 'Why don't you freshen up before you see Dr Mac?'

'Why?'

'You look a bit ... fraught ...'

Megan retreated to her dressing table, confronted by the evidence of her anguish. Her hair was wild where she had unconsciously gripped locks of it; her face was red, skin flaking, and she'd spilt coffee down her T-shirt. Even her eyes were puffy and sore, with broken blood vessels from her new habit of rubbing at them.

You look like someone heading for a Section 3 . . .

Shaken by the threat, she changed into a clean mustard cashmere sweater that was now far too big, the downy fabric enveloping her. She hadn't bothered with make-up since coming home, but she rubbed foundation into her cheeks and touched a mascara wand to her eyelashes in a vague attempt to create a mask to hide behind. She didn't trust her shaking hands with eyeliner: a dab of powder, a spritz of J'adore and a messy bun was the best she could manage. She couldn't allow Macaulay to see her looking like she had lost control.

He'll keep Luka from you even longer if he thinks you can't hold it together.

Low voices murmured, their secrets threatening, as she entered the sitting room and she saw Stef had already settled Macaulay in his usual seat.

'Don't talk about me when I'm not here, Stef,' she snapped.

Stefan had the grace to blush, but Macaulay shook his head. 'Nothing has been said that I wouldn't be happy to repeat to you. I hear you've been distressed today.'

She didn't miss his emphasis on 'distress', rather than using the simple 'upset'. 'Yes.'

'Would you like to talk about it? Stefan said it was to do with a photograph of your niece?'

'I don't think it is my niece. And now the photo's gone; someone took it.'

'Sophia could see it was upsetting you,' Stef said.

'I wanted to keep it.'

'I'm sure Sophia was trying to help,' Macaulay said.

'I want it back!' Megan heard her voice rise sharply.

'Shall I leave you to it?' Stef was already making for the door.

'Stay a few minutes, Stefan, if you will.'

Stef hadn't expected his escape to be denied and he took another couple of steps, as if he intended to defy the psychiatrist. He reluctantly took the armchair next to Megan's, looking like he wished he had a stiff drink to hand. Megan felt momentarily sorry for him. Stef wasn't cut out for this; he was too impulsive for subterfuge; careful thought didn't come naturally to him. His past made it harder for him; the half-truths he had lived with made him hate secrecy all the more.

'What happened this morning, Megan?' Macaulay's pen was poised, as usual.

He can't wait to find out what you've done wrong this time.

Megan raised her chin defensively. 'I needed to go into Stef's desk and I found the photo.'

'And you don't believe it's of Amelia?'

'No, it looks nothing like her, even though Sophia said it was.'

'Then why don't you believe her?'

'Because I remember what Amelia looked like when she was born, and she didn't have dark hair. She didn't have any hair.'

'Why would Sophia lie?'

'She didn't want me to know the photo is of my son.'

Stef slapped his palms against his thighs. 'Megan, that picture is not our child, I swear to you.'

'How can I believe you, Stef? You lied about the duck. Amelia didn't give a damn about Quackles – you said it was her favourite. It was Luka's, I know it!'

'Amelia is passionately attached to a vegetable – she's not exactly discerning!'

'Megan, remember we've talked about the ways psychosis presents itself?' Macaulay interjected. 'The delusions, making you believe things that aren't real?'

Got an answer for everything, hasn't he?

'These aren't delusions,' Megan insisted. 'I bought the toy for my son, not my niece.'

'You may not be able to distinguish between reality and delusion at the moment.'

'You just expect me to believe you, don't you?'

'I hope you will, yes. I want you to trust me.'

Megan shook her head. 'I don't trust anyone any more.'

Macaulay cleared his throat. 'We can continue our session alone now, Stefan. Thank you for staying.'

Stef was on his feet immediately, striding across the room even as he spoke. 'I'll be upstairs if you need me.'

He can't wait to get away from you.

Megan pinched the bridge of her nose to hide the tears that sprang unbidden, swallowing down the sudden swell of emotion as she acknowledged the chasm between them.

Macaulay waited until the door closed firmly behind Stef. 'Have you been taking your medication, Megan?'

'Yes,' she said woodenly, as woodenly as she now tossed the pills into her mouth.

Then she remembered – she had vomited. Less than half an hour after taking the tablets. Surely her stomach wouldn't have had time to absorb them.

Your head is clearer. That's why you were able to process the photo. You're not medicated.

The triumph lasted only a moment before she was gripped by panic. Macaulay would urine-test her in another few days – what if she failed? Her section would be revoked. Could the test tell if she'd skipped a day of meds?

'You seem rather animated, if you don't mind me saying so.'

'I was thinking about Stef.'

Macaulay chose to interpret that statement positively. 'You're lucky to have a strong marriage; a lot of my patients don't. How long have you been together?'

Megan didn't bother to correct him. She had no desire for Macaulay to know of the new cracks widening daily in her relationship. 'Nine years. We knew each other as kids, dated through sixth form, then grew apart when we went to university.' For once, she wanted to speak at length, distract him from realising she wasn't under the influence of the drugs.

'What brought you back together?'

'Selling the house after my mother died. Stef helped me tidy it up and market it properly. We got far more than I'd expected, thanks to him.'

'What did you do with the money?'

Why does he want to know?

'We're not talking millions,' Megan said guardedly. 'It was an unloved terraced house in Brockley and the property market hadn't exploded then. I invested in Stef's company. Sophia blew most of hers travelling the world and finally bought an over-priced house when she gained a little bit of sense. That's why we ended up paying for Eve's IVF courses.'

'Eve's an academic, right? She must have a reasonable salary.'

How does he know about Eve? Has someone been telling tales again?

Megan frowned. 'They have a huge mortgage and Sophia has a lot of debts. We wanted to do it. We could spare the money, and they needed it to raise Amelia.'

'Did Stefan agree?'

The insinuation ignited a flare of irritation. 'Of course he did. We're very comfortably off. Why wouldn't we want to help Sophia?'

'Some husbands might not be so keen.'

'Stef's not like that. He treats Sophia like his own sister.'

'He doesn't have siblings?'

'His brother died. That's what connected us when we met again, he understood what I was going through with my mother's death.'

Careful. He doesn't need to know about Isaac.

'You've both experienced hardship. Has it affected your relationship?'

'Before all this, I thought it made us stronger.'

'And now? Do you think your marriage is suffering?'

'Of course it is. We tiptoe around each other like strangers.'

'Stefan seems very supportive of your recovery.'

'He understands a bit about mental health.' Megan defied the voice's warning in her bid to keep Macaulay distracted. 'His brother used to self-harm.'

'Have you had any thoughts about self-harm, Megan?' His words sounded sly, at odds with his concerned expression.

'Cutting myself? No. I haven't thought about that.'

'You've never tried it?'

'No.'

'Have you been tempted? Did the idea of release through cutting ever appeal to you?'

'No, for God's sake!' Megan snapped, hating the way he seemed to be inviting her.

'That's good.' Macaulay reached abruptly into his briefcase. 'I brought you the papers on dissociation to read.'

She'd forgotten all about them.

'Hopefully they'll give you a clearer idea of the issue. Shall we talk about your dissociation? Maybe it would help if you wrote your own notes, then you can refer to them when you're struggling to know what's real and what's delusion.'

As if a few bullet points will give you a definitive guide between reality and fantasy.

Ignoring the voice once again, Megan obediently fetched a notepad and pen. It was the one she usually took to house auctions, filled with notes about dry rot, woodworm and leasehold issues. Suddenly, she yearned for the buzz of the auction room, the uncertainty of bidding, which she usually found so stressful, the tension as the amounts rose higher and a determined rival continued to raise their card.

'What are you thinking about?' Macaulay must have noticed her lack of interest in the task.

'Work. The business.'

'Do you miss working?'

'I hadn't even thought about it, but today, yes, I'm missing it.'

'What projects do you have at the moment?'

'A terrace in Whitechapel, a semi in Romford, an absolute wreck of a bungalow out in Essex somewhere and two flats in an Edwardian building in Stepney,' she rhymed off without hesitation, then paused in wonderment at her memory's sudden surge of capability. She really must have vomited up the medication before it could be absorbed.

'Will you sell them all on?'

'We usually keep flats to rent. They're easier to manage than house rentals and the income is steadier. The houses are sold.'

'That must be quite a profit margin.'

He wants to know how much you're worth. Watch him up his hourly rate accordingly if he finds out.

'The company is successful, yes,' she said carefully. She didn't discuss the business's turnover with her own sister, let alone a relative stranger.

'What made you decide to give up your own career?'

'I didn't, really. I was in a job I disliked and, when Stef proposed, I decided it was time to do something I enjoyed. My degree was in architecture so I had a lot of transferable skills.'

'You must work well together.'

'Stef's about as organised as a tsunami so he's happy that I take charge of the planning and coordinating while he's on site. It lets us both work to our strengths.'

'How did he propose?'

Megan raised her eyebrows. 'Is that relevant?'

'Happy memories are important. They help you understand that life can be like that again.'

'We had a picnic at the top of Meridian Hill. It's my favourite place in London. He proposed as the sun went down.' She toyed with the diamond set into her engagement ring. 'I didn't remember ever feeling so happy before. We'd just bought the house a few months before, the company was really starting to expand; it felt like we had everything we could ever want.'

'And what does it feel like now?'

Megan didn't reply immediately, taking the time to really consider her answer. She debated lying, saying it felt the same or that she believed contentment was still within reach, but what was the point? Eventually, she shook her head, dismissive.

'It feels like I've lost everything that mattered to me.'

That evening, with the clarity of a mind free from medication, Megan knew she wouldn't have long to abduct her phone. The voice hovered close, offering quiet guidance, reassuring her the plan wouldn't fail.

When she suggested a takeaway, to avoid the need for cooking, Stefan agreed with a delighted smile, as if he had succeeded in making her happy enough to eat. The Thai was surprisingly nice, considering she had little appetite, and she enjoyed the creamy, gentle spice of the massaman curry.

Stef was drinking bottles of Peroni. He preferred a good Malbec these days, but she suspected he was sticking to beer so she wouldn't be tempted to share the wine. Not that an open bottle of red would attract her attention at that moment; she was too focused on remembering her task.

She went along with his idea to curl up in the living room and watch the newest *Avengers* film; she hated superhero movies, but Stef was renowned for falling asleep partway through and she wanted him tired.

When they eventually went upstairs at midnight, he had already dozed off twice and was asleep within minutes. Megan sat upright, her Kindle in hand in case he woke up, and forced herself to wait a good twenty minutes before she silently slid out of bed, padding across the deep carpet to retrieve the key from her discarded jeans.

In the office, she worked by the light of the desk lamp to unlock the filing cabinet as quietly as she could, wincing at every metallic noise it made. There it was, the black screen of her iPhone sitting at the bottom of the drawer. She ignored the other items, even though her mind acknowledged such random objects as her tweezers and a pencil sharpener.

Locking the drawer again, she took the second staircase, smaller and narrower than the main one, up to her study. She hadn't visited this floor at all since she'd come home and the air smelled fusty, tinged with stale sweat, despite the efforts of the reed diffuser. She went to open the French windows, careless of the chilled night air, but found the keys were missing.

No prizes for guessing where they are. No time to retrieve them, just hurry up.

A charger was still plugged in by her easel and the phone screen flared into bright white light as she attached it. It took too long to load, uncharged for weeks, and she tapped her fingers impatiently against the unfinished canvas balanced on the easel, the stark charcoal lines showing no form, no connection. She couldn't remember what she had been attempting to sketch, but she instinctively disliked it.

Finally, the phone allowed her to enter her passcode, face ID banned after the period of disuse. She eagerly tapped the Facebook icon, watched her timeline load, ignored notifications to navigate to her profile page. As she scrolled through, noticing there had been no updates for weeks, she recognised a couple of posts and her heart leapt in encouragement.

It was only when she noticed she had scrolled back to Christmas that realisation dawned. There were no photos of Luka. No posts announcing his birth or bringing him home or even his first smile. She checked even further and found photos of herself with Sophia, Stef, a few friends, but all of them were head-and-shoulders shots. None showed her pregnancy, not a single picture featuring any sign of a bump.

There must be something.

She carried on searching, more frenzied now, yearning for a scan picture or a complaint post about morning sickness. A whole year's worth of posts, and nothing.

Winded with disappointment, she dropped into the wicker armchair and clicked on to her photos. Countless pictures of Amelia and selfies with Stef, friendly cats encountered in the street and the perfect wallpaper for a rental-flat living room, various holiday snaps and city skylines. No dark-haired baby.

She checked further back for baby Amelia, but it was a relatively new phone; she had at last admitted defeat and prostrated herself at the altar of Apple and hadn't got round to transferring pictures from her previous Samsung. The meticulous albums didn't go back far enough to cover Amelia's birth. She had nothing to compare her mental image of the mystery photo to either.

As a last resort, she scrutinised her WhatsApp and text messages, but she was mildly OCD about keeping her messages in good order and she habitually deleted any she didn't need for future reference or sentiment. As expected, there was nothing of any use and she hadn't received anything new – the last, inconsequential message was from the day before she had ended up in A&E. That struck her as slightly odd. She didn't have many close friends, the legacy of a youth spent caring rather than socialising, but she had a small circle she met for dinner and drinks regularly.

Surely one of them would have been in contact.

Defeated, frustration losing the battle to despair, Megan powered the phone off, realising she had been sitting up there for over an hour. She couldn't risk taking any longer. Creeping carefully down the stairs, she returned the phone to its prison and taped the key in the correct place. Stef was still in the same position, snoring lightly, when she slipped under the duvet.

Lying back against her pillows, she wondered how Stef had known her passcode – the date they had completed on the house, not an obvious one, like a birthday or their wedding anniversary. He wouldn't have seen her type it in; she always used the convenience of face ID. And it could only have been Stef who had deleted all the content. No one else had access, and why would they want to hide it from her?

Stef is determined to make you believe Luka is a figment of your imagination.

The voice sounded stronger tonight. Its authority wouldn't be ignored even as she tried to concentrate on her own thoughts.

If you can't find any evidence, you'll start to believe he's right.

Chapter Sixteen

Stef hesitated before pressing Sophia's name on his phone screen. He wasn't sure he wanted this conversation with her, or with anyone really, but someone needed to know what was happening in his house. Just in case . . . no, that wouldn't happen, not again. This was insurance, that was all. Sensible. Just a precaution.

'Don't tell me, my sister needs a babysitter again,' Sophia answered.

'Hello to you, too.'

'Good morning, Stefan, how are you today?' An unnervingly accurate impression of Macaulay. 'You're getting far too used to American niceties.'

'Your wife is American.'

'My wife isn't here, in case you've forgotten.' Sophia's voice quietened as she moved the phone away. 'No, it's not Mommy, babe. Mommy will call us later.'

'Listen, there's something I need to tell you. My desk lamp was on when I went into the office this morning. I wasn't even in there yesterday when it was dark. There's no reason I'd have used it.'

'Reckon Megan's been through your desk again?'

'That's what I thought. Not that there was anything else to find. There was nothing missing from the locked drawers and the key was in its usual place.'

'Maybe find it a new place, just in case. You don't want her getting hold of those knives again, not when she's having meltdowns over photos.'

'I can't believe she found the damn thing.'

'It was your fault for leaving it lying around.'

'I was busy hiding every item in the house that could be used to stab me! I forgot I even had it.'

Sophia gave an impatient sigh. 'She didn't believe it was Amelia.'

'No, she didn't. She's not stupid, after all.'

'We've been treating her as if she is. Even I find myself talking to her like she's a child.'

'She's absolutely determined that she's right and we're lying to her.'

'Well, we are.'

'We are not,' he snapped. 'We're limiting information, we're avoiding telling her things that may affect her condition, but we are *not* lying to her.'

'Keep telling yourself that, Stef, it sounds so plausible. Do you really think we're doing the right thing, using Dr Mac's programme?'

' 'Course we are. He's the best.'

'Are you trying to convince me or yourself? Look, you knew he was controversial. He must be in private practice because he was too maverick for the NHS. And because he likes being rich, presumably. God, I'd love to be rich ...'

140

'Sophia,' Stef warned, before she could go off on a tangent.

'Just saying. Anyway, what if he's too controversial? Are we only going to damage Megan more if she finds out the whole story? I've started to wonder if the longer we keep it all from her, the worse it'll be when we tell her.'

'When she finds out?' he echoed.

'She will find out, Stef, she has to, and reasonably soon. Life can't go on like this. We need to get back whatever normality is left.'

'Dr Mac says she needs to learn coping mechanisms first, to deal with the news. This dissociation thing she has, it'll make it seem a completely new situation to her. We could end up right back at square one.'

'Do you have any of your own thoughts, or are you just going to keep parroting Dr Mac?'

'I believe him.' Stef gritted his teeth.

'Why can't we tell her now, then use the therapy programme to help her deal with it all?'

'We can't tell her now! She's completely irrational, nowhere near stable, even with all the meds. She'd end up locked away in a mental hospital for fuck knows how long. I'm not losing my wife!'

'You're paying ridiculous sums of money to prevent that happening, remember?'

Stef raked his hands through his thick hair. 'Fuck, this is impossible.'

He was getting a headache and wished he'd never picked up the phone. The loss of autonomy was harder than he had imagined; the sense of relief in handing responsibility to Macaulay had become a distant memory. If only his thoughts of Isaac, the sound of his twin's voice echoing in his ears at night, could be as far away.

'Soph, one last thing?'

He could almost hear her rolling her eyes. 'Yes, I'll come round and play prison guard.'

Stef put the phone away, rubbing his eyes until he was sure he was back in control, then busied himself setting Megan's pills out on the saucer for when she came down. He had no idea why he did it, but it made him feel a little better to at least make them look more palatable.

'Good morning,' he said with forced cheer as his wife entered the kitchen a few minutes later. He watched her robotically taking her juice and downing the pills without even glancing at them.

'I'm going to the bungalow in Essex. Do you want to come?'

Megan shook her head, as he had known she would.

'I'll be going to the auction tomorrow. Everything's gone through for the Deptford sale, so it's time for the next one.'

She didn't seem to hear him. 'Is Sophia coming?'

'Yes, after Dr Mac. Your appointment's early today.' He indicated the schedule that he was sure she'd never even glanced at.

'OK.' She stared blankly at the toast he placed in front of her. No point going to the effort of eggs or bacon sandwiches. She was so thin now, the jut of every bone visible through her sweater, the lack of nutrition showing in her lank hair, her pasty skin.

Isaac had been skeletal too, at the end. It had been a battle to persuade him to eat anything. His body had become as fragile as his mind.

142

Stef poured the coffee and opened the news app on his iPad. Safer to read in silence than give his own thoughts attention.

By the time Sophia and Amelia arrived, Megan had already forgotten what had been discussed in her therapy session. The medication felt stronger today, or maybe she was just noticing it more now she had experienced how it felt to be without it. The fog was thicker, heavier, taunting her until her frustration was barely containable.

'Paint, Meggie!' Amelia declared after a brief, fierce hug. She thumped her backpack on to the dining table, spilling crayons and colouring books across the surface.

Megan dutifully began to colour the unicorn she was directed to, but it was the wrong colour. She changed to the right shade, only to be told she was colouring the wrong part of the unicorn. After several horrified screeches when her crayon touched an inappropriate part of the paper, she was eventually permitted to fill in one leg and was scolded for doing it too neatly.

She tried her best to concentrate as her niece chatted away, a stream of nonsense about buses and babies and snails, but couldn't summon the focus for anything other than the photograph of the baby. She could see it so clearly it might have been branded into her memory. Indelibly, she hoped.

'What's up?' Sophia watched her closely as she did a circuit of the room, ignoring Amelia's protest at her abandonment of the task in hand.

'I need to get out of the house. I feel like the walls are closing in on me. I want to scream.'

'How about the garden?' Sophia suggested warily.

The picture of Luka won't be in the garden.

'No, I mean out. Not here. Let's go to your house.'

'Why my house?'

Megan thought carefully about an appropriate explanation, anything other than her true intention. 'It feels less of a risk than going to a café.'

'That makes no sense.'

'None of this makes sense!' Megan's laugh sounded slightly hysterical, even to her ears. 'Please, Soph, let me come round for an hour. You don't have to entertain me.'

'Stef will go berserk if he comes home and we're gone.'

Who gives a fuck about Stef? He's chosen his side.

'Since when are you bothered about Stef's reactions? He won't be back for hours, he'll never know.'

'This feels like we're on *Prison Break*.'

'You don't have that many tattoos. Come on, Sophia. One hour. That's all. Then I'll come home and be a good patient.'

Sophia gave a martyred sigh, but Megan could see she wasn't completely against the idea.

Push her. Beg. You need that photo.

'Please,' she said again.

'All right, fine, but if Stef finds out, I'm blaming it on you. I was powerless to stop you. I was an unwilling patsy. I'll even say you made me cry.'

'Whatever you want.' Megan was already pulling her coat on. 'Shall we get an Uber?'

'If you pay. Here, log into your account.' Sophia handed over her phone and Megan was so buoyed at the thought of leaving the house that she barely glanced at the other apps until the contacts icon inexplicably drew her gaze.

Remember, Sophia promised you something . . .

144

Megan froze at the unexpected flash of recollection. Her thumb hovered over the icon. 'Did you find Stef's parents' number?'

'Shit, no, sorry. Completely forgot.' Sophia nodded to the screen. 'How long for the Uber?'

Megan reminded herself and the voice there was already a task to focus on; she didn't need another distraction. 'Four minutes,' she finally announced.

'Christ, you try getting a toddler ready in four minutes! Grab the bloody hat, quick.'

Sophia's house was a narrow mid-terrace on a busy road, steep steps making it equally awkward to juggle shopping or children, the benefit of the thin garden somewhat negated by the neighbours' cannabis habit. She freely admitted she hadn't chosen well, but she'd never been one for careful consideration.

'It's an absolute hellhole,' Sophia warned as she unlocked the faded door. 'I haven't had the energy to tidy up after Madam's gone to bed.'

'I couldn't care less.' Megan followed her sister into the cluttered, lightless hallway, sighing with relief as she closed the door against the threats of the outside world.

Amelia went running off on a tour of the living room and kitchen before returning to Megan's side, tugging insistently on her hand.

'Snail!' Amelia declared, her little face very serious, to reflect the gravity of her random announcement.

'What do you mean?'

'She wants a pet snail,' Sophia translated.

'Like one of those giant African snails?'

'Nope, those things you find in the garden.'

'Snail,' Amelia insisted again.

'No, Amelia, not today,' Sophia said gently. 'Soon, OK?'

Amelia tilted her head in contemplation, then seemed to accept her mother's promise and charged off again happily enough.

'Where's Eve?' Megan asked, following Sophia through to the galley kitchen.

'In New York, lecturing at Columbia for a few weeks.' Eve was a well-respected history academic, in high demand both in the UK and her own country. 'She flew out while you were in the neurology unit.'

Wait. That's not right.

Megan frowned. 'But you said Eve was looking after Amelia the day I came home.'

'No, I didn't.'

'You definitely did.'

'Megan, I didn't say that because Eve was on the other side of the Atlantic when you came home.'

Don't push your luck. You need to find that photo.

Megan obediently bit back the urge to argue, not prepared to sacrifice her new freedom. 'Shall I go and play with Amelia?'

'Good idea. She'll want a potato if she comes in here.'

For an hour, Megan waited for Sophia to leave her unsupervised, but her sister refused to be distracted, for once, and Megan succumbed to the simple pleasure of playing with her niece. Together they built Duplo structures, had a teddy bears' picnic and created an ear-bleeding racket with a xylophone and a tambourine until Sophia begged them to stop.

Eventually, Megan noticed Sophia stealing glances at her watch. She didn't have long left.

'That's the hour I promised.' She smiled at her sister. 'Let me sort an Uber and we'll head back to mine.'

Sophia didn't bother to hide her relief at Megan's cooperation. 'Sounds good to me.'

'Can I use the loo before we go?'

'Sure, just ignore the towels on the floor and the toothpaste marks in the sink. I wish we'd bought somewhere with a downstairs cloakroom so I don't have to be mortified every time a visitor needs to pee.'

Megan took the stairs slowly, heavy exhaustion weighing her down. She forced herself to focus on her mission. If she could coerce her unwilling limbs, she would have time to quickly search upstairs for the photo.

There was still some blood when she used the toilet, but only a small stain; if it was her period, it was taking its time getting started. She risked a quick glance in the mirror as she washed her hands and immediately wished she hadn't.

As she pulled the bathroom door closed behind her and turned towards the master bedroom, a flash of a familiar colour drew her instead across the hallway, to the tiny box room. Her feet found their own way across the threshold and her gasp left her breathless.

The warm yellow walls, the exact shade of lemon pie. The brightly coloured stencils, the comfortable nursing chair, even the mobile hanging over the cot, gently swaying as if a tiny hand had just set it in motion.

Why is Luka's nursery at Sophia's house?

Dazed, forgetting all about her search for the photo, Megan stumbled across the room, reaching into the cot. The blanket's fleece held that scent, of talcum powder and baby shampoo and just *him*. Megan stroked it against her face, inhaling Luka's smell.

'Megan, what are you doing?' Sophia's voice was too loud in the serene room and Megan dropped the blanket as if guilty. As it fell, she saw, nestled in one corner of the cot, waiting for his owner, Quackles the duck.

'Why is the nursery here?' She turned to face her sister, clutching Quack to her chest.

'What do you mean? Where else would it be?'

'Amelia has her own room.' Desperate for proof, Megan marched past her sister to the third bedroom at the far end of the hallway. This time it was decorated with unicorns, floor scattered with toys.

'It's only her playroom at the moment. She's still in the cot in the nursery. This room isn't wired for the baby cameras so she's safer in there when she tries to escape.' Sophia spoke slowly, carefully, as if addressing an inattentive child, a deep crease growing between her eyebrows. 'What's wrong?'

'I remember the nursery being at my house. For Luka.'

Sophia opened her mouth but didn't seem to know what to say. 'It's never been at your house.'

'Are you sure?'

''Course I'm sure. Megan, the nursery has been here ever since we painted it together. Remember, Stef wouldn't shut up about craving tarte au citron till we stopped for cake on the way back from B&Q? Why are you looking at me like that?'

Megan looked down at the toy she was clutching, unable to keep eye contact with her sister, unable to admit what Sophia's memory meant. She cuddled Quack close, smoothing his velvety fur against her cheek, trying to draw comfort from his scent.

'Why are you so obsessed with the duck?'

Megan felt her voice break. She hadn't cried properly in so long she almost thought she'd lost the ability to weep, but the maelstrom of the photo, the duck and now the nursery was enough to bring tears spilling continuously down her cheeks. 'Because I know I bought Quack for Luka.'

'Oh, Megan.' Sophia wrapped her arms around her, a rare hug from her usually undemonstrative sister.

The tears ran out after only a minute.

'I wish I could pour you a glass of wine.' Sophia smiled shakily. 'This is even harder, not being able to have a drink with you.'

'I hadn't even thought about wine, actually.'

'Oh God, don't tell Dr Mac I reminded you about alcohol! He'll ban me.'

'He can't ban you.'

'Don't bet on it.'

Megan frowned. 'What do you mean? Is Dr Mac controlling who's allowed to visit me? Is that why none of my friends has been in touch?'

Sophia gave a little shrug. 'Just a joke. Come on, we've got to get you home before Stef realises you've gone.'

'I'm not a prisoner.'

'Until your treatment's finished, sis, you pretty much are.'

'This is madness!'

Sophia barked a laugh. 'That's exactly what it is.'

Chapter Seventeen

Before

The party was well attended, people glad to make the effort for the rare celebration. Megan's mother could go weeks, even months, as a virtual recluse, housebound by her down periods, but the avenue looked after the family as best they could with casseroles and offers of a few hours' supervision.

Stefan couldn't help but notice their neighbours didn't offer his parents the same support for Isaac's issues, but he supposed it was different. It wasn't something to be publicly aired. The fewer people who knew, the better, as far as he was concerned.

His parents had drifted to the bar table and were chatting with various neighbours, enjoying the rare chance to socialise as a couple. Stef was starving and keen to raid the groaning buffet table, but he was determined to police his twin, keep him away from Megan. He was not prepared to tolerate any friendship developing between them.

Isaac stood close to the safety of the hedge, holding a can of lager he had yet to drink from. Stefan, on the other hand, was on his fourth beer and waiting for the warm buzz that seemed unattainable tonight. He hadn't even had a chance to talk to

Megan, who was circulating with platters of cheese and biscuits, smiling politely as she moved between the guests.

'Can I go home now?' Isaac asked.

'No.'

'I've been here half an hour. I want to go home. I can go by myself. You can tell Dad.'

'As if he'll let you go alone. Just shut up and stay put. Can't you see the 'rents are enjoying themselves for once?'

'They're drunk, of course they're enjoying themselves.'

'Ever tried it? Being happy?'

Isaac shook his head, refusing to make eye contact. 'You don't know a thing about me, do you?'

'I know enough, Isa, more than I want to. I know what you did. I heard Mum and Dad talking after you went to that mad-expensive shrink last time I was home.'

'What did I do?'

'At Cambridge.'

'I wanted to die, Stef. Don't make me talk about it; it was a difficult time for me.'

'Seemed pretty easy to lie in the bath and slit your wrists. Harder for Mum and Dad to pick up the pieces afterwards, don't you think?'

'I didn't intend them to have to.'

'Do you realise how fucked up that is? Do you even care about Mum and Dad?'

Isaac seemed to consider that. Finally, he heaved a deep sigh. 'I don't even care about myself.'

'Isaac, what the fuck went wrong in your head? Were you always like this?'

'I suppose I was. You didn't notice because you didn't want

to. I embarrass you, just like I did when we were little. You find it easier to deny my existence.'

Stefan couldn't stand the conversation another minute; the combination of beer drunk too quickly and hidden demons rearing their heads was threatening to overwhelm him, and his resolve slipped.

'I'm going to get something to eat,' he snapped. 'Stay here. Don't go near Megan.'

He strode away from his brother to load a plateful of food. Still, he kept an eye on Isaac even as he ate, and his temper only rose further when Megan approached his twin. Taking several pieces of cheese, Isaac bit slowly into them as he talked. He rarely ate – there was a good reason why he was skeletal – but it didn't stop him accepting more when Megan offered.

She laughed at something he said and Stefan's stomach clenched. Sophia and her friends had started to dance, their laughter filling the air as they sung along to the lyrics. They tried to pull him into their midst, but he shook them off impatiently, ignoring their cajoling. Their antics had captured Megan's attention – she was looking at them, rather than Isaac – and Stefan seized his chance to intervene.

'Didn't I just tell you?' he growled at his twin.

'She came over to me!' Isaac protested.

'You OK?' Stef moved close to Megan, resting his hand in the small of her back.

She frowned at him in confusion. ''Course I am. Why wouldn't I be?'

Stefan focused on his brother. 'Stay the fuck away from her, Isaac.'

'It's fine, Stef,' Megan protested.

'I was only talking to her,' Isaac whispered. 'I wasn't doing anything wrong.'

'You don't talk to her, you hear me? You don't even look at her. Understand?'

Megan's mother called from the other side of the garden, waving her empty glass. Megan hesitated, torn between keeping the peace between the twins and her responsibility to the celebrant.

'Will you two try to get along for five minutes? I'll be back. Wait here.'

Stefan waited until she was out of earshot before stepping closer to his brother, straightening his shoulders to flex the powerful muscles. 'She's not interested in you, mate.'

'She's not yours any more.' Rare stubbornness flashed across Isaac's face. 'I can talk to her if I like.'

'Why are you looking for a shag from my ex? That's just fucking weird.'

'It's not like that!' Isaac went red. 'She's nice, way too nice for you.'

'You wouldn't know what to do with someone like Megan.' Stefan stepped even closer, right in his brother's face, noses almost touching.

Isaac punched him.

It was so unexpected that Stefan ended up on his backside, not because it was a good punch or even because it connected well, but because it was the last thing he had ever thought his twin would do.

The humiliation of having been caught off guard was the last straw. Stefan scrambled to his feet and hurled himself at Isaac. They crashed back on to the lawn, Stefan's punches accurate and hard, all his energy focused on what he had been wanting to do for so long. At last, an excuse.

A crowd of partygoers formed a loose circle around them, the younger ones cheering them on as the elders advised calm and cessation.

'Stef, get off him!' Megan's cry penetrated Stefan's red mist, but he couldn't – wouldn't – stop now.

Finally, a strong pair of hands dragged him off, holding him back as he lunged again, and he realised it was his father. Megan and his mother were pulling Isaac to his feet, trying to staunch the blood rushing from his nose, fussing around him like he was a toddler.

'What the hell is this about?' his father thundered.

'Isaac threw the first punch!' Sophia piped up, thrilled at such a ruckus. 'He knocked Stef down.'

Isaac was gasping for breath, his emaciated chest heaving, and he struggled to form a sentence. 'He said—'

'I told him to stay the fuck away from Megan,' Stefan spat.

'Stefan, go home!' His mother's cheeks were burning bright red. 'How dare you behave like this?'

'No!' Isaac tore his arm free. 'I want to go. Make him stay here. I don't want him near me.'

That suited Stefan. Megan was glaring such daggers at him that he couldn't leave without explaining himself. He let his body relax and felt his father's grip loosen.

'I'll take Isaac home,' his mother said, and Stefan immediately felt guilty that he had ruined her enjoyment.

His father shook his head firmly. 'No, all your friends are here. You stay. I'll go with Isaac.' There was no question of letting him go alone. 'I'm getting a headache anyway.'

Isaac, tissue pressed to his nose, allowed his father to march him through the garden gate. For another moment, the silence remained, then the buzz of chatter started again and everyone turned away to find more food or drink.

'I don't want to talk to you,' Megan snapped as Stefan awkwardly approached her. When he continued to hover, she dragged him further down the garden, out of earshot.

'I'm sorry, Megs, I was trying to protect you.'

'I don't need protection! You're twice as strong as Isaac, you hurt him!'

'He needs to understand he can't have you.'

'You can't either! I'm not yours any more, Stef!' Megan raised her voice sharply. 'I know what you're hoping for and it isn't going to happen. You don't get any say about who I choose to spend time with! Just leave me alone, OK?'

She stormed away, leaving Stefan stammering apologies after her. He received a further glare from his mother as he slunk back towards the drinks table.

There seemed to be nothing else for it but to get as drunk as he possibly could.

Chapter Eighteen

'Did you say you were going to the house auctions today?' Megan asked suddenly, partway through mechanically nibbling her lunch, which consisted of an apple.

'So you *were* listening.' Stef was inhaling a ham sandwich he had hurriedly thrown together; he no longer bothered to ask her if she wanted one.

'Why wouldn't I be?'

'You seem to be wrapped up in your own thoughts these days.'

'Maybe that's what I want you to think.'

'What's that meant to mean?'

'Nothing. Joking. So, auctions?'

'I'm going to the Hampstead one; there are four or five properties that look decent.'

'Have you got the details?'

'You don't have to worry about the business. You concentrate on yourself.'

Don't let him patronise you like that!

Megan bristled at his dismissal. 'I'm tired of concentrating on myself. Myself is boring and frustrating and I want a distraction. Let me see the details.'

Stef took his time retrieving his briefcase from the dining table and handed her a slim document wallet. The property listings were arranged by ascending price, paper-clipped together, details neatly highlighted, obviously office manager Trisha's work.

'This one looks good.' She indicated a former council property in West Ham. 'Could be a one-month turnaround if the crew pull their fingers out.'

'I like the Plaistow wreck.'

''Course you do. Looks like it needs demolishing.' Megan reordered the papers and handed the file back to him. 'Can I come with you? Feels like forever since I went to an auction.'

'You don't like auctions,' Stef pointed out. 'They stress you out.'

'I'm on so much medication, it's impossible to get stressed at the moment.' She had dutifully taken her pills that morning, fearing Macaulay's drug test, but the numbing, draining effects were starting to fade now, by the afternoon. She was still aware of the drugs in her system, the world in slow motion, but she supposed she was either developing a tolerance or there really had been a reduction.

'Sure it won't be too much for you?'

'There's only one way to find out. I'll tell you if I'm struggling. I can always wait in the car if I need a break. Please, Stef, let me come.'

Just as it seemed he would refuse, he gave in. 'You'll need to be ready in twenty minutes.'

'I'll get changed and grab my notebook.'

Energised by her victory, she hurried upstairs to find business clothing, foreign after so long being in leggings and T-shirts. She took her time to apply her make-up properly, even attempted a quick French plait that wasn't a complete failure. Slotted pearl studs into her earlobes and selected lipstick-red patent Louboutins, created to inspire self-confidence.

Downstairs, Stef hovered by the front door, keys in hand. 'You look amazing,' he smiled.

He doesn't need to sound so surprised.

'Unusual these days, isn't it?' she retorted, immediately feeling guilty when his smile faltered.

He gave her one last appraising glance, holding out his arm to guide her down the steps, opening the car door open for her.

Maybe he'll attend to your seatbelt as well, while he's treating you like an infant.

Megan gritted her teeth, refusing to allow the voice to sour her outing. She took the particulars from Stef's briefcase again and flicked through them, letting her brain slowly adjust to thoughts that used to come naturally to her: profit margins, possible pitfalls, resale potential, transport links. She found her thought process was quicker than she had become used to, as if her synapses were learning to fire properly again.

Inside the auction house, the sheer number of people in the room gave her a brief moment of fight or flight, and she very nearly chose the latter. She had become used to solitude, she realised. She hadn't been among crowds for so long that the very sound of so many voices was overwhelming, an insistent buzz like an angry, trapped bluebottle that made her want to cover her ears. She could smell aftershaves and sweat and stale cigarette smoke, making nausea rise in her throat. Her muscles tightened, breathing becoming too quick, too shallow, and she found she had reached unknowingly for Stef's hand.

'Say if it's too much.' He squeezed her fingers, reassuringly close beside her.

'It's a shock to the system.'

'Never the nicest of places, are they?' Stef said, comfortably at home in the heady environment.

He steered her away from the pockets of bidders to a couple of solitary faded chairs. Decades of trousers rubbing against the seats had worn the covers bare in places and dubious stains had barely been scrubbed clean. Megan sat without noticing any of the detail she usually observed.

Stef waved to a few people he recognised, happy for a moment of normalcy, then turned his focus to the catalogue, pen poised. Megan concentrated on slowing her breathing, reminding herself how many times she had attended auctions.

A couple of lots went by, bidding deliberately lackadaisical at first, becoming fiercer as the main competitors gradually emerged, until the final fight to the finish saw the victor punch their card triumphantly into the air. Megan felt the atmosphere swell as polite convention masked the cut-throat desire to win; desperation born out of a glimpsed opportunity that could be lost in a moment. Tension clamped her back teeth together and, although she knew Stef loved the excitement, she could feel his body had gone rigid as he waited for his moment.

He was outbid on the first property, restraint he usually had to be forced into, and she suspected he was on his best behaviour, not wanting to upset her in any way. He took the loss in his usual fashion, blowing out a long breath as if at the end of a boxing bout before shrugging and grinning at the adrenaline rush.

'Let's get a drink while we wait for our next lot.'

Megan's throat was already dry and she nodded gratefully. 'I'll come with you.' She didn't feel secure enough to be left alone and quickly stood with him, leaving his bidding card and catalogue to mark their seats.

The queue for drinks was long, as usual, and Megan rallied herself to use the Ladies while Stef stood in line, drawn easily into conversation, as ever. She didn't have to wait for a cubicle; even in the age of equality, auctions remained mostly the domain of men. She imagined that most women had no desire to sit under the clouds of testosterone and aftershave for hours on end.

She had noticed that morning she had stopped bleeding. Out of habit, she now checked again, but it had definitely ceased.

Hold it together.

She firmly told herself she had never been regular and it might start again in another few days, as her period often did. No need to assume all was lost.

Washing her hands, she risked a glance in the mirror and had to acknowledge her efforts with make-up and clothes had paid off – she was still too thin, but her skin had some colour that looked almost natural, and her eyes seemed bigger and brighter with careful use of eyeliner and volumizing mascara. She decided she didn't look like someone who was sectioned. Though what exactly they looked like she wasn't sure. More insane, maybe – rolling eyes and bird-nest hair and regular cackles of manic laughter.

That's basically a description of your mother in her last years.

She refused to acknowledge the observation, even though she didn't need to hear it to know it was true.

160

'Megan, I thought it was you! How are you? It's been so long!'

A woman had emerged from another cubicle and stopped midstep, her arms thrown out in delight as a beam of recognition spread across her face. Megan found herself enveloped in a hug, which at least gave her the opportunity to try to put a name to the face.

'Great to see you,' she said, hiding her uncertainty with a return smile. 'How're things?'

If the woman realised her dilemma, she showed no sign of acknowledging it. 'Busy as ever, you know how it is! Wish the property market would take a mini break so I could as well! Did you and Stef sell the Deptford house?'

You know her . . . she's that estate agent Stef prefers to deal with.

Megan had no clue what the woman's name was. 'Yes, it all cleared a few days ago.'

'You know I'd have got you a higher profit.' A grin that said not to take the comment seriously. 'Stef straight back to the bidding wars, I presume?'

'As always.' Megan found it wasn't as difficult to fall into the natural rhythm of conversation as it had been recently. 'I've left him queuing for drinks.'

'What's he got his eye on?'

'I haven't been paying much attention.'

'Oh yes, you've been ill, haven't you? An operation, wasn't it? It's a good couple of months since I've seen you. How did it all go?'

Megan turned to the hand dryer to buy herself time to construct an answer. 'It wasn't pleasant, but I'm getting over it now.'

'Tell me about it! I haven't experienced the agony myself, but I can certainly sympathise. Can't have been easy.'

What are you actually discussing here?

'No, it wasn't,' Megan agreed tentatively. 'I'd better go and find Stef.'

'I'll come with you, take the opportunity to pick his brain.'

They left the Ladies together to find Stef waiting impatiently in the corridor, holding two cardboard cups of coffee, keen to return to the action. He registered Megan's companion and she saw him blow out a quick, sharp breath.

He doesn't want people to see you.

That stung.

'How's it going, Stef?' the woman said cheerfully. 'Look who I ran into in the loos!'

'Hi, Marie,' Stef said, his tone amiable, even though his face showed all the expression of a piece of granite. At least in greeting the woman by name, he had inadvertently aided his wife. 'Didn't expect to see you here. Not your usual stomping ground.'

'I'm representing my own interests today, for once. And then I find your gorgeous wife! She's looking amazing, isn't she? All that weight loss!'

Stef handed Megan her coffee. 'Too much weight loss, really.'

'She's been so strong, hasn't she?' Marie chattered on. 'I could never be that brave.'

Megan tried to catch Stef's gaze, but when he finally made eye contact she saw the flash in his eyes that always ignited when he was in competition.

He doesn't want anyone to know about the psychosis. You embarrass him.

'Yes, very brave,' he agreed, slinging his arm casually round Megan's neck. She only just managed not to pull away from him. She could feel the rapid beat of his pulse.

'I was only thinking about you two last week, wondering if everything had gone OK. Haven't seen you for ages either, Stef.'

'Are you looking at the Porter Road semi?' Stef asked. 'It would be an easy turnaround for you.'

Marie immediately snapped back into business mode. 'I was concerned at the state of the roof when I went to view.'

They fell into shop talk and Megan took the opportunity to distance herself, watching the auction room as she sipped the weak coffee. It didn't take long for Stef to shake off Marie and rejoin her. His jaw was clenched and he was breathing as if he had just finished bidding, but she said nothing until they were back in their seats and waiting for the lots to tick over to their next target.

'Do people know about my breakdown?' she whispered.

His pause to swallow coffee was just a beat too long. 'I don't think so. Can't be sure, though. You know what this industry's like for gossip.'

'I wasn't sure what Marie was referring to. She knew I'd had an operation.'

'That's what I told people who asked – that you'd needed surgery for a head injury. I didn't give any other details. I didn't think you'd want people to know.'

More like he didn't want his own status being damaged by having a mental wife.

'I'm not upset.' A lie. 'It was just unexpected.'

'I didn't expect anyone we knew well to be here.'

163

'It doesn't matter. I have to start meeting people again; it's like I've forgotten how to hold a normal conversation.'

Stef shifted restlessly, tapping his pen against the catalogue. 'Don't put yourself under pressure.'

Feels like he's the one under pressure, for once.

Chapter Nineteen

'We're not at the family intervention stage of therapy yet, Stefan.' There was an edge of irritation to Macaulay's tone.

'I'm not asking for therapy.' Stef forced himself to concentrate on the road rather than the voice emanating from the car's Bluetooth. 'Just a meeting. I don't need long. I'll come to the Grosvenor.' He wanted to make it clear this wasn't a request he expected to be denied.

'My day's rather full. How about lunch? I'll be at Kimchee at one p.m.'

Stef would certainly be picking up the bill, but he didn't care. 'See you there.'

He arrived at the popular Korean restaurant still somewhat surprised Macaulay hadn't requested somewhere more upmarket. He had expected The Ivy, or at least Bill's, but Macaulay was Californian after all; he probably preferred the casual familiarity of Korean food to the stuffiness of British institutions.

The seating comprised long dining tables like a school hall, too intrusive for Stef's taste, but the restaurant was quiet and they were permitted privacy. Macaulay wielded his chopsticks expertly as he raised dripping slices of glistening red kimchee to his mouth, savouring the spicy fermented cabbage.

'Reminds me of back home. Some amazing joints in Koreatown.'

Stef was eating his bulgogi beef slowly to hide the fact he was struggling to control the chopsticks. Megan had tried to teach him in the privacy of their kitchen but he had never mastered her elegance and usually hoped for Western cutlery. No such luck today, and he was damned if he would look a fool in front of the American.

Macaulay cleared his throat. 'Megan mentioned in our session this morning that you'd taken her to a property auction over the weekend.'

'She asked to come with me. First time she's shown any interest in the business since she came home. There was someone we knew there; she got talking to Megan in the toilets. She didn't give anything important away, but it unsettled Megan – she was asking a lot of questions afterwards.'

Macaulay waved his chopsticks dismissively. 'We can't control every variable. As you said, nothing important was given away.'

'I'm worried it triggered something. She barely said a word after we got home, even though I'd got the property she wanted rather than the one I preferred.'

'Does she talk to you much in general?'

'Hardly at all. She responds to questions, but it's like she's reading a script most of the time. She talks to Sophia and Amelia, though. Normally.'

'What do you call normal?'

166

'Like she enjoys talking to them.'

Macaulay rapidly chewed rice. 'You feel threatened by Megan's relationship with her sister?'

'Why would I feel threatened?' Stef retorted, riled by the sly inference. 'My wife loves me.'

'Does she make you feel unsafe?'

'She won't hurt me again,' Stef said defiantly. 'Not that she's anything to use unless she throws a wok at my head.'

'What did you really want to ask me, Stefan?'

Finally, they could get to the point. Stef hated picking his way carefully through every conversation with the psychiatrist. 'Is there any other treatment we can try? Something that may work better than the therapy programme.'

He knew it sounded like he had lost faith in Macaulay's methods, but he was damned if he was apologising for it.

'You're expecting results too soon. Megan has a lot to process and she's doing so at her own pace.'

'At the pace you set for her, you mean.'

'That's part of my role in her recovery.'

'I'm not seeing any recovery!' Stef realised he was in the wrong place to raise his voice and lowered it. 'Are you?'

'Some, yes. Every patient is different; I try not to compare. I'm not concerned.'

Stef thought he wouldn't be concerned either if he was getting paid by the hour. He wondered if he would be charged for Macaulay's time as well as the lunch bill.

'I want to know about any alternative treatments,' he insisted, trying to catch a particularly elusive sliver of red pepper.

'Is Megan's behaviour unstable?' Macaulay ignored the question, as he so often did.

'Sometimes. She goes from quiet to shouting in a moment if something agitates her. Like with that photo.'

'I do understand your concerns. Give me some time to analyse Megan's treatment so far and decide if a different course of action is needed.'

Stef opened his mouth to continue presenting his argument, but Macaulay was tidying up his empty dishes and signalling for the bill, his side of the discussion clearly over.

'My apologies, but I have appointments to get to. Feel free to call me if you're still worried.'

That, it seemed, was the only reassurance Stef was to receive in return for his money. Once again, he felt his twin's presence, reminding him that no amount of therapy or money had been able to save Isaac. And, once again, he shrugged it off. Megan was different. She was not Isaac; she was not her mother. History would not repeat itself. He wouldn't let it.

No matter what it took, he wouldn't lose Megan to her demons.

As the evening drew in, Megan was unexpectedly seized by the urge to cook. She had spent the afternoon attempting to read after Macaulay's very routine session, spending too long staring at the same passages over and over without absorbing anything. Instead, she daydreamed about weaning her son, puréeing fresh fruit and vegetables for him to try, showing him new worlds filled with delicious adventures. She pictured his beautiful eyes opening wide as the tastes hit his tongue for the first time, his delighted smile at the burst of flavours.

You may never get the chance to cook for him. Maybe you'll never be trusted to care for him again.

She shook her head against the premonition. She had always loved to cook, and one day she would share that with her son. They would while hours away in the kitchen as she perfected a recipe or experimented with an exotic dish she'd spotted on Facebook, giving him little tastes as he watched.

Galvanised into action, she headed upstairs and knocked on the office door.

'I want to make dinner,' she said. 'I need you to get the knives out.'

She saw Stef's flash of reluctance before he hid it behind a grin. 'Fantastic, save us from my attempts. Give me two minutes to send this email and I'll be with you.'

'I don't need supervising.'

'I'm not allowed to leave you alone with the knives, sweetheart.' He shrugged an apology. 'I'll bring my tablet down and work at the island while you get on. Won't be in your way. What're you going to make?'

'I'll throw a casserole together.'

'Brilliant. There's a fair bit of fridge gravel I haven't got through.' He was being far too enthusiastic about a simple meal. 'And there's some crusty bread to mop up the sauce.'

Megan nodded obediently, waiting as he carefully locked the computer, his screensaver a photo of them at Lake Como last year, compulsory turquoise waters and lush Alpine peaks rising above the quaint Bellagio buildings, happiness reflected in their tanned, relaxed faces, and crossed to the filing cabinet.

'I'll bring them down to you.'

He won't retrieve the key while you're watching.

The unexpected flare of embarrassment took Megan by surprise and she quickly turned away from him.

'I'll see what veg we've got.'

Her cheeks were still burning as she searched the fridge, concentrating on thoughts of flavour rather than the deep mistrust that had crept into her marriage. The circulated air calmed her as it cooled her face, and she emerged with a miscellaneous collection of vegetables, the result of Stef being responsible for the Ocado order.

She decided on a rustic ratatouille; she knew she was lacking in vitamins, plus, it didn't require a great deal of concentration. Better throw in a chicken breast to address Stef's aversion to vegetarian food.

Assembling and washing a motley crew of carrots, courgettes, peppers, aubergine and a random swede, Megan consulted the spice drawer, finding comfort in the warm, exotic smells that made her think of bazaar visits in Marrakesh, Istanbul, Mumbai.

'You look at home.' Stef laughed as he came into the kitchen. 'Much more than me, anyway.'

He had repacked the knives into their original box; Megan had insisted on keeping it because she loved its ornate lacquered finish. She ran her fingers over the textured surface, remembering her delight when Stef had surprised her with the set. She had spent hours watching YouTube tutorials to perfect her technique.

'Need any help?' Stef asked, blatantly obvious in his hope that she would decline as she efficiently stripped the necessary vegetables of their skins. The voice quietened as she became absorbed in the rhythm of her task.

'No, I'm fine.' Megan tested the knife blade against the pad of her thumb. Still sharp enough.

She halved an onion, the blade slicing through with ease, and lost herself in the routine of chopping as oil heated in the cast-iron pot. The colourful pile sizzled deliciously as it hit the hissing surface and Megan's stomach rumbled despite her lack of appetite.

Taking her time, she measured dried herbs into the mixture, added bay leaves and garlic, a pinch of saffron, checked the seasoning and ground more black pepper. Finally, she stirred the tomatoes in and she settled the bubbling stew to a simmer. Rich, enticing smells drifted across the room, causing Stef to glance up from his tasks and sniff the air appreciatively.

'God, I've missed your cooking.'

'Wait and see how it turns out first,' she replied. 'I'm out of practice.'

She turned away to wash the knife in the sink – it was too precious to leave dirty or entrust to the dishwasher. Stef was immediately on his feet, skirting the island to her.

'I'll do that, sweetheart.'

'It'll only take a second. Don't worry.'

'Here, let me.'

What's the matter with him? Since when does he ever wash up?

Megan was well aware how effectively her husband usually avoided kitchen chores. 'Stef, I can do it! You've got work to do.'

'You concentrate on stirring, I'll do the boring bits.'

Megan paused with the chef's knife dripping soapsuds. 'Why don't you want me to clean the knife?'

'I'm just offering to do it.'

'You can lock it away soon as it's dry, don't worry,' she said scathingly. She saw the hesitation in his expressive eyes. 'You don't trust me to handle them, do you?'

'Come on, Megs, we don't need to argue about it.'

'Why are you so worried? I can hardly cut my wrists while you're right there.'

His eyes fixed on the blade. Then she understood.

'You're not concerned about me hurting myself. You're worried I'll hurt you.'

Stef made eye contact, but she saw he still kept the knife in his line of sight.

'What do you think I'm going to do, Stef?' she demanded. 'Are you expecting me to attack you?'

'It's a precaution, that's all.'

'A precaution against what?'

'The psychosis. I know you wouldn't deliberately hurt me.'

'What do you mean, "deliberately"?'

Put the knife down, for God's sake, stop waving it around!

She realised she was still clutching the knife, and she placed it carefully on to the worktop.

'When the psychosis was at its worst, you weren't in control. You didn't know what you were doing.'

A hot fear rose in Megan's chest, beginning a slow burn up her throat. 'Stef, what did I do? Tell me!'

Stef hesitated, his hands paused in rare indecisiveness. Finally, he lifted his T-shirt, revealing a thin raised wound running vertically down the edge of his stomach, not quite a scar yet but certainly destined to become one.

Megan stared in horror at the cut.

You did that. You stabbed your own husband.

'No. No! I didn't! Stef, I didn't do that.'

'You came at me with the paring knife.' Stef held out his palm, showing her a shorter cut she hadn't noticed before, almost fully healed. 'I had to wrestle it off you.'

172

'No.' Megan was shaking her head so hard she was becoming dizzy. She searched her clouded memory, desperately seeking a confirmation that could not be found. 'You're lying. Why would I do that? Why would I hurt you?'

'Megs, listen to me. Try to stay calm.' Stef took her hands in his. 'Everything's fine, I promise. It doesn't hurt. You didn't mean it.'

Megan snatched herself free and backed away, catching the edge of the island, stumbling. Stef moved towards her, hands outstretched as if to contain her. She cried out, slapping at the air between them.

'I wouldn't harm you!' she cried.

'I didn't want to tell you. I'm sorry.'

'Why are you sorry? You're the one who was stabbed! And you think I'm going to do it again. That's why you don't want me handling the knives. You think I'm going to kill you!'

'We just have to be sensible, until you're well again.'

'What if that never happens?' Her voice rose to a shout. 'Is this how it would be, for ever? You spending every day wondering if today's the day I finally murder you.'

'Of course not!'

'Stop lying to me! You're scared of me! I can see it in your eyes. You think I'm mad!'

Go. Get away from him. Before you lose control.

She couldn't stay in the cloying, suffocating room a moment longer. She ran, making for the stairs with no idea where she was going. Had she been thinking, she would have made for her study, the furthest room away from Stef, but she flew straight into their bedroom and through into the en suite.

Slamming the door, she scrabbled with the lock, finally crumpling to the floor.

Chapter Twenty

Megan pressed her back against the door, not feeling the edges of the panels digging into her spine. She realised she was sobbing, but there were no tears, just a heaving chest and dry, racking sounds bursting from her tight throat.

Frantic knocking from the other side of the door made her jump, and she pushed herself harder against the oak in case Stef somehow managed to open it.

'Megs, you need to come out. Or just undo the lock so I know you're safe. Are you listening to me?'

'No!' she gasped.

'Open the door, Megs,' Stef said again, more softly this time.

'I can't,' she whispered back.

'What can I do to get you out of there?'

'Just leave me here. I'll be OK.'

'I can't leave you!' His voice had risen again. She heard him pacing the bedroom, then speaking quietly. Into his phone, she realised. Macaulay – he would be calling Macaulay for help. He was going to take her away again. She would be locked up in the Grosvenor for months.

You'll never see Luka again. You won't stand a chance of finding him after six months.

Megan heard a noise escape from her clamped lips, a low, keening moan as she realised the voice was right.

Stef was back on the other side of the door.

'Keep talking to me, Megs, so I know you're OK.'

'Don't send me back there.'

'Where?'

'The Grosvenor. I can't get locked up again.'

'You were never locked up. I know it must have felt like it—'

'Don't let him, Stef.'

'Let who what?'

'Take me away. Dr Mac. I don't want to go with him.'

She couldn't hear Stef any more. His voice faded away as the other sounds took over: a baby's frantic screams, a familiar voice yelling her name. Megan clamped her hands over her ears, but it did nothing to drown them out. Her head was about to explode. She slid lower to the floor, curling into a foetal position, felt herself begin to gently rock, a mother soothing her baby.

'Megan. Megan! You have to open the door! Megan, for fuck's sake!'

She didn't know how long had passed, but a new voice was on the other side of the door, much louder than Stef's, and insistent enough to break through the noises. Macaulay had come. She'd ruined it all.

'Go away, Dr Mac!' she managed to shout.

'I'm not Dr Mac, that's just insulting! It's me, you idiot!'

Sophia. She won't let anyone take you.

Megan hauled herself to her feet, dizzy, blood rushing to her head as she stood upright. The moment she turned the lock,

Sophia was in the bathroom with her. She seized Megan's arms, turned them over in her hands, ran her palms along her skin.

'You're OK,' she said gently. 'You're OK.'

'I haven't done anything,' Megan managed to say before she was pulled into a fierce hug.

'Is she all right?' Stef's voice rang out from the corridor.

'She's fine, Stef,' Sophia said firmly. 'Go and make coffee or enormous G&Ts, or something useful.'

Stef's footsteps almost sounded relieved as he withdrew. Megan heard the bedroom door close behind him and sank down to the floor again, against the edge of the bath. She realised both hands were gripping hanks of her hair.

'I'm here.' Sophia came to sit beside her, gently untangling her fingers and holding them loosely in her own. 'You'll be fine. Just take your time.'

'Soph, I stabbed Stef. He's got the scars, I saw them! Why don't I remember? How could I forget something so awful?'

'I don't know, Megan. I wish I did.'

'Will Dr Mac change my section? Will he lock me away?'

'Of course he won't.'

'How do you know? Stef will tell him I had another episode. I went mad.'

'You didn't go mad.'

'I lost control.'

'We all lose control, Megan. That's not psychosis, that's just human nature. I lost control with Amelia's bloody hat earlier and considered burning it on the hob. Can we get off the floor now? The bed will be much more comfortable to have a breakdown on.'

She got up and extended a hand. Megan allowed herself to be pulled to her feet, but her legs folded beneath her and she

176

clung to Sophia to remain standing. She was led to the bed and wrapped in the duvet, a soft cocoon.

'I'm scared, Soph,' she whispered.

'What are you scared of?' Sophia sat on the edge of the mattress, stroking Megan's hair with unusual affection.

'Myself.'

'Do you want to hurt yourself?'

'No, not like that. I'm scared of what I'll do.'

'You won't do anything.'

She doesn't know that.

'But I did, before.'

'You weren't on meds before, or having therapy. You're getting better, Megan, you just don't know it yet.'

'Am I really?'

'Yes, really.' Sophia tucked the duvet more securely around her sister. 'You need to rest now. Everything will be OK after you've slept.'

How can you believe her now, after everything she's already lied about?

Megan reached to grasp her sister's hand. 'You won't tell Stef I came to your house, will you?'

'That's our secret.' Sophia touched her index finger to her own lips, then to Megan's. 'He doesn't need to know. Close your eyes.'

Megan did as she was told, feeling the rigid tension beginning to slip away from her body. Exhaustion swept over her, too strong to fight, and she was unaware of Sophia silently leaving the room.

Stef leapt to his feet as Sophia entered the kitchen, grim faced and looking completely drained.

'She crashed out soon as I got her into bed; I expected it to take for ever to settle her. Please tell me you didn't make coffee.'

'I thought we'd need something a bit stronger.' Stef indicated the drinks waiting on the island. 'Who's got Amelia?'

'I thought it was high time she learned to look after herself,' Sophia drawled, before conceding, 'my friend round the corner, OK?'

She grabbed one of the balloon glasses, drained the double gin and tonic in several rapid gulps, immediately held out the glass for another. Stef obliged, free-pouring.

'Mm, pure juniper. Are we heathens? At least put a slice of lemon in it.'

He took one from the fridge, rapidly sliced wedges with the abandoned chef's knife, ignoring the pile of fresh chopped herbs already occupying the butcher's block, waiting in vain to be added to the simmering ratatouille. 'It's the medication that knocks her out.'

'Are they giving her horse tranquillisers?'

Stef shrugged. 'I didn't ask.'

She stared hard at him. 'You've happily handed all responsibility to Dr Mac, haven't you?'

'He's the one who'll make Megan better! He knows what he's doing, I don't.'

'Then you need to learn. Megan needs your support.'

'I'm giving her support! I'm doing everything possible, just like I always have!'

'By showing her the scars she gave you?' Sophia's movements were becoming sharper, carelessly handling her glass. A splash of liquid sloshed over the rim as she banged it down.

178

'I had to show her; she wouldn't believe me otherwise.'

'You shouldn't have told her at all!'

'Why are you blaming me for everything, Sophia?' Stef's voice rose to match her volume. 'I thought we were together through this, and now you're turning on me! Why?'

The words flew from Sophia's mouth with the uncontrollable fury of rapid-fire bullets, a torrent of rage. 'Because it's your fucking fault! This entire mess has happened because of you!'

Stef's body jerked as if she had slapped him.

'My life was destroyed because of you and your secret. And now it's causing Megan's life to be ruined as well.'

'Soph, I'm doing everything I can to make things right.'

'You keep telling yourself that.'

'What else do you want me to do? I can't change what's already happened! I know I made mistakes, but I thought I was making up for them.'

Sophia glared over the rim of her glass. 'You thought wrong. What you did—'

'Why are you saying all this now? Is this some kind of revenge? All these years, Soph, I've helped you, done my best to make up for it. Does that change now that you've got what you wanted from me?'

'It changes because my sister is losing her mind!' Sophia jumped up abruptly, strode over to the gin bottle and poured a near-neat glassful, ignoring his glass. Her blazing eyes burned into him as she drank, her body shaking with a mix of anger and hurt.

For several agonising moments, Stef didn't know what to say.

'I didn't think you still blamed me,' he said, barely audible, confidence slipping away from him when he needed it most.

Sophia didn't reply as she knocked back her drink. As suddenly as it had erupted, all the fight seemed to go out of her. She slumped on to the nearest stool as her body went limp and Stef saw the tears streaming down her face.

'I have to,' she rasped. 'Sometimes I just need to. I can't keep it inside; I can't stop it. I'm sorry. It was so many years ago, but it's still there. It never really goes away.'

Stef reached for her, wrapping her in his arms. He felt her body convulse as she wept pain-filled tears into his shoulder, crying out everything she had suffered.

'I am grateful to you, Stef, for everything you've done to help me. You've never said no.'

'Bit difficult for me to refuse, really,' he said ruefully, so quietly that Sophia didn't seem to hear him through her sobs.

She wasn't one to accept comfort easily and no sooner had the tears ceased than she pulled back and scrubbed her tender, salt-stained cheeks with her palms, sniffing hard.

'Jesus, you're going to think madness really does run in our family at this rate.' She choked out an unsteady laugh, then frowned and sniffed the air. 'Is something burning?'

'Oh shit, the ratatouille's still on the hob!' Stef leapt across the room to rescue the pan. It was too late; the stew had already congealed to the burnt bottom. 'Bollocks, I forgot all about it.'

'Ratatouille's bloody awful, anyway.'

'Megan's isn't. She can make anything taste amazing.'

'Well, I'm starving, so you'll just have to order the most amazing pizza you can find.'

She reached for the almost-empty gin bottle, shook it and indicated a fresh, unopened one. Stef nodded eagerly. The last thing he wanted to be that night was sober.

Chapter Twenty-One

Before

So bad was his hangover that when Stefan first heard the thud of stones hitting his bedroom window, he couldn't get out of bed to investigate. It was only the knowledge that it must be Megan that persuaded him to snatch open the curtains; they had been tossing little stones at each other's bedroom windows since they were children, before mobile phones did away with the need.

His eyes widened. Where the hell was his phone?

'Stef!' Megan's voice was loud enough to hear even through the glass.

He dragged up the sash window and leaned his torso out into the shock of the chilly morning air. 'Megs, I'm so sorry about last night.'

'Have you seen Sophia?' she interrupted.

'Sophia?' He resisted the urge to jerk his body back inside and bury himself in his warm, comforting duvet. 'No. Why would I?'

'She wasn't at home when I woke up. Did you see her before you left?'

Stefan frowned as he searched for non-existent memories, the aftertaste of the night still noxious in his mouth. 'She was dancing with the girls. She'll be passed out at one of their houses.'

'I've already checked. She's not with any of them.'

'Sure she's not sleeping it off somewhere else in your house?'

'She's missing, Stef! I can't find her. Will you help me look?'

There was no question of him refusing. 'Two minutes.'

He dragged on jeans and a hoodie, shoved his bare feet into trainers. On the landing, his parents' door was still shut and Orion confirmed no one else had yet got up by howling for his breakfast when Stefan got downstairs. He hurriedly upended a tin of Pedigree Chum into the dog's bowl and was about to run out of the front door when it occurred to him that Orion's nose, so good at sniffing out roast chicken, could be useful.

Orion was amenable to helping after he had inhaled his breakfast and delighted to see Megan. She patted him distractedly as Stefan managed to get his collar on.

'When do you last remember seeing her?' he asked.

'She was there before I put Mum to bed, but I'm not sure after that.'

'Does your dad know?'

'He's already out looking. He went to bed before Mum so he's no idea when the last sighting of her was. Don't you remember anything from later on?'

'I think she and a couple of the other girls were having a fag down the bottom end of the garden. Maybe a spliff, actually, come to think of it.'

Megan's face tightened in panic. 'What if she took other drugs? She might have overdosed or choked on her own vomit ...'

'You don't know she took anything.' Stefan grabbed her

shoulders, forcing her to look at him. 'We'll find her. Chances are she was too drunk to get to bed and she found somewhere to curl up and sleep it off. Let's go round the back and check in all the gardens on this side.'

They set off at a jog, Orion bounding happily alongside them. It took some time to peer over all the fences into the back gardens. Stefan vaulted over several to check inside sheds, but there was no sign of any semi-conscious teenagers. He could sense Megan's tension growing as they neared the end of the long avenue with no success.

'We'll check the allotments. She might have found a green-house for warmth.' He kept his tone deliberately positive, reaching to take her hand as they picked up the pace again.

No gardeners had arrived to tend their crops so early in the morning and the allotments were silent; even the scarecrows weren't rustling in the breeze, as they usually did. Stefan usually hated the watchful, motionless figures; ridiculous caricatures of humans – he had always felt like their eyes were on him when he brought Megan here. That morning, however, they were no threat to him, almost benevolent as they observed the search, silent witnesses who would never be heard.

Orion suddenly became unusually alert, straining on the end of his lead. He barked, but only once before it became a strange whine. Stefan unclipped him, expecting him to run off in pursuit of a sneaking fox, but Orion padded forward tentatively, nose outstretched. Dragonflies and crickets leapt for their lives as he plunged into the wild grasses.

Stefan saw a flash of colour amid the vegetation.

'Megan!' He ran forward after the dog, but Megan was quicker, crashing through the untamed vegetation ahead of him.

Stefan heard her cry out and saw her drop to her knees, shouting her sister's name at a bundle of clothes on the ground. And he realised it was Sophia, lying curled on her side, too still and silent.

His heart sank, wondering if hypothermia had got to her before they had or if a dodgy pill had claimed her. Megan clutched her sister's hand, begging her to wake up.

It was up to Stefan to tentatively place two fingers on Sophia's ice-cold neck, searching for a pulse he didn't think would be there.

Chapter Twenty-Two

Of course, the next day there was no mention of scars or stabbings or hiding in bathrooms. As if nothing had happened.

Stef was working from home, but Megan didn't fail to notice how keenly he avoided her, keeping to the office once he'd ensured she ate the required slice of toast and swallowed the pills, only making occasional forays for coffee. On one trip, he found her in the kitchen, scrubbing at the burnt ratatouille pan with feverish desperation.

'Leave it, sweetheart, it's beyond saving. I'll buy a new one.'

Of course he will. He'll make everything better by denying anything went wrong.

Megan put down the sponge in defeat, staring blindly into the sink.

'How long do we have to do this for, Stef?'

At least he didn't ask her what she was talking about. 'I don't know.'

'Days? Weeks? For ever?'

'I wish I could tell you.'

'I noticed you didn't disagree with for ever.'

'It won't be for ever.'

'How do you know? Because Dr Mac works miracles? He'll fix me, yes?'

'It's not about "fixing" you, it's about making you better. Let's not get into it now, Megs. We both had a difficult day yesterday and you need to be calm for when Dr Mac arrives.'

'Is that a threat?'

''Course it isn't a threat!'

'Are you going to tell him how I reacted yesterday?'

Stef didn't seem to know what reply to give to such a direct question. 'I haven't thought about it yet.'

'You've had all night to think about it.'

He indicated an empty bottle of rhubarb gin. 'Wasn't in much of a state to think.'

'Please don't tell him.'

'He won't be angry, Megs.'

'I don't give a damn if he's angry or disappointed or anything else. I care that he'll change my section.'

'He won't do that.'

'He can do whatever he pleases, Stef. He's the one in control.'

Stef cleared his throat, breaking eye contact. 'I won't say anything unless he directly asks me.' He tugged his coffee mug from under the machine. 'Shall I leave you to let him in?'

Megan didn't want him anywhere near the psychiatrist if she could help it. 'I think I can manage that.'

Stef returned upstairs and Megan resumed her frantic scrubbing. It seemed very important to save the pan. Erase any evidence of yesterday. Make it all fine again. Besides, she was damned if she was throwing away a Le Creuset pot.

Her hands were raw by the time Macaulay arrived, and she focused on rubbing lotion into them as they took up their default places in the sitting room. She could feel the tension emanating from her, as if Macaulay had a crystal ball which had already informed on her.

'How are you today, Megan?'

'Tired,' she said honestly. 'I'm sleeping like the dead, but I never feel refreshed. Can we reduce the medication more, see if that will help?'

'Not at the present time, but soon, yes.' He uncapped the fountain pen, his habitual signal that the main session was beginning. 'How are you getting along with Stefan and Sophia?'

Why is he asking that?

Megan acknowledged the loaded question and took care to answer neutrally. 'Things are awkward with Stef, but I'm enjoying spending time with Sophia and Amelia.'

'That's good. Amelia clearly brings you a lot of happiness.'

As much as Luka did.

Megan winced at the sting of the whispered words. 'She makes me laugh. Sophia's been very good with me, considering she's not the most patient of people. Eve often says the only person in the world Sophia has time for is Amelia.'

'Has Eve been in contact with you?

A strange question, but it was a safe topic, so she answered freely. 'No, she's lecturing back in New York. We don't talk regularly.'

'How did you feel when Sophia told you she was gay?'

Is he actually trying to attribute Sophia's sexuality as another root cause of your problems?

Megan frowned, immediately defensive of both her sister and herself. 'Did I have a problem with it, you mean?'

To her surprise, Macaulay laughed. Did she detect a note of mockery or was she just being paranoid? 'Have you noticed your subtle changes over the course of your therapy, Megan? How often you now answer a question with a question?'

'You think I'm being obtuse.'

'I think your independent thinking skills are returning.'

'That must be a good thing.'

'Hopefully, yes.' Macaulay made another note. 'Now, Sophia?'

'I wasn't surprised when she came out, if you must know. I suppose I already knew but hadn't given it conscious thought. She wasn't interested in any relationship for a long time, male or female.'

'Something happened to her?'

'Do you know?'

'Why don't you tell me?'

'When she was seventeen, she was ...' What word to use? Which was strong enough, violent enough, to describe the horror? 'Attacked ... abused. It damaged her, internally. And mentally.'

'Keep going.'

'I was in my first year at uni, Soph had started her A levels, wanted to be a primary teacher. She had a hell of a temper, but she was brilliant with little kids.' Megan took a sip of water to combat the sudden dryness clawing at her throat. 'We had a party for Mum's fiftieth, invited everyone on our street, schoolfriends and their parents, made it really special for her. Everyone was drunk; one of the neighbours had brought some coke. I worried Mum would have some and it would tip her over the edge, so I spent most of the night watching her when I should have been watching Sophia.'

'Do you want to tell me what happened?'

'It went on into the early hours. I hadn't seen Sophia for ages, but I needed to put Mum to bed; she'd drunk far too much and I thought it might make her sick with her tablets. I'd had a fair bit of vodka as well and I fell asleep as soon as Mum was safe. When I woke up the next day, I realised Soph wasn't in the house. She'd got her first mobile by then, but when I called it, I could hear the ringtone. I found it on the garden table.

'I checked everywhere in case she'd passed out drunk, then I went to wake Dad. He said to ask the neighbours, so I went up and down the road, but no one had seen her. Stef came out to help search. Then we found her.'

Megan gulped the rest of her water, nodded her thanks as Macaulay poured from the jug. She watched a piece of lemon bob to the top; she had found it already chopped in the fridge, evidence of Stef's drinking session. She focused on the fruit rather than looking at the doctor.

'There was a little copse of wildlife land running along the backs of the gardens, beyond some allotments.' Another pause, not enough water to ease the tightness in her throat. So long since she had talked about that awful morning. 'That's where she was. Laid on the ground, covered in scratches and grazes. Her dress was torn; she didn't have any shoes on. I thought she was dead, she was so still, but Stef found she just had a pulse. Stef covered her with his hoodie and I sat and held her hand while he ran for help. I tried to wake her up, but she wasn't responding, she was barely breathing. That's when I saw the blood. The bottom half of her dress was soaked in it, and it had run down her legs. I remember it looked black against her skin, she was so pale. I was sitting in it.'

'That must have been awful,' he said, so neutrally that she almost hated him.

'I screamed for Stef, but it was my dad that came. He scooped her up and ran. I couldn't run with him. Sophia's blood was soaking into my jeans, but I couldn't stand.'

'I assume Sophia was badly hurt?'

'No one was sure if she'd survive. She had massive internal bleeding, then infections set in. I lost count of how many times they operated. She was so badly damaged.'

'Hence why you mentioned she can't have children.'

Misses nothing, does he?

Megan didn't notice the sly dig, enveloped by the memories she had locked away many years previously. 'That was the hardest part for her. She'd always wanted kids. The attack itself was bad enough to cope with, even though she remembered nothing, but it was being sterile that affected her the most.'

'I imagine the effect on your family must have been terrible.'

'Mum couldn't cope at all. We didn't dare take her to the hospital but, in a way, that was worse. Her imagination was even more awful than the reality.' More water. 'Dad tried his best, but I think he felt violated himself. Our community had always felt secure. The usual London burglaries and car thefts, but no violence. He thought we were safe, and he blamed himself when it turned out we weren't.'

Macaulay paged back through his notes. 'You told me in a previous session that your father walked out on you, you assumed for another woman.'

'I lied. There was no one else.'

'Why did you lie?'

'I don't like talking about it.'

'We should talk about it now. Keeping secrets bottled up won't help your recovery.'

But it's OK for him to keep secrets from you.

'So he left because of Sophia's attack?' Macaulay ignored Megan's pointed silence.

'I suppose he couldn't deal with it,' Megan said reluctantly. 'He left us a note saying he needed to make a fresh start. He put money into an account every month for us, sent cards on Christmas and birthdays, but we never saw him again.'

'You didn't search for him?'

'What would have been the point? To be honest, I didn't need another relative having a breakdown and requiring care.' Megan traced circles with her finger against the condensation on her glass.

'You felt betrayed when he left?'

'Of course. Sophia was more stoical about it. I suppose she had to focus on herself. It took so long to recover from her injuries; the pain was horrific to see.' Megan felt a sob rise in her chest. 'She was so strong, stronger than I could have been.'

'I'm very glad she made a full recovery.' The words sounded hollow, even though the sentiment seemed sincere.

'She still suffers sometimes. Psychologically, she's better, especially now she has Amelia. I was relieved when Eve agreed to the pregnancy. Sophia was struggling, seeing her friends and colleagues having families while she couldn't. I felt—' Megan stopped abruptly. She had only ever admitted this to Stef. She didn't think she could say it to anyone else.

'You felt what?' Macaulay pressed.

'Like it was my fault she was suffering so much. Because I hadn't kept her safe.'

'Do you feel you owe Sophia for that night? That you have to make it up to her somehow?'

Shut up before you say something you shouldn't.

Megan ignored the voice's stern order. 'I suppose so. She stopped living completely after it happened, flunked her A levels, never made it to university, let alone teacher training. That's why she works for the drama company; she isn't qualified for anything else in education. She lost her entire future because I didn't bother to check where she was.'

The tears came now, silently. She let them run unchecked down her face, cathartic trails of quiet release. She felt completely calm. Maybe this was how the religious felt after relieving their burden in confession.

Macaulay capped his pen, his usual signal. 'That'll do for today, Megan.'

'We can carry on, if you want.' That was the first time she'd ever wanted to continue.

'It's important you have processing time. We'll pick up where we left off tomorrow.'

And just like that, the routine was over for another day. Only today, she didn't feel exhausted.

Chapter Twenty-Three

Before

The police came often to the avenue for weeks. They must have taken statements from every partygoer but, to Stefan, it felt he was their target. He wasn't allowed to return to Durham immediately, not that he had been intending to leave Megan to cope alone, but the order annoyed him. As if he were a suspect.

The first meeting was tense. It seemed he was the only one required to attend the police station to give his statement. He knew of no one else who had been summoned. He had found Sophia; he had been drunk and violent at the party. The detectives seemed convinced he knew something. He was assured it was a voluntary interview as a key witness; he was free to leave at any time and he wasn't under caution. Yet the burden of suspicion sat heavily on him, threatening to crush the air from his lungs.

He was shown into an interview room that stank of stale tobacco. The chair was deliberately uncomfortable, the floor tiles sticky against his trainer soles. There was no natural light, only strobe bulbs, and their harsh glare made him feel exposed. He drank the tea he had been given too quickly, teeth furring with tannin from the over-stewed brew, making his mouth taste foul as the thin plastic cup burned his fingers.

By the time two detectives arrived, Stefan could feel beads of sweat gathering on his hair line and he had to fold his hands under the table to hide how unsteady they had become. The air in the room was cloying, hot and heavy, and the smell of the male officer's aftershave made him feel sick. He desperately wanted water but didn't dare ask.

'I was drunk,' he said, several times. 'Absolutely hammered. I don't remember leaving the party, let alone seeing Sophia.'

'We've been told you had a fight with your twin earlier in the evening.'

'He was annoying Megan so I told him to back off and we had a bit of a scuffle.'

'And Megan is your ex-girlfriend.'

Stefan nodded confirmation. 'We're still good friends.'

'So you left the party around what time?'

'I don't remember. Late. Early hours.'

'Do you recall arriving home? Who was there?'

'My dad and Isaac. Mum stayed out later, I think.'

'Your mum says she helped Megan put Mrs Crawley to bed and you'd gone when she left to go home herself.'

'Then you've got a good idea what time I left. Why are you asking me?'

His question was ignored. 'So you went to sleep and didn't wake up until Megan came to your house for help?'

'Yes. We took my dog; he must have caught Sophia's scent when we were searching the allotments. He found her, really.'

'What were your thoughts when you saw Sophia?'

'I thought she was dead,' Stefan replied bluntly.

'Did you realise what had happened to her?'

'Not at first. I thought she'd passed out drunk or she'd got hypothermia from being out all night. Then I saw the tree branch and the blood. That was when I realised she'd been attacked.'

'We have your hoodie – we'll have to keep it as evidence.'

'Because it's got Sophia's blood on it?'

'And because it may have picked up traces of her attacker from contact with her body. We also found your phone. It was at the scene, very close to where Sophia lay.'

Stefan went rigid, his hands clenching involuntarily into fists. 'Why did she have my phone?'

'Can't you tell us that?'

'I didn't have it when I woke up. It could have fallen out of my pocket at the party. Maybe Sophia found it and was bringing it back to me. That could be why she left the garden.' He was babbling now and he knew it, but he needed to give a reasonable explanation.

'When did you last have it?'

'I don't know! When I arrived at the party, definitely, but after that, I can't remember.'

'We'll be able to check if you used it any time after you arrived.'

Stefan's fists clenched again at the implied threat. 'I've just told you, I'm not sure when I last used it. If I dropped it at the party, Sophia might have decided I needed it back immediately. Maybe she was attacked while she was on her way to my house.'

'We don't know anything for sure yet. Back to what you were telling us – what happened after you found Mr Crawley?'

'He grabbed Sophia and ran back to the house with her. We

wrapped her up in duvets and tried to stop the bleeding with towels, but it just kept leaking out of her. It was all over the living-room carpet by the time the ambulance arrived.'

'Did you go to the hospital?'

'After we'd sorted everything out at the house. Mrs Crawley couldn't be left alone, so I fetched my mum to stay with her. I tried to clean the carpet so Megan wouldn't see it. We were both covered in blood; we showered there, and my dad dropped us off at the hospital.' He realised he was gabbling again. Did that sound more suspicious than giving short answers?

'He didn't stay to support you?'

'My brother was at home – they don't leave him alone. He has mental problems.'

That caused raised eyebrows. 'What sort of mental problems?'

'I don't really know. He's scared of the entire world; he's attempted suicide in the past. He sees a counsellor.'

'And he didn't return to the party at any time after your fight?'

'No. He didn't want to go in the first place. He doesn't like crowds or socialising. They terrify him.'

'Did anyone see you when you got home?'

'Isaac did.' Stefan maintained eye contact, hoping it didn't seem defiant. 'I looked into his room; he was in bed but not asleep. He'll probably know what time it was. I said sorry for hitting him then went to bed myself.'

'Did you spend much time with Sophia during the evening?'

'No, she was having fun with her friends. I spoke to her a couple of times at the drinks table.'

'You didn't dance with her?'

'She wanted me to, kept asking, but I wasn't in the mood.

She can be hard to shake off when she's determined to have her own way.'

'And she didn't give you a hug at any point?'

'Sophia's not a touchy-feely type of person – I don't think she's ever hugged me in all the time I've known her.'

A glance between the two officers, unreadable but distinctly unsettling.

'Is there anything else you can add, Stefan? Were there any strangers at the party?'

'No, we knew everyone. There's nothing I can think of. It was just a party, everyone having fun. Apart from me arguing with Isaac, there was no drama at all.'

'If you do think of anything, you'll let us know?'

'Sure. Do you have any fingerprints or evidence from the scene?'

'We can't discuss that with you.'

'So does that mean I can go now?'

The female detective handed him a card. 'In case you get a flash of memory. We'll let you know when you can have your phone back.'

Stefan made a show of stowing it in his wallet with clumsy fingers and followed them out of the interview room, his legs weak with relief as they released him back into the foyer. He wasn't a natural liar; he was too garrulous to keep up a convincing story, but he thought they'd believed him.

The question was, how did he now deal with the guilt that was tying his guts into knots?

The month of the Easter holiday passed in a maelstrom of honourable acts, anything to not be alone with his thoughts.

Accompanying Megan to hospital visits, reassuring talks of Sophia's strength and recovery potential, helping her father pull up the old carpet and lay a new one, trying to avoid looking at the flaking, fetid stains that had dried to the colour of rust.

Part of him wanted to run back to Durham, away from it all, and behave like an ostrich for his final term of university. Megan had told him the police had found no fingerprints, no DNA, nothing that would be of any help in proving a suspect's guilt. Sophia remembered nothing of the attack, her memory fading from the start of the party. She had no recollection of leaving her garden, of lying bleeding to death on the living-room carpet, of the resuscitation-room panic or the emergency operations.

The police came again the week before Easter term began, apparently content to speak to him at home this time. Their conversation with Stefan's parents was brief, before his dad stumped off to continue ruining the gardener's careful cultivation of the rose bushes and his mum returned to her preparation of the Crawleys' daily meal.

'Looking forward to going back to university?' the female detective asked Stefan when he took his place before them in the living room, as if they were having a catch-up over beers.

'Can't wait.'

'Got a job lined up for after graduation?'

'I'm going into the City.'

'Good money, that. Will you move back home?'

'No, flat-share in the Docklands with a couple of college mates.'

'We just have a few more questions for you, Stefan, following on from your witness statement. I assume Megan Crawley has been keeping you up to speed with our investigation?'

'She tells me the important bits.'

'Then you'll be aware we haven't yet identified a suspect.'

'Yeah, I know. Sophia's going to be out of hospital soon and you still haven't found who did this to her.' He was aware of how belligerent he sounded, and he didn't care.

'It's been a rather difficult investigation – sexual attacks often are. We won't give up; the case is still very much active.'

'That's not much comfort to Sophia.'

'We understand that. Her family is, rightly, very upset.'

'I know. I'm the one who's helped Megan through this.'

'She's mentioned how supportive you've been.'

Stefan wasn't entirely sure if that statement was sarcastic or not. 'What did you want to ask me this time?'

'We were wondering if any memories had returned yet.'

'Nothing of any use. I still don't remember if Sophia was there when I left.'

'Unfortunately, no one seems to know. We hear there were drugs at the party?'

'Bit of coke. I think the sixth-form girls had some weed.'

'Did you see Sophia smoking it?'

'I don't remember.'

'Did you have anything?'

'No, I'm not into that shit. I just like a drink.' No need to mention the pill one of Sophia's friends had given him, nor the others he had gone in search of later. Oblivion had seemed a great idea at the time.

'We're finding it a bit odd that not a single person knows what time Sophia disappeared from her garden.'

'It was a party; no one was paying attention to anything except enjoying themselves.'

199

'You weren't enjoying yourself.'

'I was concentrating on getting paralytic and forgetting what a prick my brother is.'

'Do you mind if we take a hair sample from your dog?' the male detective asked abruptly, looking down at Orion, who had grown bored of the visitors and fallen asleep on the hearth.

Stefan frowned. 'What?'

'We found some fibres on Sophia's clothing; we need to compare them to his fur.'

Stefan could only shrug his consent and summon Orion to him. The female officer produced a pack containing a white plastic sheet and a small comb, laying the sheet on the floor. Orion obligingly flopped down on to it, his tongue lolling as she ran the comb through his thick, golden coat until enough had accumulated for her to pinch a sample into an evidence bag. The whole pack was sealed in yet another bag and the procedure was apparently over. Stefan couldn't tear his eyes away from the process, which was at once banal and fascinating.

'Does he go to the Crawley house regularly?' the detective asked.

'He went with me that morning while I was helping to set up the garden. And he came to the party, of course.'

A look was exchanged between the two detectives. 'You took the dog to the party?'

'We always take him out with us; he adores the attention, and it saves anyone having to leave early or nip home to let him out.'

'Do you remember seeing Sophia stroking him during the evening?'

'He loves her and Megan, he'll have followed them around all night.' Stefan realised the connection they were trying to make. 'Wait, if you found Orion's hair on Sophia, it could have come from my hoodie when I covered her with it.'

The officers' expressions altered somewhat at both pieces of news. Irritation combined with resignation. Still, the woman took care in scribbling the required information on the evidence labels and stowing them away.

'We've got your phone to return to you, if you'd sign here for us. We don't need to keep it any longer.'

'What did it show you?'

'You last used it before nine that night, though we can't trace its exact movements. Sophia's fingerprints were on it, as were yours and your brother's.'

'And half of my college, plus Megan, plus my parents,' Stefan drawled sarcastically, slipping it safely into his pocket and scrawling his signature where indicated.

'Thank you for talking to us again, Stefan. You can let your brother know we're ready for him now.'

'You want to speak to Isaac?'

'Just a short statement. We didn't take one from him in the first round of inquiries, since you confirmed he didn't spend long at the party, but we're covering all bases this time.'

'You know he's not all there, don't you?'

'Don't worry, one of your parents can sit in with him.'

'You won't get anything out of him; he only talks to people in cyberspace,' Stefan retorted, not caring how obvious his attitude was.

He thumped upstairs and entered Isaac's bedroom without knocking. Fear flashed across his twin's face as he leapt from his computer chair.

'Please don't burst in like that!'

'Cops are here to speak to you,' Stefan snapped.

'Why?'

'How should I know? Mum's going to sit in with you. So they don't scare you.'

Isaac, for once, didn't appear intimidated. 'Why would they scare me? Their questions are going to be about you.'

'Fuck off, Isaac.'

'What do they want to know?'

'When I got home. They want you to confirm you saw me. I told them you'd remember what time it was when I looked into your bedroom and apologised.' Stefan's eyes never left his twin's, winning rare eye contact from Isaac.

Isaac nodded slowly but didn't speak, gave no hint of reassurance. Defeated, Stefan snorted and spun on his heel, deliberately leaving the door open behind him as he returned downstairs to snatch a beer from the fridge. He was drinking too much, he knew he was, but he had to do something to dampen the guilt. The urge to tell Megan he was lying to the police, protecting himself with an alibi he shouldn't need but felt compelled to have, was becoming overwhelming.

He heard Isaac coming down the stairs, followed by voices as the officers greeted him, his mother replying that she didn't understand why they needed to speak to him.

Stefan closed the fridge door silently and went to sit on the step that led up into the hallway. They hadn't closed the living-room door and, if he sat very still and breathed quietly, he could hear the conversation.

'Yes, I was in bed, but I couldn't sleep. I heard my brother arrive home very late; he disturbed me when he came into my room.'

'What time was it?'

'About half past two.'

'Did you come straight home when you left the party?'

'Yes. I was upset. Stef had made my nose bleed. Everyone saw.'

'Do you have problems with crowds, Isaac? Get anxious in social situations?'

'I'm not very comfortable around people. I don't tend to socialise.'

'Then why attend the party?'

'My dad ordered me to. Besides, I like Megan Crawley, she's nice to me.'

'What about her sister?'

'I don't know her sister.'

'You grew up on the same street.'

'As I said, I'm not a sociable person. And she's younger than me, so our paths haven't crossed.'

'You didn't speak to her at the party?'

'No. She was dancing with the other teenage girls. They were all drinking.'

'Did your brother dance with them?'

'Not that I noticed.'

'You noticed they were drinking, though?'

'They were very loud – it would have been hard not to notice.'

'I suppose seventeen-year-olds are allowed to have a few drinks.'

'I don't like alcohol, it makes me feel out of control.'

'What time did you leave the party?'

'I've already told you.'

'Please tell me again.' An order disguised as a request. Stefan leaned further over the step to hear better.

'About nine o'clock, I think.'

'And you and your dad came straight home, as you've already told us. What did you do then?'

'I went to bed. I had a headache.'

'You didn't use your computer? Talk to anyone online?'

'No, just read for a while.'

'How did Stefan seem when he got home?'

'Very drunk. He could barely stand up. I just wanted him to leave me alone.'

'Was he out of breath? Did you think he was stressed or angry?'

'I couldn't tell.'

'And just to confirm, Isaac, you didn't leave the house at all, for any reason, once you returned from the party?'

'No.'

'Did your brother?'

'I don't know. I fell asleep.'

So focused was Stefan on the conversation that he hadn't heard the back door open. He leapt to his feet as a quiet cough came from behind him. Red faced, he looked at his father.

He opened his mouth to gabble a ridiculous explanation, but his father simply shook his head, pressed his finger to his lips and went back outside.

Chapter Twenty-Four

'I think you may be right, Stefan.'

Stef felt his grip tighten on the phone as the American's words registered. 'About Megan's treatment?'

'I'm becoming concerned how erratic her behaviour is. I'd expect a little more stability by now. If she reacts in the same way as we continue to fill in her memory blanks, we may be forced to consider a different section. And none of us want that, do we?'

The surge of guilt at having told Macaulay of Megan's reaction to him revealing the knife wounds made Stef feel slightly nauseous. 'No, we don't,' he said sharply.

'There's something I'd like you to consider. Have you ever heard of ECT? Electroconvulsive therapy?'

'You want to electrocute her brain?' Stef practically yelped, horrified. 'Like McMurphy? Jesus, this isn't a film! I didn't mean anything that drastic!'

'It's not as awful as it sounds. Everyone sees the procedure performed in movies and assumes the worst. It can be very successful when administered correctly.'

'She won't agree to it. And I don't blame her, to be honest.'

'She doesn't need to agree. She's under section, remember.'

'You'd do it against her will? No! That's barbaric!'

'As her next of kin, you can give permission.'

'I don't want to give permission!'

'I understand this may seem a very extreme route. I've emailed you some literature to read. Why don't you have a look before making your decision?'

'Can I discuss it with Megan?'

'Of course. She'll need to be prepared.'

'What if she refuses?'

'We'll cross that bridge if we get to it. Try to phrase it positively, as a benefit.'

'You think it is a benefit?'

'I do, but Megan may not. You'll need to persuade her it is.'

'How the hell do I do that?'

He could hear Macaulay's smile. 'You'll think of something.'

Sophia and Megan were at the dining table, making clay models with Amelia, when he arrived home.

'Stef!' Amelia leapt on him. 'Look! Baby snail!'

'You've made a baby snail? That's very clever, Ami, well done.' He professed great enthusiasm for the pitted lump she showed him. 'Are snails the latest obsession?'

'Slightly better than baking potatoes,' Sophia said. 'Time for a drink, I think. Anything good in the wine rack?'

'Megan can't have a drink, so I haven't been opening wine.'

'It's fine,' Megan insisted. 'I don't want any.'

'Grab a decent Malbec,' Sophia ordered, nodding approval as Stef held up a bottle for inspection. She accepted a large glass.

'Want to watch Peppa, Amelia?' Stef asked.

He turned the TV on and waited for her to settle on the Chesterfield, to be enthralled by the irritating pig family and unlikely to interrupt the adults.

'I need to discuss something with you both,' he said, returning to the table before he could change his mind. 'Dr Mac called. He wants to try a different course of treatment alongside your therapy, Megs.'

'What sort of treatment?'

'It's called ECT. It involves using little electrical currents to help your brain recover from the psychosis.'

Sophia went very still. Megan frowned, looking confused.

'Electricity?'

'A very low current. You'd have an anaesthetic, so you wouldn't feel a thing. Dr Mac thinks it would speed up your recovery. That's what you've wanted, isn't it?'

'Don't talk to me like I'm a child.' He'd clearly overdone keeping it simple. He hadn't meant to be condescending, but he was finding it almost impossible to word the conversation.

'This is mad,' Sophia declared. 'Are you asking Megan to agree to torture?'

'It's not torture. Don't be so bloody dramatic.'

'Sounds like *One Flew Over the Cuckoo's Nest*.'

'Apparently, it's completely different to what you see in films. She'll be asleep for it. It takes minutes. She won't know anything about it.'

'She will when she wakes up like a zombie.'

'Dr Mac wouldn't be doing it if it wasn't safe. He says it's common practice.'

'Dr Mac could tell you there are unicorns grazing on Clapham Common and you'd believe him.'

'I have read up on it,' Stef said defensively. 'He emailed me some literature.'

'Then Megan should also be allowed to read up on it.'

Stef waved his phone, irritated by Sophia jumping to conclusions, as usual. 'I've got all the information, and of course she can read it.'

'I am here, you know,' Megan interjected. 'Please stop talking over me. Let me see, Stef.'

He handed his phone to her, momentarily wondering if she would give it back or attempt to make the call to his parents she had been so insistent on previously. At least her limited focus seemed to have drifted away from that urgency. He didn't want his parents drawn into this mess.

He refilled his wine glass, which had somehow become empty during the conversation, and jiggled his feet while she read, Sophia peering over her shoulder in a way that would usually have irritated her sister.

'"I could feel a huge weight of black fog lifted from my mind,"' Sophia quoted. 'Think they paid someone to write that? It's very Shakespearean.'

'You're not helping, Sophia.'

'I'm not here to help you. I'm here to help Megan.'

'Technically, you're here to babysit me so Stef can leave the house,' Megan said drily. 'Apparently, the anaesthetic is very light and I wouldn't be intubated.'

Stef nodded encouragingly. 'The literature says it's a safe, effective alternative treatment when therapy and medication aren't achieving the desired result.'

Sophia rolled her eyes. 'You're like a walking advertisement. I hope you're charging appearance fees.'

208

'You want me to have it, don't you?' Megan ignored her sister, kept her attention on Stef.

'It's not his decision,' Sophia put in.

'Sophia, let me speak for myself,' Megan said firmly. 'I know you're trying to protect me, but I do still have some ability to make decisions.'

'You're not seriously going to do this?'

They might let you have Luka back sooner.

Megan seized upon the vague hope. 'If it'll make my recovery quicker, then yes, I will.'

'Why? Because Stef wants you to?'

'Because I want to be able to trust my own brain again. I never know whether my memories are real or not, and I hate it. There's so much I can't remember. It's constant uncertainty. You don't know how it feels – if you did, you'd do anything to make it stop.'

Sophia didn't seem to have any reply to that.

'No one will force you, sweetheart,' Stef said quickly, 'but I agree it's a good idea to try it.'

'I won't have to stay in, will I?' Panic flitted across Megan's face. 'I don't want to stay at the Grosvenor again.'

'No, you'll come home the same day.'

'I can't believe you're agreeing to it,' Sophia snapped.

Megan put Stef's phone down resolutely. 'I want my life back. That's it, decision made.'

Stef avoided Sophia's accusatory gaze, more than a little relieved at how much easier it had been than expected.

He just had to hope Megan remembered the conversation the next day.

★

Megan had anticipated her return to the Grosvenor to be traumatic and had braced herself against the insidious fear that began creeping over her the moment she looked up at the gleaming front door. What she had not anticipated, however, were the flashbacks. They took her completely by surprise, sudden assaults of uninvited mental images: ambulances and tight restraints, hovering needles and faces made anonymous by surgical masks.

The waiting room, empty but for them, was filled with sounds: crying, screaming, wailing, her own voice begging an invisible threat to leave her alone. Then a baby's cry silenced them all, a plaintive wail, and she felt Luka's warm weight against her breast, the strength of his tiny fingers trying to grasp her flesh.

'You OK?' Stef whispered, his face taut with concern.

Megan looked down to find she had tightly grasped a lock of hair and was rocking gently, as if soothing an invisible infant. She couldn't reply but she managed to nod, hoping he would assume her fear was of what lay ahead.

'Don't worry, sweetheart, you won't feel a thing. It'll be fine.'

Megan focused her gaze on the shiny floor tiles, trying to regulate her breathing, barely able to hear Stef's voice above the noises assaulting her ears.

'Megan, how are you?'

Megan realised she could hear a familiar accent amid the sounds, one she immediately recognised, and she looked up instinctively.

'Hi, Gemma.' The words caught in her throat. 'I'm a little nervous.'

'I didn't realise you were on the list till I got in this morning.'

'It was only decided a couple of days ago.'

Gemma consulted her notes, taking her time, brow furrowed in concentration. 'So it seems. Are you ready to come through to the treatment room?'

Megan stood immediately, desperate to escape the waiting room and its ghosts. 'Does Stef stay here?'

'If he wants to wait for you, he can, or he can come back.'

'I'll wait,' Stef said. He leaned over to kiss her. 'Good luck, sweetheart.'

Megan followed Gemma mechanically, expecting her legs to collapse with each step, to another ground-floor room. This one was clinical, an examination bed covered by a sterile blue sheet, surrounded by various pieces of equipment Megan didn't want to study too closely. Macaulay was waiting, making notes on a clipboard that looked considerably more official than his usual notebook.

'Great to see you, Megan. Please take a seat.'

Why does he make everything seem like a pleasant social occasion?

She ignored the observation and sat obediently on the edge of the bed.

'I have to give you a quick rundown of the rules: no alcohol or driving a vehicle for twenty-four hours after treatment, and Stefan will have to supervise you for the same amount of time.'

'I understand.'

'Are you wearing any jewellery or make-up? Any pins or grips in your hair?'

Megan shook her head.

'Do you have any questions? No? Perfect. The heart tracing you had when you arrived was clear, so we're fine to proceed. I'll see you in a few minutes to introduce you to the anaesthetist.'

211

He withdrew, and Megan watched Gemma moving efficiently around the small room. The nurse was unusually quiet, none of her normal cheerful chatter.

'Gemma, how many of these procedures are done here?'

'I don't keep count, love. A fair few.'

'So it's common?'

'I wouldn't say it's common, but it's used when necessary.'

'Does it work?'

'Depends how you define "work". It's effective in treating some of the most challenging symptoms of mental illness.' Gemma patted the bed. 'Lie back here, Megan, and take your shoes off for me. When the anaesthetist comes through, he'll give you an injection and, once you're asleep, you'll have another injection of muscle relaxant and he'll insert a mouth guard to protect your teeth. When you wake up, you'll have an oxygen mask on, but there won't be any tubes or anything. You're only out for a few minutes.'

Megan slipped off her ballet pumps and lay down until her head was resting on the waiting pillow. 'I can't believe it's come to this.'

'What do you mean?'

'I just assumed it would work – the meds and the therapy. I thought I'd do all that and I'd get my baby back. I didn't imagine I'd need electric shocks to understand whether my child is actually real or not.'

Gemma paused in her tasks, turning to face Megan fully. 'You're expecting the treatment to give you back your true memories?'

'I'm expecting it to get rid of the false ones. That's right, isn't it?'

Gemma nodded, barely moving her head. 'Just need to get some more pads for these wires, won't be a minute.'

Megan watched the door close behind the nurse, realising these ones weren't barred by entry cards. She could hear voices in the corridor and flinched, terrified that the sounds from the waiting room had followed her. As she held her breath, she realised the voices were real this time, an American and a Cornish accent together, speaking in low, urgent tones.

They're talking about you.

Sitting up, she shuffled to the end of the bed, closer to the door, to hear better. She could only just make out Gemma's insistent whisper, but the inflection was clear.

'This is wrong. There are ethics! We can't just dole out ECT because she's starting to remember things before you want her to!'

'We're within the guidelines.'

'She doesn't need this therapy! You're disrupting her memories for no good reason. You know as well as I do she'll suffer more retrograde amnesia after this; she'll end up more confused and vulnerable than she is now!'

'There's good reason for the treatment, Gemma.'

'I'm not comfortable with any of this. I'm sorry.'

Megan realised she was holding her breath.

'Gemma.' The familiar overuse of a person's name, insistence on full attention. 'This is far from the first time you've assisted with ECT. What's the problem suddenly?'

'I like this woman.' Gemma sounded exasperated. 'She's not like the others we've treated using ECT. She's strong enough to beat the psychosis; she just needs to work through it in her own way.'

213

'The medication isn't having enough effect on her.'

'Maybe because she doesn't need to be medicated.'

'She tried to stab her husband then attempted suicide – do you not think medication is rather vital?'

'At that time, yes, but now she's starting to process, be curious about what's happened to her. I can see for myself how different she is to when she was discharged.'

'To be honest, Gemma, I don't see much progress.'

'Look, your methods always raise a few eyebrows, especially when you drip-feed patients information—'

'I do not "drip-feed"; I address dissociation issues with patients in accordance with their stage of recovery and their ability to cope with the information.' Macaulay's voice became sharper. 'You need to attend to your patient. Either that, or I'll call another nurse.'

An invisible hand of fear closed around Megan's throat, permitting her only shallow gasps of air.

You'll lose all your memories of Luka if you have the procedure.

Stop this!

The voice was louder than she'd ever heard it before.

Now!

Megan moved faster than she felt capable of, clumsily grabbing her shoes as she snatched open the door.

'I don't want this!' she almost shouted, practically falling into the corridor in her haste.

Macaulay and Gemma both froze at her unexpected appearance. The psychiatrist recovered more quickly, spreading his arms in a consolatory manner, an understanding smile pasted to his face.

'The consent has already been signed and approved, Megan.'

'I'm saying no! I won't have the ECT. I refuse.'

'Under your section, we don't need your permission,' Macaulay stated calmly.

'And I don't need my brain electrocuting!'

'You may be surprised how much it helps you.'

'Where's Stef? I want my husband. Please get him for me.' Megan looked imploringly to Gemma, who gave a brisk nod and disappeared. She was gone only a few moments, returning with Stef trotting urgently behind her. In her agitation, Megan barely registered the glare Macaulay directed towards his nurse.

Stef's shirt was stained dark by several damp patches; he must have spilt the open bottle of water he clutched as he leapt to follow Gemma.

'What is it, sweetheart?' He moved towards her, arms reaching out to draw her to him. She leaned heavily against him, gripping his shirt with both hands. For that moment, he was her only protection.

'Don't let them do it, Stef. I don't want it. Make them stop, please.'

'But you agreed before.'

'Now I don't! I hadn't thought it through.'

'Dr Mac says it's the best option.'

'I don't care what Dr Mac says! Please, take me home, get me away from here. I won't do it.'

Take his water! They can't do the treatment if you've had something to drink.

She snatched his Evian bottle, not caring that she caught his skin with her nails, glugging the remaining half of the water.

She saw Stef looking at Macaulay, his eyes dark.

215

'You may as well take her home,' Macaulay finally said. 'We won't be able to do the treatment while Megan is so upset.'

'I'm not upset,' Megan snapped. 'I'm defending my decision. Can we go now, Stef?'

She started striding towards the doors, hoping Stef would be right behind her. Just as she realised she didn't have the pass to permit her escape into the world beyond, Gemma appeared beside her, tapping her card against the reader.

The two women stepped out in the fresh air as, behind them, Stef hastily gathered belongings, flustered by his lack of control over the situation. Macaulay had already gone, a child who had lost a schoolyard game.

'Thank you,' Megan whispered to the nurse.

Gemma glanced back into the building, then gave Megan's arm a squeeze.

'Don't do anything you don't want to do. Take care of yourself.'

If you're ever going to find out the truth, you need to take control of your own recovery.

As the nurse returned inside, Megan acknowledged the voice was right. The question was how to do it without anyone realising.

Chapter Twenty-Five

It was disconcerting to wake to find Stef watching her from his pillow, his hand smoothing her hair as she slept. She rubbed sleep from her eyes, sliding away from his touch as she stretched beneath the duvet.

'How are you feeling?' he whispered.

'Relieved,' she said, honestly.

'I'm sorry you had to go through that. I really thought you were OK with it.'

'I was, till I started thinking about what could happen.' She had no intention of mentioning Gemma's part in her abrupt refusal. 'Did I let you down?'

'Of course you didn't.' Stef pressed his lips to hers for a brief kiss. 'I wanted it to be your choice.'

'Can't say I'm looking forward to seeing Dr Mac today. He was annoyed yesterday. It was blatantly obvious.'

'What made you change your mind?'

'I was scared when I saw the machines,' she said blandly. 'It's not normal, having your brain electrocuted.'

'None of this is particularly normal,' Stef said with a laugh.

'You wanted me to do it, didn't you?'

'I thought it would help, yes, but it's your decision.'

'It's not really, though, is it? Dr Mac said under my section he could do the ECT without my consent. It was a threat. That he could do it any time he wanted to, if he chose. And I couldn't prevent him.'

'Megs, he isn't threatening you. I wouldn't let him.'

He is, and Stef knows it.

Megan threw back the duvet in disgust. The conversation was pointless; Stef was not going to listen.

'Fine, don't believe me. My psychiatrist wants to permanently disrupt my memories, but you're OK with that, so it doesn't matter.'

'It's not like that. I want you to have the best treatment.'

'Most expensive isn't always best! How many times have I told you that about marble worktops in rental properties?'

'But Eve said—'

'Eve?' Megan interrupted, nonplussed at the unexpected mention of Sophia's wife.

'She found me the recommendation. Dr Mac went to Cornell as well. Apparently, he was brilliant, way ahead of his time.'

'If he's that great, why isn't he still in California, making millions from Hollywood stars' breakdowns?'

'I haven't asked him,' Stef said shortly. 'I'll make breakfast. I picked up some of the Jamaican coffee beans from the Brixton café.'

Megan had no interest in her favourite coffee, but the smell was enough to stir her senses as she entered the kitchen after a concerted effort to get ready. She had dressed for the battle she was anticipating with Macaulay: professional clothes, full make-up and understated jewellery, hair carefully styled, protective shields against his force.

'You look like you're ready for the office,' Stef said uncertainly.

'Thought I'd make an effort to look more like myself today,' she replied, as if her appearance were inconsequential. 'Have you got appointments?'

'I'm meeting the crew to get the ball rolling on stripping the West Ham place. Sophia's coming over.'

Good, keep him out the way.

It was a relief to know her sister would be in the house with her. Macaulay had become a threat now, not just to her freedom but to her safety. Stef wouldn't protect her again, she knew, and she was glad when he swapped his supervision duties with Sophia and left without a backward glance.

'Ready for war?' Sophia asked, indicating Megan's appearance. It made Megan smile to know how easily her sister could read her.

'I wanted to show Dr Mac my game face today.'

'Good idea. Let him know who's boss. Those shoes are to die for. Can I borrow them?'

'What for?'

'Tesco shopping, nursery collection, sterilising bottles.'

'You can have them if you'll stay in the therapy session with me.'

Sophia's eyebrows rose. 'You don't have to be scared of him.'

'I'd feel better if you were there. Call it moral support.'

'Fine. I'll come and analyse ink blots that look like demon cats and practise deep breathing till I pass out. Will it look insolent if I bring a G&T in with me? They always have a drink in films.'

Megan stiffened as the doorbell rang.

'I'll play butler. You go into the sitting room.' Sophia took charge and bounded off to answer the door.

Megan smoothed down her shirt, pinstriped with pale pink, and drew herself to her full height, glad she had decided to wear heels, even though she would be seated. It reassured her to know she was taller than the psychiatrist in the Valentino stilettos and she enjoyed the echoing, authoritative sound of them against the floor as she strode through to the sitting room.

'Good morning, Sophia.' Megan heard Macaulay's voice drift up from the steps.

'No portable electrodes with you before I let you in?' Sophia asked.

An obliging laugh. 'Not today.'

'Nor yesterday either, I hear.'

'I'm glad Megan feels able to confide in you.'

'I'm a much more useful sounding board than my brother-in-law,' Sophia agreed. 'Come in.'

'Is your daughter here? I hear a lot about her.'

'She's quite comfortable in her madness. She doesn't need therapy.'

Megan sat up straighter as the sitting-room door opened. If she had expected any sign of anger or frustration from the psychiatrist, he gave nothing away, settling himself in his usual seat after greeting her politely. She thought he looked slightly flustered, but that was quite usual in people who had felt the full force of Sophia's personality.

'You don't mind if I sit in today, do you, Dr Mac?' Sophia asked brightly, her body language making it perfectly clear that she considered it a polite rhetorical question and would not to be taking no for an answer. She sat down next to Megan and smiled. 'Thank you.'

'I don't usually encourage an audience.' Macaulay maintained his neutral expression, but his eyes had hardened.

'I'm a good audience; I don't applaud unless instructed and I won't interrupt you for a loo break.' Sophia settled herself more comfortably. 'Pretend I'm not here.'

'Megan, do you feel unable to talk to me alone today?'

'I'd like Sophia to see a therapy session for herself.'

'Very well, if that's what you want.'

Show him you're in charge for once.

'I don't want to talk about yesterday,' Megan declared. 'I've made my decision and I'm not going to change my mind.'

'You seemed very decisive yesterday,' he agreed, making his first note.

'I'm still capable of thinking for myself.'

'You didn't feel guided in refusing the treatment?'

'No,' she said firmly. 'May we begin the session now?'

'As you wish. Perhaps with Sophia here, now would be a good time to continue our discussion of your family?'

The bastard. He knows what reaction he's going to get.

Megan felt Sophia tense as she became alert to danger and hated Macaulay for his manipulation of the situation, bringing it firmly back under his control again, taunting her brief attempt to snatch power.

'Would you like to talk more about your mother?' Macaulay asked.

'Not really. Why?'

'Perhaps there are lessons to be learned from how she reacted to trauma. You said she didn't cope with Sophia's attack.'

221

Sophia flinched as if she had been physically struck but, to her credit, she managed not to intervene.

'Our mother couldn't cope with her own issues, let alone anyone else's,' Megan said quietly.

'And I expect it became worse after your father left? More responsibility on you?'

'I had to look after them both, plus juggle university and a part-time job. It wasn't easy.'

'You felt obliged.'

'Not obliged. Of course I looked after them, they were my family.'

'You gave up a great deal of your own life for them.'

'We didn't have many other options. Stef's mum was great, but his family moved away later that same year. I understood why – his brother died in their house – but I really did struggle after they left.'

'Stefan didn't offer you any help after he graduated?'

'He severed contact. It was for the best, really. He still wanted us to get back together. I didn't have the time to keep him happy as well, so it was easier to let him go. We lost touch for several years, until Mum died.'

'Do you mind me asking how she died?'

'She finally committed suicide, when I was twenty-five. She'd been trying to do it for years.'

'You weren't surprised.' An observation rather than a question.

'Neither of us were.' Megan risked a glance at her sister. Sophia was completely rigid, gripping the arms of her chair and taking care not to look at anyone. 'She was never really a mother to us. Always a patient. We looked after her rather than the other way round.'

Macaulay glanced up from his notes, interest clearly piqued, but Sophia refused to make eye contact with him.

'May I ask, did the police ever catch Sophia's attacker?'

'No. There were no forensics so—'

'So the bastard got away with it,' Sophia interrupted.

Macaulay seemed to have forgotten all about the purpose of the therapy session; his attention was now fixed on Sophia, and Megan was relieved to not be the object of his scrutiny for once.

'Did you ever remember any details about the attack, Sophia?' he asked, his voice softer than usual.

'Clearly not, or he'd be in prison by now. I'd hardly have kept it to myself,' Sophia snapped.

'Did you have therapy?'

'They made me have counselling when I was in hospital. Using art to explore my emotions, and all that crap. I had to write words on a doll once in marker pen. "Angry. Afraid. Robbed. Violated." Shit like that. As if defacing a doll would make everything better.'

'You haven't explored getting any help as an adult?'

'I had my therapy – travelling. I saw the world, and the world healed me.' Sophia had angled herself away from the psychiatrist, neck twisted round so her eyes could burn into his. 'You won't get any money out of me, Dr Mac. I haven't got any.'

'It must have severely disturbed your mental health to be told you couldn't have children.'

He's gone too far now.

The elastic band that had become Sophia's body was on the verge of snapping, stretched beyond its capabilities. 'How is that any of your business? You're here to make my sister well, not poke around in my private life.'

223

She's going to blame you.

'I'm sorry,' Megan whispered, even though she knew words couldn't be enough to salvage the situation. 'We were talking about Mum and her problems, and your attack just sort of followed on.'

Sophia shrugged. 'Suppose it was pretty traumatic for you to go through as well. No one asked you how you were coping, did they?'

'It wasn't important.'

'Should have been,' Sophia declared, getting abruptly to her feet. 'I think that's enough therapy for me for one day. That G&T is calling my name. Excuse me.'

'I hope I didn't upset her,' Macaulay said, sounding genuinely apologetic, as the door closed smartly behind Sophia.

He knew exactly what he was doing.

Megan shot the psychiatrist as fierce a glare as she could manage. 'She doesn't talk about the attack.'

'I thought she may find it helpful, since she was here.'

'She's not the therapy type; she's learned how to cope in her own way.'

'And that's by ignoring it?'

'She hides how brittle she is behind acerbic wit, gets her attack in first. She didn't use to be like that; she was softer, more approachable. She would have been a good teacher.'

Macaulay slid his notebook into the briefcase. 'I'll go now, let you check on Sophia. Please apologise to her for me.'

She saw the psychiatrist out and found Sophia sitting at the island, swirling a glass of what smelled like a very strong gin and not much tonic.

'Are you OK?'

' 'Course I am. Takes more than that to shake me up.'

'It wasn't very pleasant for you.'

'Damn right it wasn't, but whatever, doesn't matter.'

'I'm sorry I talked about you.'

'I don't mind.'

'Really?'

'No, that was a lie. I do mind. But I understand why you wanted to talk about it. It must have fucked you up as well, even though I was too wrapped up in myself to notice at the time.'

'You were fighting for your life, not being self-absorbed.'

'That's true. Pretty heroic, when you think about it.' Sophia raised her glass and took a long drink. 'It's OK, Megan. I'm not blaming you for talking about it. If it helps you process things, then at least it's been useful for something.'

'I still feel terrible about it.'

'When I smell of gin collecting Amelia and the nursery calls social services, then it can be your fault. You can come with me in case I get kicked out.'

'What if Stef comes back?'

'Fuck it. We'll call it day release.'

Chapter Twenty-Six

Before

'I remember a lot more than you do about that night.'

Hiding on the snug's sofa, Orion lolling in his arms, Stefan nearly tipped the dog off as his body jolted with shock at the sudden words breaking the silence. Isaac had appeared unnoticed in the doorway, an unwelcome apparition.

'What the hell are you banging on about?' Stefan snapped, to cover his reaction.

'I went along with your story for the police, but there was a lot more to it, wasn't there?' Isaac, for once, maintained full eye contact, somehow much worse than his usual avoidance. 'Don't you remember Sophia bringing your phone back?'

'She did what?'

'Turned up on the doorstep, knocking loud enough to wake the dead. Not Dad – he wouldn't hear the apocalypse – but I had to go down when she started shouting up at my window, thinking it was yours.'

'Why didn't you just wake me?'

Isaac smirked. 'Because you hadn't come home by then.'

'So how could I remember if I wasn't here, genius?'

'You ran into us as I walked Sophia home. Stumbled, more accurately. You shoved me off and insisted on taking her yourself. You don't recall trying to punch me again and falling flat on your face?'

Stefan tried to make sense of the timeline, his mind racing in useless circles. 'So, if Sophia brought my phone back, why didn't I have it? Why was it found with her?'

A shrug. 'You tell me. Maybe you dropped it again after she gave it back to you.'

The sudden rush of nausea nearly overwhelmed Stefan and he gripped Orion's fur tightly until he was certain he wasn't going to be sick. His head swam, his body beginning to shiver as sweat slicked his skin.

'They say blackout memories come back, bit by bit,' Isaac continued, almost conversationally. 'Perhaps you'll start remembering some parts.'

Stefan had to escape. He was going to vomit. The house had become unbearably hot and he was lost, helpless and drowning in the sea of unwelcome revelations. Isaac grabbed his arm as he forced his way past, unexpected strength in his hold, enough to leave a red weal on Stefan's wrist that burned more than it should have done.

Dragging himself free, Stefan made for the front door, pausing only to snatch Orion's lead, not prepared to leave his dog behind. He had barely stumbled down the steps before he vomited into the shrubbery. The retriever watched him with an expression that was almost understanding, waiting patiently until he was able to stand again.

As Stefan walked along the allotments, too lost in his own fears to pay any attention to his surroundings, he failed to hear his name being called. Only when it became a shout did he finally look up, as Orion strained on the end of the lead. Megan's father stood creosoting the newly constructed garden fence, eight feet of defence against the world's wrongs, taking refuge from his broken family.

'Sorry, didn't hear you,' Stefan mumbled, trying to continue walking as if he had somewhere urgent to be. He'd had no intention of going near Megan's home in this state, yet somehow his feet had found their own way without him even noticing.

'Clearly. You look like your world's collapsed. What's up? You had another row with Megan?'

'Nothing's up. I'm not feeling well. Going for a walk to clear my head.'

Paul Crawley took his time dipping his brush into the creosote pot, precise movements that seemed to require his full attention. 'What do you know, Stefan?' His face was entirely without expression, his words flat and emotionless.

Stefan felt the words hit like a punch, hard enough to knock him down. Somehow, he managed to control his reaction, though he suspected his own expression betrayed him. 'What do you mean?'

'You've not been doing all this just because you're still in love with Megan: taking her to the hospital, helping me decorate, hovering around. So what is it?'

'I wanted to help.'

'You wanted to be kept busy so you wouldn't have to think.'

'It's not like that.'

'You're back up to Durham end of the week, that's why you need to get it off your chest. Come on, son, spit it out. Did you see Sophia that night? Did you give her drugs? What?'

'I didn't give her drugs! And no, I didn't see her. Honestly, I didn't.' Stefan took a couple of steps backwards, the air between them suddenly suffocating.

'Then what?'

'I don't know what you're talking about, Paul. I just want to help.'

'You already said that.'

'I mean it.'

'You can't keep it inside for ever, son, it'll tear you apart.'

Stefan nearly cracked at such perceptive words. He bent his head to pat Orion so Paul wouldn't see the betraying tears forming.

'You know Sophia's had a crush on you for years,' Paul said, almost gently. 'She got her hopes up when you and Megan split. Always on the phone to her friends about how good looking you are.'

'Sophia's a kid. I think of her as a little sister.'

'Was she coming on to you?'

'No!'

'We both know what she's like when she gets an idea in her head – nothing stops her. Did she get too much? Did you lose your temper with her?'

'Paul, I've never laid a finger on her, I swear.'

'It wouldn't have taken much for you to convince her to go off with you. She'd have followed you anywhere if she thought you were interested.'

'It didn't happen.'

'Why did the police find your phone with her?'

'Like I told them, I must have left it at the party. She could have been coming to return it when she was grabbed.'

229

'Yet you conveniently don't remember.'

'Why does everyone suspect me?' Stefan almost shouted. 'What have I done to make people think I'm capable of something like that?'

'Because someone's to blame for this, and you've not been yourself since it happened!' Paul thundered, his sudden volume enough to startle Stefan. 'The police found your phone at the scene, hairs from your dog on Sophia's clothes. It doesn't look good, does it?'

To Stefan's horror, tears blurred his vision and, before he could stop them, they were cascading down his face. Hot, furious tears that could not be denied or ignored, the result of too long spent on constant guard, guilt eating away at him.

'I lied. I told the cops Isaac saw me when I came home. But I didn't go to his room. I went straight to bed.'

'So you made him lie as well.'

'I didn't make him. He just went along with it.'

''Course he did. He's not all there, is he? Why the hell did you lie?'

''Cos I've no idea when I got home. I don't remember anything apart from falling into bed and not being able to get to sleep 'cos the room was spinning.'

'You were that pissed?'

Stefan rubbed his forehead hard enough to leave a stinging red mark across it. 'I took pills at the party.'

'You absolute idiot. I never imagined you'd be that stupid.'

'I never take drugs normally! I just . . . I don't know . . . I just wanted to forget everything that was winding me up.'

'Where'd you get the pills from?'

'One of the sixth-form girls. And no, before you ask, I didn't see Sophia trying any.'

'There was no trace of drugs found in her system, but some of them disappear quickly, don't they?'

'Roofies do – I remember a talk at school about them – but party drugs can be traced. I really don't think she took anything.'

'How would you know? You were so off your face anything could have happened.'

There wasn't much he could say to that.

'Why didn't you tell the truth?'

'I was scared. I can't prove where I was. The cops will think I'm guilty.'

'They will when they find out you lied.'

Nausea washed over Stefan again. 'Are you going to tell them?' he asked, feeling like he was begging for a resolution he knew wouldn't be possible.

'I don't know yet.'

There was such power in that short sentence that Stefan immediately regretted opening his mouth. He stared hard at the fence, unable to look away from the drying creosote.

Paul took a long time to dip his brush into the pot and carefully remove the excess liquid. 'Like I said, son, I've known you years. You've always been a decent kid. I don't want to think you're capable of something like that, but if you were drugged off your head . . .'

It seemed there was no ending to his words, even though Stefan waited for it. He didn't know how to reply. The silence became unbearable.

'It wasn't me, Paul,' he finally said, aware of how weak his words sounded in comparison.

'You sound like a child denying a playground scrap. Grow up, Stefan, this isn't a bloody game.'

'Think I don't know that?' Stefan retorted, his temper rising from nowhere. 'Sophia nearly died, for fuck's sake!'

'Watch your fucking mouth!'

Stefan ground his teeth, tugging Orion's lead to bring the dog back to his feet. 'I'll go. I'm just making things worse.' He noticed how grey the older man's face had become. 'You OK?'

He was shocked to see Paul's eyes fill with tears. 'I've nothing left in me, son. I'm so tired. I can't keep going much longer.'

'What do you mean?'

'You don't know what it's like. For years I've been a carer, not a husband, and I've watched the woman I love go through hell. Now I'm seeing my daughter suffer even more. And there's nothing I can do. Nothing I do will change what's happened to Sophia. It won't heal her or let her have children or save her mind from the torture she's got to live with. Can't you see that?'

Stefan had no reply to give; there was nothing he could say that would render Paul's points dismissible. He turned to leave.

'Are your parents home?' Paul asked abruptly.

'They've had to go to my grandmother's care home. I'm supposed to be watching Isaac.'

'I want to speak to him, so I know you're not lying to me.'

'Why would I lie to you?' Stefan practically yelled.

'Why would you lie to the police?' Paul snapped back.

'Isaac won't talk to you.'

'I won't be giving him the choice. Come on, before your parents get back and you end up with even more explaining to do.'

There was nothing else for it but to follow, a grim march to the gallows. They walked in silence towards the other end of the wide, elm-lined avenue, not seeing any of the sun dappling their feet through the heavy canopy of spring leaves. Stefan automatically looked for an escape route when he spotted a familiar figure ahead. Megan was walking rapidly down the street towards them, not looking up, her eyes focused on the pavement. She jumped when she realised who was in front of her, unnecessarily startled.

'Thought you were still at the hospital,' Stefan greeted her.

'Soph needed to go for tests, so I left early.' Her words came out in a rush and Stefan realised she was drunk, although her father seemed completely unaware of the fact. It was rather early, but who was he to judge?

'Why are you coming this way?'

'Bus got diverted.' More like she'd come from a pub rather than straight from the hospital, but he didn't press the issue. 'Where are you going, Dad?'

'Stefan needs a hand taking down his bookshelves. Won't be long.'

'Are you coming to evening visiting?'

Paul scrubbed a hand across his face, heavily lined with the weight of his responsibilities. 'I'll go. You have a rest tonight.'

Megan didn't argue, her need clear in the dark circles beneath her dull eyes and the stoop of her delicate shoulders. 'Thanks, Dad.'

The two men made it to Stefan's front door without any further encounters, greeted by a still, silent house.

'Is he in his room?'

'He's always in his room.'

'Come up with me so he doesn't freak out, then take Orion for a walk,' Paul instructed. 'Just round the block. I'll be gone when you get back.'

'Don't you want me to stay, just in case?'

'In case what? He's hardly going to talk to me with you leaning over his shoulder.'

Aware he would not win the argument but with no intention of doing as he was told, Stefan led the way upstairs, deigning to knock on Isaac's closed door before they both entered.

It was immediately obvious that Isaac had been crying. His eyes were red and sore and barely dried trails of tears and mucus glistened on his face. As usual, the curtains were half closed, but the sunshine was bright enough to show the room was in uproar. Furniture upended, clothes ripped from the wardrobe, belongings lying broken on the littered carpet, even books with their pages torn out. Most telling of all, Isaac's beloved computer, the screen a spider web of cracks and the gaps in the keyboard like missing teeth.

'What the hell have you done?' Stefan asked, unsure why his voice was so hushed.

'What do you want?' Isaac's voice was scratchy with the rawness that came only from intense screaming or sobbing.

'Mr Crawley wants to speak to you.'

The effect was instantaneous. Isaac scuttled like a frightened animal into one corner of his wrecked room, grabbing his duvet to huddle beneath, only the top of his head peeking out. His eyes, just visible above the cover, gleamed with an emotion that could have been mania, terror or dread, or maybe all three.

'I'm not here to hurt you, Isaac,' Paul said, so much calmer than Stefan could have managed. He seemed to have forgotten his dog-walking instructions, so Stefan silently retreated to the doorway and stayed there, barely breathing.

'What caused you to do all this?' Paul asked.

'I was angry.'

'Angry at what?'

'The world.'

'Do you know why I'm here?'

'You want me to stay away from Megan?'

'No, I'm here to talk about Sophia. About what happened to her on the allotments.'

'Why would I want to talk about that?'

'Because I know you lied to the police for Stefan,' Paul said quietly, his voice almost hypnotic as he crouched down. Isaac burrowed deeper into the protection of the duvet, trying to force himself further into the corner. 'I know you didn't see him come home that night.'

'Leave me alone. I didn't do anything.'

'You lied for your brother.'

'He told me to. He made me.'

Stefan only just managed to bite back his protest. He shot Isaac his darkest glare, but his twin didn't seem to have even noticed he was there.

'Maybe you went out again?' Paul suggested. 'Did you see Sophia wandering around drunk? Was she with Stefan?'

'I didn't go out. I didn't see Sophia or Stef.'

'Come on, Isaac, you know something. You wouldn't be behaving like this if you didn't. What are you scared of? Are you scared of Stefan?'

'He beat me up in front of everyone.'

'He won't hurt you now, not if you tell me the truth.'

'Please, stop it.'

'You like Megan, don't you? Don't you want to help us find out who hurt her little sister?'

'Stop talking.'

'Sophia didn't fight her attacker, Isaac. There was no skin under her fingernails. He must have drugged her. Does Stefan use drugs? Have you seen him with that date-rape stuff?'

'Why are you asking me these things?' Isaac sobbed, the duvet shaking violently in time with his gasps for breath.

'I'm asking because I want to know what really happened when my daughter nearly died.'

'I don't know anything!'

'You're lying, Isaac. If we'd found her half an hour later, she would have been dead. Do you know how much blood she lost? Do you know the damage she has internally? She'll never have children now. She may never recover from the trauma.'

Stefan watched, frozen, not daring to move in case the spell Paul Crawley was casting was broken.

'Shut up!' Isaac screamed, the words sounding even louder after the whispers. 'Just shut the fuck up! Stop talking about it! Get out of my room! I'm not scared of you!'

'You don't have to be scared of me. I'm not going to hurt you. But I am going to speak to the police and tell them you lied. They'll arrest you, Isaac, charge you with wasting police time. They'll take you to the station. I don't think you're going to like it there. You won't have your parents running around trying to make you better or a nice cosy bedroom to hide away in. So why not save yourself from all that and tell me the truth?'

'Get away from me!' Isaac lashed out, his limbs softened by the duvet he was still cowering beneath.

Paul glanced behind him to Stefan, noticing him for the first time. 'Did you force him to lie to the police?'

'No, I swear! He went along with it, I didn't even ask him! I just told him what I'd said.'

'You're a fucking liar!' Isaac screamed. 'I'll tell Mum and Dad what you've done!'

'As if they'll believe you!' Stefan roared back, the spell broken. 'They know you're a fucking headcase!'

'Enough!' Paul thundered. 'I don't care about whatever fight you two want to have. I care about my daughter and finding out who did this to her.'

'It wasn't me!' Stefan blurted out, unable to control his need for denial in his desperation to be believed, to be granted his innocence, even if he wasn't worthy of it. Isaac buried himself completely, the outline of his gaunt figure shaking under his shelter.

Paul looked sadly from one twin to the other. 'I hope to God it wasn't, son.'

By the time his parents returned, there was no sign of anything amiss. Stefan had stayed away from his twin, not trusting himself. Emotions coursed through him after Paul had left, feelings he couldn't quite identify but which scared him more than he could ever admit. He paced his room for hours, trying to decode them, hearing the sounds of Isaac tidying for some time before, finally, silence. Probably hiding under his duvet again.

Stefan was in the snug when he heard his parents' car in the driveway. It was late, he should have made dinner for them, but the thought of food brought the waves of nausea again and he couldn't bring himself to enter the kitchen. He stayed in the snug, cuddled up to Orion, barely returning his mother's greeting. Only days until he could leave this house and its secrets.

He heard his mother preparing dinner and her footsteps as she took a plate up to Isaac. As usual, he hadn't made an appearance, shutting himself away, not a sound heard from him, but of course his mum still made him his favourite meal.

Her cry was primal when it came. His dad's name screamed out, then Isaac's, over and over again. Stefan bolted up the stairs, already knowing what he would find. His mother shoved past him, scrambling for the phone, still howling for his father to call an ambulance, do CPR, bring him back.

Stefan looked down at his brother's body, curled on his bed, a thin trail of vomit tacky on his chin, eyes half open to stare at nothing. The popped blister packs had been dropped carelessly on the carpet beside the almost-empty vodka bottle. Isaac's fingers, curled gently towards his palms, were chalky with their residue.

Stefan tried to summon some feeling of grief, something that would acknowledge he had lost his twin, the person he was supposed to be closest to in this world.

There was nothing.

Early the next morning, as his parents sat rigid and silent at the kitchen table, staring into cold mugs of coffee made hours previously, Stefan left the house unnoticed. It was a misty morning, damp heavy in the air, uneasy weather that allowed him to bury his chin deeper into his jacket and hide his clenched fists in his pockets.

Paul Crawley was waiting for him, as arranged, eyes bleary with weekend sleep and too much whisky, the sharp tang of the Scotch easily detectable on him.

'Isaac's dead,' Stefan stated, emotionless in his announcement.

Paul's body visibly recoiled, as if a punch had connected hard. 'Dead?'

'He killed himself last night. Overdose.'

That grey tinge had crept over Paul's skin again. 'Did he leave a note?'

Stefan shook his head. 'Didn't see one, but the police said they'll send their crime scene people this morning, so maybe they'll find something.'

'Do the police need to investigate suicide?'

A shrug. 'S'pose they've got to make sure he really did it himself.'

He had expected more questions, maybe sympathy, almost certainly shock, but Paul was behaving as if he was afraid. Backing away, shaking his head, uncoordinated enough to trip over his own feet as he turned his back. Was he still drunk? He usually seemed so tightly in control; it was unnerving to see him unravel in such a way.

'I've got to go, Stefan. Need to get to the hospital.'

'It's too early for visiting.'

'Things to do first. Sorry. Must go. Sorry.'

'I'm not mourning him, Paul!' Stefan called stridently. 'You shouldn't either.'

The older man looked to have flinched again at the sharp words, but he didn't stop, didn't look back. Picked up his pace until he was almost running.

Stefan didn't follow. Whatever Paul's issue was: guilt over his last words to Isaac, horror that the avenue had lost a resident so close in age to his daughters, fear that Sophia may one day do the same terrible thing, Stefan couldn't quite bring himself to care.

He went home, to watch scenes of crime technicians, anonymous in white coveralls and latex gloves, come and go. To join his parents in their silence, although his reasons were different to theirs.

When it was finally all over, when the police had retreated, the funeral held and the inquest coroner certain to return a verdict of suicide, Stefan went to say his goodbyes.

He hadn't had a chance to bid farewell to Paul Crawley, not after he left for work one morning, never to return. Only a brief note for his family; explanation or confession, Stefan didn't know. But he knew he couldn't leave another goodbye left unsaid.

Megan had aged years when she opened the door. He hadn't seen her cry since she had told him her father was gone, abandoning them to their problems, but he could see how tightly she was keeping herself under control. The old grace was gone from her movements, replaced with a coiled tension that seemed on the verge of breaking her. Guilt stabbed at his heart and responsibility weighed down his shoulders. There was so much he should apologise to her for, beg her forgiveness for, but he couldn't tell her any of it.

'Are you off?' she asked.

'Yeah, car's all packed. Say bye to Sophia and your mum from me. Hope they'll be OK.'

Her expression said neither of them was ever likely to be OK, but she didn't voice it and he was glad of that. 'Hope you get your 2:1,' she returned.

'Might scrape it if I stay out of the college bar this term.' He tried to grin but failed and scrubbed his hand over his face instead. 'Megan—'

240

'Don't, Stef. It won't help. Go back to Durham and do your best, and enjoy your new life in the City. I'm sure I'll see you around.'

He moved forward to offer a hug, but she was already stepping back inside, denying him. She gave him a strained smile, not knowing it would be for the last time, as she closed the door.

He would not contact her again: he would change his number, delete his email account, and he would not return to Marlborough Avenue. She deserved a fresh start, away from him and the indelible stain he had cast over her life.

Stefan said a silent goodbye and walked away from it all, yet again telling himself it was the right thing to do.

Chapter Twenty-Seven

Megan was awake early, before Stef's alarm went off. She had slept badly, unable to switch off enough to relax into slumber, but rather than being dogged by lethargy, she felt energised, focused. For the first time in far too long, she knew what she was doing; her obedient passivity was quietly coming to an end.

She skipped through the shower, smoothed on a touch of concealer and a dash of eye make-up to disguise the dark circles that seemed to have become her constant companions. Downstairs, she set the coffee machine to grind and croissants to warm, assembled plates, presented slices of Swiss cheese, cured ham and her home-made tomato relish on a bread board and placed everything on the island.

'Someone's been busy this morning!' Stef appeared in jeans, clearly not planning on leaving her in Sophia's charge that day.

Don't make him suspicious.

The voice was ready for action today, chiming in stridently, refusing to allow other thoughts to distract her. 'I was awake early and I thought it was my turn to make breakfast.'

They ate together, a leisurely meal that seemed like the old days as they chatted about summer holiday plans and whether Sri Lanka was a better bet than Cambodia and Vietnam.

'Will you make more coffee?' Megan asked as she drained her mug. 'That machine is driving me mad. Almost literally.'

He laughed. 'Time for a new one?'

'One less complicated than a NASA invention would be great.'

Stef got up to follow orders, ferrying their crumb-strewn plates to the dishwasher, replacing them with fresh glasses of orange juice. He was getting careless, already becoming too used to the routine of coffee, breakfast and pills. He slid Megan's saucer of pills across to her and turned away to battle with the recalcitrant coffee machine.

It took only this momentary distraction for Megan to slip the pills into her jeans pocket. She was finishing the last of her orange juice when Stef turned around again.

'Any plans for today?' he asked cheerfully, as if she was intending to head out for lunch and shopping.

'I might try to sketch a little after Dr Mac has been. I haven't really been up to the study since I came home.' She saw his knuckles whiten as his grip momentarily tightened on the juice glass. 'What's wrong?'

'Nothing,' he said, too quickly.

The study must be where . . .

With the affirming knowledge that she was unencumbered by drugs, Megan made the mental jump almost effortlessly. 'Is that where I tried to commit suicide?'

Stef swallowed hard, giving a quick nod. 'Not that you should avoid it or anything. I mean, you don't even remember it happening. Just bad memories for me, I suppose.'

'I'll be safe, Stef, I promise.'

'I know, I'm being stupid. Ignore me.' He kissed her gently. 'I'd better get cracking – exchanging contracts today. Give me a knock if you need anything.'

Megan busied herself stacking the dishwasher as she waited for the doorbell to announce Macaulay's arrival. Today's session was set to be a double challenge: avoiding any further attempts to convince her of ECT's merits while ensuring he didn't realise she was unmedicated. She would just have to hope that taking the tablets tomorrow and over the next few days would satisfy the next urine test.

Macaulay seemed a little subdued, quietly taking out his notebook without any of his usual small talk. Perhaps Sophia's reactions had troubled him, or maybe he was frustrated his blatant attempts to connect with her problems had failed. Megan decided the latter was more likely.

He doesn't like being thwarted, does he?

She enjoyed the idea of the psychiatrist being beaten at his own game.

'What you would like to talk about today?' he asked, once he was ready.

Megan shifted in her seat, the pills burning guiltily in the watch pocket of her jeans. 'I'd like to talk about the future.'

'Anything specifically?'

'What will happen to me? I can't remain in treatment for ever, or sectioned indefinitely. Sooner or later, I'll have to go back to work, meet my friends, go to restaurants, travel. A normal life.'

'Yes, hopefully, you will.'

'At the moment, it feels very far away.'

'I'm sure it does.' Today seemed to be all about vague reassurances.

'Dr Mac, I know you're lying to me.'

Macaulay's pen stilled midword. 'Lying about what, Megan?'

'About my son.'

'As we've said before, you do not have a son. Your belief is part of your delusions.'

'Why would I imagine a baby?'

'Psychosis rarely makes any sense.'

'But I remember. I was pregnant, I gave birth, I held him in my arms. I've even seen a photo of him.'

'We agreed that picture was of Amelia.'

'No, *you* agreed. You and Stef and Sophia.'

'Yet you still think you're right and we're all wrong.'

'Yes, because you're lying to me.'

'We're not lying to you, Megan. You seem rather fixated today. Have you been taking your medication?'

Don't give him any reason to doubt you.

Megan didn't blink. 'Of course. You can check with Stef. He watches me take them.'

'That's good.'

Inwardly delighted by the clarity of her thought processes, the mental agility she'd forgotten she was capable of, Megan leaned forward.

'This doesn't change the fact that I believe I'm not being told the truth.'

'I'm sorry you feel that way.'

'I can't imagine what reason a doctor would have to conceal a baby from its mother.'

'That would certainly be a very difficult situation.'

245

'Then tell me where Luka is.'

'Luka doesn't exist, Megan. I can't make you believe me, but I will keep telling you the same thing. You do not have a son.'

'And you can keep saying it, but I still won't believe you.' Megan resisted the urge to fold her arms across her chest. It seemed a juvenile action when she was determined to show she was capable of functioning as an adult.

'Then we're at a stalemate. This is why I suggested the ECT, as a further aid to your recovery.'

'Don't threaten me.'

'I'm in no way threatening you.'

'It feels like you are. Dangling the carrot of recovery even while you're trying to use the stick of ECT.'

'That's an excellent metaphor.'

He's getting suspicious.

Megan had surprised herself with that unplanned statement, but she was careful not to show it. She had to rein herself in before Macaulay realised she was functioning too well to be medicated.

'I've been reading a lot,' she murmured. 'I enjoy metaphors. I've even written some haikus.'

'That's excellent.' Macaulay's reaction was too enthusiastic, relief at having finally steered her away from the subject of Luka.

Distract him before he starts to wonder where the sudden creative urge has come from.

'Why did you come to the UK?' she asked, aware that it was an abrupt change in subject, but it seemed in keeping with her usual disjointed thoughts.

One eyebrow twitched in surprise. 'I always said I'd like to live and work in London, so when the opportunity arose, I took it.'

'Did you work for the NHS when you first arrived?'

'Very briefly. I didn't enjoy it – too many constraints and procedures and regulations. Private practice allows me to use my strengths and my own methods rather than those dictated by seniors.'

'Did Gemma come from the NHS too?'

'You and Gemma got along well, didn't you?' He tried to get back in control by replying with a question.

He doesn't like Gemma. She's become a threat to him.

Megan felt a surge of loyalty towards her nurse. 'She was kind to me.'

'Yes, she's very good at her job. She has an excellent rapport with all patients.'

Megan didn't miss the emphasis on 'all'. 'You must have treated quite a few celebrities, being in Hollywood.'

'My practice was in Malibu, but yes, some famous names passed through the door.'

'I wouldn't have thought you'd want to leave that behind. I'm sure film stars pay much more for treatment than property developers.'

'Are you hinting at a scandal, Megan?'

'I just wondered what prompted you to give up such a successful practice.'

'If something had gone wrong, I wouldn't have been allowed to practise in this country, certainly not for the all-seeing NHS.'

He's hiding something, no matter what he says.

'Then why leave?' Megan challenged.

'Time for a fresh start. A relationship breakdown, some legal changes that made some methods difficult to use, and, of course, the fickle nature of Los Angeles. The trend shifted from therapy and meds to homeopathic methods and mindfulness, and my client list dwindled.'

Somewhat disappointed her probing hadn't unearthed any wrongdoing – she had imagined an ECT session gone terribly wrong or a psychotic patient launching a devastating attack on the defenceless psychiatrist – she glanced at her watch.

'Our hour is up, Dr Mac.'

'Do you have something pressing to do?' He raised an eyebrow at her timekeeping accuracy.

'I want to sketch today, and I'm keen to make a start while I'm inspired.'

'Haikus and art, very impressive.'

She smiled her thanks, even though she was unsure if he was being sincere, and efficiently showed him to the door, barely able to wait until he reached the bottom of the steps before closing it.

Chore done for the day, she had bigger plans than sketching. She trotted up the stairs, tapping on the office door.

'I'm going up to the study now.' She poked her head round. 'Don't worry about me.'

'Did you have a good session with Dr Mac?'

'Yes, it was very useful today.'

'Great. I was a bit worried there might be some tension after the ECT issue.'

Megan gave a grin. 'We talked through it.'

Stef laughed and turned back to his laptop, seemingly reassured that she was in good spirits. She closed the door gently and headed up to the second floor, where her easel waited.

For a few moments, she gazed at the charcoal lines of the unfinished sketch, trying to remember what she had been attempting to capture. The outline was chaotic, no style or discernible feature.

Maybe you were attempting to draw what was inside your head.

She shrugged away the voice's suggestion and dragged her attention from the easel. She hadn't come up here to draw. She had a more important task. The study was a little sanctuary and the only place where her need for order relaxed slightly. Here, she stored the various detritus of her life prior to moving into her dream house: school certificates yellowed with age, photo albums of awkward teenagers in braces and boot-cut jeans, journals she had conscientiously kept, cameras that still required film, T-shirts she no longer wore but which held too many memories to throw away. And somewhere, among it all, was her previous phone.

It took longer than anticipated to find. She kept getting distracted by a photo of her sixteen-year-old self in the arms of a more muscular, baby-faced Stef or a postcard from Sophia's Bolivia trip or keys from long-forgotten locks.

Finally, she spotted the Samsung box at the bottom of the refurbished tea chest that doubled as a side table. The battery was long since dead and she hadn't put the charger neatly in the box as she would usually have done. Where would she have put it? Was it being used to charge another device?

Your Kindle. Same connection. Come on, hurry up.

She ran down to the floor below, grabbed the lead and shot back up to the study. The phone took for ever to gain enough charge to switch on and she paced the study in her impatience before realising Stef would hear the creaking floorboards through the office ceiling. Not wanting to attract his attention, she forced herself to sit and wait until the screen eventually lit up.

It was useless as a phone, no SIM card, and they must have

changed internet provider since it was last used, for it didn't connect. Megan didn't care; the only thing she wanted was her picture file.

Completely focused, she skimmed through the images, watching Amelia in reverse, growing younger and younger until her earliest baby pictures. She tapped one, enlarging it. Her niece was tiny, a day old, still in her hospital bassinet awaiting discharge. Typically Amelia, she was bellowing her disapproval at being kept imprisoned in the small space. Her legs kicked angrily at the blanket and she glared at the camera with wide, furious eyes. The first meeting had not been a success; Amelia had screamed throughout the visit and Megan had left feeling distinctly relieved that she did not have any maternal responsibilities.

Remembering her thoughts that day felt like a punch to the gut. She had loved her new niece, of course she had, but there had been no surge of hormones, no desire for her own. It had been a relief to get away from the cries.

So what had changed? How had she gone from being happily childless to being a woman searching for any clue to her baby's existence? Had she woken up one morning gripped by the urge to procreate? Something must have changed her mind, awoken a desire she never knew she'd had, but she couldn't yet grasp what.

She realised her attention had slipped again and the phone had gone blank. Tapping the screen, she recalled the photo and hunched over to study it intently before swiping on to the next in the series.

You were right!

In the first picture, Amelia was wearing the traditional soft hat all newborns seemed to sport on their delicate heads. Further along the reel, however, the hat had been removed. Exactly as Megan had thought, Amelia had barely a wisp of hair. What little she did have was blond almost bordering on ginger. She did not have a full pelt of dark, downy fuzz. Nor were her eyes that beautiful blue-grey colour. Amelia's eyes were pure sapphire, as they still were, a piercing gaze.

The photo in Stef's desk was definitely of a different baby. And now you've got proof.

Megan clenched her fists, revelling in a brief moment of triumph before another detail caught her attention as she was about to keep scrolling for further evidence. Sitting beside Amelia, on guard against any threats, was a white fluffy duck with a bright orange beak. Quackles.

Winded, Megan sat back, her mind racing. Stef and Sophia had been telling the truth. She must have bought Quack for Amelia; if he had been a present for Luka, he wouldn't have existed at the time Amelia was born.

What is real and what isn't? How are you supposed to know?

Megan clutched her head as the voice fought for supremacy. Confusion ran in ever-decreasing circles in her mind, a dizzying kaleidoscope of thoughts that she couldn't control. Was she remembering Stef's photo correctly? She couldn't trust her memory to have preserved an accurate mental image.

Just what is there left for you to trust?

She was outside Stef's office before she realised, no memory of leaving the study or taking the stairs, but the phone was still clutched in her hand. She didn't pause to knock, and Stef spun round in surprise at the sudden intrusion.

'What's wrong?'

'I have Amelia's baby pictures.' Megan thrust the phone at him.

251

'Is this your old phone?'

'I found it upstairs. It has all the early pictures of Amelia on it. Look.'

Stef glanced at the image on the screen but said nothing, as if awaiting her next move.

'I told you she wasn't born with masses of dark hair. She's completely different from the baby in the photo you were hiding.'

'I wasn't hiding it. I told you—'

'You told me it was Amelia. Clearly it wasn't. Where is the picture? I want to compare them.'

'I'll ask Soph to find it, if that's what you want.'

'Why did you lie to me? You knew the photo wasn't of Amelia. You knew.'

'I didn't want you to be upset.'

He's getting flustered.

The voice drove Megan closer, almost nose to nose with Stef. 'Who was the baby? Was it Luka?'

'No, it wasn't Luka, for God's sake. Can we talk about this later? I'm right in the middle of something.'

'No, we can talk about it now.'

Stef shoved back his chair, rising abruptly to his feet. 'What if I don't want to talk about it?' he snapped.

Megan took a step back at his visible anger, so rare in her even-tempered husband.

'It's all about what you want! Ever since this started, I've had to tiptoe around so you don't get upset! What about what I want, for a fucking change?'

'Stef . . .' Megan was shocked by the sudden torrent, suddenly uncertain of her previous determination. 'I didn't mean—'

'I know exactly what you meant!'

'I only want to know the truth. Is that too much to ask?'

'What truth do you think you're going to find, Megan? I'm sick of you accusing me. Everything I did, all those years growing up, everything I'm doing now, to try and help you the best I can, and all you do is throw it back in my face!'

'It doesn't feel like you are!' Her voice rose to match his.

'Because you're too busy seeking out some fucking conspiracy to see how hard I'm trying!'

'I know I'm being lied to, Stef!'

'We're trying to save your life!' he almost screamed. 'Don't you understand? You came this close to death, and even closer to taking another life with you!'

Megan opened her mouth to scream back, but his words penetrated her subconscious before she could and it robbed her of volume.

Another life?

'What do you mean?' It came out hushed.

Stef shook his head violently. 'No, you're not turning this back to what you want again. I mean it, Megan!'

He strode to the door and snatched it open.

'I've had enough!'

Megan watched in disbelief as he stormed down the stairs. She heard the slam of the front door, followed by the throaty engine of the Cayenne revving, its tyres grinding heavily into the gravel as Stef spun out of the driveway.

He had left her alone.

Chapter Twenty-Eight

It took Megan a few minutes to recover from her shock at Stef's reaction. Part of her immediately wanted to rebel against every obstruction he had put in place: ransack his office, scatter knives around the house, rescue her iPhone and send out a long, rambling post about everything she'd been through, put the lock on the front door so he wouldn't be able to get back in.

She did none of those things.

Instead, she returned upstairs to the study and settled herself in the wicker armchair with her old phone and the landline handset. This time she summoned the stored numbers, pleased she had never got round to clearing the phone and selling it online. Flicking through the contacts, she found the number for Eve's Brooklyn apartment and copied it into the landline.

When she heard the international dial tone, she breathed a little more easily. As she waited for it to be answered, her eyes were instinctively drawn to the framed studio portrait of Sophia, Eve and Amelia that hung in the little gallery on the wall. Eve, very tall, slim and angular, with rectangular glasses, a long face and short, near-black hair she styled into a quiff, looked so completely different to the blond Sophia and Amelia. It seemed unfair that she had carried the child, endured a difficult pregnancy and a long, agonising labour, only to bear no resemblance to her.

Luka doesn't look much like you either.

She ignored the voice this time. She didn't like that observation.

'Hello?'

'Eve?'

'Hold on a minute, she's right here.' Eve's cousin lived in the apartment full time to take care of the place when Eve was in the UK. 'Who's calling?'

'Tell her it's Megan.'

A moment's movement, background noises growing louder. 'Megan, hi,' Eve's voice said. 'I wasn't expecting to hear from you. What can I do for you?'

'Sorry to call, but I was wondering if I could ask you a question that's been annoying me.'

'I guess.' Careful, entirely neutral.

'Exactly when did you fly out to New York?'

A pause. 'Why do you need to know that, Megan?'

'I'm trying to get a timeline clear in my head. My memory's still not great. I'm struggling to put events in order.'

'Let me think a minute. The days all blur into one when I'm here. It was ... I think it was the day before you were sent home.'

That can't be right.

Megan frowned as she processed the reply. 'You didn't leave while I was still in the neurology unit?'

'No ...'

'I'm sure Sophia said you flew out just after I had surgery.'

'Maybe she meant I was away someplace else. I was in Oxford for some lectures and then I went up to Edinburgh – easy to get confused. So, how're you feeling?'

'Confused, mostly.'

The noise level rose again: a yappy dog barking in the background, a baby fussing for attention, the clink of glasses and the chinks of cutlery against plates and easy laughter.

'Sorry, it's busy here. My cousin's got all her friends round for cocktails. Hold on, I'll go on the balcony.' Footsteps as Eve moved outside.

'I'm also calling to ask you about Dr Macaulay. Do you know him?'

Eve's tone sounded more relaxed, on surer ground. 'I know *of* him. I've met him at alumni events a few times; he has quite a reputation at Cornell.'

'For what?'

'Pushing the boundaries to achieve what others believe isn't possible.' Eve was typically forthright. She didn't censor her speech, she said exactly what she thought. 'He's always been known as a maverick, but quite brilliant. He rocked a few boats in California, I can tell you. I know people from New York who moved there to be treated by him. That's how highly regarded he is.'

'So why did he give it up to come to the UK?'

'I heard rumours of problems. Probably slept with a patient – that's what usually happens. I don't really know, but I can probably find out. Why the interest in Barnard Macaulay's background?'

'He knows everything about me, only seems fair I learn a little about him.'

'Want to discredit him?'

Megan couldn't help but grin at the conspiratorial tone. 'He tried to make me have ECT.'

'Make you?'

'I'm sectioned, so it could be done without my permission.'

'Did you go through with it?' Shock crept into Eve's voice.

'No. I had agreed, I thought it was for the best, but I couldn't do it in the end. I was too scared of what it would do to me. I mean, we've all seen—'

'*One Flew Over the Cuckoo's Nest*,' Eve finished for her, cautious again. 'Are you still experiencing episodes?'

'The psychosis is controlled by medication and the therapy sessions are helping me understand the condition and the symptoms.'

God, she sounded like a brochure for the Grosvenor Unit.

'That's good. So you feel more like yourself?'

'Not entirely, but a lot more stable. I'm much more aware of how the psychosis affects me, so I can deal with it better.'

It now felt very important to refer to it as 'the' psychosis. 'My' psychosis made it part of her, established an irrefutable link that she couldn't allow.

'It's not permanent, is it?' Eve asked.

'No, Dr Mac says I'll recover. I *am* recovering.'

'That's great to hear, Megan, really. It must have been scary for you.'

'Terrifying,' Megan admitted. 'It's awful being out of control without even knowing it.'

'I'd say I can imagine, but I really can't. You've gone through a lot.'

'So, when are you coming back to the UK?' Megan attempted a smooth change of subject, not wanting Eve to ask too many probing questions. It no longer came naturally to her and she knew Eve wouldn't be fooled for a second.

'Pretty soon,' Eve said, casually evasive. 'Listen, I'd better go before everyone drinks the apartment dry.'

'Thanks for speaking to me.'

'Anytime.' A pause. 'You're going to be OK, Megan.'

Megan hung up with more questions than answers yet feeling slightly reassured Eve had engaged in the conversation. She didn't know why, but she had expected her sister-in-law to hang up, an intuition powerful enough to invoke a feeling of deep unease, even though she couldn't fully understand why.

The voice didn't seem to have any explanation to offer, for once. With no answer forthcoming, Megan scrolled idly through her contacts, wondering who else to call while she had the chance. Her finger stilled by one name. Claudia was her closest friend from the small group she met with regularly, the one she was most likely to confide in.

'Claudia, it's me.'

'Megan? Oh my God, I didn't know when I would hear from you!'

'Sorry it's been so long.'

'You don't have to apologise! We've all been keeping our fingers crossed for you. How are you? It's been absolutely ages since we last had an update from Stef. I suppose he must be busy looking after you.'

'Yes, I suppose. I'm OK, mostly.'

'Have you recovered from the operation?'

'Which one?'

A pause ripe with confusion. 'The surgery for the bleed on your brain.'

'Oh. That. Yes, all seems to be fine now. I have a little scar and I get headaches, but there was no permanent damage, apparently.'

'You don't sound completely convinced of that.'

'I'm not convinced about anything these days.'

'What do you mean? And what other operation did you think I was talking about?'

'The hysterectomy.'

'Oh, yes.'

Megan gulped a breath of air into her suddenly empty lungs. 'So I definitely did have a hysterectomy?'

'Yes . . .' Utter confusion in Claudia's voice made the reply sound like a question again. 'I don't understand, Megan. Why would you not know?'

'I'm having some memory issues.'

'How awful! Can I do anything to help?'

'It would help to know what Stef's told you.'

'Well, he last called when you were in hospital again. He said you were quite weak and easily distressed, that you'd had some mental health issues and we should all wait till you were feeling more yourself before we got in touch with you. We had to respect your doctor's orders. I hope you didn't think we'd abandoned you.'

'Not at all,' Megan said, weakly, trying to take in the avalanche of words. 'I've not really been up to visitors anyway.'

'Just say the word when you're ready, we'll take you for the best lunch you've ever had! We've missed you! And you must be dying for a drink after so long.'

'I haven't really thought about booze, actually.'

'You're a better person than me! My nine months dry were

absolute torture. At least you didn't have hold off any longer. I had to wait ages till breastfeeding was done with.'

'What do you mean?'

'Well, you didn't have to breastfeed, did you?'

'Breastfeed?' Megan whispered, abruptly robbed of breath, barely able to speak.

'Megan, are you OK? Have I said something wrong? I'm so sorry if you didn't want to talk about it. I think I should go. I've upset you.'

Don't let her hang up, you're so close to the truth.

'No, you haven't! Claudia, don't hang up, please.'

'You seem really confused, darling, I don't want to make anything worse.'

'You're not making it worse, I promise.'

'Shall we talk about something else? What have you been reading? I'm completely hooked on *Shantaram* at the moment. A trip to India might be on the cards!' Claudia babbled away, doing her best to provide a distraction. 'Are you still there?'

'Yes, I'm here. Claudia, this question is going to sound really strange, but please don't refuse to answer—'

'What is it? Why would I refuse to answer?'

'Was I really pregnant?'

The silence went on too long; Megan checked the phone display to make sure she hadn't hung up.

'Claudia, please answer, I need to know.'

'How can you not know?' Sheer disbelief broke through the confused tone.

'I have something called dissociation. It means my brain blocks out memories, so I can't remember what's real and what isn't. So I'm not sure whether I really was pregnant or not.'

'Well, yes . . . you were. You were pregnant.'

The rush of emotions made Megan grip the chair arm, certain she was about to faint. A maelstrom of disbelief and achievement, euphoria and rage, all battling for supremacy. She realised her lungs weren't functioning and she gasped air desperately, trying to keep the threatening black spots dancing across her field of vision at bay.

'Such a neat little bump,' Claudia went on. 'I was so jealous; you hardly put on any weight and you were so good about using the stretch mark oil, not like me—'

'What was the baby's name?' Megan whispered.

Another awkward pause. 'Well, you didn't name him, did you?'

'But it was a boy.' A statement, not a question.

'Yes . . .'

'Why didn't I name him?'

'I'm sorry, Megan, I can't talk any more now. I've got to collect the kids, and I'm already late. I'll have to go.'

'Just a couple more minutes.'

'I have to go,' Claudia repeated. 'I'll call you soon. I'm sorry . . .'

The phone clicked as she cancelled the call and Megan was left with a ringing silence and a feeling of triumph. Of complete, overwhelming vindication.

Chapter Twenty-Nine

Before

The car parked outside the Crawley house was unfamiliar and Stef made a note of it as he drove past. The place had been empty since the death of Mrs Crawley a few months ago, her passing solemnly reported by a neighbour. Megan's whereabouts were unknown because Stef hadn't had the guts to ask.

Probate seemed to be dragging and he had taken it upon himself to check the property was secure whenever he had to visit his parents' old home. After so long avoiding the area entirely, it still felt horribly uncomfortable each time he returned.

He didn't come here often, only when the tenants needed help with a damp patch or dislodged roof tiles. His parents had settled in the Lake District, in a little stone cottage on the edge of Threlkeld, enjoying a quiet retirement of long walks and unhurried pints in tiny ancient pubs, and had no desire to rush down to London for home maintenance.

Taking over their responsibilities had inspired Stef to dip his toes into the housing market. His property company was in its infancy, but it took up much of his time; finding suitable investments involved long days hanging around at auctions. He liked being his own boss. He had done the obligatory stint in the City and hated every moment of being an underling. Life was more uncertain now, but he was confident he had done the right thing and was determined to make a go of it.

He should have visited last week but had been caught up in his current prize, a crumbling maisonette in the depths of a brutal Shadwell estate that was causing challenges far beyond central heating and plastering.

It took longer than expected to access and assess the old boiler and decide it wasn't worth summoning an engineer to resuscitate the ancient beast. Promising the tenants he would source a replacement before his working day ended, he retreated to the leased BMW he was struggling to afford to make the necessary phone calls.

Much haggling and disagreeing with his suppliers later, he completed the purchase and drove slowly back down the avenue. The car was still outside. With a sigh, he pulled into the kerb. No doubt it would be an estate agent attempting to take marketable photos, but he had to check, even though he dreaded venturing near the front door, near the ghosts that would certainly be waiting to greet him.

He stayed in the car as long as he could, unnecessarily shuffling paperwork into neatness as he tried to calm his thoughts. He had forcibly blocked so much from his mind in the intervening years since Sophia's attack, refused to entertain the demons that had followed him despite his escape efforts.

Isaac had been right; Stefan's blackout memories had not been permanently lost. Gradually, they had returned. Disjointed, no logical order to them, sudden, crystal-clear flashes that seemed to come only in the depths of night and jerked him awake, heart racing and dripping with sweat, Sophia's name painful on his lips as he begged her forgiveness from his empty bedroom.

They hadn't come quickly; it had taken several years before he could piece the flashbacks together into some kind of timeline. He still didn't remember everything. Parts remained stubbornly in darkness, perhaps gone for ever, conspicuous in their determined absence. But he knew enough, and now the whole sorry film was playing, uninvited, through his mind.

Weaving his way home down the silent avenue, the gentle rustling of the trees his only company, an unexpected screech of a mating fox making him jump and stumble, falling against a garden wall. Managing to right himself, he heard the voices, on the opposite side of the road, getting closer.

He saw them, Isaac and Sophia. Sophia clutched a bottle of Smirnoff Ice. Isaac, empty handed, guided her with an arm around her waist, much closer than he would ever usually get to another person. He was wrapped up warm against the night's chill in a beanie and gloves and a parka Stefan mutinously recognised as his own. Sophia was clad only in her yellow dress, stained with cranberry mixer which in the dim streetlights looked like blood. Too drunk to feel the cold.

A screech of greeting from Sophia, rushing across the road to embrace Stefan, attempting an uncoordinated kiss that he struggled to fend off. Her eyes were glazed, speech slurred.

'I brought your phone! It was in the garden! I've given it to Isaac for you.' Her arms, sticky with spilt alcohol, were suffocating, a noose around his neck, and he had to force her away.

Hurt contorted her face, her emotions awash in a sea of vodka, and Stefan tried to stammer an apology. She stumbled back as if he had slapped her.

'Sophia, come on.' Isaac stepped closer to her again, putting his arm around her. 'I'll walk you home.'

'I want Stef to walk me home!' Her inebriation made her sound very young, a child who wasn't getting her own way.

Stefan slumped against the wall, too tired for her advances, shaking his head stubbornly. 'I'm going to bed, Soph. You're just a kid; I'm not getting into anything with you.'

Hurt turned to fury in an instant, outrage at being thwarted in her pursuit of him. Stefan let it wash over him, unable to bring himself to care. Isaac could take responsibility for once. Sophia wouldn't wrestle him into a clinch on her doorstep.

Sophia fought herself free of Isaac's restraining arm. Stormed off in the direction of her own home, her heels clipping angrily against the pavement, echoing down the quiet road. Veered sideways at the last moment, disappeared down the narrow alleyway that led to the allotments. Stefan closed his eyes, fighting the waves of nausea.

'Make sure she gets inside safe.' A mumble to his twin, shoving him away as he offered a balancing hand. 'Go with her!'

No reply from Isaac as he set off at a jog in pursuit of the vanishing teenager.

'Oh, fuck off, Isaac!' he heard Sophia screech. 'I'm not interested in you, and neither is my sister, so you can stop following us around like a lost puppy!'

Stefan couldn't hear Isaac's reply, if he made one, and no further protest reverberated along the sleeping street. Relieved to have escaped, Stefan didn't bother to look back as he stumbled away in the opposite direction.

It hadn't occurred to him to ask Isaac to return his phone.

Brought abruptly back to the present as his slack hands

dropped the paperwork, spilling it into the footwell and across the passenger seat, Stef realised he was on the verge of tears. He could taste the stale alcohol and raw nausea cloying his mouth as if he were still living that night.

He leapt out of the car, needing air, needing water. Needing salvation.

'Hello?' he called loudly as he approached the ajar front door, not wanting to scare whoever was inside.

'Who is it?' a very familiar voice called back, and Stef's heart leapt, uninvited, into his throat. The demons retreated, temporarily defeated by hope.

Footsteps came from further into the house and, a moment later, Megan appeared. He immediately noticed how much shorter her hair was, a neat bob lightened by honey-coloured highlights. Apart from that, she looked like no time had passed at all.

'Oh, Stef, it's you!' For just a moment, her old smile shone, but it vanished before Stef could appreciate it. Megan crossed her arms tightly across her chest, drawing herself up to her full height. She took a step that effectively blocked his entrance to her family home. 'What are you doing here?'

He stumbled unnecessarily over his explanation. 'I was checking on my parents' tenants, saw the car and thought I'd better have a look who it was.'

'It's been a long time since you graced Marlborough Avenue with your presence.' Her words were icy, ends bitten off.

'I'm sorry I didn't stay in touch. I wanted you to have a fresh start without me. I thought it was for the best.'

'You could have done me the courtesy of explaining that.' He could see how firmly she was controlling her emotions, but she couldn't prevent tears gathering in her furious eyes, betraying her. 'Do you know how it felt, to call you and hear that message saying your number was no longer in service? The one person I thought I could always turn to.'

'I'm sorry,' he said again, useless words.

'I think that hurt more than Dad leaving. You were my last support.'

'I didn't mean to hurt you.'

'Neat cliché,' she said sharply. 'Anyway, I'm afraid I'm rather busy. Nice to see you again.'

She turned away, ready to close the door on him.

'Wait, Megs, don't walk away!'

'Why not? You did.'

He took a chance, reaching out to take her hand, preventing her from moving away. He could have expected anger at his betrayal, but this cold fury had taken him aback. He had been so absorbed in himself, in his pain, that he hadn't considered how she would suffer, abandoned all over again.

Megan froze, snatching her hand free, but she stayed within touching distance and when he took a step closer, she remained still.

'Don't think you can just turn up here and expect everything to be OK.'

'I don't think that, but I want to make everything OK. I can help you with this.' He indicated the dustsheets and pots of paint cluttering the narrow hallway.

'I don't need your help.'

'This place will never sell without a makeover. It hasn't been touched for years.'

'What do you think I'm doing?'

'I've plenty of trade contacts, they'll get it sorted in no time. And I don't mind doing a bit of labour with you.'

He could see her resolve wavering as she acknowledged the task ahead of her.

'I was sorry to hear about your mum,' he added.

Megan shrugged irritably. 'She's better off, really.'

He nodded, unable to help agreeing. 'Let me help you with the house. I can't make up for abandoning you, I know that, but at least I can make some amends.'

She shook her head firmly, refusing to look at him.

'Do you have the time to do it all yourself? What do you do now?'

'Planning office in Tower Hamlets. Boring as hell, but I needed something with flexi-time because of Mum.'

'It must have been bad before she died.'

'Hell,' she said tersely. 'Look, come in if you must. I want a coffee. If you can spare the time.'

He couldn't; he was meant to be on his way to meet his builder in Shadwell and there was, after all, good reason why they hadn't spoken in so long.

'Plenty of time.'

He sent a text to the builder as Megan boiled the kettle and assembled two mugs lightly stained with tannin.

She still remembered how he took his coffee – almost no milk and the tip of a teaspoon of sugar. It made him smile. He saw her body relaxing as she moved around the kitchen, slowly accepting his presence, guard very much up but no longer entirely hostile.

'What are you doing with yourself these days? Still in the City?' she asked as she set his mug in front of him and sat opposite him at the dusty kitchen table.

'No, I escaped last year. Started my own company, buying and renovating wrecks of houses.'

'I didn't realise you were so handy.' A barbed comment, but without any real bite.

'I'm not. I've got a good team of builders, sparkies and plumbers on hand, all collected from my local.'

'Where are you living?'

'Renting on the Isle of Dogs. Riverside balcony and a nice view of Greenwich.' He ducked his head. 'You should come and see it sometime.'

She raised an eyebrow but didn't acknowledge his cheek. 'Are you married?'

'No. There's no one at the moment, actually.'

'Oh, come on, Stef, you've never been short of female attention.'

'I haven't had the time recently. Too busy getting the company established and making a turnover. What about you?'

She shook her head. 'Just casual dating. It was hard to keep a relationship going with Mum being so unwell.'

'What went so wrong?' He made the most of the sudden thawing to keep the conversation going.

'We never managed to get her stable after what happened to Sophia. Dad leaving didn't help. The doctors tried her on all sorts of different meds, but none of them really helped. She was either completely manic or trying to throw herself on to the train line, no in between. She went into a psychiatric unit for quite a while.'

'That must have been a relief.'

'It's not the done thing to admit it, but yes, it was. Let me graduate with a decent degree, at least. I hoped she'd stay there, but you know what NHS funding is like. She had carers once she was discharged, but it was a constant battle stopping her from harming herself.'

'Were you doing all this on your own? Where was Sophia?'

'Travelling. Still is, actually. She's in the States at the moment, doing bar jobs in New York.'

'How is she?' He could hardly bring himself to ask.

'Physically, OK. Mentally, who knows? She says she went travelling to find herself, but I don't think she's got a clue what she's looking for.'

'Has she ever remembered anything about that night?'

'Not a thing. I doubt she ever will now, and it's not like there's any hope of a conviction. She won't talk about it, anyway, prefers to pretend nothing ever happened.'

A pause in conversation for them to drink their coffee, not exactly awkward, but certainly not comfortable.

'What did your mum eventually do?' Stef finally asked. 'If you don't mind me asking.'

'Hanged herself. We took everything else away, so she didn't have many other options. It wasn't me who found her; it could have been worse. The poor carer.'

'Not pleasant. I'm sorry.' An image flashed unwanted in Stef's mind, dark red against pale skin, a yellow dress stained first with alcohol, then blood. He cleared his throat uncomfortably. 'Can't be many good memories for you in this house.'

'Probably the same for yours, what with Isaac and everything.' Her eyes flicked away from his, her fingers grasping a lock of hair.

'It affected my parents more than it did me.'

'He was your twin, Stef.'

'He was a stranger to me.'

'What do you mean?'

270

Stef shrugged, realising he'd given too much away. He hadn't seen Megan for years; they were no longer part of each other's lives. She didn't need to hear about Isaac's past.

Megan sipped her coffee, shaking her head as if dislodging unwelcome thoughts. 'I always felt sorry for him. He didn't seem to fit in anywhere.'

Stef had no reply to that; even now, the memories of Megan's sympathy for Isaac made him grit his teeth. 'Do you and Sophia keep in touch?'

'An email once a month, not much information, just to let me know she's still alive. She prefers to keep her distance. I hope one day she'll come home and we'll be able to have a proper relationship again, but it's up to her, I guess.'

'So, what are your plans for the house?' He changed subject before he seemed too interested in Sophia.

'Just try and make it saleable. Even if I do a bit of painting and put some cheap carpet down, it might help.'

'I'll get my crew round soon as I can. I can't offer all day, every day, but I'm happy to help as much as I can.'

She averted her gaze again, still awkward in accepting his help. 'Thank you,' she said quietly. That was reward enough for him.

Over the coming weeks, they filled a skip with old furniture and worn carpets, stripped wallpaper and sanded doors. Stef arranged for his roofer to do repairs, used his trade contacts for a new bathroom suite. One night, he stayed until midnight varnishing the skirting boards while Megan completed another coat of magnolia. It was then he managed to glimpse Sophia's email address, as the monthly dutiful few lines arrived and the notification lit up Megan's phone, safely out of harm's way on the table. He quickly took a photo before she turned around.

In the early hours of the morning, in the safety of his bed, he wrote Sophia the truth, or what he remembered of it, seeking absolution he was unlikely to receive. Too long, too emotional, too many drafts attempted then deleted and he nearly lost his nerve and scrapped the whole idea. Half a bottle of Grey Goose helped him eventually press send, his soul bared, the whole sorry story of his idiocy, his guilt, laid down in black and white. And the final plea, which he had no right to make.

'Please don't tell Megan. She'd never forgive me for abandoning you.'

He didn't expect a reply and, when one eventually came, it took hours to work up the courage to read it. Compared to his endless sentences, Sophia's response was short to the point of bluntness.

'Some closure is better than none. Megan says you're back on the scene – if you don't fuck it up, I won't tell her.'

When he steeled himself to ask Megan for a drink, cautiously buoyed by Sophia's email, she declined unceremoniously. He asked again, was rejected again. Finally, she agreed to accompany him to the pub after a long evening stripping ancient glued-on wallpaper, staying for the one drink he had promised. The next time he asked, they shared a bottle of wine in a tiny craft bar on Brockley Road and, at last, talked like the old friends they had once been.

At the end of the project, he invited her out for dinner and the night turned into an Upper Street bar crawl that ended with her in his bed.

Stef knew then, one day, he would ask her to marry him.

Chapter Thirty

The temptation to head straight for Upper Street and wander the bars until he couldn't remember his agitation was so strong that Stef nearly hadn't made it to Sophia's house. When he did arrive, he immediately wished he'd chosen the drinking option.

'You walked out and left her?' Sophia had practically yelled in his face. 'What the hell is wrong with you?'

'I didn't know how to answer her! I had to get away before I said the wrong thing and tipped her over the edge.'

'And leaving her alone in a heightened state is highly unlikely to "tip her over the edge", is it? Come in while I get Amelia ready. Fuck knows what'll happen if I send you home on your own.'

Now he waited in the kitchen for Sophia to wrestle her daughter into clothes, unable to stay still, alternating between bouncing on the soles of his feet and biting at a ragged nail. Amelia, naked save for her nappy, found it more entertaining to slalom through the house.

He tried ringing the home phone, his fingers suddenly too

large to efficiently manage a smartphone screen, but it was engaged each time and he gave up after the third attempt.

'Amelia, I will put you in the car naked if you don't come here!' Sophia bellowed. 'We need to go!'

'I'm not having a naked toddler in my car!' Stef yelled in horror, with visions of being pulled over and arrested.

'Oh, shut up!' Sophia stormed back into the kitchen, her own phone pressed to her ear. 'Grab Amelia and force her into any clothes you can find. Hello? Megan? Yes, it's me.'

She listened to the reply.

'I know. He's here. Are you OK? Are you safe?' Another pause to listen. 'We're on our way back, just . . . don't do anything stupid. No, I'm not panicking. Yes, I'm listening to what you're saying, but I still don't want you being alone.'

Stef managed to corral Amelia into a corner of the kitchen, seizing her before she could duck past him. He grabbed the sweatshirt held loosely in Sophia's free hand and wrestled it over her head.

'Do you want to speak to Stef?' Sophia asked into the phone. She glared at him. 'She doesn't want to speak to you.'

'She doesn't have to!' Stef shot back hotly, losing his grasp on the toddler. 'Just tell her I'm sorry.'

'He says he's sorry he's such a complete and utter prick,' Sophia relayed.

She seemed more reassured as she hung up, swapping the phone for a pair of leggings seized from the radiator. Expertly flipping her daughter upside down, she thrust her into them before setting her back upright.

'She sounded fine, to be fair, not like she was on the verge of a breakdown. Maybe she was pleased to get a break from you.

274

Amelia, get your shoes on ... all right, wellies then! Hurry up! Stef, take her backpack and get the car started.'

Miraculously, both niece and uncle did as they were told, and they were on the road minutes later. With Amelia safely plugged into oversize headphones, Sophia barely waited for Stef to steer out into the traffic before she launched into her tirade.

'How did she find out about the photo?'

'Her old phone. Amelia's baby pictures were saved on it. I mean, she didn't have the original to compare so we could always convince her she remembered wrongly.'

'I've told you, we're not lying to her.'

'We've already lied about the damn photo!'

'Maybe you have, but I didn't commit to an answer.'

'Get off your high horse, Sophia.'

'If she knows, she knows. We need to just tell her.'

'We can't!'

'Yes, we can! I've had enough of it, Stef, all the secrets and the half-truths and the sneaking around. I want my family together and I want my sister back.'

'What do you think I want?'

'I don't even know any more, that's the problem.'

'I'm following the programme, like we agreed.'

'The programme's not right for her. You can throw money at the problem, but it won't be fixed until Megan's allowed to confront what caused her all the pain in the first place.'

Stef thumped the wheel in frustration. 'In case you've forgotten, that pain made her want to kill herself. What makes you think it'll be any different now?'

'Because, despite my increasing dislike of Dr Mac, he has given her some coping tools. She's regained a lot more strength than you give her credit for. You're the one who's scared now, Stef, not her.'

Stef opened his mouth to argue, then realised he couldn't. He was terrified of what might happen when they came clean. When they admitted to Megan everything that they had kept from her.

Megan had forgone coffee in favour of a glass of Sancerre and curled up in front of the living-room log burner to slowly savour it. After so long without alcohol, she didn't want to lose her clear head just when she had regained it, so she limited herself to a small measure sipped gradually.

She didn't bother to get up when she heard the key in the front door but was unable to keep from smiling when Amelia erupted into the room and cannonballed on to the sofa.

'Meggie home!'

'Thankfully,' Sophia added, close behind her daughter. 'Sure you're OK, sis?'

'Fine.' Megan raised her glass. 'Want one?'

'God, yes. I'll get it. Stay there while your husband grovels.'

Stef's expression as he strode into the room told her he was rehearsing what he was going to say in his head before he risked speaking. Trying to decide what was least likely to lead to disaster.

'I'm so sorry, babe,' was what he eventually settled on.

'Is that all you can say?' Megan ran her fingers through Amelia's silken hair as her niece snuggled close, eyes already half closed after the excitement of the rush.

'I shouldn't have left you alone.'

'I'm not a dementia patient, Stef,' she snapped, her tone

somewhat modified by Amelia who was beginning to doze in her arms.

'It was still wrong of me.'

'There's quite a lot wrong, isn't there?'

She watched him rake his hair back and transition between leaning against the door and standing upright, re-folding his shirt sleeves, anything to buy himself some thinking time.

'Just wait, Megan.' Sophia was back with glasses for herself and Stef. She scooped Amelia into her arms. 'Let me put her in the buggy so we can talk in peace. Stef, sit down, for God's sake!'

Stef, for once, didn't resist being given orders. He chose the far end of the L-shaped sofa, uncomfortably upright, as there was nothing to lean back against.

'I assume I'm doing the talking?' Sophia asked tartly when she returned. 'Or are you going to say anything?'

'We should discuss this with Dr Mac first,' Stef said, stubbornness in his voice.

'He's not going to be the one to tell her. Fuck, Stef, you're not usually a coward.'

'Stop talking as if I'm not here!' Megan raised her voice to ensure due attention was given. 'I don't give a damn what Dr Mac wants. If you have something to say, get on with it. Or shall I just tell you what I know and make it easier for both of you?'

A quick, wary glance between her husband and her sister.

'What you know?' Stef echoed.

'The photo wasn't of Amelia,' Megan stated firmly.

'No, it wasn't.'

'And I know for sure I gave birth. My friend Claudia confirmed it.'

'You spoke to Claudia?' Stef's expression was similar to the

277

one he had when he had forgotten something particularly important, like his passport as they arrived at security.

'All my contacts were still in my old phone. I called Eve as well, to find out if she was really there or if you were lying about that as well.'

'Megs . . .'

'Eve didn't have much to say really, but Claudia did. She told me I had been pregnant and I'd had a boy. She said I hadn't named the baby, but I did. I named him Luka.'

Megan looked from Stef to Sophia and back again, seeing frozen faces and tight grips on glasses. 'So why has everyone repeatedly told me I don't have a child? I want to know why you've been lying to me, and I want to know where Luka is.'

Stef gulped from his glass, taking too long to realise it was already empty, but still didn't put it down. 'We haven't lied, Megs. You don't have a child. We don't have a son.'

Megan had been expecting a spill of admittance, Stef coming clean in a rush of clichés, begging her to forgive him, and his words threw her. A sudden, terrible thought occurred to her.

'Did he die? Oh God, is the baby dead? Was that why I needed the C-section, because there were birth complications?'

'No, Megan! He's not dead, the baby's fine,' Sophia hurriedly interjected.

'Then why isn't he here with us? Has someone taken him away?' Another traumatic thought pushed its way to the front. 'Did social services take him when I tried to kill myself? Did I try to hurt him?'

'Social services haven't taken him. God, I wish you remembered! It's awful having to do this all again.'

'Again?'

'We've already been through it once, and it made you attempt to kill yourself.' Sophia's lips quirked despite the seriousness of the conversation. 'Let's hope this time goes a bit better, hey?'

'Soph, where is he? Where's the baby?'

'He's with Eve in New York.'

'Why is he with Eve?'

Sophia put her glass down firmly. 'Because he's our baby, Megan.'

Chapter Thirty-One

Before

When Sophia and Eve arrived without Amelia, Stef knew something was going on. The only time Amelia didn't come was when they had arranged a night out together, and he was certain no plans had been made.

'Wasn't expecting to see you two today,' he said as he opened a Montepulciano and poured four glasses while they waited for Megan to come down from her study.

'I texted Megan early to ask if we could pop round for a drink,' Sophia said.

'I haven't seen her today; she's been on a sketching mission all week, so she's locked herself away upstairs. Is something wrong?'

'We're not getting divorced or putting Amelia up for adoption, if that's what you mean.' Sophia picked up her glass. 'Come on, living room.'

Stef followed obediently with their drinks and hoped Megan would hurry up. He was usually perfectly content in the company of his sister-in-law and her wife, but he could sense something tonight, a tension that was never usually present.

'Sorry, sorry.' Megan came flying into the room five minutes later, fingers still stained grey with charcoal smudges. She hated to keep anyone waiting. 'I heard the bell, but I had to finish that section or I'd go mad. How are you both?'

She picked up her wine and took a long drink before settling beside Stef in the curve of the sofa, gracefully curling her legs beneath her.

'We're good.' Eve answered for them, unusually. She wasn't one for small talk.

'Why are you fidgeting like you're sitting on a cactus, Soph?' Stef asked. 'You're clearly here for a reason, so just spit it out, then we can get drunk.'

Sophia and Eve exchanged a glance.

'We've decided we want to have another baby.'

Stef blinked, surprised. 'Wow, that's fast. Amelia's not even a year old yet.'

'Better to have them close in age, get the nappies and night feeds over with together,' Sophia said, somewhat glibly.

'I suppose you want one using your eggs?' Megan didn't seem as taken aback as Stef was and he wondered if there had already been a discussion between the sisters.

'Exactly. And it's going to take some time to organise.'

'How come?' Stef asked.

'I've been advised not to carry another child,' Eve said. 'I've had problems since Amelia's birth and the doctors say it wouldn't be safe to have another pregnancy.'

'Why not wait a couple more years, see if it's possible then?'

'Because my eggs are shit quality,' Sophia said bluntly. 'The probability of them being viable is "extremely low", to quote the consultant.'

'But they're frozen, aren't they?'

'Yes, but if it turns out none of them will step up and do their job, we'll have to consider other avenues. Adoption, maybe, or another of Eve's eggs – we don't know. We're hoping it won't come to that.'

'But you can't carry a baby, right?' Stef was getting more confused by the minute. He drank some more wine in the hope it would help provide some clarity. Megan's expression was deliberately neutral, but he noticed she had sat more upright and knew she was paying close attention to the conversation.

'Nope, my uterus was shredded and now doesn't exist,' Sophia said casually – a little too casually. Stef flinched involuntarily at the description.

'So I assume you've got a plan?' Megan asked.

Sophia nodded, took a visibly deep breath. 'Eve's age would count against us, either for adoption or more IVF in the future, so we've decided to try for a surrogate.'

Megan didn't seem particularly shocked by that statement. 'Via the fertility clinic?'

'No. We didn't like the thought of that. So much that could go wrong, a stranger carrying our baby. All those ITV dramas could be right; it could end up being stolen or deformed by lack of nutrition, or born with withdrawal symptoms from a well-hidden crack habit.'

Stef couldn't help but roll his eyes at Sophia's natural flair for the dramatic. He looked to Eve, who was drinking her wine slowly and looking deeply uncomfortable, shifting continually in her seat and not looking at anyone.

'Besides, do you know how much it costs? Around £50,000. We haven't a hope of getting that much together. Getting the eggs fertilised and implanted is nearly going to bankrupt us as it is.'

'We can help you,' Stef offered. 'The full amount, if you need, for the whole package.'

'No.' Eve spoke now, steel in her voice. 'You already paid for Amelia's conception. We won't take any more of your money.'

'We're offering help, not charity.'

'We won't accept it, Stef. We appreciate the offer, and don't think we're not grateful, but no.'

'Megan, will you do it?' Sophia suddenly blurted out, then immediately looked horrified, as if the words had escaped without her consent. 'Shit. Sorry. I mean, would you consider doing us the biggest act of kindness in the world and carry our child? God, that sounds like we're in *Pride and Prejudice*. I had what to say all planned out and now I've forgotten every word.'

Megan had gone completely still while Sophia babbled on, her entire body locked with tension, gripping her wine glass so hard it looked like it could shatter. Her eyes were fixed on her sister's apologetic gaze. Clearly, this had not been discussed beforehand.

'You won't accept our money, but you'll let your sister carry your baby?' Stef asked in disbelief.

'This about family, about biology, not bank accounts,' Sophia snapped.

'It's certainly bigger than money, I agree.'

'Please,' Sophia said weakly. 'We've no one else to ask.'

'Soph, I don't think I can.' Megan had gone cold, and her hand shook slightly as she gulped blindly from her glass. 'I've never wanted children.'

'It wouldn't be your child, it would be mine. The closest I'll ever get to carrying a baby.'

'Don't guilt her, Soph,' Stef intervened.

'I'm not!' Sophia cried. 'I'm just being honest. There's no one in Eve's family who could do it and, even if there was, the red tape of having a UK surrogacy in America would be insane. Megan's the only family I've got. There is literally no one else I can ask. Unless you suggest that nice woman behind the bar at Slim Jim's would be a good person to try?'

'Then there must be other options.'

'Not with a biological connection to me.'

'And if Megan doesn't want to do it?' Stef held Sophia's gaze steadily, steadier than he felt. 'She's the only one who can make the choice, and she can't make it if she isn't completely sure, if she has any doubts. No one can coerce her.'

'We know that! No one's trying to coerce her.'

'What Stef's saying is we need to make this less emotional,' Eve said quietly. 'Megan shouldn't be influenced by what we want. It has to be solely her decision.'

'Eve, what are your thoughts?' Megan asked.

'I understand why Sophia wants a child that is genetically hers. She feels I have a stronger connection to Amelia than she does, even though that's not true. I can see it from her perspective, but I don't think we have to rush into it like this.'

'You know the reasons why!' Sophia interrupted. 'This way, the baby will still be born from my bloodline. It will be family. I can't bear it to come from some stranger's womb. And I know Megan will do everything right, she always does. She'll take care of my baby until I can. She'll give it the best start possible.'

'They're valid reasons, but we still can't use them to force Megan.'

Megan took a slower sip of wine, one of her favourites, but suddenly bitter and acidic in her mouth. She put the glass down.

'I don't want to be pregnant, Sophia. I don't think I'm cut out for childbirth. I can't even watch a woman give birth on TV without feeling a bit sick.'

'You can have an elective C-section if you don't want to push! I can understand why you don't want your bits torn to pieces.'

'Jesus, Soph, you're hardly being convincing.' Stef looked nauseated.

'I'm just saying there are plenty of options.'

'No option about carrying it for nine months, though,' Megan said.

'Megan, if there was any way I could have a baby myself, I'd do it. I never thought I'd end up like this, having to beg something like this from you. I lie awake trying to think of any other way. It's tormented me from the day the surgeons told me I'd never have children. I always hoped there'd be some medical breakthrough – I don't know, new uteruses grown in stem-cell labs or something.'

'Don't get upset, babe,' Eve said softly. 'We have to stay grounded about this.'

'It's all right for you,' Sophia retorted. 'You still have all your parts. Shit, sorry. I didn't mean that.'

Eve was used to Sophia's habit of speaking without thinking and took no offence, reaching to hold her wife's hand. Sophia squeezed it hard, fixing her gaze on her sister.

'Don't give us an answer now. Think it over. Take as long as you need.' She drained her wine. 'We'll go, give you some space. Please, just promise me you'll think about it.'

285

She barely waited for Megan's replying nod before she dragged Eve out of the front door. Left alone, Stef and Megan sat very still, staring at each other, neither knowing what to say.

They got ready for bed in silence, the weight of responsibility lying heavily on their shoulders but neither of them ready to voice their thoughts. They lay side by side, staring up at the cornicing, the loudest sound their breathing.

'Tell me what you're thinking,' Stef said eventually.

'I can't think, that's the problem. My mind's working so fast I can't focus on any thoughts.'

'Are you scared?'

'Terrified. I'm so shocked she asked me. She knows we've never intended to have children.'

'It won't be our child, though.'

'You know what I mean. Pregnancy. I've never wanted to go through it. I've always thought it seems horrific. I don't even like being around pregnant friends in case they go into labour. I refused to sit next to Claudia when she was getting close to her due date.'

'Sounds to me like you know what your decision will be.'

'It's not that simple. I have to do it. Sophia asked me to. You know what she went through.'

'Yes, and it was terrible, but that doesn't mean you should do something you don't want to do.'

'It's the only way she'll ever have a baby of her own.'

'She has Amelia.'

'You know what I mean. A biological baby.'

'Megs, plenty of women can't have children. They find other ways. Sophia will just have to accept that, for once, she can't have what she wants, and she'll have to consider alternatives.'

'It's easy for you to say that.'

'It isn't, actually. I love her too. She drives me completely mad, but I want her to be happy. That's why we helped with Eve's IVF.' Stef propped himself up on one elbow. 'Let's do some research, find out more about surrogates. There must be some excellent ones out there. We can pay – fifty grand isn't going to cause us any trouble. We can sell one of the flats if necessary.'

'Sophia doesn't change her mind when she's decided against something.'

'Then it's time she learned to be more flexible.'

Megan shook her head, burrowing deeper under the downy duvet. 'You know her better than that.'

'Megs, I'm not having you coerced into something you're fundamentally against.'

'I'm not against helping my sister.'

'You're against pregnancy and childbirth! That says it all.'

'You don't understand, Stef. I let Sophia down all those years ago. I didn't protect her. I didn't even check where she was. If I'd kept an eye on her, the attack would never have happened.'

'You don't know that.'

'I do! I've carried the guilt for so long. Maybe this is the way to get rid of it once and for all.'

'You can't do this out of guilt.'

'Yes, I can. I have to.'

'No, you don't!' Stef raised himself up on one elbow. 'Listen to me. What happened to Sophia was not your fault, and entering into something against your will is not going to make it any better, for either of you.'

Tears gathered uninvited in Megan's eyes and she rolled on to her side so Stef couldn't see. She didn't want him to know how affected she already was. It would just make him more certain about what the decision should be.

'Let's talk about it in the morning. I'm too tired to think now.'

'If that's what you want. Sleep well, sweetheart.' There was relief in his voice as he leaned over to kiss the top of her head, hoping the debate might fall by the wayside in the sensible light of morning.

Megan listened to him settle into his pillows, his body relaxing as he drifted effortlessly into the sleep she knew would not claim her that night. She didn't need to talk about it any more, not tonight, nor tomorrow.

She had already made her decision.

Chapter Thirty-Two

Megan stared, uncomprehending, at her sister. It made no sense.

'How can he be your baby if I gave birth to him?'

Sophia leaned forward over her knees, reaching to put her hand on top of her sister's, an anchoring touch.

'You were our surrogate.'

Before Megan could process what had been said, Sophia plunged on.

'You agreed to carry him using one of my rubbish eggs. We never thought it would work but it did, on the first attempt. It was like a miracle.' For once, there was no sarcasm in Sophia's voice. Her eyes shone with gathering tears.

'I didn't get pregnant with Stef?'

Another fleeting glance between them. 'My fertilised egg was implanted into you,' Sophia said.

'Did the birth go wrong?'

'He wasn't getting enough oxygen, your labour went on for so long. When his SATs dropped, they whisked you off to theatre. Soon as they delivered him, they rushed him off to neonatal

ICU. We didn't even get to touch him until he was stable. While we were following him, you started to haemorrhage on the operating table.'

'So the hysterectomy did happen?'

'Yes, sweetheart, it just happened earlier than we told you,' Stef said.

'Megan, all of it's true, I swear to you.'

Megan wasn't ready to confront that part of the story just then. 'Did you use the same sperm donor as Amelia?'

'No, a different one. Amelia's donor was horrifically expensive. Which may explain why she's so bloody entitled.'

'So I carried your baby and, when I gave birth, you took him?'

'You make it sound like I snatched him from your arms. He was in hospital with you a few days and you gave him his first feeds so he'd have the colostrum. You were so good with him.' Sophia's smile faded. 'I should have realised we weren't being fair on you, letting you care for him. Of course you were going to get attached – your hormones were going haywire. We were wrong to let you bond with him.'

'Was I normal then?'

'Emotional, but, yes, you seemed to be. Are you wondering when the psychosis started?'

Megan nodded.

'It was so gradual we aren't really sure. You were very down after we took the baby home, and you had to stay in hospital another couple of days. We had to wait till you were discharged before we could do the legal paperwork to sign him over to us, and you were definitely struggling by then. Stef said you were wandering around the house, muttering to yourself, and you weren't sleeping.'

A glare was directed at the silent Stef, a blatant signal for him to start playing his part in the conversation.

'I thought it was normal and you were just missing the baby,' he offered. 'I assumed you'd get used to not having him around, then we could get back to normal.'

'Just like that,' Megan said blandly.

'You knew the plan. We'd already drawn up and signed the agreements. You were aware all through the pregnancy that the baby wasn't yours and you were happy to hand him over to Sophia and Eve.'

'Until the psychosis started, you mean.'

'When we went to the solicitor's office, you were saying things that didn't make sense, like you had a fever. It took ages to convince you to sign the papers, and you only did it in the end because you thought we'd left the baby alone in the car.'

'I didn't want to give him up.'

'He wasn't yours to keep, sweetheart. But yes, you're right, the psychosis was telling you the baby was yours. We just didn't realise it then.'

Megan looked at Sophia. 'Did you name him Luka?'

'No. That was the name you called him by, while you were both in hospital. I didn't stop you – we hadn't agreed a name so I couldn't see anything wrong in it. I should have seen that you were struggling to understand what was reality and what wasn't.'

'So what happened after I signed him over?'

'You got worse. Manic some days, like you had all the energy in the world and nothing could tire you out. Then the next day you wouldn't get out of bed and you'd cry for hours. You were talking to yourself, having conversations like there was someone else in the room. That was when we realised we needed to get you help.'

'But I tried to commit suicide before you could?'

'It had been a bad day, that day. You just couldn't cope any more.'

'Tell me what I did.'

Sophia tried to drain the final droplets from her wine glass before answering. 'You jumped,' she said simply.

Stef stood abruptly. 'Let me get more wine.'

'You're not running away now. Sit down,' Sophia barked. 'I'll get the wine.'

Reluctantly, Stef took his seat again, clasping and unclasping his hands, shifting continually as if he couldn't find a comfortable position. Beads of sweat glistened on his forehead, highlighting the pallor of his skin and the new lines that littered his forehead.

'Why did you delete the posts and photos about Luka from my Facebook?' Megan asked.

Stef looked bewildered. 'I haven't touched your Facebook.'

'You must have. Everything's gone. There's not a single mention of him.'

'Megan, you deleted everything. You went through your phone and erased every picture from your photos, every Facebook post, all the congratulations messages. You made me watch you do it. You said you were deleting him from your life.'

'Have you got a picture of him?' Megan whispered.

Stef hesitated, transparently weighing up his options. Finally, he produced his phone and scrolled through before holding it out to her. It must have been a recent picture – Luka had grown

292

longer and broader, more robust than she remembered his little body feeling in her arms. His hair was a shock of dark, thick fuzz and his blue-grey eyes seemed bigger, an arresting colour that immediately drew attention.

'He's beautiful,' Megan whispered, holding the phone as carefully as if the baby was in her hands. 'Why did Eve have to take him to New York?'

'In case you tried to snatch him when you were released from the Grosvenor,' Sophia said bluntly as she returned with a fresh bottle of wine.

'For fuck's sake, Sophia!' Stef cried.

'You thought I was a danger to the baby?' Megan whispered, mechanically holding out her glass for a refill.

'The psychosis was, not you. It made more sense for Eve to take him to New York, where her parents could help, than hide him here or hole up in a hotel.'

'I can't believe you had to take him away from me.' Megan stared down into her wine, tears stinging at the corners of her eyes. Her triumph had faded, replaced by wretchedness gripping her in a stranglehold. 'I'm so sorry.'

'You've nothing to be sorry for. You couldn't help what it was doing to you.'

'But you've missed so much time with him, with your son. Will you tell Eve to bring him home? Are you still scared I'm out of control?'

Sophia shook her head. 'You're dealing with the psychosis, you're getting better. I feel like I'm talking to my big sister again instead of this empty shell that just looks a bit like her.'

'I don't want you to bring him back if you don't think he'll be safe. What if I hurt him again?'

Sophia reached to grasp Megan's hand, the strength of her fingers subduing the nauseating swirl of fears.

'I trust you,' she said simply.

After Megan had fallen asleep on the sofa, exhausted by wine and revelations, Stef and Sophia withdrew to the kitchen. He poured more wine, feeling like his entire world was on the verge of collapse. The thought of history repeating itself made him feel sick.

He watched Sophia make her call to New York, his hand unsteady as he drank.

'Time to come home,' Sophia said softly into the handset. 'We've told her everything. Hang on, I'll put you on speakerphone. No, it's just Stef and I.'

'How did she take it?' Eve's voice asked.

'Surprisingly well. Calmly, no shouting or tearing her hair out. She fell asleep as soon as she ran out of questions, so hopefully she doesn't try to kill Stef when she wakes up.'

'That's not funny!' Stef snapped.

'Will she carry on seeing Dr Macaulay?'

'Yes,' Stef said.

'That should be for her to decide,' Sophia said at the same time. They glared at each other across the island.

'So, you want me to check availability for the return flight?'

'I want you and our son home.' Emotion made Sophia's voice unsteady. 'Think he'll remember me?'

''Course he will. You're pretty unforgettable even to an infant. Let me go start searching for Delta seats. Love you, babe.'

'Love you too.'

'Are we doing the right thing?' Stef asked as Sophia hung up and rubbed roughly at her eyes to conceal her tears.

'What would you know about doing the right thing?'

'Stop blaming me for all this! Blame Dr Mac!'

'Oh, now you suddenly decide he's not God!'

'I trusted him!' Stef yelled, losing the fragile strands of control he had been clinging to all day. 'I believed he was the only one who could save Megan's life!'

'Keep your bloody voice down before you wake Megan and Amelia.'

Stef gritted his teeth and reined his temper in with great difficulty. 'Don't try and act as if this was all me. We both agreed we wouldn't tell her about the baby or the surrogacy or any of this other shit until she was stable and ready.'

'That time would never have come if we'd stuck to Dr Mac's schedule. He didn't want to risk the headlines if Megan succeeded in topping herself second time round.'

'You agreed,' Stef repeated, his words muffled by his tightly clenched jaw.

'When she was having daily psychotic episodes and trying to stab you with vegetable knives, yes, I did! I never imagined we would drag it out for as long as this, letting her believe she really was mad!'

'We didn't lie to her.'

'You should have that cast on a coat of arms and make it the Newman motto, you say it so often. Have you convinced yourself to believe it yet? We've stood by while Megan questioned everything she thought she knew. We've watched her lose trust in us, in herself and in her brain. And we did nothing, all because the almighty Dr Mac told us not to. He's a loose cannon, Stef. We should never have trusted him.'

'His methods have worked for other psychotic patients.'

'Other psychotic patients didn't have to hand over the foetus they had nurtured for nine months. Or find out her husband's role while she was carrying a baby that would never be hers.'

Stef inhaled a sharp breath as he drank a large mouthful of wine and nearly choked. Spraying fine droplets as he coughed, his nose and throat burning, he couldn't speak.

'We can't tell her that, Soph,' he gasped raggedly. 'She has no memory of it; she doesn't need to know. She was never meant to find out.'

'The memory will come back to her at some point. It won't be gone for ever. Imagine the betrayal she'll feel when it does come back if we keep hiding it from her.'

'But not now, not today.'

'No, not today, she's been through enough. We need to let her process this first.'

'I don't want to tell her.'

'I know you don't.' Sophia's voice softened. 'Nor do I. But she's worked it out once and she will again, even if she doesn't remember.'

'Let's wait a while, give Dr Mac some more time with her.'

'You're determined she's going to carry on seeing him, aren't you?'

'It would be worse to suddenly stop, especially after all this.'

'Then find her a different shrink. A good one who follows the rules and isn't a complete prick. Then we can get her off this damn section and back into the real world.'

'Where are you going?' Stef hadn't expected her to put her half-full wine glass down and start gathering her belongings.

'Home. I want to get ready for my wife and my son.'

'Can I do anything to help?'

'You can make sure my sister doesn't go near any balconies.'

Megan awoke expecting to be in turmoil, her brain rapidly reprocessing everything that had been said before she had fallen asleep. Instead, a sense of peace enveloped her, calm and warm, as if she had tipped her toes into a Mauritian ocean as the sun caressed her body. She had been right. Finally, she could start to trust her own mind again.

Manoeuvring herself off the sofa, suddenly starving, she padded through to the kitchen to find Stef, drunk and alone, staring into a glass of whisky. He hated whisky.

'What time is it?' she asked.

'Late. You slept hours. I didn't want to wake you.'

'You can give me my phone back now, Stef.'

He pulled himself clumsily upright. 'Yeah. OK, sure. Sorry. I'll grab it now.'

He stumbled out of the room and Megan went to the fridge, pulling out hummus and olives, goat's cheese and sun-dried tomatoes, piling them on to the dining table and returning to find crostini and breadsticks.

She didn't bother to wait for Stef, loading her plate and digging in with her fingers, relishing the explosion of juicy flavours in her mouth. She'd forgotten what it was like to feel hungry, to enjoy the taste of good food. Her senses felt revitalised, free of the numbness that had overwhelmed her for so long she had ceased to recognise it.

'Here.' Stef placed her phone by her elbow. 'The battery's still charged, somehow.'

'I took it last week, while you were asleep. I found out where the key was hidden.'

'Oh.' Clearly, he hadn't suspected ulterior motives behind her visit to his office. 'What did you want it for?'

'The photos and Facebook posts, but they were gone.'

'You still don't remember deleting them?'

'No. Maybe the memories will come back.'

Stef retrieved his whisky and joined her at the table. He didn't bother to get himself a plate, pinching tomatoes with his fingers and nibbling slowly on them.

'How angry are you?' he eventually asked.

'I'm not angry. I'm not quite sure what I feel, but it isn't anger.' Megan dug into her jeans pocket, producing the pills that were still secreted there. 'I didn't take my meds today.'

'Had you planned all this?'

'Some of it. I didn't know what I'd find, and I certainly didn't expect what I did discover.'

'Megs, you can't just stop that sort of medication. It's dangerous.'

'I know. I'll take it tomorrow, but I want lower doses until I can come off them entirely. You don't know how they make me feel, Stef. I didn't either, until I realised just how much I could do and think about without them. I'll tell Dr Mac tomorrow.'

'You still want to see him?'

'Long term, no. I don't like him, to be honest.'

'I'm becoming less keen on him myself.'

He took a sip of whisky, his grimace giving away how much he disliked the peaty spirit.

'I'm sorry, Megs,' he whispered. 'I thought I was doing the best thing for you.'

'Did you really think that? Or was it just easier to keep me in the dark? Save you having to face up to the problems. You've always preferred the ostrich approach.'

'I just wanted you to be OK, for us to be happy again.' He swallowed hard. 'I didn't want you to end up like your mum.'

'I will be OK, Stef, but it won't be because of Dr Mac. I'll be OK because I want my life back and I'll do whatever's necessary to make sure I'm never a threat to our family again.'

She saw a smile fleetingly cross his face.

'What?' she asked.

'You said "our" family. I thought maybe you wouldn't want to be in a family with me any more, after everything that's happened.'

Megan broke a breadstick in half. 'I can't say I've really thought about the future.'

The remains of the smile vanished.

'Just give me some time, Stef. I don't know what I want at this moment.'

He got up unsteadily, raking back his hair.

'I'll sleep in the burgundy room, shall I?'

Megan nodded slowly, focusing on the food before her. She didn't want to look at the tears in his eyes, the defeated sag of his shoulders, or she would forgive him there and then. And that wouldn't be honest, to herself or to him.

'That would be best.'

Chapter Thirty-Three

For the first time, they faced Macaulay as a couple.

Megan had submitted to close observation that morning as she swallowed her tablets, knowing it would be a poor decision to refuse them, as much as she wanted to. She wasn't stupid; she knew from her mother that psychiatric drugs couldn't just be suddenly terminated. There would have to be a process of withdrawal, a gradual decrease that she was prepared to accept, as long as she knew there was an end in sight.

Stef had complied with her request to bring the blister packs downstairs, and spread them on the coffee table, as if displaying a card trick, before taking his seat.

'Is there a particular reason you want to be present today, Stefan?' Macaulay asked as he went through his usual preparations. He barely glanced at the medication. 'Has something happened?'

'You could say that.' Megan decided to take the reins before Stef could. She was aware she wasn't functioning as well as yesterday. Her limbs were lead weights from the medication and her head pounded, even though the voice remained silent, but she summoned the will to concentrate on her task. 'I asked Stef and Sophia to tell me everything they'd been keeping from me.'

The familiar eyebrow twitch. 'Keeping from you?'

'About my pregnancy and the surrogacy.'

For the first time, the mask slipped. A flash of something that could have been anger, frustration or disappointment, before it was quickly disguised.

'That's unexpected. I didn't believe we were at that stage of treatment yet.'

'Megan found some photos that caused her to question what we'd told her,' Stef said slowly, each word carefully chosen. 'She contacted one of her friends, who confirmed that she had given birth. We needed to answer her questions, to make sure she didn't become distressed.'

'They needed to answer my questions because I knew I'd found out the truth,' Megan interjected.

'I'm surprised you didn't contact me, Stefan.'

'There wasn't an opportunity.' Stef's jaw was tight, teeth gritted.

'So I know everything, Dr Mac.' Megan took over again, unable to help raising her chin in triumph. 'And I don't appreciate the fact that a doctor, who I am supposed to trust, lied to me.'

'Prevented you from knowing information which could cause you to relapse,' Macaulay corrected. 'You were always going to be told about your pregnancy, Megan, but in a controlled way. A safe way.'

'Well, the world hasn't ended, has it? I haven't tried to kill anyone or myself. So I suppose we can call it a success.'

'Perhaps I should tell you a little more about why we were so cautious in revealing too much to you while you were still unstable.'

'Go on.'

'You have a specific type of psychosis called postpartum psychosis. It's a rare condition, and one I have particular interest in. I studied it in depth back in the US.'

Megan allowed herself a moment to process his words. 'It only happens after giving birth?'

'That's correct. Postpartum psychosis is a very serious mental health condition. It can cause women to hallucinate and lose their grip on reality. They often believe people are trying to harm them or their baby. This can make them become violent, either to themselves, the child or those around them. Some-times it can lead to the woman killing her baby, or someone else, in her misguided attempts to protect it.'

'And that's what I've got? Definitely?'

'Yes, you were definitively diagnosed. Your symptoms began in the days after you gave birth, although they weren't recog-nised as psychosis for a couple of weeks.'

Megan struggled to speak around the lump in her throat that had risen seemingly from the stone that had lodged itself in her stomach. 'I've never heard of it.'

'As I said, it's rather rare. This is the main reason why we decided not to reveal your surrogacy to you while you were in the early stages of treatment.'

'Early stages? You were just going to carry on indefinitely?'

'No, there was a treatment plan that Stefan signed on your behalf. Which, unfortunately, we will now have to alter considerably.'

'So you intend to keep me under the section? What if I refuse further treatment from you?'

'You're free to find another psychiatrist to treat you, but they will also adhere to the section.'

'They might not keep me on enough medication to knock out an elephant, though. I'd like to know what each tablet is, please.' Her voice brooked no argument. It was not a request.

Macaulay leaned forward cooperatively, using his fountain pen to tap each blister pack. 'These are antipsychotics called clozapine, which combine with these ones, valproic acid. These are benzodiazepines. They act as a sedative. And these are lithium – mood stabilisers.'

'Quite a cocktail. Is that standard?'

'The NHS prescription would be slightly different, but this is the combination I prefer to use in cases such as yours. It has been trialled and tested and proven successful, I assure you.'

'I don't want to take so many tablets. I'm tired of being drugged.'

'We can discuss reducing the medication, maybe remove the sedatives.'

Stef began gathering up the blister packs. 'I'll lock these away again.'

'I'm not going to crush them into your coffee or take them all at once, if that's what you're worried about,' Megan retorted.

Stef left the room without replying. She doubted he would return.

'You've kept me doped up to make sure I don't ask any awkward questions.' Megan turned to the psychiatrist, accusation making her voice higher than normal. 'I'm not prepared to submit to that any more.'

'That's not the reason you've been on all the medication.'

'I don't trust you. Doctors aren't supposed to do things like this.'

'I admit my methods aren't particularly conventional, but I do believe in them.'

'How many other women have you done this to?'

'I've treated many women with psychosis, both postpartum and otherwise.'

'And none of them have disagreed with your treatment?'

Macaulay's smile was dismissive. 'Some have, yes.'

'Is that why you came to London?'

'I told you my reasons for coming to London.'

'I don't believe you. I don't understand you, Dr Mac. You don't think what you do is wrong.'

'Of course not, otherwise I wouldn't be able to ethically practise.'

Megan gave an incredulous laugh. 'Ethics?'

'You can check, Megan. I haven't broken any laws. My work stays within the ethical boundaries.'

'You must have a very good legal team to convince yourself of that.'

'Why do we need to bring legality into it?'

Megan was enjoying baiting the psychiatrist, but it was a hollow pleasure and she convinced herself to stop.

'Sophia has lost precious time bonding with her son because of you. You made her believe that I would harm him.'

'I didn't advise her to send the child away; that was a decision made by Sophia and her wife. I merely cautioned her that the psychosis made it a possibility.'

'You have an answer for everything, don't you?' Megan sat

back and took a drink of water, feeling as if the meeting was beginning to slip from her control. She didn't want Macaulay to see that she was becoming frustrated; he would view that as victory.

'I think the time has come to discuss your attempted suicide.'

Megan felt herself sit a little straighter as her muscles involuntarily tensed. This was what she had been waiting for, for so long, but now the moment was here it was tempting to retreat to the familiar safety of ignorance.

'Tell me everything,' she forced herself to say.

Chapter Thirty-Four

Before

When Stef saw Sophia's number on his mobile screen, he was tempted to ignore it again. This was the third time she had called in the space of minutes, and he didn't want another argument about Megan. Yes, she had been quite down since she'd signed the parental order process, but that was only to be expected. She'd bonded surprisingly strongly with the baby. She'd be fine once she'd come to terms with his departure.

The phone rang yet again, and Stef gave in, snatching it up.

'Soph, I'm absolutely snowed under here, can it wait till later?'

'Megan's got the baby!' Sophia's voice was frantic, and Stef felt himself freeze.

'What do you mean?'

'She's taken him and gone! Left the house while I was in the kitchen. I don't know where she is!'

'Maybe she just went for some fresh air with him,' he said weakly, already knowing that wasn't the case.

'Stef, for fuck's sake!' Sophia screamed. 'She's snatched him. She wants him to be hers. She thinks he *is* hers! What if she harms him?'

'She'd never harm a child! Are you mad?'

'No, *she's* mad! I've been trying to tell you, but you wouldn't listen, would you? Something's wrong with her! She's losing all grip on reality.'

'Will you stop screaming at me and calm down?' Stef raised his own voice to be heard. 'Is Amelia safe?'

''Course she is. I've had to leave her with the neighbour while I go looking for Megan.'

'OK, good. Well done.' Even he was aware of how patronising that sounded but, for once, Sophia didn't rise to it. 'Where might Megan go?'

'I don't know, Stef! She's *your* wife!'

'She's your *sister*!' he yelled back, panic rising now. 'Where are you?'

'Checking the little park at the end of my street.'

'Wait there for me. Don't go running off till I get there; we need to do this sensibly.'

'Should I call the police?'

'On your own sister? No!'

'They both might be in danger.'

'She won't do anything to her nephew.'

'We don't know that!' Sophia shrieked. 'The way she's behaving, she could do anything, and not even realise it.'

'Just wait there,' Stef ordered.

He couldn't release his frustration by slamming the phone down, so he made do with pounding his clenched fist on to his desk several times before he ran for the car. Sophia's house was only ten minutes away, but driving along Balls Pond Road seemed to take hours.

He parked on double yellows, not giving a damn if he got a

ticket, and ran into the small, scruffy park. Sophia sprinted across to him, seizing his jacket, practically shaking him in her panic. Stef grabbed her by the shoulders, held her still.

'Look at me,' he ordered, needing to show her he could handle the situation. 'The baby will be fine. Megan won't have taken him far, and she'll be looking after him. They'll both be perfectly safe. We're going to find them, and we're going to take them home, OK?'

Sophia's eyes were locked on to his, desperately seeking reassurance, and he felt her make a concerted effort to slow her breathing. When he was sure she wasn't going to start shouting again, he released his grip, allowing her to step back.

'Did she take her car?' Stef asked.

'No, it's still outside my house.'

'Then she can't have gone very far. She hasn't got the pram?' A headshake from Sophia. 'I doubt she'll have got on a bus. She'll have walked. Where's nearby that she might head for? Favourite café or something?'

Sophia stared at the ground as she thought, her fists clenching and unclenching rhythmically. 'I don't know,' she whispered. 'I can't think.'

'You need to think. Come on, Soph, you two hang around this area all the time. Where do you usually go for lunch?'

'The Pavilion Café, in Victoria Park.' Sophia paled even more. 'The one next to the lake.'

She spun on her heel and started to run. Stef caught her before she crossed the road.

'Get in the car! We don't have time to run there!'

Clearly, that idea hadn't occurred to Sophia, and Stef had to drag her to the Cayenne. She wasn't capable of doing her own seatbelt and flinched violently when he reached over to do it for her, shying away from me.

'Soph.' He squeezed her hand. 'It's only me, it's OK.'

She visibly shook herself. 'Sorry. Old ghosts. You've got the same eyes as him.'

There was no suitable reply Stef could give to that comment, so he ignored it and steered the Porsche out into the traffic. It was a short drive to Victoria Park, but Sophia had unnerved him and he narrowly avoided mowing down a cyclist, who performed the traditional London retaliation and kicked the car, swearing furiously. Stef was relieved to abandon the Cayenne at the closest parking spot, but that sense of relief was immediately lost as Sophia shot out of the passenger seat and started sprinting, even before he'd turned off the ignition.

He pelted after her, telling her to slow down, wait for him, but she was fuelled by a maternal instinct he would never know and he was powerless against it. He caught up with her as she neared the edge of the boating lake. The park was quiet, a few people at the café's outdoor tables and the odd dog-walker, but no sign of a lone woman with a small baby.

Together, they hurried around the curve and there she was, by the edge of the water. Standing perfectly still, staring out over the lake, clutching the blanketed bundle tightly to her chest. Her lips moved continuously and, even though they couldn't hear what she was saying, they both instinctively knew the words would make no sense.

Sophia made to leap forward, but Stef caught her arm. 'Wait here,' he ordered. 'Don't go any closer to her. Let me.'

Amazingly, she did as he said, standing stock still as he slowly moved towards his wife. Step by gradual step, taking care not to rush, not to startle her. No sudden movements, no loud noises, even hushing the crunch of his shoes against the gravel.

'Megs?' he said gently. 'Hi, sweetheart.'

She looked up at him with a smile, surprised to see him. 'What are you doing here? I thought you were going into the office.'

'I came to find you.'

'Find me? Why?'

'Because you took the baby from Sophia's house, sweetheart.'

'Yes, I took him for a little walk. Get some fresh air.'

'But you didn't tell Sophia you were taking him or where you were going. She was worried about you both.'

'Was she?'

'You shouldn't be carrying him so far after your surgery. Is it hurting?'

She shook her head vaguely. 'I don't think so.'

'And is the baby OK?'

' 'Course he is. He's fast asleep.' She dipped her shoulder so Stef could see the child's peaceful, sleeping face. 'Why are you here, Stef?'

'I came to take you home.'

'But I like it here. I enjoyed taking Luka for a walk. I haven't been able to see him much since Sophia took him home.'

Stef forced a smile. 'Amelia will be raging that you left her behind.'

'Oh, sorry, I didn't think to bring her with us.'

'Probably best you didn't. Can I give the baby to Sophia now?'

'I want to hold him a bit longer.'

'He'll be getting cold. Sophia will take him to the car and warm him up; we can sit here for a bit if you want.'

He saw her arms tighten on the little bundle. 'But he's mine.'

Stef crouched down in front of her, forcing her to make eye contact with him. 'Megan, he's Sophia's baby.'

'Luka is mine.'

'He's not called Luka – Soph and Eve haven't decided his name yet.'

'I gave birth to him.'

'I know you did, babe, and you did so well to carry him for Sophia, but you knew all along he wasn't ever going to be yours.'

'Why are you saying these things?' Megan stood abruptly. 'Go away if you're going to talk like that.'

She began walking slowly along the side of the lake, her hand rubbing the baby's back soothingly.

'Where are you going?' Stef flapped a hand at Sophia to warn her to remain still and started after his wife.

'Away from you. You're lying to me.'

'How am I lying to you? Tell me what's wrong. Has something happened that's upset you today?'

'Sophia told me Luka isn't mine.'

'And she's right.'

'No!' Megan's voice rose suddenly, startling the baby awake. He started crying immediately. Stef saw Sophia dash forward and Megan clearly noticed as well, for she started moving more quickly, away from her sister. 'I know!'

'Know what?'

'I know, Stef. About you.'

'Megan, give the baby to me,' Stef said firmly. 'He needs his mother.'

'I am his mother!' she screamed.

'Megan, what are you doing?' Sophia cried.

Stef watched Megan look wildly around her, taking a few steps towards the path, before turning sharply and moving back towards the lakeside.

'I need to get away. I can't think with you all here! Just leave us alone. We'll be fine together.'

'Give me the baby!' Stef spoke louder, trying to cut through Megan's babbling.

She changed her hold on the child, taking him in both hands, supporting his head as she held him out in front of her.

'Why won't you leave us alone? What do I need to do to make you go away? You're not stealing him from me!'

She took another, bigger step towards the lake and, for one awful moment, Stef thought she was going to throw the baby into the murky water. He saw her arms tense, her feet set themselves, and he reacted entirely on an instinct he hadn't known he possessed. He leapt forward, wrapping them both in a bear hug. Megan screamed, an anguished sound that caused the few other park visitors to freeze, unsure of what action to take.

Stef held tight as his wife struggled to free herself, lashing out with her feet, even biting at his coat. Then, just as abruptly as it had started, the fight went out of her and she flopped limply in his arms. The baby began to howl, enraged by his treatment.

'Sophia, take him,' Stef ordered, and Sophia rushed to her son, cradling him to her breast, whispering reassurances to him.

Stef held Megan upright, feeling the sobs wracking her body, hearing her jumbled monologue to herself. He was completely out of his depth. Whatever was wrong, he didn't know how to fix it.

★

A few hours had passed since they had returned home from Victoria Park, and Megan hadn't moved since he had steered her to the Chesterfield. The coffee he had made sat untouched in front of her, as did the congealing sandwich. She hadn't even moved her head, as far as he was aware. His calm, capable wife, who always knew the right thing to say and do, was suddenly a mannequin.

At first, he sat beside her on the sofa, holding her hand, trying to gently cajole her to talk. When she remained silent, he thought perhaps she wanted space, so he retreated to a breakfast-bar stool. Still no response. He had run out of ideas and energy; he felt utterly drained.

'How about I run you a bubble bath?' he offered. 'I'll get in with you, if you want.'

That seemed to get a reaction. Megan turned to look at him. He smiled gently, extending his hand, encouraging her to go to him.

'You think I want sex?' she asked, her voice harsh and foreboding, a voice he had never heard before.

'No! I just want to make you feel better.'

'If we have sex, we can have another child, can't we?'

'Another child?' he asked, baffled.

'You've taken away my first child.'

'I haven't taken him away, Megs! He wasn't yours to keep. You knew that!'

'You made me sign papers.'

'They were the legal documents; we went through them all before you gave birth, remember?'

'You want me dead, don't you?'

Utterly bewildered, Stef got to his feet as she moved jerkily

313

towards him. 'Dead? What are you talking about? Of course I don't want you dead.'

'You wanted to throw us into the lake. Luka and me.'

'What? No!'

'I was going to swim away with him, to keep him safe from you. But you grabbed me. You took him from me again.'

'Megan, I'd never hurt you, you know that!'

'I don't know anything any more. I don't know who you are, but I can tell what you're planning. Are you going to kill me tonight, while I'm asleep? Because I'm not going to sleep. I'm going to stay awake and watch you.'

Stef was beginning to feel afraid, so out of control had the situation become in mere moments. He held out his palms, placating, as Megan moved away from him, around the other side of the island.

He watched her snatch up her phone, jerkily dragging her thumb across the screen, punching her index finger repeatedly against it.

'What are you doing?'

'Deleting everything.'

'Everything?'

'Photos. When I was pregnant. Luka's baby pictures. Face-book posts. All the messages I got. Everything. It all has to go.' She looked up momentarily, her eyes gleaming unhealthily, beads of sweat scattered across her forehead. 'Don't come near me, Stef. Don't stop me.'

'I don't know what's going on, babe, but I swear I won't harm you. Not ever.'

'You will. I know you will. You've been wanting to do it ever since we left the hospital. I can hear your thoughts, you know.'

'I think you need to see a doctor. Something's wrong. We need to get you some help.'

'No!' she screamed, slamming her phone down. 'You'll have me put in prison! I'll never see my baby again!'

Stef moved slowly round to her, his arms spread open, as non-threatening as he could be. 'Calm down, Megs, every-thing's going to be OK. No one's going to put you prison.'

'Liar!' she howled, lunging towards him.

He didn't see her weapon until it was too late. He watched in what seemed to be slow motion as she raised the paring knife and slashed. He felt the blade split his skin, a burning sensation, but no real pain. Megan swung again. Instinctively, his hand came up, blocking the next attempt. This time pain flared instantly as the well-honed knife cut into his palm. Instinctively, the other hand grabbed Megan's wrist, squeezing until she cried out in pain. The knife clattered to the floor, sending tiny droplets of his blood across the Cotswold stone flags.

Megan fled. He heard her pounding up the stairs, a door slamming, but he couldn't follow her. He grabbed a tea towel and wrapped it tightly around his hand before carefully raising his T-shirt. Blood swelled from a narrow wound several centi-metres to the left of his belly button. He could see it wasn't deep, but it was starting to hurt now. He found another tea towel and pressed it to the cut, wincing at the sting, which was sharp enough to take his breath away.

Deciding neither injury was serious enough to warrant an ambulance, which would bring all sorts of questions and prob-ably a visit from the police, he scoured the kitchen drawers for something to hold his makeshift dressing in place. The only thing he could find was clingfilm, so, inexplicably thinking of

315

the *Full Monty* scene, he wrapped several layers tightly around his midriff.

He was slow going up the stairs. He hadn't lost much blood, but he felt lightheaded and nauseous all the same. The stomach wound burned mercilessly with each step.

Megan wasn't in their master suite or the main bathroom. He had to haul himself up the smaller stairs to the second floor. Her study door was closed, and he knocked gently, expecting it to be locked.

'Megs, it's OK. I'm fine. You don't need to be scared. Let me in so we can talk. Nothing bad is going to happen.'

No reply. He tried the handle and was surprised to find it allowed him to push it down. Warily, he edged the door open. The study was a small room under the eaves where Megan kept her easel and charcoals. She hadn't done much sketching during the pregnancy, had rarely used the room, in fact, and he wondered what had driven her up here.

The French windows stood wide open, despite the cold wind, and Megan was leaning against the Juliet balcony rails, looking down on to the extension roof below.

'Are you OK?' Stef asked quietly, making no move to go closer to her.

'Did I stab you?' Her voice quivered.

'Just cut me a little. I'm OK. I know you didn't mean it.'

'Are you going to die?'

'No, of course not. I'm hardly bleeding.'

'If you die, I'll never see Luka again. I'll go to prison.'

'I'm not going to die, Megs.'

'Was I supposed to kill you?'

Stef had no idea how to answer that question. He had no

316

clue what was going on, but Megan's rambling was scaring him all over again. She didn't seem to be in control of what came spilling from her mouth. She didn't even look like his wife; her delicate features were contorted in a way he'd never seen before, a terrifying mix of rage and fear and confusion, and her eyes seemed to protrude from a face that suddenly looked skeletal.

He tightened the tea towel around his hand again, hoping she wouldn't see the blood. 'Do you think you should talk to someone?' he asked gently. 'I can call the GP. He'll come to the house to see you.'

She half turned to look at him. 'I can't.'

'Can't what?'

'I can't talk to anyone.'

'Why not?'

'Because everyone wants to kill me. I was meant to kill you so I'd be safe, but I fucked it up, didn't I?'

'What have I done to make you want to kill me?'

'You know what you did!' Her voice rose sharply.

'Do I?'

'I know, Stef! I know everything!'

'Tell me what you think you know.'

'I don't want to tell you!'

'But how can I help you if I don't know?'

'You can't help me.'

'Of course I can, babe. We're a team, we'll get through this together.'

Megan shook her head wildly. 'We're not a team. You betrayed me. You don't understand how you've made me feel.'

Stef dared to take a couple of steps into the room, encouraged when she didn't shrink away from him.

'I won't understand unless you tell me.'

'Get away from me!' Her hands flew to her throat, nails leaving angry red gouges as she clawed, as if trying to free herself from restrictive clothing only she could feel. 'I can't breathe!'

'You're hurting yourself! Megan, stop!'

Her movements stilled as he took another wary step forward. 'Why have you changed?' she demanded, hands falling limply to her sides, suffocation seemingly forgotten.

'Changed? I haven't changed?'

'You don't even look like you.'

'Don't I? What do I look like?'

'Like a monster,' she whispered, turning back to the balcony.

A heartbeat later, she jumped.

Later, Stef would have no memory of his frantic, desperate dash down two flights of stairs. He would not remember scrambling to open the bi-folding doors, unable to fit the key into the lock, trying to unlock his phone at the same time, dropping it repeatedly. He didn't recall screaming at the operator, begging for an immediate ambulance, someone to help him, unable to answer the insistent questions calmly issued.

What he remembered was his certainty that she was dead. Even as he dropped to his knees on the grass beside her, hardly daring to feel for a pulse, check for breathing, he was sure he had lost her. Even as he gave his stuttering responses to the control room operator, confirming vital signs, he didn't quite believe it. She looked dead. Grey skin, eyes closed, but no blood. No yellow dress stained dark red this time. No viscous pool of precious liquid for him to kneel in.

As he threw back his head to the skies, prepared to bargain

318

with a god he didn't believe in, he was certain, in that suspended moment, he saw another figure standing over his wife. A taller, thinner version of himself, silently watching, expressionless face forever that of a young adult. Stef squeezed his eyes shut, denying, and when he dared look again, they were alone.

'Megan,' he heard himself saying over and over again. 'Megs, can you hear me? Open your eyes for me. Megan!'

He could still hear the noise, the horrific thud of her body crashing down on to the kitchen roof that would stay with him for ever. Gripping the balcony ironwork, he had been frozen to the spot, unable to move as he watched her limp form slip down the steep tiles as gravity took charge, dropping her to the lawn below. As he stared, powerless, at her fragile, motionless body, Isaac's voice whispered in his ear.

'*You failed again.*'

'Megan, wake up!' The words came out in a howl as he fought himself not to take her in his arms, rock her back to life.

He had no idea how long it took the rapid-response car to arrive. More paramedics followed, running across the garden with spinal boards and oxygen cylinders and heavy backpacks stuffed full of equipment he was certain would fail to save Megan's life, until she was surrounded by people in green liveried overalls. Someone moved him away and he tried to resist, but he was too weak, from the blood still soaking through his T-shirt or from the certain knowledge he had once again allowed harm to befall someone he had sworn to protect.

Hours later, his wounds were cleaned in A&E, assessed to not need stitches and covered with adhesive dressings. At the same time, several floors above, Megan remained unconscious but otherwise miraculously uninjured after her plunge to the extension roof.

He'd been so sure she was dead.

'She's lucky,' the consultant had said. 'I expect she aimed to avoid the roof, but it broke her fall enough that she didn't sustain any additional damage when she hit the ground. She was already unconscious, so she didn't tense up. Fewer injuries when the body is completely relaxed. Very lucky.'

Was she lucky? Stef had wondered, noting the repetition of the word, the insistence of great fortune. She had wanted to die. What would happen when she woke up and found she hadn't?

He jumped as his cubicle curtain twitched and two uniformed police officers stepped in. Both male, broad and bulky in their stab vests and duty belts, near-identical crew cuts and neutral expressions.

'Mr Newman?'

'Yes?' Stef had no idea why they knew his name.

'We need to ask you a few questions about your injuries.'

'Why?'

'One of your neighbours called us, suggesting violence may have taken place at your address.'

'There was no crime.'

'Yet your wife is currently in intensive care.'

'She tried to commit suicide.'

'Sorry to hear that. Did you two have a row?'

'No. She's been having problems ... I don't know ... mental health stuff, I suppose. She jumped from our second-floor balcony.'

'Miraculous she survived,' the second PC observed.

'So everyone keeps saying,' Stef snapped, then realised to

show temper wouldn't look good. His past experiences dealing with police questions had left their scars and he reined himself in with difficulty.

'How long's she been struggling for?'

'Couple of weeks.'

'You didn't get her any help?'

'I didn't think I needed to. Everyone gets a bit down sometimes.'

His dressed hand was pointedly indicated to. 'Down enough to stab their husband then attempt suicide?'

'I don't know what you're talking about, Officer. As I told you, there's been no crime. I don't understand why you're here.'

The first officer spoke abruptly. 'Did your wife do this?'

'No, of course not! I was in the kitchen when she ... when she jumped. I cut myself when she ... you know ... landed on the roof.'

A doubtful raise of one eyebrow. 'In two places?'

Stef looked back defiantly, challenging the man to ask any more questions.

'The knife slipped.'

Chapter Thirty-Five

Megan could feel herself tugging repeatedly at a lock of hair as she processed everything Macaulay had revealed. She was powerless to stop the self-soothing action. Her body ran hot and cold, horror enveloping her as she realised how close she had come to harming the baby.

'Do you think I would have hurt him if Stef hadn't stopped me?' she whispered.

'You probably intended to, yes. You would have genuinely thought you were keeping him safe from other threats. The delusion was strong enough to convince you the baby would be better off with you and that the only way you would both be safe was if neither of you were alive.'

'No.' Megan shook her head frantically.

'I think I should call Stefan back in.' Macaulay paused half-way to his feet, then made his decision and crossed to the door, calling Stef's name up the stairs before returning to his seat, leaving the door open. 'As I said, Megan, you didn't harm the baby. That's the most important thing.'

'But I would have done.' Megan realised she was crying, tears streaming down her face, and she swiped clumsily at them as Stef rushed into the room, startled by Macaulay's unexpected summons. 'Stef, I tried to hurt Luka,' she sobbed.

'You didn't mean to, babe.' He grabbed her hands, squeezing them tight as she went to grasp hanks of her hair. 'He was fine, didn't know anything was wrong. Just a bit cold.'

'But I took him. I stole him from Sophia. No wonder she told Eve to take him away. How can you even stand to look at me, knowing what I tried to do?'

'Because you're my wife! I love you so much. I wouldn't know what to do without you.'

'I'm a monster.'

'You're not a monster!'

The pressure of his hands gripping hers grounded Megan, allowing her to control her breathing, bring herself down from the heights of anxiety she had inadvertently reached. She had to stay calm, or all this would be for nothing. Macaulay needed to see she was capable of self-control.

She waited, steeling herself, for the voice to begin its urgent muttering, but she could hear nothing except her own ragged breathing.

'Am I ever going to be me again?' she whispered.

She pulled away from Stef, looking back to Macaulay.

'Megan, you were being controlled by the psychosis when you intended to harm the baby and Stefan, and when you tried to commit suicide. You weren't capable of rational thought at that time. That's how powerful psychosis is, and that's why we were so reluctant to remind you of the things that led to its occurrence.'

'That still didn't give you the right to play God with me,'

323

Megan retorted, annoyed that she found the psychiatrist's words reassuring. 'Aren't you supposed to listen to me talk about my feelings? Isn't that what therapy is about? Because I don't think anyone is listening to me.'

'I'm sorry you feel that way,' Macaulay said, 'but now everything is out in the open, we can learn and move on.'

'No, you're not going to make it that simple, like nothing's happened.'

'We can still continue with your treatment.'

'All you want is Stef's money. That's why you don't want me to go to another psychiatrist.'

'I don't want that because I feel we can continue to make progress and I wouldn't want any changes to jeopardise that.'

'You're the one who's jeopardised it! I don't want to work with you any more. How can I accept help from someone I don't trust? Nothing you say will change that.'

Macaulay put his pen down, folded his hands into his lap. 'I'm sorry you feel that way,' he said again, the words glib even while his expression shone with determined empathy.

'Stef, I want you to find another psychiatrist. I understand I still need treatment, but I won't accept any more from Dr Macaulay. I mean it.'

Stef nodded, squeezing her hands again. 'I'll do my best.'

Macaulay gathered his things together, efficient movements, yet giving the impression he was in no rush, as if at the end of a pleasant dinner.

'I think it's best I leave you in peace for today, Megan. If you do choose another psychiatrist, I'll need to discharge you from my practice to theirs, but I'll make the process as smooth as I can.'

'I *will* choose another.'

'Then I'll wait for Stefan to be in touch with me. Please make sure you continue to take the antipsychotics; to stop them would be dangerous. And remember, you're still under the same section conditions.'

'I know,' Megan said forcefully. 'I've no intention of being stupid.'

'Goodbye for now, Megan.'

'Goodbye, Dr Macaulay.'

'Here.' Peering warily into the bedroom, Stef handed Megan a sheaf of papers. He looked destitute; unshaven, eyes red with burst blood vessels, still wearing the same clothes as yesterday, which smelled of dread and stale gin. 'This is the best list I could draw up of London psychiatrists. I think you should pick the one you want.'

Megan accepted the print-outs, arranging them tidily on top of the duvet. It had been easy for Stef to avoid her since Macaulay's final visit to the house; she had done little except sleep. Her body finally seemed to have realised the constant fight-or-flight mode was no longer necessary and she had been poleaxed by its natural response, to hibernate and heal. The voice was still silent and it felt like an awakening of a different kind now, to a world that was no longer full of hidden threats.

'Will you have your tablets?' Stef held his palm out. Gone was the saucer and the careful arrangement. There were, she noticed, also fewer pills.

'Where are the rest?'

'Dr Mac reduced the dosage, like you asked.'

Megan swallowed the pills and waited for him to retreat.

'Have you spoken to Sophia?' he asked, hovering. 'Maybe she can help you decide which psychiatrist you want?'

'I'd like to make a decision on my own, thank you.'

'If that's what you want. Shall I bring you some lunch up?'

'Lunch? What time is it?'

'Nearly two o'clock. You really must have needed sleep. Are you hungry?'

She was about to say no, out of habit, but realised she was starving.

'Can I have a bacon sandwich, please?'

Megan picked up the print-outs as Stef retreated, flicking through them, but was unable to summon the necessary focus, despite her best intentions. Almost all of them were men, she noted. What could men understand about such an entirely female phenomenon?

On impulse, she grabbed her phone, now never far away from her hand, and googled 'Dr Barnard Macaulay psychiatrist'. Just like the first time, a number of relevant entries immediately presented themselves, but now she could take her time scrolling through. *The New York Times* reported on a 'brilliant but unsettling tour into the deepest crevices of our psyche' and the *Los Angeles Post* told the story of his first clinic in the hills of Malibu. But one entry stood out, and that was the one she tapped.

Monstrous Minds and Invisible Enemies: A Journey into Puerperal Psychosis. It was a review of Macaulay's first book, published three years previously, and it lauded the book for its insight and for challenging such a taboo subject. Megan skimmed the plaudits, not caring for the celebration of Macaulay's 'unflinching commitment to conquering a dangerous and sometimes deadly mental illness'. The final sentence drew her attention:

'Dr Macaulay's second book, examining individual cases he has successfully treated, will include his experiences in his new London practice and further explore his commitment to rehabilitating women who have harmed or threatened those dearest to them.'

So that was why he had wanted to keep her as his patient, why he had manipulated her treatment so carefully. It wasn't because he feared she would tarnish his reputation. It was because he needed her story, and needed it to be told the way that would sell the most books.

The instinct to hurl her phone across the room almost overwhelmed her, the wave of rage taking her by surprise.

'What's wrong?' Stef asked, returning with an unappetising-looking bacon sandwich slapped on to a side plate. She had been hoping for toasted sourdough and crisp bacon dripping with fat dollops of ketchup, not this limp meat and dry sliced white.

'Read this.' Megan shoved her phone at him and watched his face tighten as he trapped his bottom lip between his teeth. 'Did you know about it?'

'No, of course not! As if I'd have let you be used as a test subject!'

'Macaulay didn't tell you?'

'Not a thing. I didn't even know he'd written a book. All the references he gave me were for articles and medical journal entries.'

'Didn't you google him?'

Stef shrugged awkwardly. 'Briefly.'

'You mean you read the first couple of entries and decided that was all you needed to know? Or did you just search for the positive reviews?'

He had no reply to that, instead handing her the phone back and proffering the unappealing sandwich again. She was hungry enough to take it and tear off a greasy bite.

'Eve should be back now,' she said.

'I know. You should ring Sophia.'

'I don't know what to say to her. I tried to kill her baby.'

'She's still your sister, Megan. That's all in the past.'

'It still feels very present to me.'

'You mean you're still getting those thoughts?' Horror glinted in Stef's eyes at the prospect of another episode.

'No, not like that! I mean I haven't dealt with what I did. Sophia should hate me.'

'Of course she doesn't hate you. Just ring her, you'll see. She's stood by you through it all, Megs. She wouldn't have done if she was harbouring a grudge.'

Megan knew he was making sense, but it still felt physically impossible to pick up the phone. She handed the empty plate back to Stef, her hunger having triumphed over her foodie prejudices, and waited for him to ferry it to the dishwasher before she reluctantly picked up her phone again.

'I was wondering whether to call you!' Sophia said after barely a couple of rings. 'Stef said you were sleeping, but I didn't know if you were angry or upset or—'

'No, I really was sleeping. It feels like I've got so much to catch up on.'

'That's good, if you're able to rest. Must mean your brain isn't going haywire.'

'Small mercies. Is Eve home? Did the baby remember you?'

'She got back a few hours ago. He didn't scream when I picked him up, so that's a positive. He's a chilled-out little thing, though maybe I'm just comparing him to Amelia, which really isn't fair on him.'

'How is Eve?'

'Pleased to be home. She wants to know when you're coming round to see us.'

'You want me to?'

''Course we do. You need to meet your nephew properly. We haven't got an attic to stick him in whenever you turn up on the doorstep.'

'I know what I tried to do to him, Sophia. You shouldn't let me near him. I'm not safe.'

'Don't be ridiculous. I want you to be an amazing aunt to him, like you are to Amelia.'

'But . . .'

'No buts. Get your coat on and tell Stef to drive you round. Right now. Strike while the iron's hot.'

'Soph, I could have killed him.'

'But you didn't. He's definitely alive. I've checked several times.'

'I snatched him.'

'Yes, I was there, remember? Oh, wait, you don't . . . sorry.'

'I don't trust myself to be around him.'

'He's hardly going to have any memory of it, is he? I can assure you he's not traumatised, apart from by Amelia constantly trying to poke him.'

'I can't do it. I can't put him at risk again.'

'Megan, listen to me. We've done wrong by you. All of us. We're a family – it's about time we started acting like it. This is the first step. Now come and meet your nephew while he's still adorable, because no doubt it won't be long before he's as mad as his sister. See you soon.'

Sophia hung up before Megan could continue with her list of reasons against the plan. Megan stayed where she was for some time, trying to find an excuse not to go, until Stef poked his head round the door again. 'Soph's just rung me.'

'Thought she might.'

'She says stop sodding about and get a move on.'

It seemed there wasn't much else to be done other than to submit. It could be a quick visit. Ten minutes of polite conversation and it would all be over.

Megan got dressed, a hoodie and leggings that had both seen better days, not bothering with make-up or her hair.

Sophia answered the door before Stef could raise his hand to knock.

'Why do you look like you're expecting me to bite you?' she asked her sister.

'I'm scared,' Megan whispered.

'Of me? I wish you had been when we were kids. Come in, for God's sake, the wind's freezing today. We can barely afford the heating bills as it is. If they go up much more, we'll have to send the kids out to work. Amelia would be an excellent debt collector, don't you think?'

Megan didn't respond to the inanely cheerful patter as she followed Sophia down the claustrophobic hallway.

'Meggie! Stef!' Amelia shrieked, barrelling into them, her little arms trying to hug both of them at once. 'Come! Look!'

'They're right in front of you, Amelia, not on the next continent,' Sophia groaned. 'Go into the living room while I put the kettle on. Eve! Megan and Stef are here!'

They settled on the sofa with Amelia crawling over them,

babbling about babies, snails and ducks, waving Quack determinedly in their faces.

'See, she was happy to be reunited with the duck,' Stef said. 'Just took her a while to get reacquainted.'

Careful footsteps sounded on the wooden stairs and a murmur of conversation between Sophia and Eve could be heard. Eve came in first, her smile not quite natural but her body language loose and relaxed, perhaps too deliberately.

'Hey, guys, how are you?' She stooped to give Stef a quick hug before wrapping Megan in a tight embrace. 'So good to see you.'

In spite of herself, Megan found she was hugging her sister-in-law back, putting her apologies and her fears into her grip.

'It's OK.' Eve spoke softly into her ear. 'It's all fine.'

'It doesn't feel fine.'

'Give it time. We're all here for you. God knows you've done enough for us. You know that, right?'

'Thank you,' Megan managed to say, her throat too tight to allow words easily.

'Mommy, sit!' Amelia ordered, breaking the hug as she dragged Eve down on to the sofa, squashing all of them together.

'Did you get the return seats sorted OK?' Stef's tone was stiff, awkward.

'Can't complain. The airline was pretty accommodating.'

'The flights must have been difficult with him being so young,' Megan said, trying too hard to make normal conversation.

'Not so bad, actually. A colleague was flying out as well, so she helped, and my mom decided she'd come back with me and see Amelia. Could've been much worse.'

'Does your mum know? What I did?'

'I told her a little, but she didn't need to know the details.'

'Thank you.'

'No one's judging you, Megan. You were sick, that's all there is to it.'

'I'm so grateful you'll forgive me.'

'Nothing to forgive,' Eve said decisively. 'We wouldn't have him if it wasn't for you.'

They all looked up as Sophia padded into the room, a tiny figure resting against her shoulder. She raised him gently, turning him so his back rested against her chest. The baby looked placidly at his audience, blinking lazily as he regarded the visitors.

'Say hello to Sawyer,' Sophia said.

'Sawyer?' Mega was momentarily thrown, still thinking of him as Luka. 'Where did that name come from?'

'After my favourite *Lost* character,' Sophia admitted with a grin. 'Though I'm telling everyone it's really after Tom Sawyer, to make it sound better.'

'Snail!' Amelia declared. 'My baby!'

'We have not named your brother Snail, for the millionth time!'

'Snail,' Amelia said stubbornly, crossing her arms and sticking her bottom lip out.

'How do you even get Snail from Sawyer?' Sophia looked at Megan in exasperation. 'I know it's a hard name for her to pronounce, but they sound nothing like!'

'Better than potato,' Megan said.

'Is it, though? People will think he's a slug. I'd rather they thought of tropical islands or floating down the Mississippi.'

'So I suppose Amelia wasn't really demanding garden creatures to raise?'

'I'm sure she would've if she'd thought of it, but no, she didn't understand why her new pet had suddenly vanished. She kept thinking I'd put him somewhere. In the microwave, perhaps.'

'It must have been very confusing for her after just getting used to the idea of sharing you and Eve.'

'And we all know how good at sharing she usually is. Do you want to hold him?'

'No, thank you. Not just yet.'

'He won't bite.'

'Not yet, Sophia.' Megan fought to keep her voice steady. 'Let's have coffee.'

'Sod coffee, we've got wine.'

'I shouldn't be drinking.'

'After everything that's happened, a glass of wine is completely forgivable. I won't get you plastered, I promise.' Hooking Sawyer back on to her shoulder, she disappeared again. 'Eve, will you battle the bloody corkscrew?'

'Forget the wine. I got a taste for Cosmopolitans again while I was home. I'll mix us up some.'

'You don't have to be afraid of holding him,' Stef said quietly as Eve went to take over.

'I don't trust myself.'

'You never put Amelia down when she was that age.'

'Everything was normal with Amelia.'

'And everything will be normal with Sawyer.'

'Did you know that's what they'd named him?' A nod of confirmation. 'Why didn't you tell me?'

Stef shrugged awkwardly. 'You so badly wanted him to be Luka.'

'Can we have our own child, Stef? And name him Luka?'

The words came out in a torrent, unplanned and completely unexpected.

Acute discomfort contorted Stef's face as he grimaced. 'Megs, we can't . . .'

Of course. How could she have forgotten the hysterectomy? Seeing Sawyer had made her womb feel like it was contorting, desperate for connection with him, but there was no womb. It hadn't been a real sensation. Even now, she still couldn't fully distinguish between reality and fantasy.

'Oh, yes,' she managed to say, as if she'd dismissed the thought. 'Sorry.'

Sophia was back, balancing the baby and two cocktail glasses of cranberry-red liquid.

'I assume you're on maternity leave from work, not just using up holidays?' Megan asked.

'Yeah, I did have to lie about that. Sorry. Couldn't really tell you at the time.' Sophia shrugged an apology.

'No, I suppose not.'

'I thought you handled all the revelations really well, sis.'

Stef coughed sharply. 'You're making it sound like an MI5 cover-up!'

'I'm a bit surprised I wasn't angrier about it, or more emotional,' Megan admitted.

'You'd still have been under the longer-term effects of the meds, wouldn't you? They'll have kept everything dulled a bit.'

Megan hadn't thought of that. She'd assumed that missing the doses that day had meant she had been completely under her own control.

'Maybe it's better they were still in my system,' she said.

'There was enough of the real you there as well.'

'None of it felt real, though.'

'That was the shock, not the drugs or the psychosis.'

'I'm not sure.'

'Because you don't trust yourself yet. And that's our fault.'

Megan shook her head. 'I'm the reason you had to keep quiet; if I hadn't done what I did, it wouldn't have ever been necessary.'

'Megs, you're not to blame,' Stef said.

'You didn't choose to have psychosis,' Eve added.

'But I put Sawyer in danger.'

'And you'll never do it again,' Eve said firmly.

'Here, hold him.' Sophia had clearly had enough of stepping softly.

'Do you trust me to?'

Sophia rolled her eyes. 'Stop fishing, for God's sake. Here.' She thrust the squirming bundle into Megan's arms before another word could be said.

Instinctively, Megan clasped him to her. He felt so right in her arms, like he was meant to fit there. He was heavier than she remembered, so much sturdier than when she had held her breast to his hungry lips for his first feed. He watched her calmly, as if he recognised her as his first caregiver, and she felt a connection she was sure she wasn't imagining. Her heart lurched and it felt like the same happened beneath her scar.

'He's so beautiful, Soph,' she breathed, extending her little finger for him to grasp. The strength of his grip surprised her. She had given him a good start in life, before it had all gone so wrong.

Megan stared into the baby's stunning eyes, feeling as if she had known him for ever, a familiarity she had not expected. It was then she realised why.

She had looked into eyes of that exact same colour before.

Chapter Thirty-Six

It took another day for Megan to make her decision. She reached it while she was baking, soothed by the familiar, repetitive actions and the homely smells. She wasn't particularly aware that she was thinking – thought had been resolutely linked to the voice for so long – and the sudden realisation made her lose control of the whisk and spatter red velvet batter across the worktop.

Careless, for once, of the mess, she snatched up her phone before she changed her mind. A notification popped up on the screen: her contraception app, reminding her that today was a safe day in her cycle. She almost laughed at the irony, deleting the reminder and opening her call list.

'Hi,' Sophia answered. 'How are you feeling?'

Megan ignored the question. 'Will you bring Sawyer round for a visit?'

'Sure,' Sophia said lightly. 'Eve's taken Amelia for a day out to make up for all the time she was away, so we're free. I'll get the little man dressed and I'll be with you. What's the urgency?'

'No urgency,' Megan said, forcing calm into her voice, not

wanting to spook Sophia into further questions. 'See you soon.'

She forced herself to wipe down the surfaces methodically, tidied up the flour and sugar that had blown themselves everywhere, set the cakes and scones out to cool. All routine, nothing to justify the tightness in her chest and the gradual labouring of breath she valiantly tried to ignore. She waited for the voice to come, to instruct her, but once again it failed to make an appearance.

'Something smells amazing.' Stef had followed his nose, his first appearance since breakfast, still a necessity to ensure she downed her pills.

'Sophia and Sawyer are on their way.'

Stef's smile wasn't quite genuine, though he disguised it well. 'Great. Are we having drinks?'

'You've done nothing but drink recently.'

'Stress relief. Are you OK? You seem on edge.'

'I took my tablets, don't worry.'

'I wasn't suggesting—'

'It doesn't matter,' Megan said impatiently.

Stef took one of the breakfast-bar stools. He'd gained weight, she noticed for the first time. His shirt buttons were straining and he looked softer around the edges, extra padding his lean frame he had never had to contend with before.

'God, the house smells like heaven!' Sophia shouted through as she clattered into the hallway. 'Please tell me I can eat whatever I want.'

She barely paused to thrust Sawyer into Megan's arms before grabbing a plate and raiding the fridge for cream and jam.

'Don't you eat at your own house?' Stef asked.

'Can't afford it. We just toss the kids a crust of stale bread whenever we remember. Get off – that one's mine!' Sophia slapped his hand away from the plumpest scone.

Sawyer began to grizzle and Megan shifted him to settle closer against her, his little head resting in the curve of her neck. He smelled deliciously of Sudocrem and warm milk and biscuits fresh from the oven. She felt him snuggle into her and closed her eyes, losing herself to the wave of calm that washed over her.

She didn't miss how closely Stef and Sophia were watching her when she next looked up. Sophia appeared perfectly relaxed, despite her focus on Megan, but Stef seemed ready to burst from his seat at any moment. Megan dropped a feather-light kiss on to her nephew's head and handed him back to Sophia before any assumptions could be formed. He didn't protest as Sophia laid him in his pram, content to watch his audience.

'He's got your nose,' she said to her sister.

'I hope that's a good thing.'

'He has the same face shape as you as well. You can tell he's yours.' Megan smiled, leaning over to extend her finger for Sawyer to grasp. 'Just his eyes that are different. Grey eyes must be rare; not a colour you see often.'

Stef clattered his plate as he cut himself a slice of cake. 'Not that rare.'

Megan caught her husband's gaze, saw him trying to avoid her scrutiny, trying to look anywhere but directly at her, as if he could deny what she had seen every day for so many years.

'Stef, the baby has your eyes. The colour is the exact same. How is that possible? How can Sawyer have your eyes?'

The colour drained from Stef's face and she waited for him to deny it, to claim mere coincidence and laugh at the chance of it. He looked frantically at Sophia, who shook her head, wordless for once, her mouth opening and closing as she fought to speak.

'Stef, I've changed my mind,' she finally stumbled out.

'You can't,' he gasped.

'I don't want to do this.'

'We agreed! You said it – no more lies.'

'Stef, don't—'

'Stop it!' Megan banged her fist on the island, then remembered Sawyer and ceased instantly, dropping her voice. 'Tell me. Now.'

Sophia buried her head in her hands, refusing to look up.

'I'm his biological father,' Stef whispered.

Megan stared at him, not comprehending his words, even though he was only confirming what she had already known.

'Sawyer's mine. I mean, he's not mine, he's Sophia and Eve's, but I fathered him. It was my sperm.'

For a moment, Megan couldn't speak, couldn't catch her breath. All the air rushed out of her as if she had been punched in the stomach, and she felt herself fold over, gripping her scar.

'How? I don't understand.'

Stef couldn't look at her. 'I donated my sperm. It was all done anonymously at the clinic.'

'Why the hell would you do that?'

'Do you know how hard it is to find willing, decent men who will genetically father a baby, knowing they'll never be a dad to it?' Sophia demanded. 'All the men we knew either refused point blank or there was something we didn't like about them – you know, a drinking problem or a bad temper or ginger genes in their family.'

'Not helping, Sophia,' Stef said between clenched teeth.

'Well, that's the truth of the situation. We couldn't find a suitable donor and we couldn't pay for a proper one.'

'We'd have given you the money!' Megan cried.

'Eve wouldn't let me. You know how weird she is about borrowing money.'

Eve had grown up in a Midwest religious sect, renouncing it before graduating high school but, although it wasn't discussed, Megan knew she still felt constrained by some of her childhood teachings. Even using alternative conception methods had taken her a long time to accept.

At least Megan now understood how hard it could be to silence old ghosts.

'She said we were already in debt to you from Amelia—' Sophia rolled her eyes at such scruples.

'We gave you that money happily – it wasn't a debt!'

'Try convincing Eve of that! And now we were further indebted because you'd agreed to be the surrogate. She was right – we'd already asked more of you than anyone ever should, and you'd been so amazing. I can't tell you how incredible you've both been to us through all this.' A sob escaped Sophia's throat, an almost unknown event that shocked Megan enough to quieten her. 'Without you, I wouldn't have any children, let alone two. I'd have spent my life watching other people playing happy families, knowing it could never be me.'

'But you took my husband's sperm.'

'He *gave* me his sperm.'

'Did you beg him? Is he Amelia's father as well?'

'No! We used a proper donation service for Amelia.' Sophia tried to grasp Megan's hand, but she snatched it away. 'Please listen to me, Megan, I was desperate. My eggs were barely viable and I had so few anyway. The chances of fertilisation were minuscule; we never thought it would happen. It wasn't meant to be like this.'

'My husband fathering my sister's baby, you mean? The baby I carried because I knew how much being a biological mother meant to you.'

'I'm so sorry.'

'Why, Sophia?'

'Why am I sorry?'

'Why, Stef? I don't understand.'

'Because I owed Sophia,' Stef said bluntly before Sophia could reply.

'Owed her for what? Did you do something?'

Another awful silence, Stef on his feet pacing the kitchen, Sophia frozen still.

'Isaac did,' Sophia eventually whispered.

'Isaac?' The mention of Stef's twin, dead for over a decade, threw her.

'It was him, Megan.' Sophia withdrew, taking herself to the other side of the room, wrapping her arms around herself as she concentrated on staring at the floor. 'Isaac attacked me.'

Megan swallowed the leaden lump in her throat with great difficulty. Her intention to confront them had not been supposed to lead to this.

'I know.'

Sophia's head shot up and Stef's body jerked as if he had been slapped.

'How do you know?' Sophia asked hoarsely.

'I could ask you the same question. You never remembered who did it, Soph. You had no memory of that night.'

'I didn't find out till after he was dead.'

'Did someone tell you?'

Another sob broke free from Sophia. She shook her head, either unable or unwilling to speak.

'I did,' Stef mumbled, barely audible in his reluctance to admit yet another secret.

Megan turned on him. 'You knew all that time and you didn't tell the police?'

'I didn't know back then!' Stef yelped. 'I really did have a complete blackout after the party. I remembered little bits over the years, after Isaac died. I only realised for sure once I had enough to piece it all together. By then it was too late.'

He buried his head in his hands.

'I fucked it up so badly, Megs. I met Isaac walking Sophia home after she'd come to return my phone. She came on to me, but I shoved her away, told her I didn't want her. I only wanted you. I left Isaac to walk her back because I was more interested in getting away from her. I left her with him, even though I knew he wasn't safe. It was my fault Soph was attacked, and it was my fault your dad left. I fucked your entire lives up.'

'Dad?' Megan echoed. This was spiralling out of control.

'He confronted Isaac the day before he died. After he topped himself, Paul was certain it was his fault, that he'd bullied him till he couldn't cope any more.'

'But Dad didn't pressure Isaac into suicide.'

'How can you be so sure?'

The lump in her throat was threatening to choke her and it took a momentous effort to force her words out.

'Because I encouraged Isaac to do it.'

Chapter Thirty-Seven

S ophia and Stef both stared wildly at Megan.

'You did what?' Stef managed to say.

'Everyone suspected you, Stef. I didn't want to believe it, but you were behaving so strangely. When the police told us you had an alibi, I knew it had to be Isaac, so I went to ask him. He admitted he'd lied for you. Burst into tears, then clammed up and wouldn't say another word.' Megan took a deep breath, trying to order her thoughts. So many years, so long refusing to acknowledge what she had done.

'I raided your parents' liquor cabinet and made us drinks, talked to him till he calmed down. He was drunk so quickly – he wasn't used to it. Finally, it all came spilling out. He still wanted me to think it was you, but he kept tripping himself up and I realised he could only have known some of the details if he was the guilty one.'

Without thinking, she reached for the cake and cut a precise slice, placing it carefully on to a plate. She picked up a fork and began dissecting it into tiny pieces, needing to look at something, focus on anything that wasn't the two people before her.

'I didn't tell him I'd worked it out. I was scared of him, to be honest. I'd seen it, the madness in him. He was ranting about leaving the world that had never understood him. He kept mentioning Cambridge, a girl who wouldn't sleep with him, how she mocked him. He attacked her too. Did you know, Stef?'

'Only from eavesdropping on my parents' conversation. I found out just before your mum's birthday party. Isaac never admitted it.'

'Well, he did to me. Told me how he'd slipped a pill into her drink, all the things he did to her.' Megan clenched her fists, tears welling in her eyes. 'He started gathering all his medication together, all these different tablets he had stashed about his room. I encouraged him, told him it was the only way out, helped him hide it all under his mattress. I even left him with a bottle of vodka to spur him on.'

'Why didn't you go to the police?' Sophia demanded.

'I couldn't decide what to do. There was no evidence – the police had told us that often enough. I thought they'd laugh at me if I told them I just knew. I was still trying to decide when I found out he was dead.' Megan found the courage to raise her eyes to her sister's. 'He'd have done it again, Soph, maybe even to me the next time. I needed to make sure we were safe.'

'And you never told me any of this?' Stef whispered.

Both sisters' eyes whipped in unison to stare at him with such intensity he dropped his head to protect himself.

'Don't you play the innocent in all this,' Megan hissed. 'If you hadn't lied in the first place, the police might have investigated Isaac more thoroughly.'

'I know it was my fault.' Stef scrubbed at his face, looking surprised to find it was wet with tears. 'I should have told the truth and I should have walked Sophia home. I was so stupid, so fucking selfish. I knew he was capable of it. I knew much more than I ever said. He'd killed animals: cats and pet rabbits. I think he even tried to poison Orion once. He assaulted more than one girl at Cambridge, I'm sure of it. If I'd spoken up, people would have known to be wary of him, but I was too proud, didn't want people judging my parents. It wasn't their fault he was like that.'

Sophia reached into the pram for her sleeping son, pressing Sawyer close to her chest as she gazed down at him. Megan felt her own fingers tighten involuntarily and she had to look away.

'What an absolute mess.' Sophia sighed, not noticing her sister's reaction. 'Even after all this time, what Isaac did is still ruining our lives.'

Finally, there were no more words. Nothing any of them could say. The cold reality lay before them, exposed, so many secrets buried for so long. Maybe they should never have been exhumed. What could they bring other than more pain?

For the first time, Megan regretted her single-minded determination to reveal everything.

She stood abruptly, making both of them jump. 'I need some time alone. I can't think. There's too much. Go home, Sophia, please.'

'Will you be OK?'

'Just go. Take Stef with you.'

'I can't leave you alone, Megs, you're still under section.'

'Then just stay away from me. I'm going for a bath. Don't follow me.'

It took a lot of energy to climb the stairs. Her muscles ached as if she'd put them under enormous strain, and she was short

345

of breath by the time she reached the master bedroom. Her head began to pound in time with her heartbeat.

She had to sit for a few minutes before she could summon the strength to run the bath. Staring down into the flowing water, watching thick, scented bath foam rise to the surface, she ran her fingers through the silky liquid. Her engagement ring glistened like the iridescent surface of the bubbles before they popped and she slid it from her finger, holding it up to the light.

Sinking into the scalding water, the temptation to simply slip beneath the surface and never rise again was so strong she had to grip the roll-top edges to prevent herself. She found she was holding her breath in preparation for an act she would not – could not – allow herself to do.

'Megan?' Sophia's voice from the doorway was almost a whisper. 'I can't go, not like this. I can't just walk away and leave you.'

'I don't want to talk any more. I'm too tired.'

'Please.' Sophia crept further into the bathroom. 'Please don't shut me out.'

'Where's Sawyer?'

'Stef's got him.'

Megan spread her hands across the surface of the foam, focusing on them so she didn't look at her sister. 'He's with his father, you mean.'

'Stef isn't his father, Megan. Not like that.'

'Biology says different.'

'Biology can say whatever the hell it wants. Stef is Sawyer's uncle, just like you're his aunt. This is probably the most fucked-up thing a family could go through, but it doesn't change that much.'

'Sophia, it changes everything!'

346

'We shouldn't have told you. I was so determined we should come clean about everything, but this was something that should have stayed buried. I didn't realise until it was too late.'

'More secrets,' Megan said dully.

'Isn't every donor a secret?'

'Not like this.'

'No,' Sophia admitted. 'Not like this.'

'Does Eve know about Stef?'

'No, I said I'd got a dodgy loan off the internet and I'd pay it all off. She still went mad, of course.'

'She hasn't worked it out, like I did?'

'The donor was my choice this time, so I showed her a random profile of a Croatian man from the fertility clinic's list and she accepted it. A lot of Croatians seem to have grey eyes so she hasn't noticed anything amiss. And I suppose she doesn't look into Stef's eyes that often.' Sophia sighed. 'Yet more secrets, I know.'

She sat on the floor, leaning back against the bath, looking straight ahead.

'Can I tell you how it happened? Please? Then you might understand a bit more.'

Megan sank deeper into the bath, tempted to use the water to block out the sounds of Sophia's voice. When she didn't reply, Sophia took it as permission.

'Stef came round at the wrong time. I was in a complete meltdown when he arrived. I'd asked every male acquaintance I could think of and none of them was willing to be a donor. Eve had said she'd put a stop to the whole thing if I took any more money from you, so I really had tried to take out some ridiculous internet loan and been refused because my credit was so bad from travelling. I couldn't stop crying. Every way I turned, I was being blocked, and the thing I wanted most in the world was not going to happen. I just lost it.'

'What's that got to do with Stef?'

'He tried to comfort me – you know how panicky he gets when women cry – and I lashed out at him, told him all of this was because of Isaac and because he didn't stop him.'

Sophia drew a shaky breath, as if preparing herself for battle, and when she spoke again the words flew, savage yet liberated, like caged animals finally released from captivity.

'I said the most awful things, Megan. I didn't mean it, but I couldn't control it. Everything I'd kept inside me since the attack came spilling out, and Stef took the full force of it. And you know what he's like – he just wants to make everything better. He blurted out the offer to help me, and I should have said no. I know now and I knew then, I should have refused, but I couldn't. I couldn't lose my only chance. So I agreed, and then Stef was trapped. He couldn't back out. He wanted to, once he realised what he'd agreed to, but he didn't dare.'

'You always get what you want in the end, don't you?'

'I know I'm selfish. It was so wrong of me to let Stef be the donor. I suppose I never actually believed it would happen. I was certain the eggs would fail so I convinced myself it wouldn't be an issue, there was never going to be a baby anyway. Then it happened, so easily, and it was too late to stop it. It tormented me, whenever I let myself think about it, but it was already done and I couldn't take it back.'

A thought occurred to Megan. 'What if Eve finds out?'

'She can't ever know! She'd leave me if she knew what I did, and probably take Amelia with her!'

'What Stef did,' Megan corrected.

348

'He's not to blame, Megan, can't you see that? He's about as much use as a chocolate fireguard sometimes, but he's loyal. He thought he was making things right, and that's all he ever wants, to make everything all right, to make up for the past.'

'But I do blame him.'

'You shouldn't. You should blame me. If anyone's going to be cast out of your life over all this, it should be me, not Stef.'

'You're my sister! You're the only family I have left.'

'And he's your husband; he's as much your family as I am. Stef's been there practically all our lives. He hasn't cheated on you. He hasn't broken his vows.'

'It feels like he has.'

'I know it does, but if you really think about it, all he's done is try to help me. I convinced him, I rushed him into it; it's me you should hate. Stef's tried his best, for both of us.'

Megan couldn't listen to any more. Her headache had become a stabbing pain, shooting across her forehead at the same time as a deep ache lanced through the haematoma scar. She realised her hands were clutching her abdomen, the irrefutable evidence that had convinced her of Sawyer's existence and now convinced her Stef's betrayal was twofold because there would be no more babies, not between them. She had already unknowingly carried her husband's first and perhaps only child.

She didn't know how long she lay there, long after Sophia had crept out, after she heard the unsteady footsteps of Stef checking on her, though he had the sense not to speak.

However long she stayed, cocooned under the warm duvet of bubbles, it would never be long enough to save her from having to face up to a reality she could never even have imagined.

Chapter Thirty-Eight

Somehow, she slept, but it wasn't restful sleep. Her dreams were punctured by replays of the revelations, jumbled words shouted in Stef and Sophia's voices. Macaulay looming over her, electrodes in hand. Sawyer, in the arms of a faceless stranger, being carried away from her as she tried to run towards him. Her dad, crying, begging her to forgive him. Isaac, standing over Sophia's bloodied body, promising their lives would never know a moment's peace from him, swearing his revenge for her rejection of him.

When she eventually woke, a startled return to consciousness with the sounds still ringing in her ears, her body ached as if she had fought for her life. To her surprise, Stef lay beside her. His puffy, reddened eyes and pale skin told her he hadn't slept.

'You were shouting,' he said. 'What were you dreaming about?'

'Isaac,' she admitted. 'He wanted to hurt us, me and Sophia, because I'd refused a date with him.'

'He can never hurt anyone again.' There was a fierceness in his voice she couldn't help but find reassuring. 'How many times did he ask you out?'

'So many. He didn't seem to understand it was a lost cause. It was awful, having to say no each time. I felt sorry for him.'

Megan realised then what the churning in her gut was. It wasn't nausea at Stef's sins; it was the silent guilt she had carried since she was nineteen years old, since she led a man to his death without a moment's hesitation.

'I'm the reason your twin's dead.'

Stef shook his head violently. 'I never mourned him. The world was safer without him. You were right; he would have attacked again.'

'I still had no right to play God. I should have gone to the police.'

'They wouldn't have done anything. Like you said, there was no evidence. They thought Isaac was a sad case who needed help, like everyone else.'

They were silent for too long, both lost in their own memories, unwilling or unable to bridge the gap between them.

'All I've ever wanted is to protect you,' Stef finally whispered. 'That hasn't changed, and it never will.'

'But you've just been playing a part.'

'It was never an act, Megs, I swear to you.'

'How can I ever trust you now?'

'I won't do it again.'

She couldn't prevent a laugh at the childish statement. 'Of course you won't do it again!'

'Not the donor thing, I mean the rest of it. Hiding things from you. Not answering your questions. It'll never happen again.'

'I'm glad I didn't manage to ring your parents. Imagine how worried they'd have been.'

'It was pretty hard preventing you. You were so determined it had to be them looking after the baby.'

Megan found she was unconsciously tracing the path of her scar as it stretched across her abdomen.

'Stef, the hysterectomy – it definitely happened?' From nowhere, she was seized by a sudden hope. 'Is the scar really just from the C-section and you haven't told me because you're worried I'll want another baby?'

'No, it's true. They couldn't control the bleeding. We nearly lost you.'

'So there's no way we can have children naturally?'

'Not really . . . Megs, do you actually want a baby, or do you just want the feeling you had when you looked after Sawyer for those first few days?'

Confronted by the damning question she had not yet summoned the courage to ask herself, Megan couldn't reply.

'More importantly, I suppose I should ask, do you even want a child with me?'

Another question she couldn't answer.

'Megan, look at me.'

It was a struggle to raise her eyes to his, to look into the eyes Sawyer had inherited, that had given away the final lie. Stef reached to take her hand and she allowed him, even though her instinct was to pull away.

'We've all got secrets – you, me and Sophia. None of us is so different from each other.'

She opened her mouth to argue, throw back all his crimes, then realised she couldn't. He was right.

All three of them had sinned.

★

It was the last time she would ever visit the Grosvenor Unit. She could feel Stef's eyes on her as she climbed the steps, leaving him waiting in the car. He had offered to accompany her inside, but she needed to do this alone. She needed to prove she could.

She was shown into a different room by a nurse she didn't recognise, this one not suiting the cornflower-blue uniform as well as Gemma. It took a moment to realise she was in Macaulay's personal office, an inner sanctum she suspected patients were not usually permitted to see. Macaulay sat to attention at an enormous mahogany desk; behind him, the wall was filled with framed certificates and photographs of the psychiatrist receiving awards, shaking hands with familiar Hollywood faces, posing with other white-coated men.

'Please take a seat, Megan.' He smiled and indicated to the comfortable leather chairs in front of the desk. 'Would you like tea?'

'No, thank you, I won't be staying long. I've come to arrange my discharge from your care to my new psychiatrist.' She kept her tone brisk, business-like, determined to remain detached.

'Yes, I received Stefan's email. You didn't have to come all this way to complete the paperwork in person.'

'You always insisted on face to face. Why change now?'

'As you wish. How are you?'

'Getting better, no thanks to you and your methods.'

The mask was firmly in place and he showed no reaction. 'I haven't broken any rules, Megan.'

'You manipulated me into believing that my own memories were a lie. You convinced me I couldn't trust myself. You took away any sense of belonging or security I may have had.'

'I made the decision not to tell you about your childbirth

experience, yes, but only due to the mental distress it would have caused you.'

'That shouldn't have been your decision to make.'

'Psychosis sufferers are not generally capable of making their own decisions.'

'But when it became clear I *was* capable, you still didn't allow me that courtesy.'

'As I've said, I believe in my treatment programme.'

'If it wasn't for Stef and Sophia realising I was going to find out on my own, you'd still be lying to me.'

'Not lying, no.'

'Covering up, then, if you prefer a more palatable phrase.'

'You must have had a lot of information to process in a short space of time.'

'Yes, I did, as it happens. Probably not ideal to find out all at once, I grant you, but I didn't expect there to be quite so many revelations.'

'What do you mean?'

'It turns out Stef donated the sperm to fertilise Sophia's egg, so biologically he's the baby's father. Did you not know?'

'No.' For the first time, genuine shock was displayed. 'My God, I was never told that.'

'Bit of a shock for me as well.'

'How do you feel about it, if you don't mind me asking?'

'I don't want to discuss it,' she stated, brooking no argument. She would not confide in him again.

Macaulay seemed at a total loss. 'Why would Stefan do that? He adores you, that's been clear all along.'

'He had his reasons. I'm just not sure whether they're good enough.'

'Are you going to do anything?'

'Leave him, you mean? I suppose most women would.'

'If he had a reason, maybe you'll come to accept it.'

'Maybe I will, in time.'

'And how are things between you and Sophia?'

'Strained at the moment, but we'll be OK. We have to be. There's Amelia and Sawyer to think about. They'll get us through this.'

'Stefan loves the children as well, Megan.'

'He should probably love one more,' she said tartly.

'I presume he never intended to be a father figure to the baby?'

'No. I doubt Sawyer will ever know his parentage, just the same as any other donor baby. He'll only know Uncle Stef.'

'That will be for the best. Knowledge like that could prove very damaging.'

'It already has.'

'I hope it won't lead to any setbacks in your recovery.'

Megan had been concerned about the same thing, but she had no intention of letting him know that. 'It won't be for you to deal with, even if it does.'

'Have you met your new psychiatrist yet?'

'Tomorrow. She stood out above the rest by virtue of being a woman.'

'If that makes you more comfortable.'

'You'll never know what it's like to feel like this. No man will. At least a woman can have true empathy.'

'I hope it works out for you, Megan.'

'Thank you,' she replied stiffly.

'I'm sorry we couldn't complete your treatment.'

'Yes, I'm sure you are.' She thought of the second book he was waiting to publish and felt a little surge of glee that she had disrupted him. 'May I ask you a question?'

'Of course.'

'All through this, I've been hearing a voice. My own voice, only inside my head. Was that the psychosis talking to me?'

'I can only assume it wasn't a voice; it was self-talk. We all do it. We just don't usually notice it until it becomes negative.'

'So, it's normal?'

'In many ways, yes. Only when the self-talk turns disturbing does it become a problem.'

She wasn't about to discuss that aspect with him. 'Anyway, I think it's gone now. I haven't heard it since I found out Sawyer really did exist.'

Macaulay spread his hands. 'That's not to say it won't return.'

'If it does, at least I'll know what it is.' Megan glanced behind her to the closed door. 'I'd like to say goodbye to Gemma, please, to thank her for everything she did.'

'I'm afraid Gemma is no longer employed at the Grosvenor. She resigned last week.'

Megan stared at him. 'Resigned or was sacked?'

'I didn't fire her. She was ready to move on, find a new challenge. I believe she's returning to the NHS.'

'You don't have forwarding details for her?'

'She didn't wish to keep in contact.'

'Understandable,' Megan murmured, her mind replaying the scene of the attempted ECT of its own accord. She blinked hard to chase away the unwanted images.

'Gemma was perfectly happy in her work.' A note of challenge entered Macaulay's voice.

'If you say so.'

'We can agree to disagree.'

'Of course, that's much easier than actually admitting you're in the wrong.'

'I'm sorry you feel that way.'

Megan had had enough of the mind games, the battle for power. She no longer cared enough to play along.

'You were always the one in control, Dr Macaulay.' She stood up, moving the chair back into place. 'I'll be going now.'

Macaulay stood, moving around the enormous desk. 'Goodbye, Megan, and good luck.'

'By the way, I've ordered your book.'

Surprise registered in his face, at her knowledge of the book's existence or the unexpected purchase, she wasn't sure. 'You have?'

Megan nodded, buttoning her coat before pushing her hands in her pockets so he wouldn't extend his for a handshake.

'Who knows? Maybe it will be useful.'

As she left the office, closing the door carefully behind her, a hint of a smile tugged at the corners of her mouth.

That showed him.

The voice sounded like it was smiling too.

Acknowledgements

So many people have ridden the rollercoaster with me on the road to publication and my heartfelt thanks and gratitude go to every single one them:

My superstar agent, the inimitable Liza DeBlock, who swept me from the slush pile with the best voicemail ever and swore to champion Megan's journey – she has more than lived up to that promise. Also, to all at Mushens Entertainment for making me feel so welcome.

My editor, Bea Grabowska, for taking the time to find out what a watch pocket is and for being all-round wonderful to work with. Thanks also to Katie Sunley for her editorial input, to Sarah Day for a wonderful first experience of copyedits and to all at Headline Accent for their support and guidance.

All the experts who helped me grow and develop as an author over the years: Kerry Hudson and her WoMentoring Project; Tammy Cohen, the mentor who always told me I would make it one day; Erin Kelly and Michelle Davies for the Curtis Brown Creative education; Jericho Writers for the amazing opportunities their Summer Festival of Writing has offered.

My parents, Linda and Bob, for the delight and joy they have shown at each and every step of this very long process. There isn't a day goes by that I am not proud to be their daughter.

The A-Team of friends, supporters, beta-readers and advisors: Kim, Ellie, Christina, Shivani, Rachel, Sabrina, Amy, Mike, Jo, Neil and Sam, Frank and Ami, and the August Club (Andrea, Aaron, Jelena, Jo, Edna and Randy). Every one of them believed they would see this book published even when I faltered. Many bottles of Prosecco and pints of cider have been consumed in the interest of literary dedication and procrastination.

The best pub quiz team in the world (presumably) – the multi-talented Manfreds – for the endless stream of encouragement and plot twist suggestions.

The bestest puppas a woman could have in her life – Coco, Nanci, Nala-lion, Roxy, Zep, Betsy and Poppalina – for all the snuggles, boops and snack supervision.

And to Lee, who insists on bringing Marvel and football into my life, bests me at quizzes, steals the dogs' affections, and makes me complete.